QUEEN OF THE DAWN

WORKS BY
H. RIDER HAGGARD

Parliamentary Blue-Book
REPORT TO H.M.'s GOVERNMENT ON THE SALVATION
ARMY COLONIES in the United States, with Scheme of
National Land Settlement. [Cd. 2562.]

Political History
CETEWAYO AND HIS WHITE NEIGHBOURS

Works on Agriculture, Country Life and Sociology

RURAL ENGLAND (2 vols).	A GARDENER'S YEAR
THE POOR AND THE LAND	REGENERATION
A FARMER'S YEAR	RURAL DENMARK AND ITS LESSONS

Book of Travel
A WINTER PILGRIMAGE

Novels

DAWN	JOAN HASTE
THE WITCH'S HEAD	DOCTOR THERNE
JESS	STELLA FREGELIUS
COLONEL QUARITCH, V. C.	THE WAY OF THE SPIRIT
BEATRICE	LOVE ETERNAL

Romances

KING SOLOMON'S MINES	THE YELLOW GOD: AN IDOL OF AFRICA
SHE	
ALLAN QUATERMAIN	MORNING STAR
MAIWA'S REVENGE	THE LADY OF BLOSSHOLME
MR. MEESON'S WILL	QUEEN SHEBA'S RING
ALLAN'S WIFE	RED EVE
CLEOPATRA	THE MAHATMA AND THE HARE
ERIC BRIGHTEYES	MARIE
NADA THE LILY	CHILD OF STORM
MONTEZUMA'S DAUGHTER	THE WANDERER'S NECK-LACE
THE PEOPLE OF THE MIST	
HEART OF THE WORLD	THE HOLY FLOWER
SWALLOW	THE IVORY CHILD
BLACK HEART AND WHITE HEART	FINISHED
	WHEN THE WORLD SHOOK
LYSBETH	MOON OF ISRAEL
PEARL MAIDEN	THE ANCIENT ALLAN
THE BRETHREN	SMITH AND THE PHARAOHS, AND OTHER TALES
AYESHA: THE RETURN OF SHE	SHE AND ALLAN
BENITA	THE VIRGIN OF THE SUN
FAIR MARGARET	WISDOM'S DAUGHTER
THE GHOST KINGS	HEU-HEU, OR THE MONSTER

QUEEN OF THE DAWN

THE WORLD'S DESIRE
(In collaboration with Andrew Lang)

Queen of the Dawn

A Love Tale of Old Egypt

By

H. Rider Haggard

Wildside Press
Berkeley Heights • New Jersey

Wildside Press
PO Box 45
Gillette, NJ 07933-0045
www.wildsidepress.com

CONTENTS

QUEEN OF THE DAWN

Queen of the Dawn

CHAPTER I

THE DREAM OF RIMA

THERE was war in Egypt and Egypt was rent in two. At Memphis in the north, at Tanis, and in all the rich lands of the Delta where by many mouths the Nile flows down to the sea, a usurping race held power, that whose forefathers, generations before, had descended upon Egypt like a flood, destroyed its temples and deposed its gods, possessing themselves of the wealth of the land. At Thebes in the south the descendants of the ancient Pharaohs still ruled precariously, again and again attempting to drive out the fierce Semitic or Bedouin kings, named the Shepherds, whose banners flew from the walls of all the northern cities.

They failed because they were too weak, indeed the hour of their final victory was yet far away and of it our tale does not tell.

Nefra the Princess, she who was named the Beautiful and afterwards was known as Uniter of Lands, was the only child of one of these Theban Antefs, Kheperra, born of his Queen, Rima, daughter of Ditanah, the King of Babylon, who had given her to him in marriage to strengthen him in his struggle against the Shepherds, also called the *Aati* or "Plague-bearers." Nefra was the first and only child of this marriage, for shortly after she was born Kheperra the King, her father, with all the host that he could gather, went down Nile to fight the Aati who marched to meet him

1

from Tanis and from Memphis. They met in a great battle in which Kheperra was slain and his army defeated, though not before it had slaughtered such numbers of the enemy that, abandoning their advance on Thebes, the generals of the Shepherds, returned with the remnant of their troops whence they came. Yet by this victory Apepi, the King of the Shepherds, became in fact Pharaoh of all Egypt. Kheperra was dead, leaving behind him but one infant girl, and so were numbers of the great Theban lords, others of whom hastened to submit to the ruler of the North.

The Shepherd people too, like the Egyptians of the South, were weary of war and would not fight again. Therefore, although they were defeated, no cruelties were inflicted upon the followers of Kheperra, nor was great tribute asked of them; also they were allowed to worship their ancient gods in peace, and this in the northern as well as the southern lands. Indeed, by now, although the god of the Shepherds was Baal, to whom they gave the name of Set because already it was well known upon the Nile, the Shepherd kings re-built the temples of Ra and Amen and Ptah, of Isis and of Hathor, that their forefathers had de-stroyed when first they invaded Egypt, and themselves made offerings in them, acknowledging these divinities.

Only one thing did Apepi demand of the conquered Thebans, namely that Rima the Queen of dead Kheperra, and the babe Nefra, his daughter and lawful heiress of Upper Egypt, should be given up to him, hearing which Rima hid herself away with the child, as shall be told.

Now of the birth of Nefra the Princess there were strange stories. It was said that after she came into the world, a very fair babe, gray-eyed, light-skinned, and black-haired, and the rites had been accomplished, she was laid upon her mother's bosom. When Rima had looked upon her and she had been shown to the King her father, in a weak voice, for she had suffered much, the Queen demanded to be left alone, so earnestly that the physicians and women thought it best to appear to obey her and withdrew themselves behind certain curtains that divided the birth-chamber from another, where they remained silent.

The night had fallen and the birth-chamber was dark, for as yet Rima could bear no light near to her. Yet of a sudden one of the women, a priestess of Hathor named Kemmah, who had nursed the King Kheperra from his birth and now was to fill that office to his child, having remained awake, saw a light glowing through the curtains, and being frightened, peeped between them. Behold! in the birth-chamber, looking down on the Queen, who seemed to be asleep, were two royal and glorious women or so Kemmah swore and believed, from whose robes and bodies flowed light and whose eyes shone like stars. Queens they seemed to be, no less, for there were crowns upon their heads and they glittered with jewels which only queens could wear. Moreover, one of them held in her hand the Cross of Life fashioned in gold, and the other a looped sistrum with gems strung on golden wires, such as is used to make music when the priestesses walk in procession before the statues of the gods.

This glorious pair, at the sight of whom the knees of the watcher trembled and the power of speech left her, so that she could say no word to wake the others, bent down—first she who held the Cross of Life and then she who held the sistrum—and whispered into the ear of the sleeping Queen. Then she who held the Cross of Life very gently lifted the babe from the mother's breast, kissed it, and laid the Cross upon its lips. This done she gave it to the other goddess, for now the watcher knew that they must be goddesses, who also kissed it and shook above its head the sistrum, which made a tinkling music ere she laid the infant back upon its mother's breast.

Next instant both were gone and the room that had been filled with brightness grew black with night, while the priest-ess who had seen, being overcome with fear, swooned away until the sun was risen.

Nor was she the first to speak of this matter which she deemed holy and fearful, being afraid lest she had but dreamed or should be held a teller of tales who took the names of the gods in vain. Yet on the morrow the Queen called for her husband and said that a very strange vision had come to her during the night which she described in these words:

"It seemed to me that when weak with pain I had fallen asleep, two glorious ladies appeared to me clothed in the garments and wearing the emblems of goddesses of Egypt. One of these, who bore in her hand the symbol of Life, spoke to me in my dream, saying, 'O Daughter of Babylon, by marriage Queen of Egypt and mother of Egypt's heiress, hear us. We are Isis and Hathor, ancient goddesses of Egypt, as you know, who of late, since you came to this land, have worshipped in our temples and made offerings on our altars. Be not afraid, for although you were bred to the service of other gods we come to bless her who is born of you. Know, O Queen, that great troubles await you and bitter loss that shall leave you desolate, nor with all our strength can we save you from these, for they are written in the book of fate and must befall. Nor, for a while that to mortals must seem long, can we free Egypt from the bonds with which the Shepherds have bound her, as they bind the feet of their own sheep for slaughter, though the time shall come when she will shake them loose, like a bull breaking through its net, and grow greater than ever she has been. As every living thing suffers for its sins, so must Egypt suffer for her sins who has not been loyal to herself, her faith, or the lessons of the past. Yet in the end, if only for a while, her troubles shall pass like summer clouds, and from behind them shall shine out the bright star of her glory.'

"Now I answered that vision or that goddess, saying: 'These are heavy words you speak to me, O divine Lady. With Egypt indeed I have little to do, who am but the wife of one of its kings, a princess sprung from another land.

Egypt must find the fate that she has shaped, but as a woman I would learn that of my lord whom I love and of the child that has been given to us.'

"'The fate of this lord of yours shall be glorious,' answered she who bore the symbol of Life—'and in the end, that of your child shall be happy.'

"Then she seemed to bend down and to take the babe in her arms and to kiss it, saying: 'The blessing of Isis the Mother be upon thee. The strength of Isis be thy strength, and the wisdom of Isis be thy guiding star. Fear not! Be not faint-hearted, O Royal Child, since always Isis is at thy side, and however great thy danger, never shalt thou come to harm. Long shall be thy day and peaceful at the last, and thou shalt see thy grandchildren playing round thy knees. If only for a while, thou shalt bind together that which is divided and thy name shall be Uniter of Lands. Such are the gifts that Isis gives to thee, O Lady of Egypt.'

"So that goddess spoke, holding out the babe in the hollow of her shining arm to the divine sister who stood at her side. She took the child; she too kissed her on the brow and said: 'Behold! I, Hathor, goddess of Love and Beauty, bestow upon thee, the Princess of Egypt, all that I have to give. Beautiful exceedingly shalt thou be in body and in spirit. Loved exceedingly shalt thou be, and through love thou shalt make smooth the path of millions. Turning neither to right nor left, forgetting crookedness and policies, follow thou Hathor's star and thine own heart, rejoicing in Hathor's gifts and leaving all else to Heaven that sees what thou canst not see and works to ends thou dost not know. Thus, O Royal Child, shalt thou sow happiness upon the earth and beyond the earth garner its harvest to thy breast.'

"Thus in my dream those goddesses seemed to speak, and lo! they were gone."

Kheperra the King listened to this tale and made light of it.

"A dream indeed," he said, laughing, "and a happy dream

since it prophesies naught but good to this babe of ours, who it seems is to be beautiful and wise, a very Flower of Love and a Uniter of Egypt, if only for a while. What more could we wish for her?"

"Yes, Lord," answered Rima heavily, "it prophesies good to the child, but, as I fear, ill to others."

"If so, what of it, Wife? One crop must fall before another can be sown and in every crop there are weeds as well as wheat. Such is the law to which all that lives must bow. Nay, do not weep over a phantasy born of pain and darkness. They call me, I must go, for soon the army starts to fight those Shepherds and to conquer them."

Yet Kheperra thought more of this tale than he chose to say, so much indeed that he went to the high priests of Isis and of Hathor and repeated it to them, word for word. These priests, not knowing what to believe, inquired if any had seen aught in the birth-chamber, and thus came to learn of the vision of the Lady Kemmah for, to them, as her superiors, she must tell all.

Now they were astonished indeed, and rejoiced, because they were sure that such a wonder had happened as was not told of in Egypt for generations. Moreover, they caused the words of the dream and the vision of Kemmah to be written down in full and sealed by the Queen and Kemmah, also by themselves as witnesses, in three different rolls, one of which was given to the Queen to keep for the Princess Nefra, while the others were hidden away in the archives of Hathor and Isis. Yet both they and the magicians whom they consulted were frightened at that part of the dream which told of great troubles and bitter loss that were to befall the Queen and leave her desolate.

"What loss," they asked, "could befall her, when happiness and prosperity were promised to her child, save that of the King her husband?—unless, indeed, other children were to be born to her whom Heaven would take away."

Still of these terrors they said nothing, only letting it be known that Isis and Hathor had appeared and blessed the new-born Princess of Egypt. Yet they were true enough, for very soon King Kheperra marched to the war and within two moons came the evil tidings that he was slain, fighting gallantly in the van of his troops, and that his army, although not crushed, was too weak from loss of men and generals to renew the battle and was retreating upon Thebes.

Rima the Queen heard the tidings, which indeed her heart seemed to have taught her before they were spoken. When she had listened to them, all she said was:

"That has happened which the great goddesses of Egypt foretold to me, and so without doubt shall the rest of their words be fulfilled in due season."

Then, according to the Babylonian fashion she withdrew herself to her chamber with the child, and there mourned many days for the husband whom she loved, seeing none save the Lady Kemmah who tended the babe.

At length the army reached Thebes, bringing with it the body of King Kheperra, that had been embalmed, though rudely, on the field of battle. She caused the wrappings to be loosed and for the last time looked upon her lord's face all shattered and marred with wounds.

"The gods have taken him and he died well," she said, "but my heart tells me that as he has died in blood, in a day to come, so in blood shall perish that usurper who brought him to his death."

These words were repeated to Apepi and caused him to go in fear through all his life, for his spirit told him that they were inspired by the god of Vengeance, as did the magicians whom he consulted. Indeed, when he remembered that Queen Rima was by birth of the royal Babylonian House, he grew more afraid than he had been before, because in his family, the Babylonians, to whom once his forefathers had been subject, were held to be the greatest wizards in the world. Therefore he was not surprised at the tale of the vision of Rima which came to her on the night of the birth of her child, though he could not understand why the goddesses of Egypt should appear to a Babylonian.

"If Babylon and Old Egypt come together, what chance will there be for us Shepherd kings who sit astride of the mouths of Nile? Surely our state will be as that of the corn between the upper and the nether millstone and we shall be ground to fine flour," he said to his wise men.

"Those stones grind slowly, and after all flour is the bread of peoples, O King," answered the chief of them. "Did not the dream of the wife of dead Kheperra tell—if report be true—that long years would go by before the Egyptians shake off our yoke, and did it not say that this Princess of Egypt who has been born to dead Kheperra and the Babylonian should be a Uniter of Lands? Bring hither the Babylonian widow and her daughter, the Royal Princess, O King, that these things may be accomplished in their season, though as yet we know not how."

"Why should I admit to dwell in my house one who, inspired by the devils of Babylon, has prophesied that I shall die in blood? Why should I not rather kill her and be done, and her babe with her?" asked Apepi.

"Because, O King," answered the chief of the Wise Men, "the dead are stronger than the living, and the spirit of this royal lady will smite more shrewdly than can her flesh. Moreover, we think that if the oracle of those Egyptian goddesses be true, this child of hers cannot be killed. Make them captives, O King, and hold them fast, but do not leave them at large to move mighty Babylon and the world against you."

"You are right," said Apepi. "It shall be done. Let Rima, the widow of King Kheperra, and her daughter Nefra, Princess of Upper Egypt, be brought to my Court, even if an army must be sent to fetch them. But first try to lead them hither by peaceful words and promises, or if these fail, bribe the Thebans to deliver them into my hand."

CHAPTER II

The Messenger

Rima the Queen heard through her spies that Apepi, King of the Shepherds, purposed to take her and her child and to hold them captive. Having learned that this was the truth, she summoned a council of such lords as remained in Upper Egypt, and of the high priests of the gods, to ask them what she should do.

"Behold," she said, "I am a widow. My lord and yours fell fighting bravely against the North, leaving his heir, this royal infant. When it became known that he was dead, his army would fight no more but fell back on Thebes, and therefore the Shepherds claim the victory. Now, as I hear, .they claim more: namely, that I who was the wife of your king, and our daughter who is your Royal Princess, should be delivered up to them, saying that if this is not done, an army shall be sent to take us. What is your mind, O Lords? Will you defend us from Apepi, or will you not?"

Now some answered one thing and some another. They showed that the people would fight no more, since the King of the Shepherds offered them better terms than ever they could hope to win in battle, and that after the sight of so much blood they longed for peace whoever might be called Pharaoh of Egypt.

"I perceive that I and your Princess have naught to hope from you, Lords, for whom and for whose cause my husband and her father gave his life," said Rima quietly, adding, "But what say the priests of the gods he worshipped?"

Now these answered with many smooth words. One declared that the will of Heaven must be obeyed; another

9

that perchance she and the Princess would be safer in the
court of King Apepi, who swore to treat them both with all
honour; a third, that it might be well if she would appeal
to her mighty father, the King of Babylon, for succour, and
so forth.

When all had finished, Rima laughed bitterly and said:

"I perceive, O Priests, that the gold thrown by the
Shepherd king is so heavy that it can travel many leagues
of air into the treasuries of your temples.   Let me be plain.
Will you help me and your Princess to escape from bondage,
or will you not?   If you will stand by me, I will stand by
you to the last, and so I swear will my daughter when she
comes to the years of knowledge.   If you reject us, then we
wash our hands of you, leaving you to go your ways while we
go ours, to Babylon or anywhere, save to a prison in the
house of the Shepherd kings, where certainly your Royal
Princess would be done to death that Egypt might be left
without a lawful heir.   Now I pray you consult together.   I
withdraw myself that you may talk freely.   But at noon,
that is within an hour, I will return to you for your answer."

Then she bowed to that company, who bowed back to
her, and went away.

At the appointed time of noon, accompanied only by the
Lady Kemmah, the nurse who bore the Princess in her arms,
she returned to the Council Hall entering it through the
side door by which she had departed.   Lo! it was quite
empty.   The lords and priests had gone, every one of them.

"Now it seems that I am alone," said Rima the Queen.
"Well, such is often the lot of the fallen."

"Not altogether, Queen," answered the Lady Kemmah,
"since the Royal Princess and I are still the companions
of your Majesty.   Moreover, I think that in yonder empty
chairs I see the shapes of certain of the gods of Egypt who
perchance will prove better counsellors than those who have
deserted us in the hour of need.   Now let us talk with them
in our hearts and learn of their wisdom."

So there they sat awhile, gazing at those empty chairs

and at the painted pictures of divinities upon the walls beyond, each of them putting up supplications in her own fashion for help and guidance. At length the Lady Kemmah lifted her head and asked:

"Has light come to you, Queen?"

"Nay," answered Rima, "naught but darkness. This only do my gods tell me—that if we stay here those false lords and priests certainly will seize us and deliver us into the power of Apepi, as I think that they have been bribed to do. Have yours aught else to say to you, nurse Kemmah?"

"Something, Lady. It seems to me that the divine queens of Heaven, godmothers of this royal babe, Isis and Hathor whom I serve, have been whispering in my ears. 'Fly,' said the whisper, 'fly fast and far.'"

"Aye, Kemmah, but whither shall we fly? Where can the Queen of the South and her babe, the Royal Princess of Egypt, be hidden away from Apepi's spies? Certainly not here in the South where, being fearful or suborned, all would betray us."

"Nay, Queen, not in the South, but in the North where perhaps none would search for us, since the lion does not seek for the buck at the door of its own den. Hearken, Queen. There is a certain aged holy man named Roy, a brother of my grandfather, sprung from an old line of Theban kings. This great-uncle of mine, whom, when a girl, I knew well, was inspired by the gods and became the prophet of a secret brotherhood called the Order of the Dawn, which has its home by the pyramids that stand near to Memphis. There he and this brotherhood, which is very powerful, have dwelt these thirty years or more, since none now dares to approach those pyramids, and least of all any of the Shepherds, because they are haunted."

"By whom?" asked Rima.

"It is said by a spirit that appears as a beautiful bare-breasted woman, though whether she is the *Ka* of one who is buried in the tombs where my uncle lives, or a ghost from hell, or the shadow of Egypt itself shaped like a woman, is not known. At least because of her no man dares approach those ancient pyramids after night has fallen."

"Why not? Since when have men been afraid of a beautiful unveiled woman?"

"Because, Queen, if any looks upon her loveliness he goes mad and wanders off to perish miserably in the wilderness. Or perchance he follows her up to the crest of one of the pyramids, and falling thence, is crushed to powder."

"An idle tale, as I think, Kemmah. But what of it?"

"This, Queen: that there in those tombs, could we come to them, we might dwell safely enough with my uncle, the Prophet Roy. No man has courage to approach the place, save from time to time some young fool who longs to look upon the loveliness of that ghost and meets his death, or having seen her goes thence a raving madman. Even the wildest Bedouin of the desert dare not pitch his tent within a mile or more of those pyramids, while the Shepherd kings and their subjects hold the place accursed because two of their princes have found doom there; nor would they draw near to it for all the gold in Syria. Also they fear the magic of this brotherhood which is protected by spirits and have sworn to leave it unharmed. At least, such is the tale that I have heard, though doubtless there is more of it that I have not heard."

"Here then it seems we might rest in peace," said Rima with a little laugh, "at any rate, for a while until we found opportunity to escape to Babylon, where doubtless the King my father would welcome us. Yet how can we do so, bearing a babe with us, now when there is war all along the frontiers and none can cross the Arabian deserts. But, Kemmah, how are we to know that your uncle would receive us, and if he will, how are we to reach him?"

"As to the first question, Queen, the answer is easy. Strangely enough it chances that only this day I have received a message from the holy Roy. The captain of a corn boat sailing from Memphis to Thebes brought it to me. He told me that his name is Tau."

"What did he say to you and where did you meet him, Kemmah?"

"Last night, Queen, I could not sleep, being full of fears for you and the babe, so I rose before the dawn and going out, I stood on the private quay in the palace garden watching the sun rise, that I might make my prayer to Ra when he appeared in the heavens. Presently, as the mist thinned, I saw that I was not alone, for quite close to me a stalwart man who had the air or at least wore the dress of a seafarer, was leaning against the trunk of a palm, staring at the Nile beneath, near to the bank of which was moored a trading ship. He spoke, saying that he waited for the mist to clear and the wind to rise, that he might sail on to the trading quay and there deliver his cargo. I asked him whence he came and he answered—from Memphis of the White Walls, having permission from the Governor of Thebes and from him of Memphis to trade between the two cities. I wished him good fortune and was about to leave to make my prayer elsewhere, telling him my purpose, when he said:

"'Nay, let us pray together, for I too, whose name is Tau, am a worshipper of Ra, and see, the god appears,' and he made certain signs to me which I who am a priestess understood.

"Our prayer finished, again I prepared to go, but he stayed me, asking me for news as to the state of Thebes and whether it were true that the Queen Rima had died of grief because of the loss of her husband Kheperra, who fell in the battle, or as some said, had been killed with her child. I answered that these things were not true, words at which he seemed glad, for he thanked the gods and said that without doubt the Princess Nefra was the lawful heiress of all Egypt, North and South together. I asked him how he knew the name of this princess. He replied:

"'A learned man told it to me, a holy hermit to whom I confess my sins, which alas! are many, who dwells in the wilderness nigh to the Great Pyramids and among the tombs. He told me also that he knew the name of this royal child's nurse who was a kinswoman of his, and that it is Kemmah, a lady of high blood. Yes, and he charged me with a message for this Lady Kemmah, if I could find her in Thebes, because he said he dared put nothing in writing.'

"Here this Tau, the captain of the ship, stopped and stared at me and I stared back at him, wondering whether he were setting any trap for my feet.

"'It would be very dangerous, O Tau,' I said to him, 'if perchance you gave this secret message to the wrong woman. There may be many Kemmahs in Thebes. How will you know that you find the right one, or that she whom you are told is the nurse of the princess is in truth that nurse?'

"'It is not so difficult as it seems, Lady. As it chances, the holy hermit gave to me the half of an amulet of lapis lazuli on which is cut a charm or spell or prayer. He said that on this half the signs read, "May the living Ra protect the wearer of this holy thing at the last nightfall. May that protected one travel in the boat of Ra and——" Here, Lady, the writing ceases but the holy hermit said that the Lady Kemmah would know the rest, and again he looked at me.

"'Does it perchance run,' I asked, "'and may Thoth find the balance even and may Osiris receive this protected one at his table to feast with him eternally"?'

"'Yes,' he said, 'I think that those were the words, or something very like them, that the Holy One repeated to me. Still I cannot be sure because my memory is bad, especially where prayers or writings about the gods are concerned. Since you, Lady, a stranger, know the end of the charm, doubtless it is a common one worn by thousands between Thebes and the sea. She whom I have to find not only knows the charm, but wears its other half, and how to seek her out I cannot think. Can you help me, Lady?'

"'Perhaps,' I answered. 'Show me this amulet, O Tau.'

"He looked round him to see that we were alone. Then he thrust his hand into his garments and from somewhere drew out the upper half of a very ancient tablet carven over with writing, that was fastened about his neck by a woven string of woman's hair. This tablet was broken or sawn asunder in the middle, not straight across but so as to leave a jagged edge with many points and hollows. I looked at it and knew it at once, since years before Roy the Hermit and my great-uncle had given me its counterpart, bidding me send it to him as a token if ever I had need of help. Then from where it hung upon my breast, I drew out that counterpart and set it against the half that Tau the Sailor held before me. Lo! they fitted exactly, since the stone being very hard had worn but little during the passage of the years.

Tau looked and nodded his head.

"'Strange that I should meet you thus, Lady Kemmah, and quite by chance—oh! quite by chance. Still, the gods know their own business, so why should we trouble ourselves about such things? Yet there might be another half that fitted on to this broken charm that has been lent to me. So before we go farther, tell me the name of the sender and where he dwells and aught else that you know about him.'

"'His name is Roy,' I answered, 'who in the world was known as Roy the King's son, though that king died long ago, and as you have said yourself, he lives beneath the shadow of the pyramids. For the rest he is the holy Prophet of a great brotherhood, has a long white beard and hair, is very handsome and pleasant-spoken; can see in the dark like a cat because he has dwelt so much among shadows, has knees that are hornier than the feet of a desert man, because of his continual kneeling in prayer, and when he thinks that he is alone, converses much with his own double, the *Ka* that is always at his side, or perchance with other ghosts, which tell him everything that passes in Egypt. At least, such were his appearance and custom many years ago when he gave me this half of the amulet, but what they are now, I cannot say."

"'The description will serve, Lady. Yes, it will serve

well enough, though now the holy Roy has lost most of the hair from the top of his head and is too thin to be called handsome, having something of the air of an ancient and half-famished hawk. Yet without doubt we speak of the same man, as the joined amulet bears us witness. Therefore, Lady Kemmah, whom I have met by chance, yes, quite by chance, just by waiting for you where the holy Roy told me I should do, hearken to my message!'

"Here, Queen, the manner of this seaman changed, and from being light and easy like to that of one whose words conceal a jest, became quick and intent. His pleasant, smiling face changed also, for of a sudden it seemed to grow fierce and eager, the face of one who has great things to carry through and whose honour hangs upon their doing.

"'Listen to me, Nurse of Royal Ones,' he said. 'The king whom once you dandled on your knees lies in his tomb, slain by the Shepherd spears. Would you see her who is sprung from him and the lady who gave her birth follow by the same road?'

"'Your question seems foolish, Tau, seeing that where they go, I must accompany them,' I answered.

"'I know that you would not,' he went on, 'and not for your own sake only. Yet the danger is great. There is a plot to take all three of you; it was revealed to the holy Roy. In this city dwell traitors who are parties to the plot. Soon, to-morrow mayhap, or the next day, they will come to the Queen and tell her that she is in peril and that they purpose to hide her away in a safe place. If she is persuaded by them, soon she will find that this safe place is in the prisons of Apepi at Tanis, if ever she lives to reach them—and then—do you understand? Or if she is not persuaded, then they will drag her away by force with the babe and deliver them up to the Shepherds.'

"I nodded my head and answered:

"'It would seem that time presses. What is your plan, Messenger?'

"'This: Presently I sail on to the city and there deliver a certain cargo to merchants who await it. Also I have passengers on board, travellers from Siout, farmer folk flying from the Shepherds. There are three of them: a woman of middle age not unlike to you in face and form, Lady Kemmah, who passes as my sister; a fair young woman who passes as my wife and nurses in her arms a baby girl of some three months. As such at least I shall describe them to the officers on the quay, nor will those two women question my words. Yet being changeable, they will desert me here for other friends and the place where they slept will be empty. Again, do you understand, Lady Kemmah?'

"'I understand that you propose that the Queen and I and the babe should take the place of these three upon your boat. If so, when and how?'

"'To-night, Lady Kemmah, I am told there is a religious feast in this city in honour of the god of Nile, to celebrate which hundreds will row out upon the river bearing lanterns and singing hymns. To avoid all these craft I purpose to bring my ship back to this wharf, since I must sail down Nile with the south wind that springs up ere the dawn. Shall I perchance find two peasant women and a babe waiting among those palms an hour before the rising of Ra?'

"'Perchance, Messenger. But tell me, if so, where would that journey end?'

"'In the shadow of the Great Pyramids, Lady, where a certain Holy One awaits them, since he says that although the lodging be poor, there alone they will be safe.'

"'That thought has come to me also, Tau. Yet this flight is very dangerous, and how know I that in it there is not some trap? How know I that you yourself are not in the pay of the Shepherds, or in that of the Theban traitors, and sent to tempt us to our doom?'

"'A wise question,' he answered. 'You have the message and you have the token of the amulet and you have my oath sworn upon the holy name, to break which will consign me everlastingly to hell. Still, a very wise question

when there is so much at stake, and by the gods, I know not
how to answer it!'

"We stood still awhile, staring at each other, and my
heart was full of doubt and fear. Once we were in this
man's power, what might not befall us? Or rather what
might not befall you, O Queen, and the royal child, since
it is true, Queen, that for myself I cared and care little."

"I know it, Kemmah beloved," answered Rima. "But
to your tale. What happened?"

"This, Queen. Of a sudden Tau the Messenger seemed
to grow uneasy.

"'This place is quiet and lonely,' he said. 'yet certainly
I feel as though we were being watched.'

"Now, Queen, we stood back from the private quay by
the single palm that stands in the open place, whither we
had withdrawn when we began to talk, for there we could
not be seen from the river and I knew that none could over-
hear us. In the hollow to my left stands that old shrine surmounted by the shattered statue of some god, which once,
it is said, was the gateway of a fallen temple; the same,
Queen, in which you often sit."

"I know it well, Kemmah."

"This shrine, Queen, was still half hidden by the morning
mist, and although it was out of earshot, Tau gazed at it
earnestly. As he gazed the mist departed from it like a
lifted veil, and following his glance, I saw that the shrine
was not empty, as I had thought. For there, Queen, kneeling in it as though lost in prayer, was an aged man. He
lifted his head and the full light fell upon his face. Lo! it
was the face of the holy Roy, my great-uncle, somewhat
changed since last I had seen him many years ago when he
gave me the half of the broken amulet, but without doubt
Roy himself."

"'It seems that here also dwells a hermit, Lady Kemmah, as well as in the shadow of the pyramids,' said Tau,
'and one whom I think I know. Is yonder man perchance
the holy Roy, Lady Kemmah?'

"'The holy Roy and no other. Why did you not tell me that you had brought him with you on your ship? It would have saved me much trouble of mind. I will speak with him at once.'

"'Aye, speak with him and satisfy your heart as to whether I be a true man or a false, Lady Kemmah.'

"I turned and ran to the shrine. It was empty! The holy Roy had gone, nor was there anywhere that he could have hidden himself.

"'The ways of prophets and hermits are very strange, Lady Kemmah,' said Tau. 'Alone of all men, they, or some of them, can be in two places at once. Now perchance I shall find you to-night, here by this shrine?'

"'Yes,' I answered, 'I think that you will find us. That is, if the Queen consents and nothing hinders us, such as death or bonds. But stay! How can we come by those country women's garments? There are none such in the palace, and to send out to buy them might awake doubts, for the Queen is well watched.'

"'The holy Roy is very foreseeing,' said Tau with a smile, 'or I am; it matters not which.'

"Then he went to where I first met him and from behind a stone drew a bundle.

"'Take this,' he said. 'In it I think you will find all that is needful, clean clothes though rough, that it will be safe even for a royal babe to wear. Farewell, Lady Kemmah; the river is clear of mist and I must begone. Guided by the spirit of the holy Roy which, as he can be in two places at once, doubtless will companion you also, I will return to find—my sister, my wife, and her infant babe—one, nay, two hours before to-morrow's dawn.'

"Then he went, and I went also, full of thoughts. Yet I determined to say nothing of the matter to you, O Queen, till I heard what answer those lords made to your prayer to-day."

"Have you looked in the bundle, Kemmah?" asked the Queen.

·· "Yes," answered Kemmah, "to find that all is as this Tau said. There are two cloaks and other garments such as farmer women use in travelling, suited to your size and mine, also the winter dress of a little child."

"Let us go to look at them," said the Queen.

CHAPTER III

The Escape

THEY stood in the private apartments of the palace. Eunuchs guarded, or were supposed to guard, the outer gates, for the Queen Rima was still surrounded by the trappings of royalty, and at the door of her chamber stood the giant Nubian, Ru, he who had been the body-servant of King Kheperra, he who after slaying six of the Shepherds with his own hand had rescued the body of his master, throwing it over his shoulder and bearing it from the battle as a shepherd bears a lamb. The Queen Rima and the Lady Kemmah had examined the garments brought by Tau the Messenger, and hidden them away. Now they were consulting together, near to a little bed on which the infant princess lay asleep.

"Your plan is very dangerous," said the Queen, who was much disturbed and walked to and fro with her eyes fixed upon the sleeping babe. "You ask me to fly to Memphis, that is, to walk into the jaws of the hyena. This you do because a messenger is come from an aged uncle of yours who is a hermit or a high priest, or a prophet of some secret sect, and who, for aught you know, may have been dead for years and now be but a bait upon a hook to catch us."

"There is the cut amulet, Queen. See how well the pieces fit and how that white line in the stone runs on from one to the other."

"Doubtless they fit. Doubtless they are the halves of the same talisman. But such holy things are famous and so is their story. Mayhap someone knew that the priest

21

Roy had given you one half of this charm and took the other
from his body, or stole it to be used to deceive you and to
give colour to the offer of a hiding place among the dead.
Who is this Tau of whom you never heard before? How
came he to find you so easily? How is it that he can pass in
and out of Thebes without question, he who comes from
Memphis, holding all the threads of these plots between his
fingers, if plots there be?"

"I do not know who he is," said Kemmah. "I know only
that when these same doubts crossed my mind, this messenger showed me the holy Roy himself in proof of the truth
of his message, and that then I believed."

"Aye, Kemmah, but bethink you. Are you not a priestess, one soaked in the mysteries and magic of the Egyptians
from your childhood, like to this uncle of yours before you?
Did you not see the vision of the Egyptian goddesses Isis
and Hathor blessing my child, which after all is but an old
tale retold of those who spring from the bodies of kings?
How comes it that no one else saw those goddesses?"

"How comes it that you dreamed of them, O Queen?"
asked Kemmah drily.

"A dream is a dream. Who can give weight to dreams
that come and go by thousands, flitting round our heads
like gnats in sleep to vanish into the darkness whence they
rose? A dream is a dream and of no account, but a vision
seen with the waking eye is another matter, something that
springs from madness—or perchance from truth. And now
you have another vision, that of an old man who, if he lives
at all, dwells far away, and on this unstable cloud you ask me
to build a house of hope and safety. How can I be sure that
you are not mad, as indeed the wise men of my country say
that most of us are in this way or in that? You behold
gods, but are there any gods, and if so, why are the gods
of Egypt not the same as those of Babylon, and the gods
of Babylon not the same as those of Tyre? If there be
gods, why are they all different?"

"Because men are different, Queen, and every nation of

them clothes God in its own garments: aye, and every man and woman also."

"May be, may be! Yet a stranger's tale and a vision are poor props to lean upon when life and safety hang in the balance and with them the crown of Egypt. I'll not trust myself and the babe to this man and his boat lest soon both of us should sleep at the bottom of the Nile, or lie awaiting death in some Shepherd dungeon. Let us bide where we are; your gods can protect us as well here as by the Pyramids of Memphis, should we live to reach them. Or if we must go, let these gods send us some sign; they have still many hours in which to travel from their heaven."

Thus spoke Queen Rima wildly in her doubt and despair. Kemmah listened and bowed her head.

"Let it be as the Queen pleases," she said. "If the gods desire, doubtless they will show us a path of escape. If they should not desire so to do, then we can remain here and await their will, since the gods are still the gods. Now, Lady, let us eat and rest, but let us not sleep till that hour is past when we should have embarked upon the ship of Tau the Messenger."

So they ate, and afterwards, taking a lamp, Kemmah walked through the palace and found it strangely silent. All seemed to have departed; as one weak old slave told her, to attend the feast of the god of Nile and to sail in boats upon the river.

"Such things would not have been allowed to happen in the old days," he said querulously, "for then, who ever heard of a palace being deserted by those who were in attendance upon Majesty in order that they might enjoy themselves elsewhere? But since the good god Kheperra was killed by those Shepherd dogs in the battle everything seems to have changed. Nobody thinks anything of service; everybody thinks of himself and what he can get. And there is money going, Lady Kemmah, I tell you there is money going. Oh! sitting in my corner I have seen plenty of it being passed from hand to hand. Where it comes from

I do not know. I was even offered some myself, what for I do not know, but refused it, for what do I want with money who am so old and draw my rations from the stores, as I have done these fifty years, also my summer and winter garments?"

Kemmah contemplated him with her quiet eyes, then answered:

"No, old Friend, you want nothing with money, since I know that your tomb is provided. Tell me, you are acquainted with all the palace doors, are you not, and the gates also?"

"Every one of them, Lady Kemmah, every one of them. When I was stronger it used to be my office to lock them all, and I still have the second set of keys, which no one has taken from me, and remember the tricks of the inner bolts."

"Then, Friend, grow strong again; even if it be for the last time, go lock those doors and gates and shoot those bolts and bring the keys to me in the private apartments. It will be a good trick to play upon these revellers who are absent without leave when they return and find that they cannot get in to sleep off their drink till after the sun has risen."

"Yes, yes, Lady Kemmah, a very good trick. I will get the keys and go, following the round as I used to do and shooting the inner bolts that I named after all the gods of the Underworld, so that I might never forget the order in which they came. Oh! I will light my lantern and go at once, as though I were young again, and my wife and little children were waiting to receive me at the end of my round."

The half of an hour later the old man reappeared at the private chambers, announcing that all the gates and doors were locked, and that strangely enough he had found every one of them open and the keys missing.

"They forgot that I had their twins," he said, chuckling, "also that I knew how to shoot the inner bolts; I whom they look upon as a silly old fool only fit for the embalmer's bath. Here are the keys, Lady Kemmah, which I shall be glad to be rid of for they are a great weight. Take them and promise not to tell that it was I who locked the doors and forced all those idle people to sleep out in the cold. For if you do they will beat me to-morrow. Now if you had a cup of wine!"

Kemmah fetched drink and gave it to the aged man, mixed with water that it might not be too strong for him. Then, while he smacked his lips refreshed by the liquor, she bade him go to the little gatehouse of the private apartments and watch there, and if he should see any approaching the gate, to make report to Ru, who kept guard at the door which was at the foot of the eight stairs that led to the antechamber of the apartments.

This, encouraged by the wine and by a sense that once more he was taking part in the affairs of life, though what these might be he did not understand, the old fellow said that he would do and departed to his station.

Then Kemmah went and talked earnestly with the giant Ru, who listened, nodding his head, and as he did so girt his armour of bull's hide upon his mighty frame. Moreover, he looked to see that his javelins were loose in their sheath and that the edge of his great bronze battle-axe was sharp. Lastly he set lamps in the niches of the wall in such fashion that if the door were forced their light would fall upon those coming up the stair, while he, standing at the head of it, would remain in shadow.

These things done, Kemmah returned to the Queen, who sat brooding by the bed of the child, but of them to her she said nothing.

"Why do you carry a spear in your hand, Kemmah?" asked Rima, looking up.

"Because it makes a good staff to lean upon, Queen, and one that at need may serve another purpose. This place seems very still and fateful and who knows but that in the stillness we may hear some god speaking ere the dawn, telling us whether we should take ship with Tau, or bide where we are?"

"You are a strange woman, Kemmah," said the Queen, and once more fell to her brooding till at length she sank to sleep.

But Kemmah did not sleep; she waited and watched the curtains that hid the stair on which Ru kept guard. At length in the intense silence of the night that was broken only now and again by the melancholy note of some dog howling at the moon, for all the inhabitants of the city seemed to be absent at the festival, Kemmah thought she heard the sound as of gates or doors being shaken by some-one trying to enter them. Rising softly she went to the curtains beyond which Ru was seated on the topmost stair.

"Did you note anything?" she asked.

"Aye, Lady," he answered. "Men try to enter by the gates, but find them closed. The old slave reported to me that they were coming and has fled to hide himself. Now go up to the top of the little pylon above this door and tell me if you can see aught."

Kemmah went, climbing a narrow stair in the dark, and presently found herself on the roof of the pylon some thirty feet above the ground, where in times of trouble a watchman was stationed. Round it ran a battlement with openings through which arrows could be shot or spears thrown. The moon shone brightly, flooding the palace gardens and the great city beyond them with silver light, but the Nile she could not see because of the roofs behind her, though she heard the distant murmur of those who kept festival upon its waters, from which they would not return until the sun had risen.

Presently in the shadow of one of the great gateways she saw a group of men standing and, as it seemed to her, taking counsel together. They moved out of the shadow and she counted them. They were eight in all, armed every one of them, for the light shone upon their spears. They came to some decision, for they began to walk across the open court towards the private door of the royal apartments. Kemmah ran down the stairs and told Ru what she had seen.

"Now were I standing on that roof perhaps I might put a javelin into one or more of these night birds before they come to the doors," he said.

"Nay," answered Kemmah. "They may be messengers of peace, or soldiers who will guard the Queen. Wait to smite till they show themselves otherwise."

He nodded and said:

"Yonder door is old and not of the strongest. It can soon be battered in and then perhaps there will be fighting—one man against eight, Lady Kemmah. What if aught should happen to me, Lady Kemmah? Is there any other way by which the Queen and the royal babe may escape?"

"Nay, for the doors into the great hall where the Council was held are barred; I have tried them. There is no way save by leaping from the palace wall at the back, and a babe's bones are tender. Therefore, Ru, nothing must happen to you. Pray the gods to give you strength and cunning."

"Of the first I have plenty, of the second I fear but little. Still I will do my best and may Osiris be good to him on whom my axe falls."

"Hearken, Ru. Should you scotch those snakes or cause them to run, make ready to fly with us and be not astonished if instead of a Queen and a waiting-lady, you see two peasant women and a peasant's babe."

"I am not easily astonished, Lady, and I weary of this Thebes since the good god my master fell and all these upstarts began to plot with Apepi, as plot they do. But whither will you fly?"

"I think that a ship waits us by the private quay, and its captain, one Tau, will meet us two hours before the dawn, that is before so very long, in the shadow of the old shrine. You know the place."

"Aye, I know it. Hush! I hear footsteps."

"Parley with them as long as you may, Ru, for there are things to be done."

"Yes, there is plenty to be done," he answered as she fled back through the curtains.

The Queen woke at her step.

"Your gods have not come, Kemmah," she said, "or given any sign. So I suppose it is fated that we should stop here."

"I think that the gods—or devils—are coming, Queen. Now off with those robes and be swift. Nay, talk not, I pray, but do as I bid you."

Rima glanced at her face and obeyed. Within a very little time, all being prepared to their hands, the three of them were changed into farmer women and a farmer's babe. Then Kemmah took a sack and thrust into it all the ancient priceless jewels, the regalia of the old Pharaohs of Egypt, and these were not few; also a sum in gold.

"This gear of crowns and sceptres and gems and gold which you have got together so carefully will be too heavy for us to carry, Kemmah, who have that which is more precious to bear between us," and she glanced at the child.

"There is one yonder who will carry it, Queen, one who carried something else on his shoulder out of the battle. Or if he cannot, then I think it will not matter who takes the gathered wealth of the Pharaohs of the South."

"You mean that our lives are at hazard, Kemmah?"

"That is what I mean, no less."

Rima's beautiful but sorrow-stricken face and eyes seemed to take fire.

"I would that they might be lost," she said. "Have you ever thought, Friend, of the wonderful things that may lie behind the gates of death, the glories and the harmonies and the eternities, or failing these, the rich darkness of everlasting sleep? Life! I weary of life and would put all to the hazard. Yet there is the babe born of my body, the Royal Princess of Egypt, and for her sake——"

"Yes," said the quiet Kemmah, "for her sake!"

There came a thunder of noise upon the door beyond the curtains.

"Open!" shouted voices.

"Open for yourselves. But know that death waits those who would violate her Majesty of Egypt," answered the deep guttural voice of Ru.

"We come to take the Queen and the Princess to those who will guard them well," cried one without.

"What better guard can they have than death?" asked Ru in answer.

There was a pause. Then came blows upon the door, heavy blows as of axes, but still it held. Another pause and a tree trunk or some such weighty thing was brought and driven against it, and presently with a crash it fell, burst from its hinges. Rima seized the child and ran into the shadows. Kemmah leapt to the curtains and stood there looking between them, the spear she carried raised in her right hand. This was what she saw.

The giant Nubian stood on the topmost stair in the shadow, for the light of the lamps in the niches struck forward. In his right hand he held a javelin, in his left he grasped the handle of his battle-axe and a small shield made of the hide of a river horse. Grim and terrible looked the Ethiopian giant outlined thus against the shadow.

A tall man with a sword in his hand scrambled over the fallen door, the moonlight shining on his armour. The javelin flashed and the man fell in a heap, his mail clattering upon the bronze hinges of the door. He was dragged aside. Others rushed in, a number of them. Ru shifted his battle-axe into his right hand, lifted it, leaned forward and waited, advancing the shield to cover his head. Blows fell upon the shield. Then the axe crashed down and a man sank in a heap. Ru began to sing some wild Ethiopian war chant and as he sang he smote, and as he smote men died beneath the blows of that terrible axe driven with the weight of his mighty arm. Yet they pressed forward, for they were desperate. Death might be in front of them, but if they failed death was also behind at the hands of their confederates.

The stair was too wide for Ru to cover. One ran under

his arm and appeared between the curtains, where he stood staring. Kemmah saw his face. It was that of a great Theban lord who had fought with Kheperra in the battle and now had been suborned by the Shepherds. Rage seized her. She sprang at him and with all her strength drove the spear she held through his throat. He fell, gasping. She stamped upon his face, crying "Die, dog! Die, traitor!" and die he did.

On the stairway the blows grew fewer. Presently Ru appeared, laughing and red with blood.

"All are dead," he cried, "save one who fled. But where is the knave who slipped past me?"

"Here," answered Kemmah, pointing to a still form in the shadows.

"Good. Very good!" said Ru. "Now I think better of women than ever I did before. Yet, hurry, hurry! One dog has escaped and he goes to call the pack. What is that? Wine? Give me to drink. Aye, give me wine and a cloak to cover me. I am no seemly sight for queens to look on."

"Are you hurt?" said Kemmah as she brought the goblet.

"Nay, not a scratch; still no seemly sight, though the blood be that of traitors. Here's to the gods of vengeance! Here's to the hell that holds them! This garment is scant for one of my size, but it will serve. What's that sack you drag to me?"

"No matter what it is. Carry it, Ru. You are no warrior now, you are a porter. Carry it, O glorious Ru, and lose it not, for in it lie the crowns of Egypt. Come, Queen, the road is clear, thanks to the axe of Ru."

Rima came, bearing her babe, and at the sight of the red stair and of those who lay upon it or at its foot, shrank back and said in a wavering voice, for she was almost bemused with doubts and terror:

"Is this the message of your gods, Kemmah?" and she pointed to the stains upon the floor and walls. "And are these their messengers? Look at them! I know their faces. They were the friends and captains of dead Kheperra, my lord. Why, O Ru, do you slay the friends of him who was Pharaoh, who came here doubtless to lead me and his child to safety?"

"Aye, Queen," said Kemmah, "to the safety of death or of the prison of Apepi."

"I'll not believe it, woman, nor will I go with you," said Rima, stamping her foot. "Fly if you will, as well you may do with all this blood upon your hands; here I stay with my child."

Kemmah glanced at her, then as though in thought she looked down at the ground while Ru whispered in her ear:

"Command me and I will carry her."

The eyes of Kemmah fell upon that great lord whom she had slain with her own hand, and she noted that from beneath his breastplate there projected the end of a papyrus roll that had been thrust upwards when he fell. She bent down and took it. Opening it swiftly she read, as she who was learned could do well enough. It was addressed to the dead man and his companions and sealed with the seals of the high priest and others. This was the writing:

"In the names of all the gods and for the welfare of Egypt, we command you to take Rima the Babylonian, wife of the good god Pharaoh who is not, and her child, the Royal Princess Nefra, and to bring them to us, living if may be, that they may be delivered to King Apepi in fulfilment of our oath. Read and obey."

"Can you read the Egyptian writing, Queen?" asked Kemmah. "If so, herein is a matter that concerns you."

"Read you. I have little skill," answered Rima indifferently.

So she read, slowly, that the words might sink into the mind of the Queen.

Rima heard and leaned against her, trembling.

"Why did I ever come to this land of traitors?" she moaned. "Oh! would that I were dead."

"As you will be if you stay here longer, Queen," said Kemmah bitterly. "Meanwhile it is the traitors who are dead, or some of them, and now tell their tale to Kheperra, your lord and mine. Come. Come swiftly, there are more villains left in Thebes."

But Rima sank to the ground, swooning. As she fell Kemmah snatched the child from her and looked at Ru.

"It is good," said the giant. "Now she can talk no more and I will carry her. But what of that sack? Must we leave it behind? Life is more than crowns."

"Nay, Ru, set it on my head, for thus peasants bear their burdens. I can hold it with my left hand and clasp the child with my right."

He did so and lifted the Queen in his great arms.

Thus they passed down the stair, stepping over the dead and out into the night.

Across the open space they went, heading for the palm trees of the garden. The babe wailed feebly but Kemmah stifled its cries beneath her cloak. The weight of the treasures in the sack pressed her down and the sharp edges of the jewelled crowns and sceptres cut into her brow. Still she staggered on bravely. They reached the shadow of the palms where she paused for a moment to look back and get her breath. Behold! Men—numbers of them—were running toward the doors of the private apartments.

"We did not leave too soon. Forward!" said Ru.

On they went, till at length before them in the glade they saw the ruined shrine. Kemmah staggered to it and sank to her knees, for she was spent.

"Now, unless help comes, there is an end," said Ru. "Two half-dead women I might carry, also the sack upon my head. But how about the babe? Nay, that babe is the Princess of Egypt. Whoever dies, she must be saved."

"Aye," said Kemmah faintly. "Leave me, it matters not, but save the child. Take her and her mother and go to the quay. Perchance the boat is there."

"Perchance it is not," grumbled Ru, staring about him.

Then help came. For as before from behind a palm appeared the sailor Tau.

"You are somewhat early, Lady Kemmah," he said, "but fortunately so am I and so is the down Nile wind. At least here you are, all three of you. But who is this?" and he stared at the giant Nubian.

"One who can be vouched for," answered Ru. "If you doubt it, go look at the stair of the royal apartments. One, too, who, if there be need, can break your bones as a slave breaks sticks."

"That I can well believe," said Tau, "but of bone-breaking we can talk afterwards. Now follow me, and swiftly."

Then he threw the sack over his shoulder, and putting his arm about Kemmah, supported her forward to the quay.

At the foot of the steps was a boat, and at a distance on the Nile appeared a ship riding at anchor, her sail half hoisted. They entered the boat, and seizing the oars, Tau rowed them to the ship. A rope was cast which he caught and made fast to the prow of the boat, drawing on it till they came alongside the ship. Hands were stretched out to help them; soon they were all aboard.

"Up anchor!" cried Tau, "and hoist the sail."

"We hear you, Lord," answered a voice.

Three minutes later that ship was gliding down the Nile before the strong south wind. Nor was it too soon, for as they passed silently into the night they caught sight of men, some of whom bore lanterns, searching the palm grove that they had left. They laid the women and the child in the cabin. Then Tau said:

"Now, Breaker of Bones, you may have a tale to tell me, and perchance a cup of wine and a bite of food will looes your tongue "

Thus did Queen Rima, Nefra, Royal Princess of Egypt, the Lady Kemmah and Ru the Ethiopian escape from Thebes and from the hands of traitors.

CHAPTER IV

THE TEMPLE OF THE SPHINX

FOR day after day the ship of Tau journeyed on down Nile. At night, or when the wind would not serve, it was tied up to the bank, always in as uninhabited a place as might be but never near a town. Twice this happened in the neigh-bourhood of great temples that had been wrecked by the Shepherds in the first fury of their invasion and not as yet repaired. Yet after it was dark, out of these desolated fanes or of the sepulchres around them issued men who brought food and other things to sell, but who from the signs that they made, Kemmah, being initiated, well knew to be priests, though of what faith she did not know. These men would talk with Tau apart, showing him much rever-ence, then on this pretext or on that he would bring them into the cabin where the infant princess lay asleep, whom they would look upon fearfully, and even adore upon their bended knees as though she were divine; then rising, depart blessing her in the name of the gods they worshipped. Moreover, never did they seem to take payment for the food they brought.

All of these things Kemmah noted, as did Ru, although he appeared so simple, but of them Rima the Queen took but little heed. Ever since her lord the Pharaoh Kheperra had been slain in the battle, her spirit had left her, and the dis-covery of the treason of the lords who had been his counsel-lors and generals, whereof Ru had slain six and Kemmah one in the fight upon the stairs of the Theban palace, seemed to have crushed her very soul so that now she cared for nothing save to nurse her child.

When she woke from her swoon to find herself upon the ship she asked few questions and from Ru she shrank, although she loved him well, saying that he smelt of blood. Nor would she speak much to Tau because, as she declared, she trusted no man any more. To Kemmah only did she talk freely at times, and then mostly as to how she might escape out of this accursed Egypt with her child, back to her royal father, the King of Babylon.

"So far the gods of Egypt have not served you so ill, Queen," said the Lady Kemmah, "seeing that they brought you and that Royal One"—and she waved her hand toward the babe—"out of the net of traitors, and when escape seemed impossible, safe on to this ship, doing this after you had declared that you had no faith in them."

"Mayhap, Kemmah. Yet those gods decreed that my royal husband should be killed and that those whom he and I trusted should prove themselves the foulest of all men who sought to betray his wife and child into the hands of enemies, whence we were saved only by your wit and the strength and courage of an Ethiopian. Also it is not for me, a stranger, that they work, but for Egypt's royal seed that was born of my body. Nor is this to be wondered at, seeing, although as Pharaoh's wife I made offerings upon their altars, they are no gods of mine. I tell you that I would get me back to Babylon and ere I die bow my knee again in the temples of my forefathers. Take me back to Babylon, Kemmah, where men are not traitors to the bread they eat and do not strive to sell the seed of those who died for them into captivity or death."

"This I will do if I may," answered Kemmah, "but alas! Babylon is far off and all the lands between are ablaze with war. Therefore take heart, Queen, and wait with patience."

"I have no heart left," answered Rima, "who desire but one thing—to find my lord again whether he sits at the table of your Osiris, or rides the clouds with Bel, or sleeps in the deep darkness. Where he is, there would I be and nowhere else, and least of all in this accursed Egypt. Give me my child to nurse, that I may hold her while I may. We love that most that we must leave the soonest, Kemmah."

Then Kemmah gave her the babe and turned away to hide her tears, since she was sure that sorrow was eating out the life of this bereaved widow and daughter of kings.

Once when they were off Memphis which they strove to pass at early dawn before men were abroad, there was danger. Officers came to their ship from a boat, bidding it lie to, a command that Tau thought it best to obey.

"Now play your parts well," he said to Kemmah, "remembering that you are my sister and that the Queen is my wife who lies sick. Go tell her to forget her woes and be as crafty as a serpent. As for you, Ru, hide that great axe of yours, though where you can find it easily, remembering that you are a slave whom I bought for a great sum in Thebes that I may make money by showing off your strength in market-places, and that you can talk little or no Egyptian."

The boat came alongside. In it were two officers, young men who seemed to be sleepy, for they yawned, and a common fellow who rowed it. The two officers climbed to the deck and asked for the captain. Tau appeared, very roughly clad, and in a coarse voice inquired of their business.

"It is your business that we want to know, Sailor," said one of the officers.

"That is easy to tell, sir. I am a trader who take corn up Nile and bring cattle down. There are a number of calves forward there, bred by the best southern bulls. Are you perchance buyers? If so, you might like to look at them. There is one that has the 'apis' marks upon it, or something of the kind."

"Do we look like cattle dealers?" asked the officer haughtily. "Show me your writings."

"Here they are, sir," and Tau produced a papyrus sealed by the trade masters at Memphis and other cities.

"A wife and child, a sister—which means another wife

grown old—and so many crew. Well, we seek two women and a child, so perhaps we had better see them."

"Is it necessary?" asked the other. "This does not look like a queen's warship such as we were told to search for, and the stench of those calves is horrible after a night of feasting."

"Warship, sir? Did you talk of a warship? Well, there is one following us down the river. We saw her once, but being of such deep draught, she got stuck on a sand bank so that I do not know when she will reach Memphis. She seemed to be a very fine ship with a multitude of armed men on board of her. But it was said that she was going to stop at Siout, the frontier city of the South, or what used to be its frontier city before we beat those proud-stomached Southerns. But come and look at the women, if you will; come and look at them."

This information about the warship seemed to interest the two officers so much that they followed Tau thinking little of the two women. He took a lantern and thrust it through the curtains into the cabin, saying;

"May an evil spirit take this thing! How badly it burns."

"An evil stink has taken it already," answered one of the officers, pinching his nostrils between his finger and thumb as he peered between the curtains. In the low light the place was very dark and all that the officers could see was Kemmah in dirty garments seated on a sack—little did they know that this sack contained the ancient and priceless royal ornaments of Upper Egypt—and engaged in mixing milk and water in a gourd, while beyond on a couch lay a woman with dishevelled hair and holding a bundle to her breast.

Just then the lantern went out and Tau began to talk of finding oil to relight it.

"It is needless, Friend," said the chief officer, "I think that we have seen enough. Pursue your voyage in peace and sell the calves at the best price you can get."

Then he turned to the deck where, as ill luck would have it, he caught sight of Ru squatted on the boards and trying to look as small as he could.

"That is a big black man," he said. "Now did not some spy send a message about a Negro who killed many of our friends up yonder? Stand up, fellow."

Tau translated, or seemed to do so, and Ru stood up, rolling his big eyes till the white showed and grinning all over a silly face.

"Ah!" said the officer, "a very big man. By the gods! what a chest and arms. Now, Captain, who is this giant and what are you doing with him on board your trading boat?"

"Lords," answered Tau, "he is a venture of mine in which I have put most of my savings. He is mighty and performs feats of strength, for the sight of which I hope to get much money down in Tanis."

"Does he?" said the officer, much interested but with suspicion. "Well, fellow, perform a feat of strength."

Ru shook his head vaguely.

"He does not understand your tongue, sir, who is an Ethiopian. Stay, I will tell him."

Then he began to address Ru in unknown words. Ru woke up and nodded, grinning. Next instant he sprang at the two officers, seized one of them with either hand by the neckbands of their garments and lifted them from the deck as though they had been infants. Next, roaring with laughter, he stepped to the side of the ship and held them out over the Nile as though he were about to drop them into the water. The officers shouted, Tau swore and tried to drag him back, yelling orders into his ear. Ru turned round astonished, still holding the two men in the air before him and looking at the belly of the ship as though he meant to throw them into it.

At length he seemed to understand and dropped them to the deck, on which they fell flat.

"That is one of his favourite tricks, sirs," said Tau as he

helped them to their feet. "He is so strong that he can carry a third man in his teeth."

"Is it?" said an officer. "Well, we have had enough of your savage and his tricks, who, I think, will land you in prison before you have done with him. Keep him off now while we get into the boat."

Thus was the ship of Tau searched by the officers of Apepi.

When the boat had gone and once more the ship was slipping past the quays of Memphis unobserved in the mists drawn by the rising sun from the river, Ru came near to the tiller and said:

"I think, Lord Tau, for a lord or count I hold you to be, although it pleases you to pass as the owner of a small trading boat, that you would have done well to let me drop those two fine fellows into the Nile that tells no stories of those it buries. By and by it will be found that there is no warship such as you talked of so wonderfully, and then——?"

"And then, Breaker of Bones, it may go hard with those officers who chattered of such a ship like finches in the reeds and while they did so let the real prize slip through their fingers. For this, indeed, I am sorry, since those young men were not bad fellows in their way. As for dropping them into the Nile, it might have been well enough, though cruel, had there not been a witness. What would that boatman who rowed them to the ship have reported when he found that they returned from it no more?"

"You are clever," said Ru admiringly. "I never thought of that."

"No, Ru. If my brain were added to your brute strength and uninstructed honesty, why, you would rule the world of brutes. But they are not, and therefore you must be content to serve in the yoke, like a bull, which is as strong as you, are, or stronger."

"If it is brains that make the difference, why do you not rule, Lord Tau, who are also a likely man though not so big as I am? Why are you carrying fugitives upon a dirty little merchant ship instead of sitting upon a Pharaoh's throne? Tell me, who am but a simple black man bred to war and honesty."

Tau with much skill steered his ship through a fleet of barges poling up Nile laden with fodder. Then calling to a sailor to take his place, for now the river was open with no craft in sight, he sat himself down on the low bulwark, and answered:

"Because mayhap, friend Ru, I also choose to serve. Being stupid, like most honest men, especially if they are strong and one of a simple race that understands nothing except love from which is born mankind, and war that keeps down its numbers, you may not believe me when I tell you that the only true joy in life lies in service of this sort or of that. Pharaohs are served, which is why they are often so blind and so satisfied and being but vain bubbles blown along by a wind they cannot see, springing, although they know it not, from the poisoned breath of multitudes; for the most part they do more harm than good and are themselves the slaves of slaves. With him who serves it is otherwise, for, setting aside self-seekings and ambitions, he works humbly for that which is good and in this work finds his reward."

Ru rubbed his brow, then asked:

"But whom does such an one serve, Lord?"

"He serves God, Ru."

"God? There are many gods that I have heard of in Ethiopia, in Egypt, and in other lands. What god does he serve and where does he find that god?"

"He finds him in his own heart, Ru, but what his name may be I cannot tell you. Some call it Justice, some call it Freedom, some call it Hope, some call it Spirit."

"And what do those call it who serve only themselves and their own lusts, careless of all those fine things, Lord?"

"I do not know, Ru, and yet I know that name. It is Death."

"Yet they live as long as other men, Lord, and often reap a finer harvest."

"Aye, Ru, but very soon their day is done and then, if they have not repented, their souls die."

"So you believe that souls can live on, as the priests seem to teach."

"Yes, Ru, I believe that they can live longer than Ra the sun himself, longer than the stars, and from age to age reap the fruits of honest service. Yet of these matters do not ask me but ask one whom you will soon meet and whose disciple I am."

"I don't wish to, Lord, seeing that my brain swims already, but tell me, if it please you, to what end is all this service of yours that causes you to sail up Nile and at great risk to rescue certain ladies and a certain babe?"

"I am not sure, for true service is its own end. Moreover, it is not for me to ask of ends, who am sworn to obey without doubt or question."

"So you also have a master, Lord. Who is he?"

"That you will learn ere long, Ru. Yet do not think to look upon some king or enthroned high priest surrounded with pomps and ceremonies. Ru, I will instruct you, who are so ignorant. Doubtless you believe that Egypt and the world are ruled by the strength you see, by Pharaohs, by armies, and by wealth. Yet it is not so. There is another strength you do not see which is its guide and conqueror, and its name is Spirit. The priests teach that to every man there is given a *Ka* or a double, an invisible something that is stronger, purer, more enduring than he is. Something that perhaps from time to time looks upon the face of God and whispers of God's will. Now if this be a parable, yet in a sense it is true since always such a spirit is at the elbow of everyone who lives. Or rather there are two spirits, one of good and one of evil; one that leads upwards and one that leads downwards."

"I say again that you make my head swim, Lord. But tell me, where and to what is your spirit leading you?"

"Towards the gates of peace, Ru; peace for myself and peace for Egypt; towards a land where you would find little occupation for in it there is no war. Look, yonder are the Great Pyramids, the homes of the dead, and mayhap of their souls which do not die. Come, help me lower the sail since we must drift past them slowly, to return when night has fallen and land certain passengers. There, perhaps, Ru, you will learn more of the meaning of all this talk of mine."

Night had come. At its approach he who was called Tau had rowed his ship back to a certain landing place which now, at the time of the rising Nile, was not so very far away from the Great Pyramids and the Sphinx that sits near to them staring eternally into nothingness. Here they disembarked, all of them, under shelter of the darkness and of a bed of reeds.

Scarcely were they on shore when they saw boats, which great lanterns hung at their prow and stern showed to be full of armed men, rowing down Nile. Tau watched them go by and said:

"I think some messenger has told those officers at Memphis that there was no warship following us from Thebes and that now they search for a certain trading boat on which travelled two women and a babe. Well, let them search, for the birds are out of their hands and where they nest no Shepherd will dare to come."

Then, having given directions to the mate of the boat, a very quiet, secret-faced man, as were all those on board of her, he took Rima the Queen by the hand and led her into the darkness, being followed by Kemmah, who bore the child, and by Ru the Ethiopian, who carried upon his shoulder the sack that contained the jewels of the Pharaohs of Upper Egypt.

For a long while they trudged forward, first between groves of palm trees and then over desert sands, till at length the waning moon rose and they saw a wondrous

sight. In front of them appeared the enormous shape of a
lion cut from the living rock whose face was not that of a
beast but of a man, wearing the headdress of a god or king,
and staring towards the east with solemn, terrifying eyes.

"What is that?" asked Rima faintly. "Have we reached
the Underworld and is this its god? For surely yonder
dreadful smiling countenance must be that of a god."

"Nay, Lady," answered Tau, "it is but the symbol of a
god, the Sphinx which has sat here for countless ages.
Look! Behind it stand the pyramids outlined against the
sky, and beneath it are safety and rest for you and for your
child."

"Safety for the child, perhaps," she said, "and for me,
as I think, the longest rest of all. For know, O Tau, that
Death looks at me out of those solemn smiling eyes."

Tau made no answer; indeed, even his calm spirit seemed
to be frightened at those words of evil omen, as was Kemmah, who muttered:

"We go to dwell among sepulchres and it is as well, for I
think that soon they will be needed."

Even Ru was frightened, though more by the gigantic
figure of the Sphinx towering above him than by the Queen's
words, which he scarcely seemed to understand.

"Here is that which turns my heart to water and loosens
my knees," he said in his savage imagery. "Here is that
with which no man, not even I, can fight, and therefore for
the first time I am afraid. Here is Fate itself, and what can
man do in the face of Fate?"

"Obey its decrees, as all must," answered Tau solemnly.
"Forward now, for the temple of this god is open, and leave
the rest—to Fate."

They came to some steps about fifty paces from the out-
stretched paws of this mighty monument, and descending
them, found themselves facing what seemed to be a huge
granite block in a wall. Taking a stone which lay at hand,
Tau knocked upon this block in a peculiar fashion. Thrice
did he repeat this rhythmic series of blows, each time with

some difference. Then he waited, and behold, presently
in a silent fashion the great stone turned, leaving a narrow
opening through which he beckoned them to follow him.
They entered to find themselves in dense darkness and to
hear sounds as of passwords being given and received.
Next lamps appeared floating towards them through the
darkness and they perceived that these were borne by men
clothed as white-robed priests who yet carried swords like
soldiers and wore knives thrust through their girdles.
There were six of these priests and a seventh who appeared
to be a leader of them, for he walked ahead. To this man
Tau spoke, saying:

"I bring you that I went forth to seek," and he pointed
to the royal child sleeping in the arms of Kemmah and to the
Queen and behind her, to the gigantic Ru on whom the
priests looked doubtfully.

Tau began to tell them who he was, but the leader of the
priests said:

"It is needless. The Holy Prophet has spoken to me of
him. Yet let him understand that he who reveals the secrets of this place dies terribly."

"Is it so?" said Ru. "Well, already I feel as though
I were dead and buried."

Then one by one the priests made obeisance to the babe,
and this done, motioned to them to follow.

On they went, down a long passage that seemed to be
built of blocks of alabaster, till they came to a great hall,
of which the roof was supported by huge columns of granite,
in which hall sat solemn statues of gods or kings. Crossing
it, they reached a gallery, out of which opened chambers
that served as dwelling rooms, for in them were window-
places, which chambers, it seemed, had been made ready
for them, since they were furnished with beds and all things
necessary, even to clothing such as women wear. Moreover, in one of them a table was set with good food and wine.

"Eat now and sleep," said Tau. "I go to make report to
the Prophet. To-morrow he will speak with you."

CHAPTER V

THE SWEARING OF THE OATH

EARLY on the following morning Kemmah was awakened by a ray of sunshine striking upon her bed through a window-place in the chamber.

At least we are not dwelling in a tomb, she thought to herself with gratitude, for tombs have no windows; the dead do not need them.

Then she looked at the Queen Rima who lay in another bed with the babe near by, and saw that she was sitting up, staring before her with rapt eyes.

"I see that you are awake, Kemmah," she said, "for the sun shines upon your eyes, for which I thank the gods because it shows me that we are not in a grave. Hearken, a dream has visited me. I dreamed that the good god my husband, Kheperra who is dead, came to me, saying:

"'Wife, you have accomplished all things; you have brought our child to a place where she will be safe, a holy place where the spirits of those who were great in Egypt before her protect and will protect her. Fear not for the child who is safe in their keeping and in that of those about her on the earth. Make ready, Wife beloved, to return to me, your Husband.'

"'That is my desire,' I answered. 'But tell me, Lord, where shall I find you?'

"Then, Kemmah, in that dream of mine the spirit of King Kheperra showed me a wondrous and beautiful place of which the memory has faded from me, saying:

"'Here shall you find me, where are no wars or fears or troubles, and here shall we dwell together happily for many an age, though what will chance to us in the end I do not know.'

"'But the child. What of the child?' I asked. 'Must we lose the child?'

"'Nay, Beloved,' he answered, 'presently she will be with us.'

"'Then, Lord, is she also doomed to die to the world before she has known the world?'

"'Not so, Beloved, but here there is no time, and soon her hour there will be accomplished and she will be counted of our company.'

"'Yet she will never know us, Lord, who died when she was without understanding.'

"'The dead know everything; in death all that seems lost is found again; in death all is forgiven, even those priests and princes who would have betrayed you to the Shepherds are forgiven, for some of them whom the axe of Ru sent hither, stand by me and ask pardon of you as I speak. In death are life and understanding. Therefore come hither swiftly and without fear.'

"Then I awoke, happy for the first time since Ru bore the body of King Kheperra out of the battle."

"A strange dream. A very strange dream, Queen. But who can put faith in such visions of the night?" exclaimed Kemmah, for she was frightened and knew not what to say, adding:

"Now rise, if it pleases you, and let me dress you in these garments that have been provided. Afterwards we will call the Lord Tau, for I am sure he is no sailor man but a lord, and explore this place, which it would seem might be worse, for here are good food and light and friends and dark caverns where we may hope to hide ourselves away if foes should come."

"Aye, Kemmah, I will rise, though it should be for the last time, for I would look upon the face of this wondrous Roy the prophet who has brought us here and then commend my child to him ere I pass farther than he can follow."

"From all that I have heard of Roy I think that would be far indeed, Queen," said Kemmah.

A while later, when they were seated at their morning meal that was served by priestesses who now appeared for the first time, came Tau, praying them to follow him into the presence of Roy, the prophet and his master.

They obeyed, Rima leaning on the arm of Tau, for now she seemed too weak to walk alone, Kemmah bearing the babe, and Ru bringing up the rear. Presently they heard sounds of singing, and entering a great hall lit by little window-places set high up near the roof and by an opening to the East, saw that in it were gathered a number of men and women, all clad in white robes, the men to the right and the women to the left. At the head of the hall was an altar and behind the altar, in a shrine of alabaster, a life-sized statue of Osiris, god of the dead wrapped in the trappings of the dead. In front of this altar in a chair of black stone sat an aged man clad in white priestly garments over which hung strange-shaped, mystical jewels of gold and gems.

He was a wonderful old man, or so thought Ru staring at him with round eyes, for his beard was long and white as snow, his hands were thin as those of a mummy, his nose was hooked and his eyes were black, piercing, and full of fire. Though she had not seen him in the flesh for many years, Kemmah knew him at once to be none other than the king's son, her great-uncle, Roy the Prophet, whose fame for holiness, secret power, and magic was told of throughout Egypt. Indeed, she remembered that just so had he appeared to her in the ruined shrine that was in the palace gardens at Thebes when she sought a sign that Tau was a true messenger and not one who set a trap.

They drew near while all the company stared at them in silence. Suddenly Roy lifted his head, studying them with his piercing eyes, then in a strong, clear voice asked of Tau:

"Who are these that you bring into the Chapter of the secret Brotherhood of the Dawn, to enter which without authority is death? Answer, O my son in the spirit."

Thrice Tau made reverence and said:

"O Holy One, O Home of Wisdom, greater than all kings, voice of Heaven upon earth, hear me! On the day of full moon before the last you commanded me, saying:

"'Priest of our Brotherhood, become a merchant. Sail up Nile to Thebes, and before dawn on the day that you reach the ancient city enter the garden of the palace and take your stand behind a palm tree that grows near to a forgotten shrine. There you will find a woman, a nurse of kings in whom my blood runs. Speak to her. Show her this half of a broken talisman, and if she can show its other half, declare to her that you are my messenger charged with a certain mission. Set out that mission, and if she doubts, pray to me, sending your prayer through space, and I will hear you and come to your aid. Then when she doubts no more, fulfil that mission as shall be made clear to you.'

"I heard your commands, O Holy One, and behold! the mission is fulfilled. Before you appear Rima the Babylonian, daughter of Ditanah the King of Babylon and widow of Kheperra, Pharaoh of Upper Egypt; Lady Kemmah, the royal nurse, your kinswoman, and the royal babe Nefra, Princess of Egypt."

"I see them, my son, but what of the fourth, the mighty black man, as to whom I gave no command?"

"This, Father: that without his help sent by the gods none of us would be here to-day, seeing that he held the door against traitors and with that axe of his, slew them all, eight in number."

"Not so, my son, unless my spirit told me falsely, the Lady Kemmah, my kinswoman, slew one of them."

Now Ru, who had been listening amazed, could contain himself no longer.

"That is right, O Prophet, or O God," he broke in, in his big voice. "She killed one of them who slipped past me, their captain as I think, with the shrewdest thrust ever driven by a woman's arm—also another escaped. But your sight must be very good, O Prophet, if you can see from here to Thebes and take note of one blow among so many."

A faint smile flickered on the face of Roy.

"Come hither, Ru, for so I think you are named," he said.

The giant obeyed and of his own accord knelt down before Roy, who went on:

"Hearken, Ru the Ethiopian.   You are a gallant man and a true-hearted.   You slew those who slew your King Kheperra and bore his body from the battle.   By your gift of strength and skill in war you saved your lord's child and the Queen her mother from prison and death.   Therefore I number you among our Brotherhood into whose company hitherto no black man has ever entered.   Afterwards you shall be instructed in its simpler rites and take the lesser oaths.   Yet know, O Ru, that if you betray the smallest of its secrets or work harm to any of your fellow servants of the Dawn, you shall die thus," and leaning forward he whispered fiercely into the Negro's ear.

"Have done, I pray you, Prophet," exclaimed Ru in lively terror and springing to his feet.   "I have seen and heard of many things but never of such a one as this, in Ethiopia or in Egypt, in war or in peace.   Moreover, such threats are needless, since I never betrayed any one except myself, and least of all those whose bread I eat and whom I love," and he glanced towards the Queen and the child.

"I know it, Ru; yet sometimes folly betrays as well as craft.   Hearken!   You are appointed bodyservant and guard to the Royal Princess of Egypt as you were to her father before her.   Where she goes, there you go; when she sleeps your bed is without her door.   If she fights you stand at her side in battle, shielding her with your life.   If she wanders by day or by night, you wander with her, and when at last she dies, you die also and accompany her to the Underworld.   For this shall be your reward—that the blessing and the strength that are on her shall be on you also, and that you shall serve her to all eternity.   Retire."

"I ask no better fate," muttered Ru as he obeyed.

"Kinswoman, bring me the child," said the Prophet.

Kemmah came forward bearing the sleeping babe and at Roy's bidding held it up to be seen of all, whereon everyone in that company bowed the knee and bent the head.

"Brothers and Sisters of the Company of the Dawn, in the person of this child behold your Queen and Egypt's!" cried Roy, and again they bent the knee and bowed the head.

Then he breathed upon the babe and blessed it, making over it certain mystic signs and calling upon gods and spirits to guard it through life and for ever. This done he kissed the infant and handed it back to Kemmah, saying:

"Blessed be you also, O faithful woman. Aye, and you shall be blessed, and later instructed in our mysteries and numbered of our Company. Go in peace."

Now Roy had spoken to all that company save to the chief of them, Rima the Queen, who sat in front of him in a chair that had been given to her, watching him with empty eyes and listening to his words as though they dealt with far-off matters that moved her not. Yet when he had finished she lifted her head, saying:

"Words and blessings for the slave. Words and blessings for the nurse. Words and adoration for the babe in whom run the royal bloods of Egypt and of Babylon. But what words for the Queen and mother, O Prophet, at whose bidding she and that which was born of her have been brought to this darksome place and habitation of conspirators plotting to ends unknown?"

Now Roy arose from his throne before the altar, a tall, ethereal shape, and advancing to the stricken queen lifted her hand and kissed it.

"For your Majesty I have no message," he said, bending his venerable head, "seeing that already you hold communion with one who is greater than I," and he turned and bowed to the solemn statue of the god Osiris which stared at them from beyond the altar.

"I know it," she answered with a sad smile.

"Yet," he went on, "it is reported to me that in this night that is gone, your Majesty dreamed a dream. Is it not so?"

"It is so, Prophet, though who told you I do not know."

"It matters not who told me. What matters is that I am charged to say to your Majesty that this dream was no phantasy bred of human hopes and longings but the very truth. Learn, O Queen, that this world and its sufferings are but a shadow and a show, and that beyond them, like the pyramids towering above the sands and palm trees at their base, stands the eternal verity whose name is Love. The sands are blown away and having borne their fruit, the palm trees are torn up by the tempest or grow old and die, but the pyramids remain."

"I understand and I thank you, Prophet. Now lead me hence for I am weary."

On the third night from this day Rima the Queen, knowing that the fever which consumed her had done its work and that the time was at hand for her to bid farewell to the world, sent a messenger to Roy the Prophet saying that she would speak with him. He came and she addressed him thus:

"I know not who you are nor what is this Brotherhood of the Dawn of which you speak, and to what ends it works, nor why you have brought the Royal Princess hither, nor what gods you serve, I who take but little count of the gods of Egypt, although it is true that when my child was born two of them seemed to appear to me in a vision. Yet I will add this: my heart tells me that you are a most righteous man and a prophet of power appointed by Fate to fulfil its will; also that you and those about you plan good and not ill for the Princess, who, if there is justice in the world, should one day be the Queen of Egypt. There then I leave this matter in the hands of Heaven; I who, having done all that I can do, find myself dying, unfortunate and powerless.

Those things will happen which must happen and there is
no more to be said.

' "Now I demand an oath of you, Roy, and of the priest
Tau, and of all the Brotherhood under you. It is that when I
am dead you will embalm my body with all the skill of the
Egyptians, and that afterwards, when there is opportunity,
you will cause it to be conveyed to Ditanah, the King of
Babylon, my father, or to him who sits in his place, with
these my dying words written in a scroll on its breast,
accompanied, if may be, by my daughter, the Royal Princess of Egypt.

"I demand an oath of you, further, that those who bear
my body shall say to the King of Babylon that I, the dead
daughter of Babylon, aforetime wife of the King of Egypt,
call upon him in the name of our gods and by our common
blood to avenge the wrongs that I have suffered in Egypt
and the death of my lord beloved, my husband, King
Kheperra. I call upon him under pain of the curse of my
spirit, to roll down in his might upon Egypt and to smite
these Shepherd dogs who slew my husband and took his
heritage, and to establish my daughter, the Princess Nefra,
as Queen of Egypt, and to seize those who were traitors
to her and would have given her to doom and me with her,
and to slay them. This is the oath which I demand of
you."

"Yet, Queen," answered Roy, "it is one that is little
to my liking, seeing that if fulfilled it may breed war and
that we, the sons and daughters, of the Dawn—for Harma-
chis whose image is the Sphinx that watches at our door,
is the god of Dawn—seek peace and not war. Forgiveness,
not vengeance, is the law we follow. It is true that if may
be we desire to depose the usurping Shepherd kings and
to restore Egypt to the line of its rightful rulers, of whom
the Princess Nefra is the heir, or if as yet this is refused to
us by the gods, to unite the North and South so that Egypt
may grow greater and cease to bleed from the wounds of
war."

"That is what the Shepherds seek also," said Rima faintly.

"Aye, but their ends are other than ours. They would rivet a yoke upon the neck of Egypt; we would loose that yoke and not by the sword. The Shepherds are many, but the people of Egypt are more, and if the two races can be mingled, then the good Nile wheat which we sow will smother the foreign Shepherd weeds. Already something has been done; already these Shepherd kings bend the knee to the gods of Egypt whose altars once they overthrew, and accept Egypt's laws and customs."

"It may be so, Prophet, and in the end all may come about as you desire. But I am of blood different from that of you soft Egyptians and I have suffered grievous wrong. My husband has been slain; those whom he trusted have striven to sell me and my child to slavery and therefore I seek for the justice that I shall never see. Not with soft words and far-sighted plottings would I win that justice, but with spears and arrows. My body is weak and I am near my end, but my soul is aflame. I know, moreover, that all your hopes are centred on this child of mine, as are my own, and my spirit tells me how they may best be brought to harvest. Will you swear the oath? Answer, and quickly. For if you will not swear, mayhap I may find another counsel. What if I take the babe with me, Prophet, to plead our cause in the Courts above, as I think I can still find the means to do?"

Now Roy considered her, reading her mind, and saw that it was desperate.

"I must take counsel of that which I serve," he answered. "Perchance It will give me wisdom."

"And what if I and mayhap another die while you are taking counsel, Prophet? You think that you can remove the babe, who do not know that a mother's will is very strong and that we Babylonians have secrets of our own, especially at the hour of death, with which we have the power to draw after us those who are born of our bodies."

"Fear not, Queen Rima. I, too, have my secrets, and I tell you that Osiris will not take you yet."

"I believe you, Prophet. On such a matter you would not lie. Go, take counsel with your gods and come back quickly."

"I go," he said, and went.

A little before the hour of dawn Roy returned to that death chamber and with him came Tau, also she who was the first priestess of the Order of the Dawn. Rima awaited him, supported with pillows upon her bed.

"You spoke truly, Prophet," she said, "seeing that now I am stronger than when we parted yesterday. Yet be swift, for this strength of mine is but as the brightness of a dying lamp. Speak, and shortly."

"Queen Rima," he replied, "I have taken counsel of the Power I serve, who guides my feet here upon the earth. It has been pleased to send an answer to my prayer."

"What answer, Prophet?" she asked eagerly.

"This, Queen: That I, on behalf of the Order of the Dawn over which I rule, and in the presence of those who stand next to me in that order"—and he pointed to Tau and to the priestess—"should take the oath that you desire, since thus our ends can best be brought about, though how they will be accomplished was not revealed. I swear, therefore, in the name of that Spirit who is above all gods, also by your *Ka* and mine, and by that child who here and now we take for queen, that when there is opportunity, which I think will not be for many years, your body shall be borne to Babylon and your message delivered to its king, if may be—by your daughter's lips. Moreover, that nothing may be forgotten, all your desire and this oracle are upon this roll which shall be read to you and sealed by you as a letter to the King of Babylon, and with it our oath, sealed by me and by Tau who comes after me."

"Read," said the Queen. "Nay, let the Lady Kemmah, who is learned, read."

So with some help from Tau, Kemmah read.

"It is truly written," said Rima. "There on the roll the matter is set out well and clearly. Yet, add this— that if my father, the royal Ditanah the King, or he who sits upon his throne after him, denies this my last prayer, then I call down the curse of all the gods of Babylon upon his people, and that I, Rima, will haunt him while he lives and ask account of him when we meet at last in the Underworld."

"So be it," said Roy, "though these words are not gentle. Yet write them down, O Tau, for the dying must be obeyed."

So Tau sat himself upon the floor and wrote upon his knee. Then wax mixed with clay was brought and drawing from her wasted finger a ring on which was cut the figure of a Babylonian god, Rima pressed it on the wax, while Kemmah took a scarab from her breast and sealed as witness.

"Set one copy of this roll with the ring among the wrappings of my mummy that the King of Babylon may find it there, and hide the other in your most secret place," said Rima.

"It shall be done," said Roy, and waited.

At this moment the first rays of the rising sun shot like arrows through the window-place. With a strange strength Rima took her child and held her up so that the golden light fell full upon her.

"The Queen of the Dawn!" she cried. "Behold her kissed and crowned of the Dawn. O Queen of the Dawn, rule on triumphant through the perfect day, till night brings you to my breast again."

Then she embraced the child, and beckoning to Kemmah, gave it into her arms. A moment later, murmuring, "My task is done. My Lord awaits me," she fell back and died.

CHAPTER VI

Nefra Conquers the Pyramids

Strange, very strange indeed was the book of Life as it opened itself to the child Nefra, Royal Princess of Egypt. Looking back in after years to those of her infancy, all she could remember was a vision of great pillared halls, where stone images stared at her and the carved or painted walls were full of grotesque figures which seemed to pursue each other everlastingly from darkness into darkness. Then there were visions of white-robed men and women who from time to time gathered in these places and sang sad and mellow chants, of which the echoes haunted her sleep from year to year. Also there was the stately shape of the Lady Kemmah, her nurse whom she loved well yet feared a little, and that of the gigantic Ethiopian named Ru, who always seemed to be about her day and night, carrying a great bronze axe in his hand, whom she loved entirely and feared not at all.

Foremost among them, too, was the awful apparition of an aged man with a white beard and black, flashing eyes whom she came to know as the Prophet and whom all worshipped as though he were a god. She remembered waking up at night and seeing him bending over her, a lantern in his hand, or in the daytime meeting her in the dark temple passages and passing by with words of blessing. To her childish imagination, indeed, he was not human but a ghost to be fled from; yet a kindly ghost withal, since sometimes he gave her delicious sweetmeats or even flowers that a Brother carried in a basket.

Infancy passed by and there came childhood. Still the

same halls were about her, peopled by the same folk, but now, at times, with Kemmah her nurse and guarded by the giant Ru and others, she was allowed to wander outside of them, most frequently after night had fallen and when the full moon shone in the sky. Thus it was that first she came to know the lion shape of the terrible Sphinx, lying crouched upon the desert. In the beginning she was afraid of this stone creature with its human face painted red, its royal headdress, and its bearded chin, though afterwards, when it grew familiar to her, she learned to love that face, finding something friendly in its smile and its great calm eyes that stared at the sky as though they would search out its secrets. Indeed, at times she would sit on the sand, sending Kemmah and Ru to a little distance, and tell it her childish troubles and ask it questions, furnishing the answers for herself, since from the great lips of the Sphinx none ever came.

Then beyond the Sphinx rose the mighty pyramids, three principal ones that pierced the very sky, with temples at the base of them wherein dead kings had once been worshipped, and others that were smaller which, she fancied, must be their children. She worshipped those pyramids, believing that the gods had made them, till Tau, her tutor, told her that they were built by men to be the graves of kings.

"They must have been great kings that had such graves; I should like to look on them."

"Perhaps you will some day," answered Tau, who was a most learned man and her instructor in many things.

Besides herself there were other children of the Order, born of the wedded brothers and sisters. These were formed into a school, Nefra among them, which school was taught by the Instructed among the Brotherhood. Indeed, nearly all of them had learning, for the full members of the Order of the Dawn were no common folk, although their servants and those who tilled the flat lands not far from the Sphinx having their habitations upon the borders of the great Necropolis were, or seemed to be like, any other husbandmen. To look on them, none would have known that they were partakers in mysteries which they were sworn by solemn oaths not to reveal, and indeed never did reveal, even under the fear of death or torture.

Soon Nefra became the head of this school, not because of her rank but for the reason that she was by far the cleverest of all its pupils, and her quick mind drank up knowledge as a dry fleece of wool drinks up the dew. Yet if any visited that school and watched the children listening to the teacher, or seated on their stools, copying the picture-writing of the Egyptians upon potsherds or fragments of papyrus, save that she sat at the head of a line of them and for something different in her face, they would have found nothing to distinguish her from the other little maidens who were her companions. She wore the same plain robe of white, the same simple sandals to protect her feet from stones and scorpions, while her hair was tied with a stem of dried grass into a single tress after just the same fashion. Indeed, it was a rule of the Order that she should carry on her person no robe or ornament which might reveal that she was not as other children were.

Yet the instruction of Nefra did not end with her lessons in this school, for when these were done or in times of holiday she must learn a deeper lore. Tau, accompanied by Kemmah her nurse, would take her to a little private room that once had been the sleeping place of a priest of the temple in ancient days and there teach her many secret things.

Thus he taught her the Babylonian tongue and writing, or knowledge of the movements of the stars and planets, or the mysteries of religion, showing her that all the gods of all the priests were but symbols of the attributes of an unseen Power, a Spirit that ruled everything and was everywhere, even in her own heart. He taught her that the flesh was but the earthly covering of the soul and that between flesh and soul there reigned eternal war. He taught

her that she lived here upon the earth to fulfil the purposes
of this almighty Spirit that created her, to whom in a day
to come she must return, perchance to be sent out again to
this or other worlds; though what those purposes might be
was not known even by the wisest man who breathed.
And while he taught thus and she listened, watching him
with eager eyes, sometimes the old prophet Roy would steal
into the chamber and listen also, adding a word here or
there, then hold out his hand in blessing and steal away.

Thus, though outwardly Nefra was as are other merry
children, inwardly her soul opened like a lotus lily in the
sun and she was different from them all.

So the years went on till from a child she grew into a
maiden, tall and sweet and very fair. It was at this time
in her life that Roy himself and Tau, in the presence of
Kemmah only, revealed to her who she was, namely, none
other than the Royal Princess of Egypt by right of blood
and the appointment of Heaven, and told her the story of
her father and her mother and of the kings and queens who
went before them; also of the divisions in the land.

When she heard these things Nefra wept and trembled.

"Alas! that it should be so," she said, "for now no longer
can I be happy. Tell me, holy Father, whom men name
Home-of-Spirits that, they say, hold converse with you in
your sleep, what can a poor maid do to right so many
wrongs and to bring peace where there is but bitterness and
bloodshed?"

"Princess of Egypt," said Roy, for the first time giving
her her title, "I do not know because it is not revealed to
me or to any. Yet it is revealed to me and to certain others
that in some way unforeseen you will do these things. Aye,
and it was revealed in a dream to your mother, the Queen
Rima, when you were born, for in this dream that part of
the Universal Spirit whom here in Egypt we know as
Mother Isis appeared to her and amongst other gifts gave
to you, the royal child, the high name of Uniter of Lands."

Here Kemmah thought to herself that another goddess

appeared as well as Isis and gave to this same child different'
gifts, and though she said nothing Roy seemed to read her
thoughts, for he went on:

"As to this dream and certain mysteries by which it was
accompanied, the Lady Kemmah, your nurse and instruc-
tress, is commanded to inform you; also to show to you the
record of all these matters which at that time was written
down and sealed, and with it another record of a certain
oath which I and others swore to your mother, the Queen
Rima, upon her deathbed, concerning a journey which you
must make at the appointed time. Enough of these
matters. Now I am commanded to tell you that on a day
to come which shall be declared when it is known to me,
it is our purpose with such state as we can compass, to
crown you, standing as you do on the threshold of womanhood, as Queen of Egypt."

"How can that be?" asked Nefra. "Kings and queens
are crowned in temples, or so I have been taught, and in the
presence of multitudes of courtiers, with pomp and shoutings. But here——" and she looked about her.

"Is not this a temple and one of the most ancient and
holiest in Egypt, Nefra?" asked Roy. "And for the rest,
listen. We seem to be but a humble Brotherhood, the inhabitants of tombs and pyramids which few dare approach
because they hold them haunted and deadly to the life and
soul of any stranger who dares to violate their sanctity.
Yet I tell you that this Order of the Dawn is more powerful
and more far-reaching than the Shepherd king himself and
all those that cling to him, as you will learn shortly when
you are sworn of it. Its disciples are everywhere, from the
Cataracts of Nile down to the sea; aye, and in lands beyond
the sea, and, as we believe, in Heaven above; and one and
all they obey the commands that issue from these catacombs, accepting them as the voice of God."

"Then if so, Holy Prophet, why do you not sit at Tanis
openly, instead of in secret in these tombs?"

"Because, Princess, visible power and the trappings of

power can only be won by war, and we are sworn to wage no war, we whose empire is of the spirit. It may be that in the end it is decreed that war must be waged and that thus all will be accomplished. Yet it is not our Brotherhood that will lift its banners or, save in self-defence, bring men to their deaths, for we are sworn to peace and gentleness."

"I rejoice to hear it," said Nefra, "and now, Master, I pray you let me go to rest, for I am overwhelmed."

A year or more after this day of the revealing of secrets, but before the ceremonies which it foretold, a terrible thing happened to Nefra.

Now it was her custom to wander about the great graveyard that surrounded the pyramids where in their splendid tombs so many of the ancient nobles and princes of Egypt had been laid to rest a thousand years or more before her day, so long ago indeed that none remembered the names of those who slept beneath these monuments. On these wanderings of hers it was her pleasure to go unaccompanied save by her body-servant, Ru, for Kemmah, who now grew aged, had no strength for such rough journeys over tumbled stones and through deep sand.

Moreover, at this time Nefra loved to be alone, that she might find time to think in solitude over all that had been revealed to her as to her history and fate, and the unsought greatness that had been thrust upon her.

Further, being very vigorous in body as she was in mind, she wearied of being cooped up in the narrow precincts of the temple and its neighbourhood and longed for exercise and adventure. By nature she was a climber, one of those who love to scale heights and thence look down upon the world below. Thus it became her pleasure to scramble to the top of great monuments and even of some of the smaller pyramids, which she found she could do with ease, since her feet were sure and no dizziness ever overtook her.

All of these fancies of hers were reported to Kemmah by

Ru and others who watched her, and to Roy and Tau by
Kemmah when she found that the young princess would not
listen to her chidings, but for the first time in her life turned
upon her angrily, reminding her that she was no more a
child to be led by the hand and would have her way.

These consulted of the matter, and, it would seem, according to their rule, made divination, taking counsel of
that Spirit who, as they declared, guided them in all
things.

The end of it was that the Prophet Roy bade his great-
niece, the Lady Kemmah, to trouble the Princess no more
about this business, but to suffer her to walk where it pleased
her and to climb what she would, because it was revealed
to him that whoever took harm, she would take none.

"It is not wise to thwart her as to such a little thing,
Niece," he went on, "seeing that there is no danger to her
and none of the Shepherds or other enemies dare to approach
this haunted place. Also, she goes forth guarded by Ru
to talk, not with any man, but only with her own heart
amid the holy company of the dead."

"There are always some who will dare that of which all
others are afraid, and who knows whom she may meet and
talk with before all is done?" answered Kemmah.

"I have spoken, Niece. Withdraw," said Roy.

So, having triumphed, Nefra, who was young and head-
strong, continued her wanderings and indeed did more.

Now there was a family of Arab blood among those who
served and were sworn to the Brotherhood of the Dawn,
who from generation to generation had been climbers of the
pyramids. These men alone, by following certain cracks
in their marble casings and clinging to knobs or hollows
that had been worn in them by the blowing of sand during
hundreds or thousands of years, had the art and courage
to come to the crest of every one of them; nor until they had
done so were they accounted fit to take a wife. With the
Sheik of these men Nefra often talked, and for her pleasure
at different times he and his sons scaled every one of the

pyramids before her eyes, returning safely from their dizzy journey to her side.

"Why cannot I do as you do?" she asked of this sheik at length. "I am light and surefooted, and my head does not swim upon a height; also I have limbs as long as yours."

The Captain of the Pyramids, for so he was commonly called, looked at her, astonished, and shook his head.

"It is impossible," he said. "No woman has ever climbed those stone mountains; that is, except the Spirit of the Pyramids herself."

"Who is the Spirit of the Pyramids?" she asked.

"Lady, we know not," he answered. "We never ask her, and when we see her in the full moon upon her journeyings, we veil our faces."

"Why do you veil your faces, Captain?"

"Because if we did not we should go mad, as men have done who looked into her eyes."

"Why do they go mad?"

"Because too much beauty breeds madness, as perchance you may find one day, Lady," he answered; words that brought the colour to Nefra's brow.

"Who and what is this spirit?" she continued hastily. "And what does she do?"

"We are not certain, but the story tells that long, long ago there was a maiden queen of this land who would not marry because she loved some man of a humble station. Now it came about that strangers invaded Egypt, which was weak and divided, and conquered. Then the king of the strangers, seeing the beauty of this queen and that he might build his throne upon a sure foundation, wished to take her to wife, even by force. But she fled from him and in her despair climbed the greatest of the pyramids, he following after her. Reaching its crest she hurled herself thence and was crushed, seeing which faintness took hold of the king, so that he, too, fell to the ground and died. After this they buried both of them in a secret chamber of one of the pyramids—which is not known, but I think it must have been the second since there the spirit is most often seen."

"A pretty tale," said Nefra, "but is that the end of it?"

"Not quite, Lady, since to it hangs a prophecy. It is that when another king follows another Queen of Egypt up the pyramid whence this one fell, whichever it may have been, and there wins her love, the avenging spirit of her who threw herself thence will find rest and no more bring destruction upon men."

"I would see this spirit," said Nefra. "As I am a woman she cannot make me mad."

"Nor being a woman, Lady, do I think that she will appear to you. Nevertheless, it may be her pleasure to possess your soul for her own purposes," he added thoughtfully.

"My soul is my own and no one shall possess it," answered Nefra in anger. "Nor indeed do I believe that there is such a spirit, who think that what you and other foolish men have seen was nothing but a moon-cast shadow travelling among the graves. So tell me no more such idle tales."

"There are one or two mad fellows living among the tombs who know more of that mooncast shadow than I do, Lady. Still it may be as you say," replied the Sheik, bowing courteously after the ancient fashion of the East to a superior. "Yes, maybe you are right. Have it as you will," and he turned to go.

"Stay," said Nefra, "it is my wish that you who have more skill and knowledge of them than any other man, should teach me to climb those pyramids. Let us begin upon the third, which is the smallest, and at once. The others we can conquer afterwards when I am more accustomed to the work."

Now the man stared at her and began to protest.

"Have you not the commands of the holy prophet Roy and of the Council of the Order to obey me in all things?" asked Nefra presently.

"That is so, Lady, though why we should obey you I do not know."

"Nor do I quite, Captain, seeing that you can climb pyramids and I cannot, and you are therefore greater than I. Still, there are the orders and you know what happens to those who break the commands of the Council. Now let us begin."

The Sheik reasoned and prayed and almost wept, but all that happened was that Nefra exclaimed at last:

"If you are afraid to go up that pyramid, I will go by myself. Then, you know, I may fall."

So the end of it was that the afflicted Sheik summoned his son, a lissom youth who could climb like a goat, bidding him bring with him a long rope made of twisted palm fibre, which rope he fastened round Nefra's slender waist. But now there was more trouble, for Ru, who had been listening to all this talk amazed, asked him what he was doing binding his lady like a slave.

The Sheik explained, while Nefra nodded assent.

"But it cannot be," said Ru. "My duty is to accompany this Noble One everywhere."

"Then, friend Ru," said Nefra, "accompany me up the pyramid."

"Up the pyramid!" said Ru, puffing out his cheeks. "Look at me, I pray you, Mistress, and say whether I am a cat or a monkey that I can climb up a slope of smooth stone from earth to heaven. Ere we had gone the length of that rope I should fall and break my neck. Rather would I fight ten men single-handed than be so mad."

"It is true. I think that you will make no good scaler of stone mountains, friend Ru," said Nefra, surveying the Ethiopian's mighty form which had grown no smaller with the passage of the years. "Now cease from talking, for we waste time. If you cannot go up the pyramid, stand at the bottom of it, just beneath me, and if I slip and fall, catch me as I come."

"Catch you as you come! Catch you as you come!" gasped Ru.

Without more words Nefra went to the foot of the third

pyramid, up which the Sheik, who also seemed to be empty of speech, began to mount by the way he knew, having the end of the rope that was about Nefra tied round his middle. She followed him, her feet bare and her robe tucked up about her knees, as he bade her, while after her came his son watching her every movement.

"Hearken, men," groaned Ru. "If you suffer my Lady to slip, you had better stop on that pyramid for the rest of your lives, for if you come down I will kill you both."

"If she slips, we shall slip also. The gods bear me witness that it is no fault of mine," answered the Sheik who was lying on his face upon the slope of the pyramid.

Now it is to be told that Nefra proved an apt pupil at this game. She had the eye of a hawk, the courage of a lion, and was sure-footed as an ape. Up she went, setting her hands and feet exactly where her guide had done, till they had conquered half the height.

"It is enough for to-day," said the Sheik. "No beginner of our race comes farther at the first trial; that is the rule. Rest here awhile, and then descend. My son will place your feet where they should go."

"I obey," said Nefra, and turned herself round as her guide had done above her, to see nothing beneath her save a sheer gulf of space and Ru, grown small, standing on the sand at the bottom. Then for the first time she grew dizzy.

"My head swims," she said faintly.

"Turn about again," said the Sheik, nor could his quiet voice quite conceal the agony of his fear.

She obeyed, and her strength came back to her, her flesh obeying the will within.

"I am well again," she said.

"Then, Lady, turn once more, for if you do not do so now you never will."

For the second time she obeyed, and lo! she no longer feared the height, the spirit within her had conquered her

mortal tremblings. After this the descent was easy, for
she could see where to place her hands and feet in the fissures
of that hot and shining marble; moreover, the young man
beneath, who, knowing every one of them, was able to keep
his face to the pyramid, guided her as to where to set them.
So they came safely to the ground, where Nefra sat a little
while, panting and smiling at Ru who mopped his brow
with his robe, his big eyes starting from his head, for never
before had he been so frightened.

"Have you had enough of the pyramids, Lady?" asked
the Sheik as he loosed the rope from about her.

"By no means," answered Nefra, springing up and clapping her sore hands. "I love the work and never shall I
have had enough of them till I can climb them all alone
by moonlight, as it is said that you can do."

"Isis, Mother of Heaven!" exclaimed the Sheik, throwing
up his hands, "this is no mortal maid; this is a goddess;
this is the Spirit of the Pyramids herself appearing in
earthly form."

"Yes," said Nefra, "I think that is what I am—the
Spirit of the Pyramids. Now will it please you to meet me
here to-morrow at the same time, when I hope that we may
be able to reach the top of the smallest of them."

Then having put on her sandals, before the unhappy man
could answer, she departed at a run followed by Ru, who
was so astonished that he could not speak.

This was but a beginning, for what Nefra promised, that
she performed. At this time all the strength of her young
and burning nature was directed to one thing only—the
mastery of those pyramids. It was a small ambition,
yet to her, in the day of her dawning womanhood, it was
everything. She had been told that by birth she was Queen
of Egypt. It moved her little, for dwelling amid those
deserted temples and tombs the royalty of Egypt seemed to
her a dream, or at least something far away. But the
pyramids were near, and what she desired was to be Queen

of the Pyramids which, she was also told, her far-off an-
cestors had reared up to be their tombs. Moreover, that
story of a spirit which haunted them had stirred her. She
did not believe in the Spirit, but since youth is credulous
over matters that have to do with love, she believed the
story. She saw that fair young queen, such a one as she
was, who had also learned to climb the pyramids, flying
to the top of the tallest of them and thence hurling herself
to doom to escape one whom she hated and who had
humbled her country to the dust, thus bringing conquered
and conqueror to a common doom. Also she found something beautiful, something that touched the heart in the
pendant of this story, namely, that in a day to come another
young and lovely queen would fly up one of those pyramids
pursued by another alien lover, and that there on the verge
of dizzy death, their hate would melt in the fires of passion,
thus bringing blessings on the land for the rule of which
they fought.

As yet Nefra knew nothing of love, still Nature was at
work in her, as it is in the smallest child, and she understood
something of the meaning of this beautiful fable, and the
dim thoughts that sprang from it warmed her sleeping soul.
Meanwhile she had but one desire—to achieve that which
seemed to be impossible to woman, to conquer the pyramids,
not understanding in those days that the thing was an
allegory and that she, whose strong spirit could enable her
to dare so many dangers and to overcome them with her
young body, might also in time to come meet subtler perils
and tread them beneath her conquering feet.

Moreover, at this time the desire of prayer and the mystery of communion with That which is above mankind,
That which the dwellers upon earth called God, came home
to her, not from any teaching of Roy or Tau, but, as it
were, out of her own soul. Above all things she yearned
for this communion, and there fell upon her one of the
strange fancies, some would call them madnesses, which
often enough possess those who are passing from childhood

into the fulness of life, or from the fulness of life into the twilight that precedes the darkness of death. This was her particular dream, or illusion, or vision of the Truth, that she could best make her prayer to and come into closest communion with the Spirit which brooded over her and all the world, in utter solitude upon the summit of those pyramids. It was a folly, perhaps, yet a noble folly. At least in the end she reaped its fruit, for within a year she learned to climb them all and this quite alone.

The Sheik of the Pyramids and his sons who had instructed her, the art and craft of whose family it had been for generations to scale these stone mountains for praise and reward on days of festival, were astonished and abased to see themselves equalled or outpassed in their peculiar business by a mere maiden.

At the beginning of the adventure they had been summoned before the Council of the Order, who had grown alarmed at the reports of Ru and Kemmah as to this vagary which had seized upon one whose life was precious, and asked as to its peril. They replied that there was none for those to whom the gift was given, since not for six generations had a single man among them come to his death from following this business. Yet, they added, that to those who were not of their family, it was fatal, since many had tried to share their secret and its fruits, but all of them had perished miserably, an answer that frightened the Council. Yet because of the revelations of Roy, they did nothing to restrain Nefra, who went her way about the matter and took no harm at all, till at length by day or even by night when the moon was at its full, she could reach the top of any of the pyramids as quickly as the Sheik or his sons.

Then that family abased themselves before her and, gathering together, prayed her to accept the captaincy and leadership of them all, since she had outpassed them all. But Nefra only laughed and said that it was nothing and she would not, and ordered that they should be given rewards such as she had to bestow. Thereafter she had the freedom of the pyramids and was allowed to climb them when and how she liked without the attendance of the Sheik or his sons.

Yet of this at last came trouble.

CHAPTER VII

The Plot of the Vizier

NEFRA, as has been said, when the fancy took her made a custom of climbing one or other of the pyramids, generally at the hour of the rising or the setting of the sun, and, standing there upon the topmost flat coping-stones, of praying in that glorious loneliness. Or perchance she would not pray but content herself with looking down upon the world beneath, reflecting the while upon what fortunes it might have to offer her, or on such other matters as come into a maiden's mind.

Now this habit of hers became known, not only among the members of the Order and their dependents, but to many who dwelt or journeyed beyond the boundaries of what was called the Holy Ground, upon which no stranger dared to set his foot. Nor was this strange, seeing that her slender form thus poised between earth and heaven and outlined against the sky at dawn or sunset could be seen from far away, even from the Nile itself when it was in flood. Most held it to be that of the Spirit of the Pyramids herself whose appearance thus heralded trouble in Egypt, for there were few indeed who believed it to be possible that any woman could adventure herself in this fashion, or find the strength and skill to climb up marble like a lizard.

Soon the story of the marvel spread far and wide and even came to the Court of King Apepi.

One evening Nefra, having climbed the second pyramid in this fashion, descended as usual and because the light was failing chose a somewhat shorter route that brought her

to the ground, not by the southern face where Ru was waiting to receive her, but just round the angle on that face
which looked towards the west where the light of the dying
day still shone. Having leapt lightly to the sand, she looked
about for Ru and instead of him saw four men approaching
her, of whom at first she took little note, thinking in the
fading light that these were the Sheik of the Pyramids and
his sons who came to inquire of her about the new road she
had found upon the western face of this pyramid. So she
stood still and they drew near, then hesitated a little as
though they were afraid of her, till presently a voice called
out:

"Woman or spirit, seize her! Let her not escape us!
Think of the great reward and seize her!"

Thus encouraged, with a bound they came at her. Understanding her peril Nefra turned to fly up the pyramid
again and already was some feet above the sand when the
first of the men caught her by the ankle and dragged her
down.

"Ru!" she cried in a clear and piercing voice. "To my
aid, Ru. I am snared, Ru!"

Now as it chanced Ru was very near, only just round the
angle of the pile indeed, because having lost sight of Nefra
in the shadow as she descended, feeling disturbed, he was
advancing to the western face where the light was better
to discover if perchance she were there. He heard her cry
for help; he rushed forward and, turning the corner, saw
Nefra on the ground, while round her were the four men,
three of them binding her with a rope while the fourth was
tying a linen bandage across her face.

With a roar he leapt upon them holding his great axe aloft.
He who had the bandage saw him first, a black, gigantic
figure whom doubtless he took for some terrible guardian
spirit and strove to leap past him and fly. The axe flashed
and down he went, dead, cloven through and through.
Then the other men who at first thought that a lion had
roared, saw also, and for a moment stood amazed. In-

stantly Ru was on them. Letting fall the axe he gripped
the two who were nearest, seizing each of them by the
throat. He dashed their heads together, and putting out
his mighty strength, cast them far away to right and left
in such fashion that where they fell, there they lay, stone
dead. The fourth man had drawn a knife either to stab
at Ru or to kill Nefra; but when he saw the fate of his fellows
all courage left him and, screaming with fear, he let fall the
knife and fled away. Ru snatched the knife from the sand
and hurled it after him. A yell of pain told him that his
aim was true, though because of the shadows he could no
longer see the man. Ru would have started in pursuit,
but Nefra, struggling from the ground, cried:

"Nay. Bide here, there may be more of them."

"True," he answered, "and the dog has it."

Then, without more words, snatching up Nefra and holding her to his breast with his left arm as though she were
but a babe, he found his axe and, without waiting to look
at the dead, sped away with her along the western base of
the pyramid, till presently they were among tombs where
they could be seen no more.

"This is the end of those tricks of yours, Lady," he said
roughly, for he was shaking, not with fear, but at the thought
of what she had escaped.

"Had it not been for you, it might have been worse,"
answered Nefra. "Still, I have learned my lesson. Set me
down now, O most dear Ru, for my breath has returned to
me."

When presently all this tale was told to Kemmah and
to the Council of the Order, fear and dismay took hold of
them; even Tau the Wise was dismayed. Only Roy the
Prophet remained undisturbed.

"The maid will take no harm," he said. "I know it
from those who cannot lie, and therefore it is that I have
permitted her to follow her fancy as to the climbing of the
pyramids, for it is ill to cross or to coop up such a one as
she, as it is good that she should learn to look upon the face

of dangers and to overcome them. Still, doubtless this is the beginning of perils and henceforward we must be upon our guard."

Then he sent out men to bring in the dead whom Ru had slain and to search for the wounded man and, if he could be found, to capture him alive. This, however, did not happen, for when the light came again of that man there remained only certain bloodstains upon the sand which after a while were lost, showing that he had been able to staunch his hurt, and, by walking upon stones, to leave no tracks behind him.

The dead, however, told their own story, for they were of the Shepherd race and two of them wore garments such as were used in the Court of King Apepi. The third, it would seem, was a guide, though of what people could not be known, seeing that it was on his head that the axe of Ru had fallen, and who could tell aught of whence he came upon whose head the axe of Ru had fallen?

So the bodies of those woman-thieves were thrown to the jackals and the vultures, that their *Kas* might find nothing to inhabit, and their souls with all solemnity were accursed by Roy in a Chapter of the Order, that from age to age they might find no rest because of their double crime. For had they not violated the pact of generations and entered the Holy Ground which was the home of the consecrated Order of the Dawn, and there striven to steal away or perchance to murder a certain lady who in the world without was not known by any name?

There the matter ended for a space, except that at dawn or sunset Nefra was no longer seen standing upon the crests of pyramids.

Yet some while later a sick and sorry man with a bandaged back, who from time to time coughed up blood as though from a pierced lung, staggered into the Court at Tanis, where his face was known, and being admitted, told his tale to a great officer, who listened to it wrathfully and commanded a scribe to write it down word for word.

When it was finished that officer cursed this man because he had failed in his mission.

"Is that my fault?" asked the man. "Was it right to send those who are born of women to capture a spirit or a witch?—since no maid in whom warm blood flows can run up and down pyramids faced with smooth and shining stone, as flies run up and down a wall, which we saw this one do. Is it right to expect them to fight and overcome a black devil from the Underworld, larger than any who walks the earth, whose voice is the voice of a lion and whose hands can crush skulls as though they were pomegranates? Is it right to command them to enter a haunted place peopled by gods and wizards and the ghosts of the dead? A fool was I to listen to you and your promises of great reward, and fools were my companions, as doubtless they think in the Underworld to-day, for who is there in Egypt that does not know that to violate the Holy Ground of the Order of the Dawn is to court death and damnation? Now give me my price that I may divide it among my children."

"Your price!" gasped the high officer. "Were you not wounded, it should be rods. Go, dog, go!"

"Where am I to go," asked the man, "I who am accursed?"

"To the home of all who fail—to hell," replied the officer, making a sign to his servants.

So they threw him out, and to hell or elsewhere he went very shortly. For that knife of his which Ru had cast after him with so good an aim was poisoned. Moreover, it had struck him beneath the shoulder and pierced his lung.

The officer went into the private chamber where sat King Apepi with some of his counsellors and his young son, the Prince Khian, the heir apparent to his throne. This Apepi was a big, fleshy man still in middle age, with the hooked nose of the Shepherds and black, beady eyes, one who was violent in his temper, revengeful and fierce-natured like all his people, yet very anxious-minded, a fearer of evil.

Very different from him was his son, Khian, born of an Egyptian mother with royal blood in her veins, whom Apepi had married for reasons of policy. More—he had loved her in his fashion, and when she died in giving birth to her only child, Khian, had taken no other queen in her place, though of those who were not queens he had many about him. And now this child Khian had grown up to manhood. He was gentle-natured and soft-eyed, showing but little trace of the Shepherd blood, strong and hand-some in body and quick in mind, one, too, who thought and studied, a soldier and a hunter, yet a lover of peace, by nature a ruler of men who desired to heal the wounds of Egypt and make her great.

Before these appeared the old Vizier Anath, and told his tale, reading what had been written down from the lips of the wounded man.

Apepi listened earnestly.

"Do you know, Vizier, who this mad girl is who has a fancy for climbing the Great Pyramid? he asked at length.

"No, your Majesty, though perhaps I might hazard a guess," answered the Vizier in a doubtful voice.

"Then I will tell you, Vizier. She is no other than the only child of Kheperra, the Pharaoh of the South, who fell in the battle years ago. I am sure of it. It is known that such a child was born, for as you may remember, with the help of certain bribed Thebian nobles, we tried to capture her and her mother, the Queen Rima the daughter of the King of Babylon. It would seem that her gods fought for her, since both of them escaped, and of those who went to take them only one was left alive. The rest, he swore, were all killed by a black giant who guarded them. Now there was such a giant for he fought at the side of Kheperra and bore his body out of the battle. More, he was seen upon a trading boat going down the Nile, and with him were two women and a child, doubtless disguised. By craft these three slipped through the hands of my officers at Memphis, who afterwards were degraded for their negligence, and it was reported that they had made their way to Babylon. Yet our spies tell us nothing of their coming to Babylon, which is strange if Queen Rima and her daughter, who is called Princess of Egypt, reached the Court of King Ditanah with whom now and again we have been at war for many years. Therefore, either they are dead or they are hiding in Egypt."

"It would seem that this is so, Pharaoh," said the Vizier, and the other councillors nodded assent.

"Of late," went on Apepi, "a wind of rumour has sprung up which blows from the Cataracts to the sea, and whispers in the ears of men in every city and village on the Nile. This rumour says that the Queen of Egypt lives and ere long will appear to take her throne. It says, moreover, that she shelters among that strange Brotherhood of learned folk who have their home in the tombs of the old pyramids near Memphis and who are called the Order of the Dawn. It was to find out the truth of this matter that, somewhat against my counsel, you, Vizier Anath, sent certain bold fellows under promise of great reward to spy upon this Order which has no traitors, and to get sight of this wondrous maiden who can climb the pyramids and who, rumour says, is none other than the Princess of Egypt herself, though for aught I know she may be but a juggler."

"Or a spirit," suggested the Vizier, "since it seems impossible that a woman can perform such feats, and as to this matter there is a legend."

"Or even a spirit, though for my part I put little faith in spirits. Well, the men go; they creep into the Holy Land, as this place is called; they see the climber descending a pyramid; though I gave no such order, they seize her, which shows that she is flesh and blood; she calls aloud, a black giant—mark! again a black giant—rushes roaring to her rescue. He slays three of these men as though they were but children and hurls the man's own knife after the fourth, wounding him sorely, so that the maiden escapes and the Order of the Dawn is put upon its guard. Now I say that this maiden is no other than Nefra, Princess of Egypt, still guarded by that Ethiopian who bore her father's body from the battlefield."

When the murmur of assent had died away, Apepi continued:

"I say also that this business is very dangerous. Let us look it in the face. What are we Shepherds? We are a race that generations ago entered Egypt and took possession of its richest lands, driving its king back to Thebes and usurping the throne of the North. This I still hold, and the South also in a fashion, for we have corrupted its chief nobles and its high priests, binding them with chains of gold. Yet we are in peril, having been much weakened by ceaseless wars with Babylon; also, many of our people have intermarried with Egyptians, as indeed I did myself, so that the Shepherds are becoming stained to the colour of the dwellers on the Nile. Now these Egyptians are a stubborn and a subtle folk, also they are loyal to their old traditions and to the blood of the kings that ruled them for thousands of years. If one day they should learn certainly that a queen of that blood lives, it well may be that they will rise like the Nile in flood and sweep us into nothingness. Therefore I say that this queen must be destroyed and with her the Brotherhood that is called the Order of the Dawn."

In the silence that followed the Prince Khian rose from the chair in which he was seated below the throne, and making obeisance, spoke for the first time, saying:

"O King my father, hear me. As is known to you I study many things that have to do with the traditions and the mysteries of ancient Egypt, and amongst others from certain instructed men and from old writings I have learned much of this Order of the Dawn. It is an old order and its members are peaceful folk who fight with the spirit and not with the sword, a very powerful order, moreover, for although none know them, it has adherents by the thousand throughout Egypt, perhaps even in this Court, and, it is reported, in far lands as well, especially in Babylonia.

Further, it is headed by a mighty prophet, an ancient man named Roy, if indeed he be a man; one who holds commune with the gods, and like all those over whom he rules, is protected by the gods. Lastly, by treaty made with our forefathers, the first of the Shepherd kings, and renewed by every one of them, even by yourself, my Father, the Holy Ground of graves where this order dwells in the shadow of the pyramids, is sacred and inviolate. Under pain of a dreadful curse, which curse it would seem has fallen swiftly upon those four who, somewhat against your counsel, and certainly against mine, broke the pact and entered this land, and there, not satisfied with spying, tried to do violence to a certain lady or spirit. Yet under oath and custom it may not be entered, nor may any harm be worked to the dwellers in the tombs. Therefore, Pharaoh my father, I pray you think no more of bringing destruction on this order and on a maiden whom you believe to be the daughter of Kheperra, since if you attempt it I am sure that you will bring destruction upon yourself and upon many of those who serve you."

Now the King grew angry.

"Almost might one think, Prince," he said with a sneer, "that you yourself had been sworn of this Order of the Dawn. What are oaths and treaties when our throne itself is at stake? There is disaffection in the land. Babylon harasses us continually, and why? Because she says that we have worked wrong to one of her princesses who married Kheperra, or have done her to death. You do not know it, but I have it in a recent letter from her King. I say that all this nest of plotters must be destroyed, whether it be your will or not."

The Prince Khian seated himself again and was silent, but Anath the Vizier said:

"O Pharaoh, a thought has come to me: is there not another way? Can you not walk a gentler road and gain your ends without breaking faith with the Order of the Dawn, which indeed is greatly to be feared, since, like the

Prince Khian, I hold that it is protected by Heaven itself?
You believe that this Lady of the Pyramids is the lawful
child of Kheperra, and it may be so. If this can be estab-
lished, here is my plan. Send an embassy to Roy the
Prophet and demand that this lady should be given to you
in marriage and become your lawful queen, as she well may
do, seeing that now you have none. Thus would you tie
all Egypt together in the bonds of love and keep your hands
unstained."

At these words Khian laughed aloud and the councillors
smiled. But Apepi stared at Anath, then dropped his
fierce eyes and considered awhile. At length he lifted
them again and said:

"You are wise in your fashion, Anath. A lion's cub can
be tamed as well as killed, although it must be remembered
that if tamed, still at last it grows into a lion and longs
to walk the desert and fill itself with wild meat, as did its
begetters from the first of time. Why should I not wed this
maiden—if she lives, as I believe—and thus unite the
House of the Shepherd kings and that of the old Pharaohs of
the land? It would put an end to many differences and
thereafter Egypt might be one and at peace, able also to
look Babylon in the face. Only, what says the Prince
Khian? I am not so old but that children might be born
of such a union, undertaken in the hope that the eldest of
them, like to the Pharaohs of old times, should wear the
double Crown of North and South without question or dis-
pute; for ever it was the law of Egypt that the right to
royalty came through the mother born of the true race of
Pharaohs, and thus has dynasty been linked to dynasty
from the beginning."

Now the Vizier and all there present looked at Khian,
wondering what he would answer, because upon this answer
in the end might hang his inheritance to the crown of the
North.

For a little while he made none. Then suddenly he
laughed again and said:

"It seems that the case stands thus. *If* there lives one who is the heiress of Kheperra, the dead Pharaoh of the South, and therefore of the ancient royal blood of Egypt that ruled for thousands of years before we Shepherds seized a portion of their inheritance, and *if* she consents to wed my royal father, the King, and *if*, having wed him, a child is born of this marriage, I, the present apparent heir, under such a solemn treaty of union may be dispossessed of my heritage. Well, here are many Ifs, and should all of them be fulfilled a score of years or so hence, does it so greatly matter? Do I so much desire to be King of the North and the inheritor of wars and troubles, that for the sake of such a rule I should seek to prevent the healing of Egypt's wounds and the welding together of her severed crowns? Man's day is short, and Pharaoh or peasant, soon he is forgot and perchance, in the end, it will be better for him if he has been a bringer of peace rather than the wearer of a ravelled robe of power that he does not seek."

"Truly I was right when I said that you must belong to yonder Order of the Dawn, for not so in a like case should I have answered the King my father, Khian," said Apepi, astonished. "Still, let that be, for each man dreams his own dreams and feeds upon his own follies. Therefore I take you at your word, that as the heir apparent to my throne you have nothing to say against this plan, to my mind wild enough, yet one of which trial may be made, even if in the end it should damage you. Now hearken, Khian, it is my will to send you, the Prince of the North, on an embassy to this prophet Roy and to the Council of the Order of the Dawn. Will you, who are wise and politic, undertake such a mission?"

"Before I answer, Pharaoh, tell me what words would be put in the mouth of your ambassador. Would these be words of peace or war?"

"Both, Khian. He would say to the People of the Dawn that the Pharaoh of the North was grieved that against his will the pact between him and them was broken by certain

madmen in his service who every one of them had paid
the penalty of their crime, in atonement of which he
brought gifts to be laid as offerings upon the altars of
whatever gods they worship. He would inquire whether
it is true that among them shelters Nefra, the child of
Kheperra and of Rima, the daughter of the King of Babylon,
and if he discovers that this is so, which may prove impossible, for perhaps she might be hidden away and all
knowledge of her denied, he would declare in the presence
of their Council, and of the maiden herself, if may be, that
Apepi, King of the North, being still a man of middle age
and one who lacks a lawful queen, offers to take this maiden,
Nefra, to wife with all due solemnities, and having obtained
your consent thereto, to swear that a child of hers, should
she bear any, shall by right of birth after my death wear
the double crown of Egypt as Pharaoh of the Upper and
the Lower Lands. All of these things he would prove by
writings sealed with my seal and your own, which would
be given to him."

"Such are the words of peace, O King, which I hear
and understand. Now let me learn what are those of
war."

"Few and simple, it would seem, Khian. If this maiden
lives and the offer is refused by her or on her behalf, then
you would say that I, the King Apepi, tear up all treaties
between myself and the People of the Dawn whom I will
destroy as plotters against my throne and the peace of
Egypt."

"And if it should be proved that there is no such maiden,
what then?"

"Then uttering no threats, you would return and report
to me."

"Life at this Court is wearisome to me since my return
from the Syrian wars, Pharaoh, and here is a new business
to which I have a fancy—I know not why. Therefore, if
it pleases you to send me, I will undertake your mission,"
said Khian after thinking for a while. "Yet is it well that

I should go as the Prince Khian, seeing that although the throne is in your gift and you can bequeath it to whom you will, hitherto I have been looked upon as your heir, and this Order of the Dawn might be mistrustful of such a messenger, or even make strange use of him? Thus he might remain as a hostage among them."

"Which mayhap I should ask you to do, Khian, as a proof of my good faith until this marriage be accomplished. For understand one thing. If the Princess Nefra lives, it is my will to wed her, because, as I see, she and she alone is the road to safety. He who crosses me in this matter is my enemy to the death; whether he be the prophet Roy or any other man, surely he shall die."

"You are quick of decision, my father. An hour ago no such thought had entered your mind, and now it holds no other."

"Aye, Son, for now, thanks to Anath, I see a ship that will bear me and Egypt over a rising flood of troubles which soon might overwhelm us both, and after the fashion of the great, I embark before it be swept downstream. Vizier, when you espied that ship, you did good service, and for you there is a chain of gold and much advancement. Nay, keep your thanks till it has borne us safe to harbour. For the rest, if you, Khian, think this mission too dangerous— and it has dangers—I will seek another envoy, though you are the one whom I should choose. I doubt whether you will deceive these keen-eyed magicians by taking another name and pretending that you are not Khian, but an officer of the Court, or a private person. Still, do so if you will."

"Why not, Pharaoh?" answered Khian, laughing, "seeing that, if all goes well, it is your purpose to make of me a very private person, for then I who this morning was the heir apparent, or so it pleased you to say, shall be but one of many king's sons. If that chances I would ask whether I who shall have lost much may retain my private estates and revenues that have come to me through my mother or by the endowment of your Majesty? For I who do not greatly care for crowns could wish to remain rich with means to live at ease and follow those pursuits I love."

"That is sworn to you, Khian, here and now and upon my royal word.   Let it be recorded!"

"I thank the King, and now by permission I will withdraw myself to talk with that wounded man before he dies, since perhaps he can tell me much that may be useful upon this business."

Then the Prince Khian prostrated himself and went.

When he had watched him go, King Apepi thought to himself:

Surely this young man has a great heart.   Few would not have winced beneath such a blow, unless indeed they planned treachery, which Khian could never do.   Almost am I grieved.   Yet it must be so.   If that royal maiden lives, I will wed her and swear the throne to her children, for thus only can I and Egypt sleep in peace.   Then he said aloud:

"The Council is ended and woe to him that betrays its secrets, for he shall be thrown to the lions."

CHAPTER VIII

THE SCRIBE RASA

WITHIN thirty days of the holding of this Council, a messenger appeared on what was acknowledged to be the frontier of the Holy Ground that was marked by the highest point to which the Nile rose in times of flood, and called to one who was working in the field that he had a writing which he prayed him to deliver to the Prophet of the Order of the Dawn.

The man came and, staring at the messenger stupidly, asked:

"What is the Order of the Dawn and who is its prophet?"

"Perchance, Friend, you might make inquiries," said the messenger, handing him the roll and with it no small present. "Meanwhile I, who may always be found at dawn or sunset seated at my prayers in yonder group of palms, will bide here and await the answer."

The farmer, for such he seemed to be, scratched his head and, taking the roll and the present, said that he would try to serve one so generous, though he knew not of whom to ask concerning this order and its prophet.

On the following day at sunset he appeared again and handed to the messenger another roll which he declared he had been charged by some person unknown to give to him for delivery to the King Apepi at his Court at Tanis. The messenger, mocking this peasant, said that he had never heard of King Apepi and did not know where Tanis might be; still out of kindness of heart, he would try to discover and make due delivery of the roll after which the two smiled at each other and departed.

Some days later this writing was read to Apepi by his private scribe. It ran thus:

"In the name of that Spirit who rules the world, and of his servant Osiris, god of the dead, greeting to Apepi, King of the Shepherds, now dwelling at the city of Tanis in Lower Egypt.

"Know, O King Apepi, that we, Roy the Prophet and the Council of the Order of the Dawn, who sit in the shadow of the ancient pyramids built long ago by certain kings of Egypt, once members of our order, to serve as tombs for their bodies and to be monuments to their greatness on which all eyes might gaze till the end of the world; we who from age to age drink of the wisdom of the Sphinx, the Terror of the desert, have received your message and given it consideration. Know, O King, that although of late we have suffered grievous wrong at the hands of some who seem to have been your officers, for which wrong those unhappy ones paid with their lives, as all must do who attempt to violate our sanctity and to peer into our secrets; in obedience to the precepts of our Order, we forgive that wrong and having put it aside as a matter of small account, we will receive the ambassador whom you desire to send to us to discuss matters of which you do not reveal the purport. Know, O King, further, that this ambassador, whoever he may be, must come alone, for it is contrary to our rules to admit more than one stranger beyond the borders of the Holy Ground. If after learning this it be still your pleasure to send that ambassador, let him appear before the next full moon in the same grove of palms where this roll was delivered to your messenger. Here one of those who serve us will find him and guide him to where we are, nor shall he suffer any harm at our hands."

When Apepi had heard this letter, he sent for the Prince Khian and asked him privately whether still he dared to adventure himself unaccompanied among the people of

the Order of the Dawn and in a place which all men swore
was haunted.

"Why not, Father?" asked Khian. "If mischief is
meant against me, an ambassador's guard would be no protection, nor are ghosts or spirits to be frightened away by
numbers. If I go at all I would as soon go alone as in company. Also it is plain that thus only can this embassy
be carried out, because yonder Brotherhood will not receive
more than a single man."

"As it pleases you, Son," replied Apepi. "Go now and
make ready. To-morrow the writing shall be delivered to
you by the Vizier together with my instructions; also a
guard will be waiting to conduct you to the place appointed
by this prophet. Go and return in safety, remembering our
bargain and bringing this maiden with you in charge of
women of her own people, if so it may be, for thus shall
you earn my favour."

"I go," said Khian, "to return, or perchance not to return, as the gods may direct."

So, everything having been made ready and the roll con-
taining the offers and the threats of King Apepi given into
his keeping, together with offerings of gold for the gods of
the Children of the Dawn and presents of jewels for the
Princess Nefra, if it should be proved that she was the
wondrous maiden who dwelt among them, Khian departed.
Yet he did not travel as the Prince, but rather as a Scribe
of the Court, Rasa by name, whom it had pleased the King
to choose to be his envoy upon a certain business. Leaving
Tanis so secretly that few discovered he had gone, he sailed
up Nile in a ship whose sailors had never seen him, and
although they had orders to obey him in everything, took
him to be what he said he was, a messenger, Rasa by name,
travelling upon the royal business. Even the guard that
accompanied him, six in number, were soldiers from a distant city who had never looked upon his face.

His journey ended, he reached the landing place in the
afternoon upon the day appointed and was escorted by the

soldiers who bore the gold and other gifts, also his travelling
gear, to the grove of palms which the messenger had described, as to which there could be no mistake, for no other
was in sight. Here he dismissed the guard, who left him
doubtfully and yet were glad to go before evening came,
for like all Egypt they believed this place to be haunted
by the ghosts of the mighty dead, also by the Spirit of the
Pyramids whose eyes drove men to madness.

"Now, as we are ordered by Anath the Vizier," said the
captain of the guard, "we and the ship in which you have
travelled, my Lord Rasa, depart to Memphis where we may
be found when we are summoned, though we are not sure
that you will ever need a ship again."

"Why not, Captain?" asked Khian, or Rasa.

"Because this place has an evil repute, my Lord Rasa,
and it is said that no stranger who crosses yonder belt of
sand ever returns."

"If so, what happens to him, Captain?"

"We do not know, but it is reported that he is walled up
in a tomb and left to perish there. Or, if he escapes this
fate and is as young and well-favoured as you are, perchance
he meets the beauteous Spirit of the Pyramids who wanders
about in the moonlight, and becomes her lover."

"If she is so fair, Captain, worse things might happen to
a man."

"Nay, Lord Rasa, for when he kisses her on the lips, she
looks into his eyes and madness takes hold of him, so that
he runs after her, till at last he falls on the sand raving and,
should he live at all, remains thus all his days."

"Why does he not catch her, Captain?"

"Because she leads him to one of the pyramids, up which,
being a spirit, she can glide like a moonbeam but whither he
cannot follow. And when he sees that he has lost her,
then his brain boils and he is no more a man."

"You make me afraid, Captain. This would be a sad
fate to happen to a learned scribe, for such is really my
trade, just when he had won favour at the Court. Still, I

have my orders and you know the doom of him who dis-
obeys, or even does not carry out, the commands of his
Majesty Apepi."

"Aye, Lord Rasa, I know well enough, for this king is
very fierce, and if he has set his mind on anything, ill to
cross. Such a one, if he is lucky, is shortened by a head,
or if he is unlucky, is beaten to death with rods."

"If so, Captain, it would seem better to run the risk of
the ghosts, or even of the terrible eyes of the Spirit of the
Pyramids, rather than to return with you, as I confess that
I should wish. About my neck I have a holy charm which
is said to defend its wearer from all tomb-dwellers and other
evil things, and to this and to my prayers I must trust
myself. Soon I hope to see you again upon the ship, but
if you learn that I am dead, I pray of you, lay an offering
for my soul upon the first altar of Osiris that you find."

"I'll not forget it, Lord Rasa, for know that I like you
well and could have wished you a better fate," answered
the captain, who was kind-hearted; adding, as he departed
with his company, "Perchance you have offended Pharaoh
or the Vizier, and one or other of them has chosen this way
to be rid of you."

"That man is as cheerful as a bullfrog croaking in a pool
in a night of storm," thought Khian to himself. "Well,
perhaps he is right, and if so, what will it matter when
those pyramids have seen the Nile rise another hundred
times?"

Then he sat himself down upon the ground, resting his
back against the bole of one of the palms, and contemplated
the mighty outlines of these same pyramids, which hitherto
he had only seen from far away, thinking to himself, as
Nefra had thought, that those who built them must have
been kings indeed. Also he reflected, not without pleasure,
for he was a lover of adventures and new things, upon the
strangeness of his mission and of the manner in which it
had been thrust upon him.

If this royal maiden lives, he thought, and I succeed

it means that I lose a crown, and if I do not succeed, then
it is also possible that I shall lose the crown, since my father
never forgives those who fail. Indeed, it would be best for
me if there is no such lady, or that I should not find her.
At any rate, there is some girl who climbs pyramids, because before he died that woman-thief swore to me that
he saw her. He swore to me also that she was very beauteous, the loveliest lady that ever he beheld, which almost
proves to me that she cannot have been the princess, for
as the gods do not give everything, princesses are always—
or almost always—ugly. Moreover, they do not climb
pyramids but lie about and eat sweetmeats. Perhaps
after all she whom the dying thief believed he saw, if he
saw any one, is a spirit, and if so, may it be given to me to
behold her, to do which I would take my chance of madness.
Meanwhile, these Children of the Dawn are strange folk,
to judge from all that I can learn concerning them, yet it
is said, most kindly, so perhaps they will not murder me,
even if they guess or know that I am the Prince Khian.
What would be the use, seeing there are so many who are
princes, or who can be made princes by a decree and a
touch of a sceptre?

Reflecting thus, Khian fell asleep, for the afternoon was
very hot and he had found little rest upon that crowded boat.

While he was sleeping Roy the Prophet, the lord Tau,
and the Princess Nefra were taking counsel together in a
chamber of the temple where they dwelt.

"The messenger has landed, Prophet," said Tau; "it is
reported to me that he is already seated in the grove of
palms."

"Is aught else reported, Tau, that is, as to his business?"
asked Roy. "If so, speak it out, since a command has
come to me that the time is at hand when our Lady of
Egypt here"—and he pointed to Nefra—"should be taken
into our full counsel."

"Yes, Prophet. A certain brother of ours who is one of
the Court of King Apepi—look not astonished, Princess,

for our brethren are everywhere—informs me by the fashion that is known to you that this business is one which concerns a certain lady very closely. To be brief: When four men strove to carry off this lady, Ru the Ethiopian made a mistake, for he killed three of them but suffered the fourth to get away, though wounded to the death. This man reached the Court at Tanis and before he died made a report which, added to other rumours, assured King Apepi that a certain babe who escaped from his hands in Thebes long ago—dwells among us here and is no other than the heiress of the ancient line of the Pharaohs of Egypt."

"It seems that this king is a shrewd man," said Roy.

"Very shrewd," answered Tau, "and quick to decide; so much so that on a hint given to him by his Vizier Anath, also a shrewd man, he determined at once not to kill a certain lady, as at first he thought to do, but to make her his queen and thus, by promising their heritage to her offspring, to unite the Upper and the Lower Lands without war or trouble."

Now Nefra started, but before she could speak Roy answered:

"The scheme has merits, great merits, for thus would our ends be attained and many sorrows and perils melt away like morning mist. But," he added with a sigh, "what says Nefra our Princess, who after to-night's ceremony will be our Queen?"

"I say," answered Nefra coldly, "that I am not a woman to be sold for the price of a crown, or of a hundred crowns. This man, Apepi the Usurper, is one of the fierce Shepherds who are the enemies of our race. He is a thief of the desert who has stolen half Egypt and holds it by force and fraud. He, who is more than old enough to be my father, slew my father, the Pharaoh Kheperra, and strove to slay me and my mother, the Queen Rima, the daughter of Babylon. Having failed in this, now he seeks to buy me whom he has never seen, as an Arab buys a mare of priceless blood, and for his own purposes to set me at the head of his household.

Prophet, I will have none of him. Rather than enter his palace as a bride I will hurl myself from the tallest pyramid and seek refuge with Osiris."

"Here we have the answer that I foresaw," said Roy with a little smile upon his aged lips; "nor is it one that causes me to grieve, since whatever its gains, such a union would be unholy. Fear not, Princess. While the Order of the Dawn has power you are safe from the arms of Apepi the Wolf. Tell me, Tau, according to the report that has reached you, is this all that the King of the North has to say to us?"

"Nay, Prophet. When the roll that yonder messenger bears is opened, I think that in it will be found written, that if the heiress of Egypt is not delivered to him, then he proposes to take her by force, or if he cannot do so, to send her down to death, and with her, notwithstanding his treaties, every one of the Children of the Dawn from the most aged to the babe in arms."

"Is it so?" said Roy. "Well, if a fool strives to drag a sleeping snake from its hole, that snake awakes, puffs out its head, and strikes, as mayhap Apepi will find before all is done. But these things are not yet; time to talk of them when the royal hand is thrust into the hole to grip the deadly hooded snake. Meanwhile, this envoy from Apepi must be granted the hospitality which we have sworn to him, and brought from the palm grove where he sits alone. Would it please you, Princess, to throw a man's robe over that woman's dress of yours and go to lead him here? Ru and the Lady Kemmah would accompany you, keeping themselves out of sight? If so, being clever, you might learn something from the man, who finding but a gentle youth sent to guide him, would fear no trap, and perhaps even speak freely to such a one."

"Yes," answered Nefra, "I think that it would please me; that is, if you are sure that there is no trap or ambush, since the walk to the grove is pleasant and I have been cooped up of late."

"There is no ambush, Lady," replied Roy. "Since what happened awhile ago by the pyramids our frontiers have been well guarded; also your every step will be watched, although you do not see the watchers. Therefore fear nothing. Learn all you can from this envoy and bring him to the Sphinx where he will be blindfolded and led before us."

"I go," said Nefra, laughing. "To-morrow I shall be called a queen and who knows whether afterwards I shall be suffered to walk alone."

So she went accompanied by Tau who summoned Ru and Kemmah in one of the courts of the temple and there gave certain orders to them and to others who seemed to be awaiting him. This done he returned to Roy and looking him in the face, said in a low voice:

"Do you, O Prophet, who know so much, chance to have learned what may be the name and quality of this envoy from Apepi?"

Now Roy looked him in the eyes and said:

"It comes into my mind, how or whence does not matter, that although he travels as a simple officer of the Court, called I know not what, the man is no other than the Prince Khian, Apepi's heir."

"So I think also," said Tau, "and not without reason. Tell me, holy Prophet, have you learned aught concerning this Khian?"

"Much, Tau. From his boyhood he has been watched by those at Apepi's Court who are our friends, and their report of him is very good. He has his faults like other men in youth, and he is somewhat rash. Had he not been so, never would he have undertaken this mission under strange conditions. For the rest he is more Egyptian than Shepherd, for in him the mother's blood runs strong; and if he worships any gods at all, of which, he being a philosopher, I am not sure, they are those of Egypt. Further, he is learned, brave, handsome of body, and generous in mind; something of a dreamer, one who seeks that which he will never find upon the earth, one, too, who longs to heal Egypt's wounds. Indeed, he seems to be such a man as, had I a daughter, I would choose for her in marriage if I might. This is the report that I have concerning the Prince Khian. Is yours as good?"

"In all things it is the same, Prophet. Yet why does he come hither upon such an errand, seeing that, if it succeeds, it may cost him his succession to the Crown? I fear some trap."

"I think, Tau, that he comes for adventure, and because he seeks new things; also because he is drawn to our doctrines and would study them with his own eyes and ears, not knowing that he may find more than he seeks."

"Is it in the hope that he will do so, Prophet, that you have put it into the mind of the Princess Nefra to meet him yonder in the palm grove?"

"It is, Tau. When I said that such a marriage as this Apepi proposes had many merits, what I meant was, not that she should be thrown to the Shepherd lion, but that a marriage between her and the Prince Khian would have those merits. How could Egypt be better tied together? Even if we are strong enough to wage it, we are haters of war, and would not attain our ends by death and bloodshed. Yet to propose such a thing would defeat itself, since, as she told us, this Lady Nefra is not one to be sold or driven. Her heart and nothing else is her guide, which she will follow fast and far."

"The heart of woman goes out more readily to princes than it does to humble messengers. What if this one who sits among the palm trees does not please her?"

"Then, Tau, all is finished and we must find another road. Let Fate decide after she has judged, not of the Prince but of the man. We cannot. Hearken. This envoy, however named, comes to learn what thousands know already, whether or not the daughter and heiress of Kheperra shelters among us. We can deny or we can confess. Which shall we do?"

"If we deny, Prophet, certainly he will discover the truth otherwise and set us down as liars and cowards. If we confess, he and the world will know us for true men and brave, and that the oath which we swear to the goddess of Verity is no empty form. So whatever we may lose, we shall win honour even from our foes. Therefore, I say confess and face the issue."

"So say I and the rest of the Council, Tau. To-night before the delegates from all Egypt and elsewhere, the Princess is to be crowned its Queen in the great hall of the temple, a matter that cannot be hid, since the very bats will twitter it throughout the land. Therefore it seems wise to me that this messenger should be present at the ceremony and if he will, make open report of it to Apepi. There is another thing of which he must also make report, Tau: namely, whether the new-crowned Queen will take this Apepi as a husband."

"Already we know the answer, Prophet, but after it—what?"

"After it—Babylon. Listen, Tau. Apepi will send an army to destroy us and to capture the Queen, but he will find nothing to destroy, for the Order has its hiding places, and in Egypt are many tombs and catacombs where soldiers dare not come, while the Queen will be far away. If Apepi seeks a curse, let the curse fall upon him, as fall it shall when a hundred thousand Babylonians pour down on Tanis in answer to dead Rima's prayer and to right her daughter's wrongs."

"Be it so," said Tau. "Those who seek the face of War must be prepared to look him in the eyes, for such is the rule of God and man."

Nefra, wrapped in a long cloak, approached the grove of palms, followed by Ru and the Lady Kemmah, who grumbled at the business.

"The day is hot," she said, "and who but fools would walk so far in the blaze of the sun? To-night there are ceremonies in which you, Princess, must play the greatest part. Is it fitting that you and I should weary ourselves thus when the work of making ready your robes and jewels is not finished? What is this new madness? What do you seek?"

"That which, as you have instructed me, is sought of all women, Nurse, namely—a man," answered Nefra in her sweet, mocking voice. "I believe that there is a man in yonder palm grove and I go to find him."

"A man, indeed! Are there not men in plenty nearer home, if tombs can be called a home while one is still living beneath the sun? Still, it is true that most of them are gray-bearded dotards and the rest but priests or anchorites who think of nothing but their souls, or husbandmen who toil all day and dream all night of how much mud Nile will yield at its next rising. Well, there are the palms and I see no man, nor can I walk any farther in this accursed sand. Here is the statue of a god, or perchance of some king whose name no one has heard for a thousand years. At least, god or king, he gives shade and in it I will sit as, if you are wise, you will do also while Ru hunts for this man of yours, though when he sees a black giant grinning at him with a great axe in his hand I think that he will run away."

"So do I," said Nefra, "yet, Ru, come with me, as indeed you must."

Then walking somewhat to the right she entered the grove of palms at its end and stepped softly along it, bidding Ru keep himself as much hidden as possible. Presently, seated against the trunk of one of them she saw an officer who wore upon his robe the lion badge of the Shepherd kings, having by his side certain packages, and behold! he was fast asleep. Now a thought took her and she commanded Ru to approach him softly, and having carried off the packages, to go and hide with them behind the statue where Kemmah sat. Then, she said, he was to follow her with Kemmah and the gear in such fashion, if might be, that the officer did not see them as she led him toward the statue of the Sphinx.

This Ru did without awakening Khian, for although he was so large, like all Ethiopians he could move softly enough at need—an art that they learn in tracking enemies and game. He vanished with his burden behind the statue, whence she knew well he was watching her in case of danger, but Nefra, leaning against another palm, studied the sleeper closely. At the first glance she was aware that never before had she beheld such a man as this officer, one at once so handsome and so refined of face.

If his eyes, which I cannot see, are as good as the rest of him, he is beautiful, thought Nefra. Also he looks like one whose spirit guides his flesh and not his flesh his spirit; and as she thought, something new, something she had never felt before stirred her serenity and frightened her a little, though in what way she was not sure.

So for many minutes they remained, the weary Khian sleeping and Nefra watching him. At length he stirred, stretched out his arms as though to clasp a dream, yawned, and opened his eyes.

They *are* as good as the rest of him! reflected Nefra as she slipped behind the palm and hid there, which they were, being large, brown, and somewhat melancholy.

Now Khian remembered the packets which contained the presents and the gold and began to search for them eagerly.

"By the gods, they are gone!" he said aloud in a voice that, although anxious, still was soft and pleasant. "How can this have happened and I not know it, seeing that they lay under my hand? Truly they are right who say that this place is the home of ghosts."

Nefra stepped forward, closely muffled in her long cloak, and asked:

"Is aught amiss, Sir? And if so, can I aid you?"

"Yes," said Khian, "by restoring to me certain articles which I suppose you have stolen, young man. That is, if you are a man," he added doubtfully, "for your voice——"

"—Is breaking, Sir," replied Nefra, trying to make it as hoarse as possible.

"Then it has broken the wrong way. Breaking voices should grow gruff, not soft as a girl's. But let that be. Restore to me my goods lest I should—well, kill you——"

"And perchance thereby lose them and much else for ever, Sir."

"You do not seem very frightened. Tell me, who are you?"

"Sir, I am the guide appointed to lead you—if you be Apepi's officer—to where you must lodge before you are brought into the presence of the Council of the Order of the Dawn. Knowing that you were alone and thinking that you might be alarmed if armed men came, I, as a young person who can frighten no one, was chosen to fill this office by the Council."

"That is very kind of the Council. But meanwhile, Young Person, where are the goods which my servants set by my side before they departed?"

"Sir, they have gone on before you. As you said just now, this is a home of ghosts and ghosts can carry gold and garments very fast."

"Then they might have carried me also, though on the whole I am glad they did not, for, Young Person, you amuse me. Well, I suppose that I must take your word for it, as to the goods, I mean, and if I find that you have lied, I can always kill you afterwards, or if I don't, the Order of the Dawn can, since they will have lost their presents. What next?"

"Be pleased to come with me, Sir."

"Good, Young Person. Lead on, I follow."

CHAPTER IX

THE CROWNING OF NEFRA

So THIS pair started upon their long walk, Nefra being careful to lead her companion wide of that overthrown statue behind which hid Kemmah and Ru.

"Do you live in this place?" asked Khian presently.

"Yes, Sir, here and hereabouts," replied Nefra with vagueness.

"And might I ask what is your office when you are not escorting travellers, who must be rare, and arranging for the transport of their baggage by uncommon means?"

"Oh! anything," replied Nefra still more vaguely, "but generally I run errands."

"Indeed! And where to?"

"Oh! anywhere. But tell me, Sir, are you acquainted with the pyramids?"

"Not at all, Friend, except from a distance. The pyramids, it would appear, are now the private property of that Order you mentioned, to which, by the way, I, who also run errands, have a message to deliver. None may approach them. Indeed, I have heard that some unfortunate men who wished to explore their wonders not long ago, came to a terrible end. According to the story a black lion rushed out of one of them, killed three of those men, and mauled the fourth so badly that afterwards he died. Or it may have been one of your ghosts that rushed out. At any rate, the men died."

"What a strange tale, Sir. I wonder that we did not hear of it, but living quite secluded as we do, we hear nothing, or at least very little. But they are beautiful, those

99

pyramids, are they not, standing up thus against the evening sky in majesty? Look how their sharp outlines seem
to cut into the heavens. Also from them the great dead
seem to speak to us across the gulfs of Time."

"I perceive, Young Person, that you have imagination,
which is unusual in those who run errands and guide travellers. Yet I dare to differ from you. These stone heaps
undoubtedly are beautiful with a beauty that crushes the
mind, though not so much so as are mountains chiselled
out by Nature and capped with snow, such as I have seen
in Syria. But to me they speak not of the mighty dead
whose memories they glorify, but of the thousands of forgotten ones who perished in the toil of their uprearing, that
in them the bones of kings might find a house deemed to
be eternal and their names preserved among men. Was it
worth while to leave monuments to be the marvel of generations at the cost of so much doom and misery?"

"I do not know, Sir, who never thought of the matter thus.
Yet there is this to be said. Mankind must suffer, so I
have been told who am but an ignorant——"

"——Young person," suggested Khian.

"And generally it suffers to no end," went on Nefra as
though she had not heard him, "leaving naught behind,
not even a record of its pain. Here at least something remains which the world will admire for thousands of years
after those who caused the suffering and those who suffered
are lost in darkness. Suffering that has purpose, or that
bears fruit, even though we know not the purpose and never
see the fruit, may be borne almost with joy, but empty,
sterile suffering is a desert without water and a torment
without hope."

Khian looked at the speaker, or rather at her hood, for
he could see nothing else, and remarked:

"The thought is just and finely put. They instruct those
who run errands well in this land."

"The brethren of the Order are learned, so even the young
can pick up crumbs of knowledge from their feasts—if it

pleases them to look for them, Sir— but forgive me, how are you named?"

"Named?—Oh! I am called Rasa the Scribe."

"Is it so? I did not guess your trade because among us scribes carry palettes at the girdle, not swords; also their hands are different. I should have thought that you were a soldier and a hunter and a climber of the mountains of which you spoke, not a copyist of documents in hot palace rooms."

"Sometimes I am these things also," he replied hastily, "especially a climber—when I was in Syria. By the way, my guide, I have heard strange stories of another climber, one who scales these pyramids. It is said at Tanis and elsewhere that they are haunted by a spirit who runs up and down their sides at night, and even in the daytime also. I say by a spirit, for woman she cannot be."

"Why not, Scribe Rasa?"

"Because, or so the tale tells, this climber is so beautiful that those who look upon her go mad, and who could be made mad by the sight of any woman? Also what woman could clamber over those smooth and mighty monuments like a lizard?"

"If you are a scaler of mountains, Scribe Rasa, you will know that such feats are often not so difficult as they seem. There lives a family of men in this place that for generations has been able to conquer the pyramids by day or night," she replied, leaving the first part of his question unanswered.

"Then if I stay here long enough I will pray them to teach me their art, in the hope that at the top of them I might meet this spirit and be made mad by drinking of the Cup of Beauty. But you have not answered me. Is there such a spirit, and if so, can I see her?—to do which I would give my—well, a great deal."

"Here before us is the Sphinx which I thought, Scribe Rasa, being one so curious, you would have noticed as we approached it. Now put your question to that god, for they say that he solves riddles sometimes, if he likes the asker, though never yet have *I* wrung an answer from those stony, smiling lips."

"Indeed? I have sundry problems that I seek to solve and one of them is what may be hidden by that long cloak of yours, my young guide with an instructed mind."

"Then you must propound them at another time, after the needful prayers and fastings. And now, your pardon, but I am commanded to blindfold you because we have come to the entrance of the sanctuaries of the Order of the Dawn, of which no stranger may learn the secret. Will you be pleased to kneel down, for you are very tall, Scribe Rasa, and I can scarcely reach your head."

"Oh! why not?" he answered. "First my packages are stolen; then I am thrown to the crocodiles of curiosity, and now I must be blindfolded, or perhaps beheaded by a 'young person' who has driven me as mad as though she were the Spirit of the Pyramids herself. I kneel. Proceed."

"Why do you talk of a poor youth who earns his bread by following the profession of a guide as 'she,' also as a thief or perhaps a murderer, and compare him to the Spirit of the Pyramids, Scribe Rasa? Be so good as to keep your head still and not try to look over your shoulder as you are doing, lest I should hurt you with the bandage. Fix your eyes upon the face of the Sphinx in front of you and think of all the riddles you would like to ask of its divinity. Now all is ready, I begin"; and very deftly and softly she tied a scented silken cloth, warm from her own bosom, about his head, saying presently:

"It is finished. You may rise."

"First I will answer your question, knowing that you cannot be wroth with one who is blinded. I call you 'she' because by accident I forgot and looked down instead of up and thus saw your hands, which are those of woman; also the ring you wear, which is an ancient signet; also a long lock that escaped from beneath your hood while you bent over me; also——"

"Kemmah," broke in Nefra, "my task is finished and I go to ask my fee from the gatekeeper. Be pleased to guide this scribe or messenger into the presence of the holy Prophet and let the man with you bear his goods, which all the way he has accused me of stealing from him, so that they may be checked in his presence."

He who was called the Scribe Rasa sat in the presence of the Prophet Roy, of the Lord Tau, and of the elders of the Council of the Order of the Dawn, venerable, white-robed men. Roy spoke, saying:

"We have read the roll, O Envoy Rasa, which you bring to us from Apepi, King of the Shepherds, at this time sitting at Tanis in the Land of Egypt. Briefly it contains two questions and a threat. The first question is whether Nefra, Royal Princess of Egypt, the child and heiress of the Pharaoh Kheperra, now gathered to Osiris whither he was sent by the spear of Apepi, and of Rima the daughter of the King of Babylon, lives and is dwelling among us. To that question you will learn the answer at a certain ceremony this night. The second question is whether this Royal Nefra, if she still looks upon the sun, will become the wife of Apepi, King of the Shepherds, as he demands that she should do. To this doubtless the Royal Nefra, if she lives, will give her answer when she has considered of the matter, for then there is a queen in Egypt, and a Queen of Egypt chooses whom she will as husband.

"After this comes the threat, namely, that should there be a certain Lady to refuse this offer and should it be refused, Apepi, King of the Shepherds, violating all treaties made between his forefathers and himself with our ancient Brotherhood of the Children of the Dawn, will in revenge destroy us root and branch. To this we reply at once and afterwards will write it in a roll, that we do not fear Apepi, and that should he attempt this evil thing, every stone of the great pyramids would lie lighter on his head than will the curse of Heaven that he has earned as a man foresworn.

"Say to Apepi, O Ambassador, that we who seem but a weak band of hermits living in solitude far from the world and there practising our innocent rites, we who have no armies and who, save to defend our lives, never lift a sword, are yet far more powerful than he, or any king upon the earth. We do not fight as kings fight, yet we marshal hosts unseen, since with us goes the Strength of God. Let him attack if he will to find naught but tombs peopled with the dead. Then let him set his ear to the ground and listen to the tread of armies who rush to stamp him down to doom. Such is our message to Apepi, King of the Shepherds."

"I hear it," said Khian, bowing respectfully, "and glad am I to learn, O Prophet, that it is your intention to write it in a roll, for otherwise King Apepi, a violent man who loves not rough words, might make him who delivered it by word of mouth, shorter by a head. Be pleased, therefore, to remember, O Prophet and Councillors, that I, the Scribe Rasa, am but a messenger charged to deliver a writing and to carry back the answer; also to collect certain information if I can. Of the matter of treaties between the Shepherd kings and your Order I know nothing, nor is it one that I am commanded to discuss. Of threats uttered against you, or what may be the end of these threats, I know nothing, whatever I may guess. Be pleased, therefore, to write down at your leisure all you have to say, that it may be delivered to King Apepi in due season. Meanwhile, grant me safety while I dwell among you, and with it as much liberty as you can, since, to speak truth, these temple tombs of yours have something of the air of prisons, nor do I love bandages upon my eyes, seeing that I am an ambassador, not a spy charged to report upon the secrets of your dwelling place."

Roy looked at him with his piercing eyes and answered:

"If you will swear to us upon your soul to reveal nothing that you may learn of these poor secrets of ours that lie outside the matters of your commission; also not to attempt

to depart from among us until such time as we think fitting
and our written answers are prepared, we, for our part,
will grant you liberty to come and go among us as you will,
O Messenger, who tell us that you are named Rasa and a
scribe by occupation. This we grant because, having gifts
of discernment, we believe you to be an upright man, although perchance you have been commanded to travel
under another name than that by which you are known at
the Court of Tanis, one, too, who has no desire to bring
evil upon the innocent."

"I thank you, Prophet," said Khian, bowing, "and all
these things I swear gladly. And now I am charged to
deliver offerings to your gods in atonement for a crime
against you that was wrought recently by certain evildoers."

"Our god, Scribe Rasa, is the Spirit above all gods who
rules the earth and whose raiment we behold in the stars
of heaven, one to whom we make no offering save those of
the spirit. Nor do we accept presents for ourselves who
being a Brotherhood in which each serves the other, have
no need of gold. Therefore, Ambassador, be pleased to
take back the gifts you bring and on our behalf to pray
the King of the Shepherds that he will distribute them
among the widows and children of those men who came by
their death in seeking, at his command as we suppose,
to do violence to one of us and to discover our secrets."

"As regards this new god of yours," answered Khian,
"if it be lawful, Prophet, I would pray of you, or of any
whom you may appoint, to instruct me, a seeker after
Truth, in his attributes and mysteries."

"If there is opportunity it shall be done," said Roy.

"As touching the matter of the presents," went on
Khian when he had bowed acknowledgment of this promise,
"I have naught to say, save that I pray that you will re-
turn them with your written answer and, if possible, by
another hand than mine. You who are so wise and aged,
Prophet, may have noted that great kings do not love

to have gifts thrown back into their faces with words like to yours, and, in such cases, are apt to blame their bearer."

Roy smiled a little and without comment on this matter, said:

"This night we invite you to a ceremony, Scribe Rasa. Go now, eat and rest till, at the appointed hour, you are summoned, if it be your pleasure to attend."

"Surely it is my pleasure," answered Khian, and was led away.

It was near to midnight, and Khian, having arrayed himself in garments that he had brought with him, such as scribes wear upon occasions of festival, lay upon the bed in his chamber, thinking of the strange place in which he found himself and its still stranger inhabitants. He thought of the wondrous hawk-eyed old prophet, of his grave-miened councillors as they had appeared gathered in that tomb-temple, of the ceremony to which he was to be summoned, if indeed he had not been forgotten, and what might be its occasion. He thought also of how his father, Apepi, would receive the proud answer of these anchorites; of the smile upon the face of the mighty Sphinx which that day he had seen for the first time, and of other things.

But most of all did he think of the guide who had led him from the palm grove and afterwards bandaged his eyes. This guide was a woman, a young woman with beautiful hair and hands, on one of which she wore a royal ring. That was all he knew of her who for aught he could tell might be very ugly, as the ring might be one she had found or stolen. Yet this was certain, that however common her face or humble her station, her mind was neither. No uninstructed peasant girl could harbour her thoughts or clothe them in her words. Much indeed did he long to see that guide unveiled and to discover the mystery of one who had so sweet a voice.

At this point a deep, gruff voice asked leave to enter, which he gave. As he rose from the bed there appeared before him in the lamplight a black man more gigantic than any he had ever seen, who carried in his hand an enormous axe.

"I pray you tell me, who are you and what is your business with me?" Khian inquired, staring at him and rubbing his eyes, for at first he thought he must be dreaming.

"I am your guide," said the giant, "and I come to take you with me."

"By Set, another guide, and very different from the last!" exclaimed Khian. "Now I wonder if this ceremony is that of my execution," he added to himself. "Surely the man and his axe would be well suited to such a purpose. Or is he but another of the ghosts that haunt these pyramids?" Then he addressed Ru, for it was he, saying:

"Sir Giant on the Earth, or Sir Spirit from the Underworld, for I know not which you are, I feel no wish for a journey in your company. I am tired and prefer to stop where I am. I bid you good-night."

"Sir Envoy, or Sir Scribe, or Sir Prince in disguise, or Sir Soldier, for that at any rate I am sure that you are because of your bearing and the scars on you, which were never made with a stylus, however tired you may be, you cannot remain upon that bed. I am commanded to lead you elsewhere. Will you come or must I carry you as I did your baggage?"

"Oh! So you were the thief who stole my parcels and left a smooth-tongued wench behind you to conduct me across the sand!"

"A wench!" roared Ru. "A wench——" and he lifted his axe.

"Well, Friend, what else was she? Not a man, that I'll swear, and between man and woman there is no halfway house. Tell me, I pray you, for I am curious. Sit down and take a cup of wine, for this place is cramping to one of your stature. These monks of yours seem to have very good wine. I never tasted better in my—in the King's Court. Try it."

Ru took the cup which he proffered to him and drained it.

"I thank you," he said. "The worst of dwelling with hermits is that they are so fond of water, though they have plenty of good stuff stored away in some grave or other. Now let us be going. I tell you I am commanded——"

: "So you said before, Friend Giant. By whom are you commanded?"

"By her——" began Ru, and stopped.

"Her, who or what? Do you mean the lady who guided and blindfolded me? Stay. Take one more cup of this excellent wine."

Ru did so, answering as he set it down:

"You are not far from it, but my tongue is tied. Come, Prince."

"Prince!" he exclaimed, holding up his hands. "Friend Giant, that wine must be getting into your head if it can reach so far in so short a time. What do you mean?"

"What I say, though I should not have said it. Don't you understand, Prince, that these tomb dwellers are wizards and know everything although they pretend to know nothing? They think me a stupid Ethiopian, just a black fellow who can handle a battle-axe, which perhaps is all I am. Still, I have ears and I hear, and that is how I come to know that you are a certain Prince, and a soldier like myself, though it pleases you to pretend to be a scribe. Still, I have not mentioned it to any one else, not even to—— But never mind. Be sure—she knows nothing. She thinks you are just what you say—a fellow who scribbles on papyrus. Now talk no more; come, come. Time passes. Afterwards you shall tell me what wars go on in Egypt to-day, for in this place I hear nothing of battle who before I became a nurse was a warrior"; and seizing Khian by the hand—he dragged him away down sundry dark passages, till at length, at the end of one of them, he saw light gleaming faintly.

They entered a great hall of the temple. It was roofed and the moon's rays shining through the clerestory win-

dows and the high-set opening at its end, showed Khian
that in it were gathered a multitude of men or women—
he could not see which because they were all draped in white
robes and wore veils upon their faces, that gave them a
ghost-like air. At the head of this hall, on a stage lit with
lamps, also white-robed but unveiled, sat the Council of the
Order of the Dawn. In the centre of their long, curved
line was a shrine half hidden by a curtain and in front of
this alabaster shrine stood an empty chair with sphinx-
headed arms. Nothing more could be seen in that dim
light. When Khian entered there was silence in the hall;
it was as though his appearance had been awaited for some
rite to be begun.

"We are late," muttered Ru and dragged him forward
up a kind of aisle, all present turning their veiled heads and
staring at him as he went by, through eyeholes cut in the
veils. They came to a seat set in front of the stage or dais,
but at a little distance, so that he could see everything that
happened there. Into this seat Ru thrust him, whispering
that he was not to move. Then he departed and presently
reappeared upon the dais where he took his stand upon the
left-hand side of the shrine to the right of which stood the
tall, white-haired Kemmah.

"Let the entrance be shut and guarded," said Roy presently, and movements behind him told Khian that this
was being done. Then Roy rose and spoke, saying:

"Brethren and Elders of the holy, ancient, and mighty
Order of the Dawn, whereof the Council at this time has its
home amid these tombs and pyramids and is sentinelled
by the watching Sphinx, the symbol of the rising sun, hear
me, Roy the Prophet. You are summoned hither from
every nome and city in Egypt, from Tyre, from Babylon
and Nineveh, from Cyprus and from Syria, and from many
another land beyond the sea, being the chosen delegates of
our Brotherhood in those towns and countries, among
which it dwells to kindle light in the hearts of men and to
instruct them in the laws of Truth and Gentleness, to over-

throw oppressors by all righteous means and to bind the
world together in the service of that Spirit whom we worship,
who, enthroned on high, makes of all gods its ministers.

"Why have you been called from so far away? I will
tell you. It is that you may take part in the crowning of
a Queen of Egypt, the true descendant of the ancient
Pharaohs who for thousands of years have sat upon her
throne, and a sworn neophyte of our Order, vowed to its
faith and to the execution of its duties, the daughter and
heiress of King Kheperra and of Queen Rima of the royal
House of Babylon, now both gathered to Osiris. We, the
Council of the Dawn, among whom this Queen to be has
sheltered from her infancy, declare to you upon our oaths
that she who presently will appear before you is none other
than Nefra, the Princess of Egypt, the daughter and only
child of Kheperra and Rima, as her nurse, the Lady Kemmah, who stands before you, can testify, for she was present
at her birth and has dwelt with her till this hour. Are you
content, Councillors and Elders of the Dawn, or do you
demand further proofs?"

"We are content," answered the audience with one voice.

"Then let Nefra, Princess of Egypt and heiress of the
Two Lands, appear before you."

As Roy spoke these words the curtain in front of the
alabaster shrine was drawn, and standing within it, glittering in the lamplight, appeared Nefra. So lovely did she
seem in her coronation robes upon which shone the royal
emblems and jewels of the ancient kings, so stately in her
youthful, slender grace, so fair of form and countenance,
that a sigh of wonder went up from that veiled gathering,
while Khian stared amazed, and as he stared became aware
that Love had gripped him by the heart.

The figure in the shrine stood quite still, so still that for
a while he wondered if she were human, or perchance
Hathor, goddess of Love herself, or a statue fashioned by
some great artist. Suddenly his doubts were ended, for
behold! she smiled, then stepped from the shrine and was

led to the carven chair in which she took her seat. Thrice
the veiled company bowed to her, Khian with them, and
thrice she bowed back to them. Then, advancing to the
side of the chair, Roy addressed her.

"Princess of Egypt," he said, "you are brought before
this gathering of true and pure-hearted men from many
lands that in their presence you may be anointed and
crowned the Queen of Egypt. Not thus should this holy
rite have been performed, but the times are difficult and
dangerous, and a foreign king of desert blood holds half
the land and rings it round with swords. Therefore here in
secret and at midnight in a place of ghosts and tombs, and
not beneath the sun in the presence of thousands at Memphis or at Thebes, must your hand grasp the sceptre and
Egypt's crown be set upon your brow. Yet know that
presently from the Cataracts to the sea and far away beyond
the sea, aye, and in the Court of the Shepherd King himself,
the news will fly that once more Egypt has a Queen. Do
you accept this royalty, great as may be its burdens and
its perils?"

"I accept it," said Nefra in her sweet, clear voice that
Khian seemed to know again. "Unworthy as I am, I
accept that which comes to me unsought and undesired,
brought to me by right of blood. Nor do I fear its perils
and its burdens, for the Strength that led me to the throne
will safeguard me there."

There was a faint murmur of applause—even Khian
found himself murmuring applause—and as it died away,
Roy took an alabaster vase of oil and dipping his finger into
it, made some sign upon her brow. Then appeared Kemmah and gave to him a circlet of gold from which rose the
royal uræus, and an ivory sceptre surmounted with gems.
This circlet he set upon her head and the sceptre he placed
in her right hand. Then he bowed the knee to her, and
said:

"In the name of the Spirit that rules the world, I, Roy
the ancient, son of your great-grandsire, appointed prophet

of the Spirit during my life days, before this company of brethren and officers of the Order of the Dawn, anoint and declare you, Nefra, Princess of Egypt and sister-elect of the Order of the Dawn, being a woman come to full estate, Queen by right divine and human of the Upper and the Lower Lands, and call down upon you the blessing of the Spirit. As yet you have no Court nor armies and your prerogatives are usurped by others, yet learn, O Queen, that you are acknowledged in a million hearts and that if anywhere your glance falls upon five talking together, three of them in secret are your faithful subjects. Of the future we know nothing because it is hid from men, yet we believe that in it much joy awaits you with length of days, and that the crown which now we set upon your head in secret in time to come shall shine openly before the multitudes of earth. In the name of Egypt and of the Order of the Dawn to which you are sworn, O Queen, I, Roy the Prophet, do you homage."

Then kneeling down, while the company prostrated itself before her as though she were a goddess, Roy touched the new-made queen's fingers with his lips.

With her sceptre Nefra signed that he and all should rise. Then she stood upon her feet and said:

"At such a time as this what can I say to so many great ones who have gathered here to do me honour, and for Egypt's sake to crown me Egypt's queen, I who am but an untaught maiden? Only one thing, I think. That I swear I will live and die for Egypt. I have been told that at my birth Egypt's goddesses appeared in a dream to my mother and gave to me a certain title, that of the Uniter of Lands. May this dream come true. May I prove to be the Uniter of the Upper and the Lower Lands, and when I pass to join my fathers, leave Egypt one and great. Such is my prayer. Now I thank you all and ask of you leave to go."

"Not yet, O Queen," said Roy. "An ambassador has come to us from the Court of the Shepherd King at Tanis, he who sits before you, bringing messages that to-morrow must be considered by you in Council. Yet there is one of them to which we think an answer should be given here and now, before all this company. Apepi, King of the Shepherds, being unwed, demands the hand of your Majesty in marriage, promising to your children the inheritance of all Egypt. What says your Majesty?"

Now Nefra started and bit her lip as though to keep herself from the uttering of rash words. Then she answered:

"I thank the King Apepi, but like others, this matter must be considered with the rest, seeing that it is a great one to Egypt and to Egypt's Queen. Let King Apepi's envoy"—here she glanced swiftly at Khian—"be pleased to accept our hospitality in this secret place until once more the full moon shines above the pyramids, while I take counsel with myself and with some that dwell far off. Meanwhile, let messengers be sent to King Apepi to inform him how it comes about that the return of his ambassador is delayed. Or if it pleases him, let that ambassador make his own report at once to his master, the King Apepi."

Now Khian rose, bowed, and said:

"Nay, Lady and Council of the Dawn, the command given to me, Rasa the Scribe, was that with my own hands I should bear back the answers to those questions which were written in the roll of my commission. Here then I bide till these are delivered to me. Meanwhile, if it pleases you to send messages to King Apepi, it is not in my power to say that they shall not be sent. Do as you will."

"So be it," said Nefra.

Then she rose, bowed, and departed, led by the Lady Kemmah and escorted by the Council.

Thus ended the midnight crowning of Nefra as Queen of Egypt.

CHAPTER X

THE MESSAGE

ON THE morrow Khian slept late, being very weary, and in his sleep was visited by dreams. They were fantastic dreams of which, when he awoke, he could remember little, save that they had to do with pyramids and men with veiled faces and with a giant who bore a great axe, and with palm trees through which the wind sighed gently, till presently it changed to the voice of a woman, just such a voice as that of the messenger who had guided him from the grove, just such a voice as that of the royal lady who had sat upon the throne in the temple halls.

Yet, alas! he could not understand what this voice said, and in his dream, growing angry, he turned to the giant with the axe, bidding him interpret the meaning of the song. Behold! the black giant was changed into that Sphinx who sat upon the sands, before which he had been blindfolded. He stared at the Sphinx and the Sphinx stared back at him. Then of a sudden it opened its great stone lips and spoke, and the sound of its voice was like to that of the roll of distant thunder.

"What is it thou wouldst learn of me, the Ancient, O Man?" asked the rolling voice. Now in his dream Khian grew frightened and answered at hazard:

"I would learn how old thou art and what thou hast seen, O Sphinx."

"Hundreds of millions of years ago," answered the lips of stone, "I was shaped in the womb of Fire and cast forth in the agony of the birth of the world. For tens of millions of years I lay beneath deep water, and grew in their darkness. The waters receded and lo! I was a mountain of which the point appeared amidst a forest. Great creatures crept about my flanks, they roared round me in the mists, thousands of generations of them, now of this shape and now of that. The mists departed; I looked upon the sun, a huge ball of flaming red that day by day rose up over against me. In its fierce heat the forests withered and passed away in fire. Sands appeared out of it that, driven by great winds, shaped me to my lion's shape. A river rolled at my feet, the river Nile. New beasts took refuge in my shade in place of the reptiles that were gone; they fought and ravened and mated and bore their young about me.

"More millions of years went by and there came yet other beasts, hairy creatures that ran upon two legs and jabbered. These passed and behold there were men, now of this colour and now of that. Tribe by tribe these men butchered each other for food and women, dashing out the brains of their enemies with stones and devouring them, cooked first in the rays of the sun, and then with fire which they had learned to make.

"These passed away and there appeared other men who wore garments of skins and killed their prey with flint-headed arrows and spears. Yonder in the cliff you may find their graves covered with flat stones. These men worshipped the sun and me, the rock upon which his rays fell at dawn. Thus first I became a god. Again there was war around me and my worshippers were slain, they and their fair-haired children were all slain. Still their dark-hued conquerors worshipped the sun and me. Moreover, they were artists and with hard tools they fashioned my face and form as these appear to-day. Afterwards they built pyramids and tombs and in them kings and princes were laid to rest. For generation after generation I watched them come and go, till at length there were no more of them, and white-robed priests crept about the ruins of their temples as still they creep to-day. Such is my history, O Man, that is yet but begun, for when all the gods are gone and none pour offerings to me or them, still lost in memories I, who was from the beginning, shall remain until the end. Yet was it of this that thou wouldst ask me?"

"Nay, O Sphinx. Tell me, what is the name of that wind among the palm trees of which the sound is as the voice of woman? Whence comes it and whither does it go?"

"That wind, O Man, blew at the begetting of the world and will blow until its death, for without it no life can be. It came from God and to God it returns again, and in heaven and earth its name is *Love*."

Now Khian would have asked more questions, but could not for suddenly all his dream vanished and his eyes opened to behold, not the face of the Sphinx, mighty and solemn, but the ebon features of the giant Ru.

"What is love, O Ru?" he asked, yawning.

"Love!" answered Ru, astonished. "What do I know about love? There are so many sorts of love; that of men for women, or of women for men, which is a curse and a madness sent into the world by Set to be its torment; that of kings for power which is the father of war; that of merchants for wealth which breeds theft and misery; that of the learned for wisdom, a bird which never can be snared; that of the mother for her child, which is holy; and that of the slave for him or her he serves, which is the only sort I know. Ask it of Roy the Prophet, though I think he has forgotten all love save that of the gods and death."

"It is of the first that I would learn, O Ru, and of it I think that Roy can tell me nothing, who, as you say, has forgotten all. Whom shall I ask of this?"

Ru rubbed his black nose and replied:

"Try the first maiden whom you meet when the moon is rising over the waters of the Nile. Perhaps she can tell you, Lord. Or if that will not serve so fine a noble, try her whom you saw seated on the throne last night, for she has studied many things and perhaps love may be among them. And now, if it pleases you to rise, the Council awaits you presently, but not, I think, to talk to you of love."

An hour later Khian stood before Roy and his company.

"Scribe Rasa," said the Prophet, for although Ru in his cups had revealed that his true dignity was known, this was not given to him, "we have written in a roll our answers to the letter of the King Apepi, which are such as we told you they would be. As to the matter of the marriage that is offered by the King to that royal lady whom you saw crowned Queen of Egypt but last night, we have added that you, his messenger, shall learn her answer from her own lips on the night of the first full moon after that of her crowning, since she must have time to consider this great business. Now we pray you to add to this letter of ours any that it pleases you to send, making report of what you have heard and seen among us, which report shall be borne faithfully by our messenger to the Court of your master, the King who sits at Tanis."

"It shall be done, Prophet," said Khian, "though what will chance when this report reaches the King Apepi, I cannot tell. Meanwhile, is it still your will that I should abide here among you till that moon shines, having liberty to move to and fro within your boundaries?"

"Such is the will of the Queen Nefra and of us her councillors, Scribe Rasa. That is, unless it pleases you to be gone at once."

"It does not please me, Prophet."

"Then remain among us, Scribe Rasa, remembering the oath that you have sworn, that you will reveal no secret of our hiding places, or our doctrines, or our company, or aught save of that business with which you have to do."

"I will remember it," answered Khian, bowing.

For a while he lingered, talking of little things with the Lord Tau and other members of the Council in the hope that Nefra herself would appear to take part in their deliberations. At length, as she did not come, he went away because he must, and was guided back to his chamber by Ru.

"I am going to write a letter, Friend Giant," he said, "which letter in the end may bring about my end. However, that is some way off, a month away indeed, and meanwhile, after it is finished, I desire to study the pyramids and all the other wonders of this place. Now yesterday a certain youth was my guide who seemed very intelligent. If he can be found I should be willing to pay him well to continue in that office while I remain a guest among these graves."

Ru shook his great head and answered:

"Lord, it is impossible. That youth is one of those idlers who stand about waiting for food to fall into their mouths, and if it does not come, move elsewhere. He has moved elsewhere, or at least I have not seen him this morning, and as I do not know his name I cannot inquire where he has gone."

"So be it," answered Khian, "though, friend Ru, you will forgive me if I compliment your honesty by saying that you do not lie very well. Now be pleased to tell me, as this one is lacking, how I can find another guide."

"That is easy, Lord. When you are ready, put your head out of the door and clap your hands. In this place there is always someone listening and watching, and he will summon me."

"That I can well believe. Indeed, here I feel as though the very walls listened and watched."

"They do," replied Ru candidly, and departed.

Khian wrote his letter. It was but short, yet, although so skilled a scribe, it took him a long time, since he knew not what to say or leave unsaid. In the end it ran thus:

"From the Scribe Rasa to His Majesty, King Apepi, the good God:

"As commanded I, the Scribe Rasa, have come to the habitations of the Order of the Dawn who dwell in certain ruined temples and tombs beneath the shadow of the Great

Pyramids, and been received by their prophet Roy and the members of their Council. I presented the letter of your Majesty to this Council, also the gifts your Majesty was pleased to send, which gifts they refused for religious reasons. I have learned that the royal Nefra, daughter of Kheperra who once ruled in the South, is living here in the keeping of the Brethren of the Dawn. Last night I saw this princess, who is young, crowned with much ceremony as Queen of all Egypt before a great company of veiled men who, I was told, were gathered from all over the world. The Council of the Dawn send herewith an answer to the letter of your Majesty which has not been shown to me. As touching your Majesty's proposal of marriage, however, the Lady Nefra, seated on a throne and speaking as a queen, said to me that she would consider of the matter and give me her answer to be handed to your Majesty at the time of the next full moon, until when I must abide here and wait in patience. Here then I stay, having no choice in the matter, that I may fulfil the commands of your Majesty and on the appointed day bear back the answer of the Lady Nefra, though whether this will be in writing or by message, I do not know.

"Sealed with the seal of the Envoy of your Majesty,

RASA THE SCRIBE.

When Khian had copied this letter and done it up into a roll, wondering much what Apepi his father would say and do when he read it and that by which it was accompanied, he ate of the food that was brought to him and afterwards went to the door of his chamber and clapped his hands, as he had been directed to do. Instantly from the recesses of the dark passage appeared Ru accompanied by a white-robed man whom Khian knew for one of the councillors. To this councillor he gave the roll that he had written to be despatched together with the answer of the Council to King Apepi at Tanis. When he was gone Ru led Khian through the great hall where Nefra had been

crowned and thence, meeting no one, by a secret doorway
to the desert beyond.

"Where have all those gone whom we saw last night?"
asked Khian.

"Where do the bats go, Lord, when the sun arises?
They vanish away and are no more seen, yet they are not
dead but only hidden. So it is with the Company of the
Dawn. Search for them among the fishermen of the Nile;
search for them among the Bedouins of the desert; search
for them in the Courts of foreign kings; search where you
will, yet be sure that neither you nor all the spies of the
Shepherd king will find one of them."

"Truly this is a land of ghosts," said Khian. "Almost could
I believe that those veiled ones were not men but spirits."

"Perhaps," answered Ru enigmatically; "and now, where
would it please you to wander?"

"To the pyramids," said Khian.

So to the pyramids they went, walking round all of them,
while Khian marvelled at their greatness.

"Is it possible that these stone mountains can be
climbed?" he asked presently.

Ru led him round the corner of the second pyramid and
there, seated on the sand and playing pipes that made a
wild music, were three men, the Captain of the Pyramids
and two of his sons.

"Here are those who can answer your question, Lord,"
he said, then turning to the men added, "This lord, who
is an envoy and a guest, desires to know whether the
pyramids can be climbed."

"We awaited you," said the Captain gravely, "as we
have been commanded to do. Is it now your pleasure to
see this feat performed?"

"It is," answered Khian. "Moreover, the climber will
not lack a present, though I who am a scaler of mountains
hold the thing to be impossible."

"Be pleased to stand back a little way and watch," said
the Captain.

Then he and his two sons threw off their long robes and clothed only in a linen garment about their middles, ran to that pyramid which was in front of them and separated. One son disappeared to the north and the other to the south, while the father began to spring up the eastern face as a goat springs up a precipice. Up he went, high and higher yet, while Khian watched amazed, till at last he saw him gain the very crest. Lo! as he did so there appeared with him the two sons who, unseen, had travelled thither by other roads. Moreover, presently there appeared a fourth figure clad in white.

"Who is the fourth?" exclaimed Khian. "But three started to climb, and now, behold! there are four."

Ru stared at the top of the pyramid, then answered stupidly;

"Surely staring at those polished stones has dazed you, Lord. I see but three, doubtless the Captain and his two sons."

Khian looked again and said:

"It is true that now I also see but three. Yet there were four," he added obstinately.

Presently the climbers began to descend, following one another down the eastern face. At length they reached the ground safely, and having donned their robes, came to Khian, bowing, and asked him whether he were now satisfied that the pyramids could be climbed.

"I am satisfied that this pyramid can be climbed, though of the others I know nothing," he answered. "Yet before I give you the reward you have earned so well, tell me, Captain, how it comes about that you and your sons, who were three at its base, became four upon its crest?"

"What does my Lord mean?" asked the Sheik gravely.

"What I say, Captain; neither more nor less. When you stood upon the top yonder, with the three of you was a fourth, a slender figure clad in white. I swear it by all the gods."

"It may be so," answered the Sheik imperturbably,

"only then, as we saw no one, it must have been given to my Lord to perceive the Spirit of the Pyramids herself who accompanied us, invisible to our eyes. Had this chanced when the full moon shines, it would not have been so wonderful, since then she is apt to wander, or so it is reported, but that he should have seen her in the light of day is most strange and portends we know not what."

Now Khian began to ply the man and his sons with questions about this Spirit of the Pyramids and whether she would be visible if they came to look for her when the full moon shone, but from them learned nothing, since to every question they answered that they did not know. Next he inquired of them whether they would teach him how to climb the pyramids as they did, if he paid them well. They replied that except by order of the Council they would not, because the business was very dangerous, and if aught happened to him, his blood would be on their hands. So in the end he made them a large present, for which they thanked him with many bows, and, just as the sun began to set, departed back to the temple.

As they went side by side, Khian, who was lost in thought and wonder, heard Ru mutter:

"A second whom the gods have smitten with the desire to climb the pyramids. Who could have believed that there were two such mad people in the world? What does it mean? Surely such folly must have a meaning, for among my people, the Ethiopians, they say that the maddest are always the most inspired."

Twice or thrice he muttered thus, till at last Khian asked him suddenly:

"Who, then, was the other fool to whom the gods gave the desire to climb the pyramids? Was she perchance that one whom I saw standing with the Sheik and his sons upon yonder crest?"

"No, I think not," answered the startled Ru confusedly. "Indeed, I am sure not, since to-day she has other business to attend. Also, I should have known——" Then he remembered and stopped.

"So there is a lady who loves this sport! Well, I have heard as much before, and, friend Ru, as you seem to know her, if you will arrange that I can follow it in her company, you will find youself growing richer than you are."

"Here is the door to the temple," answered Ru, with a grin, "and, by the way, the second prophet, Tau, bade me to pray you to eat with him and others this night."

"I obey," said Khian, hoping in his heart that one of those others would be the lovely lady whom he had seen crowned as Queen of Egypt. Yet this was not so, for at that meal were only Tau and with him three aged councillors, who, when they had partaken sparingly, slipped away, leaving him and his host together. Then these two began to talk, each of them seeking knowledge of the other.

Soon Khian learned that this Tau, the second Prophet of the Order, though not Egyptian by blood, had been born to a high station and great wealth. He had been a warrior and a statesman also, and, it seemed, might have become a king, either in Cyprus or Syria, where he would not say. Far and wide he had travelled about the world, acquiring the languages of many peoples and much learning, and studying religions and philosophies. Yet in the end he had abandoned all and become one of the Priesthood of the Dawn.

Khian asked him why he who, as he understood, might have sat upon a throne and mingled with the great ones of the earth while children grew up about him had chosen instead to dwell in tombs with the brethren of a secret order.

"Would you learn? Then I will tell you," answered Tau. "I have done this because I seek peace, peace for Egypt and the world and peace for my own soul, and in pomps and governments there is no peace but only strivings that for the most part end in war to win more wealth and powers that we do not need. Scribe Rasa," he added, looking at him keenly, "were you other than you are, a prince, for instance, I think that perhaps, had you instruction in our philosophy, in the end you might prove to be such another as I am, or even as is Roy the Prophet, and turning your back upon what the world calls greatness, might follow in this same path of peace and service."

"Were I such a one, Priest Tau, it might be so, though other roads run to peace through service than those that lead there by monasteries or tombs, and each must follow that which lies open to his feet."

"That is true and well spoken, Scribe Rasa."

"Yet," went on Khian, "being athirst for knowledge I would learn of these mysteries of yours and of how their servants may attain to this peace and help to call it down upon the world. Is it possible while I sojourn here that one could be found to instruct me in them?"

"I think that it is possible, but of this matter we will talk again. Sleep well, Scribe Rasa, and take counsel with your heart before you enter on this difficult path."

Then he rose and Ru appeared to lead Khian back to his chamber.

CHAPTER XI

The Fall

ON THE following morning Khian was informed by Ru that orders had been sent to the Captain of the Pyramids to instruct him in the art of scaling them, should he so desire. So presently, accompanied by Ru, he went out and at the foot of the smallest of the pyramids found this man and his sons awaiting him. Awhile later, having been stripped of most of his garments and removed his sandals, he began his lesson, much as Nefra had done, with a rope tied about his middle. Like her, being young, active, and very bold, accustomed to the scaling of heights moreover, he proved an apt pupil, climbing two thirds of the height of the pyramid, that is, as far as he was allowed to go, turning about, as Nefra had done, and descending again with but little help from his guide. Yet trouble came, for when he was within some forty feet of the ground, to which the Sheik who was beneath him had descended already and there stood, talking to Ru, Khian called to him above who held the rope to throw it down as it was no more needed, and at the same time undid the noose from about his middle.

Thus freed the rope slid away, but, although Khian did not notice this, it caught upon the marble but a little below him. Continuing his descent carelessly enough, in setting his foot upon a certain knob of this marble, his heel rested upon the rope that twisted round beneath his weight, causing him to slip and lose his balance.

Next instant he was sliding down the face of the pyramid, and, as he slid he turned so that now his head pointed towards the ground. The Sheik saw, as did Ru. Together

they bounded forward to catch him in his fall. In a second
he was on them, but the weight of his body struck between
them, forcing them apart although they grasped him as he
came. Do what they would, his head hit the ground, not
so very hard indeed, but, as it chanced, where a stone
fallen from the pyramid was hidden just beneath the sand,
and though he never felt the blow, of a sudden his senses
left him, for he was stunned.

When they returned, dimly and as at a great distance he
heard a voice speaking, though who spoke he could not see
because his eyelids seemed to be glued together with blood,
and for this, or some other reason, he was unable to open
them.

"I think that he is not dead," said the voice, which in
truth was that of a physician. "The neck does not seem
to be broken, nor indeed any limb. Therefore unless the
skull is cracked, which I cannot discover for the blood
from the cut makes search difficult, I hold that he is but
stunned and will come to himself in time."

"The gods send that you are right, Leech," answered another voice, a woman's voice that was full of doubt and
fear. "For three long hours has he lain senseless in this
tomb and so still that almost I think—— Oh! see, he stirs
his hand. He lives! He lives! Feel his heart again."

The physician did so, and said:

"It beats more strongly. Trouble not, Lady. I believe
that he will recover."

"Pray that he does, all of you," went on the woman's
voice, in which now was hope mingled with anger. "Ill did
you pyramid-climbers guard him who tangled the rope
about his feet. As for you, Ru, was not your great
strength enough to hold so light a weight falling from but
a little height?"

"It seems not, Lady," answered the deep voice of Ru,
"seeing that this light weight of his knocked me down
and the Sheik with me, and almost tore my arm out of its
socket. Full forty feet he came like a stone from a sling."

At this moment Khian opened his lips and very faintly
asked for water. It was brought to him. A soft hand
lifted his head, a vase was held to his lips. He drank,
sighed, and swooned again.

Once more he awoke or was awakened by the sharp pain
that seemed to stab his head from side to side. Now he
could open his eyes and, looking about him, saw that he
was back in his chamber at the temple, for upon a stool lay
possessions of his own. At the foot of the couch a curtain
had been drawn and beyond the curtain he heard two women
talking.

"How goes he, Kemmah? Has he awakened?" asked a
sweet voice that he knew again, for it was the voice of the
guide who had led him from the palm grove, the voice, too,
of her whom he had seen crowned as Queen of Egypt.

Khian strove to lift his head, to look past the end of the
curtain, but could not because his neck was stiff as a stone;
so he lay still and listened, his heart beating for joy because
this fair, royal lady had been at the pains to visit him that
she might learn his state.

"Not yet, child," answered the Lady Kemmah, "though
it is true that it is time he did. The learned leech, our
brother, said that he can find no great hurt and that he
should wake within twelve hours, but twenty have gone
by and still he sleeps—or swoons."

"Oh! Kemmah, do you think that he will die?" asked
Nefra in tones that were full of fear.

"Nay, nay, I hope not, though when the head is hurt
one never can be sure. It would be most sad, for he is a
fine man. Never did I see one more perfect in his body or
more comely in his face, though half his blood is that of the
accursed Shepherds."

"Who told you about his blood, Kemmah, and whence
it sprang?"

"The birds of the air or the blowing wind. Are you the
last to learn what all here know—that this guest of ours is
no palace scribe or officer, but the Prince Khian himself,

who, if you take Apepi as a husband, will be your step-son?"

"Have done with your talk of Apepi, on whom be the curse of all the gods of Egypt, and of his own as well. For the rest, I guessed, but I did not know, though I was sure that this Rasa could be no common man. Save him, Kemmah! For if he dies—oh! what am I saying? Come, let me look on him. As he sleeps there can be no harm and I will make the sign of health upon his brow and pray for his recovery to the Spirit that we worship."

"Well, then, be swift, for if the leech or Tau should come, they might think it strange to find the Queen of Egypt in a sick man's chamber. Still, have your way, but be swift. I will keep watch without."

Now although Khian shut his eyes close so that he could see nothing, with his ears he heard the curtain drawn aside, heard, too, a light footfall by his bed. More, he felt soft fingers make some sign upon his brow, a loop it seemed to be with a line drawn through it, perchance the Loop of Life. Then she who had drawn the sign seemed to lean over him and, setting her lips close to his face, to murmur holy words of which he could not catch the drift or meaning. And as she murmured, ever those lips drew closer to his own, till at length for one second they touched his own and swiftly were withdrawn. Then came a sigh and silence.

Now Khian opened his eyes, to see other eyes gazing down at him, and in them tears.

"Where am I? What has chanced?" he asked faintly. "I dreamed that I was dead and that some daughter of the gods breathed new life into me. Oh! now I remember, my foot turned on that accursed rope and being careless and over-sure, I fell. It matters not, soon I shall be strong again and then I swear that I will climb those pyramids one by one more swiftly than does the spirit who inhabits them."

"Hush! Hush!" murmured Nefra. "Nurse, come here. This sick one is awake and speaks, though foolishly."

"Soon he will be asleep again for good if you stay at his side talking of pyramids," answered Kemmah who had entered the place unseen by either. "Have you not had enough of pyramids, both of you? Would that those vain fools of kings had never built them to bring trouble to the greater fools that come after."

"Yet I will climb them," muttered Khian.

"Begone, child, and bid Ru bring the leech, and swiftly," went on Kemmah.

With one quick glance at Khian, Nefra glided away. Kemmah watched her go, saying to herself as she turned to minister to him:

"How strange a thing is love that can send so many to their deaths, or by its strength draw the dying back to life again. But of the love of these two what will be born?"

Then she gave Khian milk to drink and bade him lie still and silent.

Yet he would not obey who, having drunk, asked her dreamily:

"Think you, good Nurse, that the Spirit of the Pyramids of whom all talk in this holy land is as fair as that lady who has left us?"

"The Spirit of the Pyramids! Can I never be rid of these pyramids? Who, then, and what is this Spirit?"

"That is just what I would find out, Nurse, even if I lose my life in seeking it, as it seems that already almost I have done. My soul is aflame with desire to look upon this Spirit, for something within tells me that until I do so never shall I find happiness."

"Here the story runs otherwise," answered Kemmah. "Here it is said that those who look on her, if there be such a one, find madness."

"Are they not perchance the same thing, Nurse? Are we ever happy except when we are mad? Can the sane be happy, or the wise? Is your holy Prophet Roy happy, who is the sanest of the sane and the wisest of the wise? Are all those death-awaiting Whitebeards who surround him happy? Have you ever been happy, except perhaps years ago when sometimes you were mad?"

"If you ask me, I have not," answered Kemmah, remembering certain things and trembling beneath the thought of them. "Perchance you are right, young sir. Perchance, as drunkards think, we are only happy when we are mad. Yet if you will be guided by me, you will cease to seek a spirit in the skies, or near them, and content yourself with following after woman upon the earth."

"Who knows, Nurse," replied Khian with all the solemnity of one whose brain still reels, "that in seeking after the Spirit I may not find the woman, as in seeking after a woman, some have found a spirit? Who knows that they are not the same thing? I will tell you—perhaps—when I have climbed those pyramids by the light of the full moon."

"Which has already shone," interrupted Kemmah angrily.

"There are more full moons to come, Nurse. The sky is as peopled with full moons unborn as the sea is with oysters that will be eaten, and the pyramids will stand for a long while to welcome climbers," answered Khian faintly.

"To Set with the pyramids and your silly talk!" burst out Kemmah, stamping her foot. Then she ceased, noting that Khian had once more swooned away.

"A fool!" she thought to herself as she ran to find help. "Indeed, the first of fools who would hunt a ghost when the loveliest of flesh and blood lies to his hand. Yet were I thirty years younger I think that I might find it in my heart to go mad with this spirit-seeking fool, as I think also another is in the way of doing. What did he say? That in searching for the Spirit he might find the woman? Well, perhaps he will; perhaps after all this moonstruck prince is not such a fool as he seems. Perhaps those who climb the pyramids find joy at the top of them, and joy is better than wisdom. So at least some come to believe when we grow old and have left it far behind."

Very soon Khian, who was young and strong and though shaken by the shock of his fall, as the physician said, quite unhurt in his brain or his bones, rose recovered from his bed. Indeed, within five days, once more he was climbing the pyramids by the help of the Captain and his sons, for it would seem that this passion had grown upon him during his swoon. Also that swoon, when he shook off the last of it, left no memory of what he had said or done while it endured. From the moment when he set his foot upon the cord and slipped, until at last he rose from his bed, he remembered nothing, not even the visit of Nefra to his chamber or his talk with Kemmah, though it is true that these came back to him in after days. So where he had left off, there he began again, namely, on the slope of the pyramid, which very soon he mastered, as in due time he did the others, like Nefra before him.

Day by day, from dawn until the sun grew too hot for the work, he laboured at those pyramids, so hard that at last the Captain and his sons were almost outworn and declared that they had to do with a devil, not a man. Yet they spoke well of him, as did all others, holding that he who after such a fall dared to persevere and conquer, must be great-hearted. For they did not understand that, from the moment of his slip, of his fall he remembered nothing.

Meanwhile, though he knew it not, at the Court of King Apepi it was believed that he was dead. The tidings of his fall from the pyramid and, it was added, of his death, for dead he seemed to be, had overtaken that messenger, a Brother of the Dawn named Temu, who bore the answer from the Council of the Dawn and Khian's own letter, as he embarked upon the Nile, and he had spread it abroad and carried it to the Court at Tanis. When Apepi heard this news he was grieved in a fashion, since he had loved his son a little, at least when he was younger, though not much because in his fierce and selfish heart there was small room for any love save of himself.

Soon, however, his grief was swallowed up in wrath at that
which was written in the letter from the Brotherhood of the
Dawn, which he swore to destroy root and branch unless
Nefra, whom they had dared to crown Queen of Egypt, were
given to him in marriage. Moreover, he believed that
Khian had not come to his end by a chance tumble from
the pyramid, but that he had been done to death at the
decree of this Brotherhood, that the heir to the Crown of
the North might be removed because he stood in the path
of her who had been consecrated Queen of all Egypt. But
of all these things Apepi wrote nothing to the Council
of the Dawn.. Indeed, he seized their messenger, Temu,
and kept him in a safe place where he could communicate
with none, and meanwhile made certain plans and preparations.

During the weeks which followed his recovery Khian did
more than climb the pyramids. Thus he received instruction in the faith and worship of the Brotherhood of the
Dawn, as it had been promised that he should do. In the
evening, in a little lamp-lit hall, he was taught by Tau, or
by Roy the Prophet, or sometimes by both of them together. Moreover, he shared this instruction with another
pupil, Nefra the neophyte.

There he sat at one end of a table with ink and papyrus
in front of him, while at the other end, with Kemmah
behind her and the gigantic Ru standing in the shadow as a
guard and sentinel, sat the young Queen simply clothed in
white as a neophyte should be, so placed that he could
see her face in the rays of the lamp and she could see
his, and yet too far away for them to talk together. At
the centre of the table in carved seats sat Roy and Tau,
or one of them, expounding the secret mysteries of their
Order, and from time to time asking or answering questions.

So pure and beautiful was the faith they taught that very
soon it possessed the heart of Khian. In its outlines it was

simple, that of the existence of one great Spirit, of whose attributes all the gods they knew were ministers, a Spirit who for its own purposes sent them forth into the world, whence in due time it would draw them back again. Moreover, these holy and learned men taught their pupils of those purposes, declaring that the greatest of them was to promote peace upon the earth and to do good to all that breathed. Yet there were other parts of this doctrine which were not so plain and easy, for these had to do with the methods by which that Spirit could be approached of those who still dwelt upon the earth, with forms of prayer and hidden rites also, that would bring the Worshipped into communion with the worshipper. Further, there were many rules of life and great principles of politics and government, all of which were a part of the law.

Khian hearkened and found this doctrine good, for therein was that which fed if as yet it did not satisfy his hungry soul. On a certain day at the end of the last lesson, he rose and said:

"O holy Prophets Roy and Tau, I accept your teaching; I would be sworn as the humblest of the Brethren of the Order of the Dawn. Only for a certain reason which I must keep secret, of your temporal policies I say nothing either good or ill, neither do I bind myself to them. In the spirit I am yours; in the flesh and for the purposes of the flesh, as yet I am the slave of others. Is it enough?"

Roy and Tau consulted together while Nefra watched them curiously and Khian sat lost in thought, his head bowed upon his hands. At length the old prophet spoke, saying:

"Son, the time you can give to study and preparation being short and your heart being set upon the truth, it is enough. Here in these tombs also we learn many things, and amongst them that men are not always what they seem to be. Thus it well may chance that by blood, birth, and duty you are bound with chains you cannot break, even to satisfy your soul. It well may chance, moreover, that it is not for you to take the vows of celibacy and abstinence, or to swear that you will lift no sword in war, since perhaps it is decreed that your mission in the world must be otherwise fulfilled. Further, what we say to you, we say to our sister who with you has listened to the words of Life. Her feet also are set upon a road that is high and difficult. Therefore, exempting both of you from much to which others must bow their heads, to-morrow we will absolve you from your sins, swear you to our precepts, to break which will bring a curse upon your souls, and number you among our company in earth and Heaven."

So it came about that on the next day at a great ceremony in the temple hall, Khian the Prince and Nefra the Queen received at the hands of Roy the Ancient absolution of all evil that they had thought or done, and thereafter were sworn as full members of the Order of the Dawn, vowing themselves to accept its law as their guiding star and to pursue its holy ends eternally. Separately they knelt before its white-robed High Priest while far off on the confines of the great hall and out of hearing of their speech the brethren watched them as witnesses, and received forgiveness and benediction with words of whispered counsel, then withdrew and seated themselves side by side while all that company chanted the ancient hymn of welcome to their souls reborn. By slow degrees the loud, triumphant music grew less and died away, as, headed by Roy, those who sang departed from the temple, till at last there was a great silence, and in the silence they sat alone.

Khian looked about him and noted that even Ru and Kemmah were gone; in that great and solemn place they were quite alone, stared at by the cold statues of gods and ancient kings.

Khian looked at Nefra and asked:

"Of what are you thinking, Sister?"

"I am thinking, Brother, that I have heard wonderful words and received holy blessings which should have changed me from a sinful maiden into a saint like Roy, and that yet I feel much the same as I did before."

"Are you sure that Roy is so great a saint, Sister? I have seen him once or twice grow wrath like others. Also does the absence of temptation, of which there can be little after ninety, make a saint? For the rest, doubtless you feel as you did before, because it is not possible for snow to grow whiter than snow."

"Or fire hotter than fire. But have done, Brother. Is this a time or place for pretty speeches? Hearken, for as we are now both bound in the bonds of the same great oath we can speak our minds to each other, fearing no betrayal. These rites have changed me little, if at all, who always have known the doctrines of the Dawn that from childhood were instilled into my heart, although, until I attained my present age, under its law I could not be admitted to the full fellowship of the order. Behold! I am still no spirit but a woman as before, full of mortal purposes. Thus," she added slowly, considering him with her large eyes, "my father was slain by one I hold to have been the usurper of his rights; one, too, who, I think, would have murdered me if he could, and for those deeds I desire to repay him. Also to them of late he has added deadly insult, for now this slayer of my father and would-be murderer seeks to take me, the orphaned child, in marriage, and for that affront, too, I would repay him."

"Bad, very bad, Sister," answered Khian, shaking his head sadly, perhaps to hide a certain twitching of the corners of his mouth. "But, if I may ask, did you confess these black sins to the holy prophet Roy, and if so, what did he say of them, Sister?"

"I did, Brother, who could think of nothing else to confess, or at least not much, and what he answered makes me believe that you are right in holding that the holy Roy is still not so holy as he might be. He said, Brother, that such thoughts were born of my ancient blood and natural, and that it was right that those who committed great crimes for cold, base purposes should suffer for the crimes, and that if I were the means of bringing punishment upon this man, it would be because it had been so decreed by Heaven. Therefore he did not set me down as sinful in this matter. But enough. Tell me, Brother, if it pleases you, do you find yourself changed at heart?"

"I find my feet set upon a better and a higher road, Sister, for now I know what to worship—I who worshipped nothing because I could believe in nothing—also, how this new god should be worshipped. For the rest, no one killed my father or sought to murder me and therefore I do not wish to be avenged upon any one—at present. Yet, Sister——" and he paused.

"I am listening, Brother, who feel sure that you cannot be quite so good as you would have me understand."

"Good! No, I am not good; I only hope to become good if I can find someone to help me—no, not Roy, or Tau, or Kemmah, or the whole Council of the Dawn—someone quite different."

"A goddess from on high," suggested Nefra.

"Yes, that is well said—a goddess from on high—we will talk of her presently. But first what I want to say is that in following after righteousness I have fallen into a very deep pit."

"What pit, Brother?" asked Nefra, looking up at the roof of the temple.

"One out of which I think you alone can help me. But I must explain. First you should know that I am a liar. I am not the Scribe Rasa. The Scribe Rasa, an excellent man and a master of his trade, died many years ago when I was a boy. I am——" and he hesitated.

"—The Prince Khian, son of Apepi and heir apparent to the Crown of the North," suggested Nefra.

"Yes, you have got it quite right, except that I do not think I am any longer heir apparent, or at any rate I shall soon cease to be so. But may I ask, Sister, how you came to know my style and title?"

"We know everything in the House of the Dawn, Brother, also, as it chances, you told me them yourself when you were sick—or was it Kemmah?"

"Then it was very wrong of you to listen, Sister, and I hope that you confessed that sin with the others. Well, now perhaps you see the pit. The Prince Khian, the only lawful son of King Apepi—at present—has been sworn a member of the Order of the Dawn, which order it is the purpose of King Apepi to destroy, as is not wonderful, kings being what they are, seeing that it has just crowned a certain lady Queen of all Egypt and thereby in a sense declared war against him, the usurper. Now tell me, what can I do who on the one hand am the Prince Khian and on the other something much higher and better—a brother of the Order of the Dawn?"

"The answer is simple, Brother. You must make peace between Apepi and the Order of the Dawn."

"Indeed, and how? By praying a certain sister to become the Queen of King Apepi? Thus only can such a peace be made, as you know well."

"I never said it," answered Nefra, flushing. "Moreover, it does not please me to listen to such counsel—even from a brother."

"Nor would it please even a brother to give such counsel, for if it were taken, that brother would soon be numbered among those who make their prayers and swing their censers in the heavenly shrine whereof we are instructed in the mysteries."

"Why?" asked Nefra innocently. "If he gave it not, I could understand, for then a certain king might be wrath. But if he gave it, why?"

"Because then a certain queen might be wrath, one who, as you, Sister, have told me, loves vengeance. Or at least, because he himself, if that counsel were taken, would be so weary of the world that he could tread it no more."

Now for a while there was silence between them and,

beneath the shadow of their white hoods, each of them sat staring at the ground.

"Sister," said Khian at last, and as she made no answer, repeated in a louder voice, "Sister!"

"Forgive me, I had almost fallen asleep after last night's vigils. What is it, Brother?"

"Only this. Would you be minded to help a poor prince out of the pit of which I have spoken by dragging him up with a silken rope of—well, of love which all members of this company owe to one another—and making him a king?"

"A king! A king of what? Of these tombs and the dead in them?"

"Oh, no! Of your heart and the life in it. Hearken, Nefra. Together we may stand against my father, Apepi, but apart we must fall, for when he comes to learn the truth he will kill me, and if he can lay his hands on you, drag you whither you do not wish to go. Moreover, I love you, Nefra. From the moment when I heard your voice yonder by the palm trees and knew you for a woman beneath your cloak, I loved you, though then I thought you but some simple girl. What more is there to say? The future is dark; great dangers lie ahead. Mayhap it will be necessary to fly to far lands and leave all these pomps behind us. Yet together would they not be well lost?"

"Then what of Egypt, Prince Khian? What of Egypt and the mission laid upon me and the oath you heard me swear in this very hall?"

"I do not know," he answered confusedly. "The road is dark. Yet with love to light our feet we shall find a way. Say that you love me and all will be well."

"Say that I love you, the son of him who slew my father, that murderer who seeks to make me his. How can I say this, Prince Khian?"

"If you love me, Nefra, you can say it, because it will be the truth, and have we not heard that to hide the truth is the greatest of sins? Do you love me?"

"I cannot answer. I will not answer. Ask it of the

Sphinx. Nay, ask it of the Spirit of the Pyramids, and by her word I will abide, for that spirit is my spirit. One day still remains to us. Ask it to-morrow of the Spirit of the Pyramids, if you dare to seek and find her beneath the moon."

Then suddenly she rose and fled away, leaving him alone and wondering.

CHAPTER XII

THE SPIRIT OF THE PYRAMIDS

THAT night Khian slept little; his thoughts would not let him sleep. They filled his mind with problems and as in a mirror showed him the pitfalls that lay about his feet. He, the Prince of the North, was sworn a brother of the Order of the Dawn, which his father, the King, threatened to destroy, and how did these two offices agree? Could he smite with the one hand and defend with the other? Nay, it was impossible. Therefore he must cease either to be a prince, or to be a brother. There his path was clear. Let the rank go; indeed, had it not already been taken away from him with his own consent? Therefore, why should he trouble about it now? Henceforth he was nothing but Brother Khian of the Order of the Dawn. Nay, he was something more—an ambassador who awaited a certain answer which must be conveyed to the King who sent him on his mission. It was as to a matter of marriage; as to whether a royal lady would become the wife of that king or would choose to face his wrath.

Here again his task was easy. He must deliver the answer, whatever it might be, after which his duty came to an end and he would remain nothing more than a Brother of the Order of the Dawn, and perhaps a Prince. If that answer were such as the King desired, then doubtless he, the ambassador, would be allowed to go his ways in peace, though no more as heir to the throne of the North. But if it were very different; if, for example, it announced that this lady refused the King in favour of the ambassador

140

who chanced to be his son—what? Why! Death—no less—death or flight!

Yet at this thought Khian was not dismayed, he even smiled a little as it crossed his mind, remembering the teachings of his new philosophy, that all was in the hands of Heaven and that naught happened save that which must happen. He did not desire to die who now had so much for which to live, but if death came that philosophy taught him not to be afraid. Nor did he write himself down a traitor to his duty, because he knew that in any case Nefra would have refused this monstrous marriage, of which she had spoken to him as an insult. Moreover, as yet he did not know that any thought of him would weigh with her. He had offered her his love, but she had not accepted this gift. She had said that she could not answer, that he must ask the "Spirit of the Pyramids" whether she, Nefra the Queen, loved or did not love him, Khian the Prince. What could such words mean? There was no Spirit of the Pyramids; everywhere he had inquired of this legend and learned that it was built of air. How could he ask of a spirit that which a woman refused to tell, and where should he find this oracle?

He was told to seek it by the light of the full moon among the ancient graves. Well, that on his part nothing might be lacking, he would seek like any simple fool, and if he found nothing, would understand that Nothing was his answer. Then, seeking no more, he would demand from Roy the writing that he must bear to King Apepi and depart sore-hearted to accomplish its delivery. This done he would abide the wrath of the King and, should he escape, would wander away to such distant place as Roy or the Council might appoint and there preach the doctrines of the Dawn or do such things as he was commanded, turning his heart from woman and the joys of life.

Soon he would know; soon all would be finished in this way or in that, for on the morrow of the night of full moon the young Queen must give her answer to the demand of

Apepi and he, the ambassador, must bear that answer back
to Tanis.   Meanwhile this was certain—he who had never
loved before worshipped the maiden Nefra with body and
with spirit and above all earthly things desired her as his
wife; so much so that if he were to lose her he cared not what
else he might lose, even to life itself.

It was the appointed time and Khian, quite alone,
for as an admitted brother now he could pass where he
would, unquestioned and unwatched, wandered to and fro
among the tombs which surrounded the greatest of the
pyramids.   He was sad-hearted who believed his to be but
a fool's errand; moreover, all his troubles weighed upon his
soul.   The vast solemnity of the place, too, with its endless
streets of graves above which the pyramids towered eternally, crushed him.   What a spot was this for a love quest,
here surrounded by the monuments which told of the end of
all human things.   Hundreds of years ago those who slept
within these tombs had ceased from mortal loves and
hates, and as they were, soon he would be also, perchance
before another full moon shone in yonder sky.   He wondered whether they looked upon him now with calm, invisible eyes; not one, but ten thousand spirits of the pyramids.

He sat him down upon a stone in the midst of that deep
silence which was only broken from time to time by the
melancholy howlings of some jackal seeking food, and
watched the shadows creep across the sand.   At length,
growing weary, he covered his face with his hands and
brooded on the mystery of all things, as was natural in such
a place, and whence men came and whither they must go,
a problem that not even Roy could solve.

He heard nothing, yet suddenly, why he did not know,
he was moved to let fall his hands and look about him.
Surely something stirred yonder in the shadow of a great
tomb.   Perhaps it was a night-haunting beast.   Nay, it
seemed too tall.   It came out of that shadow and for a

moment could be seen flitting to the shelter of another tomb
where it vanished.   Surely it was a white-veiled woman or
a ghost.

Khian was frightened, his hair rose upon his head.   Yet
springing to his feet he followed it.   He came to the tomb
where it had disappeared.   It was gone.   Nay, there it was
far away, shaping a course, it would seem, toward the
second pyramid, that of the Pharaoh Khafra.   Again he
followed, but fast as he went, that figure went faster, now
hidden and now seen, so that when at length it reached the
north face of the second pyramid called *Ur-Khafra*, or
"Greatest Khafra," it was a spear's cast in front of him.

Surely, he thought, it would halt there.   But it did not.
It began to glide up the face of the pyramid and then, at
the height of a tall palm tree, it disappeared.

Now Khian more than once had climbed this second
pyramid by its northern face and knew that there was no
opening in it.   Therefore it would seem that what he had
seen was indeed a ghost which had melted away as ghosts
are said to do.   Still, to satisfy himself, though fearfully,
he climbed after it and when he had scaled some fifty feet of
the steep side, stopped astonished, for behold! there in the
pyramid was what seemed to be an open door beyond which
a passage ran downwards.   Moreover, in that passage
lamps were set at a distance from each other.   He hesitated,
for he was much afraid, but at length, thinking to himself
that ghosts need no lamps and that but one, man or woman,
had entered in front of him, he grew courageous and followed.

For some five and thirty paces this passage ran downwards
steeply between walls of granite, then for another thirty
paces it ran on upon the level, ending at last in a large chamber hewn from the living rock and roofed with great painted
slabs of stone leaning against each other to bear the mighty
weight of the pyramid above.   In this darksome place,
sunk into the rock, stood a sarcophagus of granite and
naught else.

Khian crept down the passages by the light of the lamps,

his footsteps echoing against their walls of stone, and from the shelter of a huge half-opened granite door peeped into the tomb chamber. It was lit by one lamp that stood upon the sarcophagus whereof the feeble rays shone like a star in the black gloom of the vaulted hall. This gloom he searched with his eyes. In vain; he could see no one, the veiled shape he had followed was not; or perchance it had departed by some farther door into the bowels of the pyramid.

Muttering a prayer for protection against the spirit of the Pharaoh upon whose rest he broke, and drawing his bronze sword lest he should find that he had been lured into this dreadful place by evildoers, Khian crept forward through the gloom, very carefully, for there might be pitfalls in the rocky floor. Coming at length to the sarcophagus he stood irresolute, for of a sudden his courage seemed to fail him.

What if in truth he had been following a ghost and that ghost should spring upon him from behind! Nay, he would be brave. Did ghosts set lamps in niches? Their shapes showed that they were ancient lamps, it was true; perhaps the same that were used by the builders of the pyramid a thousand years before, or by those who bore the body of the king to its last resting place. Yet lamps did not burn eternally, unless indeed they were ghostly lamps; the oil in them must be new and set there by human hands. The thought gave him courage and he stood still who had meditated flight. There was a sound at the far end of the hall, a rustling sound that checked the beating of his heart. In the darkness appeared a cloud of white which floated forward. The ghost was upon him!

He stood where he was—perchance because he could not stir. The white-veiled shape drew near and halted. Now only the width of the tomb was between them and he stared at it over the flame of the lamp but could see nothing because the face was covered, like the face of one new-dead. In his terror he lifted the sword as though to stab at this unearthly thing. Then a soft voice spoke, saying:

"O Seeker of the Spirit of the Pyramids, would you greet her with a sword-thrust, and if so, why?"

"Because I am afraid," he answered. "That which is veiled is always terrible, especially in such a place as this."

As he spoke the veil fell, and in the lamplight he saw the form and the beautiful, flushed face of Nefra.

"What is the meaning of this play, O Queen?" he asked faintly.

"Does Khian, the heir of the King of the North, name me Queen?" she asked in a mocking voice. "Well, if so, he is right, since here above the bones of him who, history tells, was my forefather and of whose throne I am the heritor, so I should be called. Prince Khian, you sought the Spirit of the Pyramids who never was except in fable, and you have found a queen who is both flesh and spirit. If still you have aught to say to her, speak on, since time is short and soon she may be missed."

"I have nothing to say except what I have said already. Nefra, I love you well and I would learn of you whether you love me. I pray you play with me no more, but let me hear the truth."

"It is short and simple," she answered, raising her head and looking straight into his eyes. "Khian, if you love me well, I love you better, for of this treasure woman has more to give than man."

His mind reeled beneath the weight of her words and his body with it, so that he must rest his hand upon the stone of the tomb to save himself from falling. Yet his first thought was angry and broke from his lips in a sharp question.

"If that be so, Nefra, what need to bring me to this dreadful place of death to tell me that it is so? What need to make me follow a dream and a ghost that I might find a woman? Surely the jest is ill-conceived."

"Not so much so as you think, Khian," she answered gently. "Yesterday I could not tell you what I longed to speak, because, being what I am, I must lay the matter before others, I, who am not the mistress of myself, but the servant of a cause. Therefore I sought time till I had learned that what I desired was the will of those who are set above me and, as they declare, of Heaven which is set above them. Had it been otherwise, you would have seen no Spirit of the Pyramids to-night and no Queen Nefra ere you departed to-morrow, and thus would have had your answer which I should have been spared the pain of speaking."

"Then Roy and the rest approve, Nefra?"

"Aye, they approve; indeed, it seems that from the first they hoped for this and therefore brought us together as much as might be, because they trust that so Egypt may once more be united and that thus their policy may prosper through our love."

"Much must happen before that can be," said Khian sadly.

"I know it, Khian. Great dangers threaten us. Indeed, I think that they are near. It is for this reason that, playing the part of a ghost, I have led you to this ancient sepulchre, believed of all to be haunted by the dead, that you may learn its secret and at need make of it your hiding place, Khian. Now I will show you the trick of the door in the casing of the pyramid, revealed to me by right of birth and to certain others by right of office, for from generation to generation this secret has descended as an inheritance in the family of the Captain of the Pyramids who are sworn not to disclose it, even under torture. Look, Khian."

Lifting the lamp Nefra held it above her head and pointed to the end of the tomb chamber, where by its light he saw a large number of great jars set against the wall.

"Those vessels," she added, "are filled with wine, oil, grain, dried flesh, corn, and other sorts of food; also, nearer to the entrance, as I will show you, are more jars of water which from time to time is renewed, so that here a man, or indeed several men, might live for months and yet not starve."

"The gods defend me from such a fate!" he said, dismayed.

"Aye, Khian, yet who knows? That jackal is safest which has a hole to run to when its hunters are afoot."

"Sooner would I be killed in the open than go mad here in the darkness with the dead for fellowship," he answered doubtfully.

"Nay, Khian, you must not be killed; now you must live on—for me and Egypt."

She set down the lamp in its place and moved to the foot of the tomb. He did likewise, so that there they met and stood a little while, gazing at each other in the midst of a silence that was so deep that they could hear the beating of their hearts. Speech had left them, as though they had no more words to say, yet their eyes spoke in a language of their own. They bent towards each other like wind-swayed palms, nearer and nearer yet, till of a sudden she lay in his arms and her lips were pressed upon his own.

"Beloved," he said presently, "swear that while I live you will wed no man but me."

She lifted her head from his shoulder and looked at him with her large and beautiful eyes that were aswim with tears.

"Is it needful?" she asked in a new voice, a deep, rich voice. "You have little faith, Khian, and I ask no such oath from you."

"Because it would be foolish, Nefra, for who, having loved you, could turn to others? Yet there are many who will seek the fairest lady on the earth and Egypt's Queen. Indeed, has not one sought her already? Therefore, I pray you, swear."

"So be it. I swear by the Spirit that we worship, both of us; I swear by Egypt which, if Roy be right, we shall rule in the days to come; and I swear by the bones of my forefather who sleeps within this tomb that I will wed none but you, Khian. While you live I will be faithful to you, and if you die then swiftly I will follow you, that what we have

lost on earth, we may find in the Underworld. If I break
this, my oath, then may I become as is he who sleeps beneath my hand to-day," and she touched the tomb with her
fingers. "Aye, may my name be blotted from the roll of
Egypt's royal ones and may Set take my spirit as his slave.
Is it enough, O faithless Khian?"

"Enough and more than enough. Oh! how shall I thank
you who have given life to my heart? How shall I serve
you whom I adore?"

She shook her head, making no answer, but he, loosing her
from his arms, sank to his knees before her. He abased
himself as a slave; he lifted the hem of her robe and kissed
it, saying:

"Queen of my heart and rightful Queen of Egypt, I,
Khian, worship you and do you homage. Whatever I have
or may have, I set beneath your feet, acknowledging your
Majesty. Henceforth I, your lover who hope to be your
husband, am the humblest of your subjects."

She bent down and raised him.

"Nay" she said, smiling, when once more he stood upon
his feet, "you are greater than I and it is the woman who
serves the man, not the man the woman. Well, we will
serve each other and thus be equal. But, Khian, what
of Apepi who is your father?"

"I do not know," he answered. "Yet, father or not, I
pray that he may not try to come between us."

"I pray so also, Khian. To-night is happy, never was
there so happy a night; but to-morrow—oh! what of to-
morrow?"

"It is in the Hands of God, Nefra, therefore let us fear
nothing."

"Aye, Khian, but often the paths of God are steep and
rough, or so my father and my mother found. Like us they
loved each other well, yet this Apepi was their doom.
Come, we must go, for alas! all sweet things have their
end."

So once more they clung and kissed, and then hand in

hand went down the darksome ways of that House of Death to the moonlit world without.

When they had climbed the steep ascent and were come to the mouth of the passage, Nefra stopped and by the light of the last lamp, for she had extinguished the others as they went, taught Khian how, by pressing a certain stone which swung upon a pivot, the place could be closed at will and, if need were, made fast from within by the aid of a bar and pins of granite, which the builders of the pyramid had used to shut out the curious while they went about their work upon the secret burial chambers at its heart. Also she showed him a great hanging door of granite that those who brought the Pharaoh to his burial a thousand years before had forgotten or neglected to let fall as they departed, leaving him to his eternal rest.

"See," she said, "if that wedge of stone were knocked away the great door would fall. Therefore touch it not, lest we should be shut into this Pyramid of Ur and lay our bones with those of the mighty Khafra, its architect. Look, yonder in that niche, where perhaps once stood the priest or soldier who was guardian of the door, are the jars of water of which I spoke, and by them oil and lamps and wicks of reed and fuel and means of raising fire, with other needful things."

Having shown him all and made sure that he understood, Nefra quenched the last lamp and set it in the niche. Then they crept out on to the side of the pyramid where thrice she made Khian close and open the swinging stone, until he had mastered the trick of it, after which, with a wedge of marble that fitted in a socket hollowed to receive it and yet could be withdrawn in a moment, she made the stone fast, so that now none could tell it from those around unless they had the secret and knew in which course of the casing blocks it lay. This done, they descended to the ground just by a fallen block that marked where the seeker for the swinging stone must mount. Crossing the paving that surrounds the pyramid, they reached the temple of the Worship of

Khafra to the east and kept in its shadow lest they should be seen by some night wanderer. Here, too, they parted with sweet murmured words of farewell, Nefra taking one path homewards and Khian another.

Slowly he made his way through the vast, moonlit wilderness of tombs, his heart filled with a great joy, for had he not won all that he desired? Yet with this joy was mingled fear of what the morrow might bring forth. Then would be handed to him, the ambassador, the written answer of Nefra to the demand of Apepi, his father, that she should give herself to him in marriage. Now he knew well what that answer would be, but what he did not know was how Apepi would receive him when, as duty demanded, he delivered it to him. There was but one hope—that he might prove content that his son should wed this queen without a throne instead of himself, seeing that the reason of such a marriage was political and nothing else, and he, Khian, was his father's heir. Had Apepi seen Nefra, almost certainly things would befall otherwise, for he knew his father's nature and that he would desire to possess himself of beauty such as hers. Happily, however, he had not seen her and therefore might be content to let her go, who was naught to him if he could secure her heritage for the House of the Shepherd kings.

Yet Khian doubted whether events would thus shape themselves. It well might be that when he learned, as learn he would certainly through his spies or otherwise, that his son was betrothed to the high lady whom he had sought for himself, that he would hold that this son, who was also his ambassador, had played the traitor to him, which in a sense was true. If so, he might be very wrath and terrible in his rage, who was cruel-hearted. Moreover, he might desire vengeance. What vengeance? Perhaps the death of the traitor, no less, and if still she would not marry him, the death of Nefra also. For was she not Egypt's lawful Queen and, while she lived, could he sit safe upon his stolen throne?

As he picked his way among the tombs by the moonlight

Khian knew in his heart that he and Death were face to face.
Dark imaginations possessed him. Almost could he see
that grisly shape stalking ahead of him while, wrapped in
the long, hooded cloak that he used as a disguise, his shadow,
cast by the moonlight on the sand, to his sight took the
very shape of Osiris in his mummy wrappings—yes, of
Osiris the god of death. Yet if so, was not Osiris also the
god of resurrection and the king of life eternal? If indeed
doom awaited him and Nefra, at least beyond the grave
lay joy and peace for thousands of thousands of years.

So Roy taught and so he believed. Still, coming fresh
from the lips of his love, those warm and human lips with
her sweet words echoing in his ears, he shivered at these
sad and solemn thoughts. For who could be sure of what
lay over the edge of the world? Oh! who could be quite
sure?

Khian came to the private door of the Temple of the
Sphinx. As he approached it, from beneath its arch appeared the gigantic shape of Ru who looked at him with
curious eyes.

"Have you been seeking the Spirit of the Pyramids, Lord,
that you wander abroad so late?"

"Who else?" asked Khian.

"And did you find her, Lord, and look upon her face that
men say is so beautiful?"

"Yes, Ru, I found her and looked upon her face. Nor
does rumour lie as to her beauty."

"And are you already mad, Lord, as they say those become on whom that Spirit smiles?"

"Yes, Ru, I am mad—mad with love."

"And being mad, Lord, are you prepared to pay the price
of her embrace and to follow her into the Underworld?"

"If need be, I am prepared, Ru."

The giant stood pondering, his eyes fixed upon the sand.
At length he lifted his head, saying:

"Lord, I am but a fool of a fighting man, yet to us of the

Ethiopian blood foresight comes at times. I tell you because I like you well that I see it written upon this sand that
for your own sake and that of another, you would be wise
this very night to fly fast and far across the sea to Syria or
to Cyprus, or up Nile to the south, and there lie hid awaiting better days."

"I thank you, Ru. But tell me, at the end of that writing on the sand, do you see the symbol of Osiris?"

"No, Lord, not that for you or for another. Yet I do
see the signs of blood and many sorrows near at hand."

"Blood dries and sorrows pass, Ru," and leaving the
Ethiopian still staring at the ground, Khian entered the
temple and sought his chamber.

CHAPTER XIII

The Messenger From Tanis

The Council of the Order of the Dawn was summoned to meet early in the morning on the morrow of that night of full moon when the Prince Khian, in searching for a spirit, had found a woman and a lover. At daybreak, those who watched the frontier of the Holy Field had reported that a messenger had come by boat from King Apepi and waited in the grove of palms to be escorted under safe-conduct into the presence of the Council. It was added that when he was asked what had chanced to the priest Temu who had been sent bearing writings from the Council to the King of the North at Tanis, this messenger replied that he had died of sickness at the Court, and therefore could return no more, or so he had heard. Then it was ordered that the man should be led before the Council at its meeting, there to deliver his message or the writings that he bore.

At the appointed hour Roy the Prophet and all the Council of the Dawn assembled in the temple hall, whither came also every member of the Order to hear the answer of Nefra the Queen to the demands of the King Apepi, and with them Khian under his name and title of Rasa the Scribe, the envoy from the King of the North. Lastly, royally arrayed and for the first time wearing the crowns of Upper and Lower Egypt, appeared Nefra herself attended by the Ethiopian, Ru, for a body-servant, and the Lady Kemmah, her nurse. She took her seat upon the throne that was set to receive her, the same throne that she had filled upon the night of her coronation, whereon the Council and the company rose and made obeisance to her.

At this moment it was announced that the messenger from King Apepi waited without with the letters of the King. It was ordered that he should be admitted, and he entered, guarded by two priests.

Khian looked at him as he came up the dusky hall, thinking that he might know him again as one of the King's Court at Tanis, and saw a thickset man of middle height who limped as he walked, and was wrapped round with shawls that even covered the lower part of his face, as though to protect himself against the cold of the winter morning. Suddenly this man's glance fell upon Khian watching him, whereon he started and turned his head. Next it fell upon Nefra seated in pomp and youthful beauty upon the throne and illumined by a ray of light that struck full upon her through one of the high-placed window openings of the hall. Again the man started as though in wonder, then limped on towards the dais. Arriving in front of it he bowed humbly, drew from his robe a papyrus roll which he laid against his forehead before handing it to one of the priests who mounted the dais and gave it to Nefra. She received the writing and passed it on to the Prophet Roy who sat upon her right hand.

Having opened and studied it, Roy read the writing aloud. It was short and ran thus:

"From Apepi the Pharaoh to the Council of the Order of the Dawn:

"I, the Pharaoh, have received your letter, also one from my envoy, the Scribe Rasa. Your messenger, who gave the name of Temu, reached this Court sick and after lingering for many days, has died. Yet before he died he told my officers that the envoy whom I sent to you, Rasa the Scribe, was dead, having fallen from a pyramid. I demand to know the circumstances of the death of this scribe, my servant, holding that he has been murdered among you.

"Of what is written in your letter I say nothing till I learn the answer of the Lady Nefra to the offer of marriage with

me, the Pharaoh, which I have made to her, for according
to that answer I shall act. This roll I send by a faithful man
but one who, being humble in his station, knows nothing of
the matter with which it deals, for the reason that I will not
trust another of my high officers among you. Deliver your
answer to this man and let him return at once, for if accident
overtakes him also, I, the Pharaoh, shall smite.

"Sealed with the seal of Apepi, the good god, Pharaoh of
the Upper and the Lower Lands, and with the seal of his
Vizier Anath."

Having read Roy cast down the writing, for his rage was
great, and motioned to the messenger to fall back. This he
did readily, as though afraid, taking his stand among the
shadows of the lower part of the hall where he leaned against
a pillar after the fashion of one who is lame and weary.

Then Roy spoke, saying:

"The King Apepi sends us no answer to those things that
we wrote to him, but accuses us of the murder of his envoy,
the Scribe Rasa, and tells us that our messenger Temu is
dead of sickness, which we do not believe, to whom it is given
to know if aught of ill befalls one of our brethren. Be
pleased to appear, Scribe Rasa, that this messenger from
King Apepi and all here gathered may see that you are
not dead, but living. Come hither, Scribe Rasa, and take
your stand by the throne that all may behold you."

So Khian mounted the dais and stood by the throne,
and as he came Nefra smiled at him, and he smiled at her.
Then Roy went on:

"Queen Nefra, the time has come when you must make
answer to the demand of King Apepi that your Majesty
should give yourself to him in marriage. What say you,
Queen Nefra?"

"Holy Prophet and Council of the Dawn," answered
Nefra in a clear and quiet voice, "I say that I thank the
King Apepi, but that I will not give myself in marriage to
him who brought my father to his death and by treachery

would have taken my mother and myself that he might bring us also to our deaths. It is enough."

"Let the words of her Majesty be written down that she may seal them with her seal and that certain of us may seal them as witnesses. Let them be written down forthwith and given to the envoy of King Apepi, Rasa the Scribe. Also let a copy of them be given to this messenger, that thus we may be certain that they come to the eyes of King Apepi."

It was done, Tau writing them with his own hands, after which they were sealed, copied, and made fast in rolls. Then Roy commanded that the messenger of King Apepi should advance and receive the copy.

But when they searched for him that messenger was gone. During the long writing and sealings he had slipped away unnoted, telling those who guarded the door that he had his answer to the message and was dismissed. There was talk of following him, but Tau said:

"Let him be. The man grew frightened and ran, thinking that if he stayed, here he might die, as our brother Temu is said to have died at Tanis. That he has left the roll matters nothing, since what his ears have heard his tongue can tell."

So that messenger departed and, save Roy, none thought of him more.

Khian was summoned to a private chamber, that of Roy. There he found the prophet himself and with him the lord Tau, some of the elders of the Council, and Nefra attended by the Lady Kemmah. When he was seated Roy spoke, saying:

"Our Queen has told us a story, Prince Khian, for so you are, as we have known from the first. She says that while wandering among the tombs last night, as at times it is her fancy to do, she chanced to meet you, Prince Khian, who were taken with a like desire, and that you spoke together alone. If so, what did you say to the Queen and what did she say to you?"

"Holy Prophet, I said that I loved her and desired to be her husband, which were the truest words that ever passed my lips," answered Khian boldly. "As to what she said to me, let her tell you if she will."

Now the blood came to the brow of Nefra, and looking down, she murmured:

"I said to the Prince Khian that I gave gift for gift and love for love, desiring him and no other man to be my lord. Now I pray your blessing on this choice of mine, my Master in the spirit, and with it the consent of the Council of the Order to our betrothal."

"The blessing you have in full measure, Sister and Queen, and the consent I think will not be withheld. Know that we have hoped and prayed that so it would befall, and even made the happening easy, in the trust that thus, without war or bloodshed, Egypt that is severed in twain may once more become one land, acknowledging one throne. Moreover, it seemed to us who have watched you both that you two are well-fitted to each other, and we believe that you were appointed to come together. That is our answer."

"I thank you, Father," said Khian, and Nefra also murmured, "I thank you."

"Aye," went on Roy, "doubtless your hearts thank us in their happiness, yet, Prince and Queen, there is more to be said. Troubles are ahead of you and us, nor can you be united until these are overcome. Apepi threatens us. When he learns that he has been rejected, he will be very wrath, and when he comes to understand why and for whom his suit has been refused—and such a matter cannot be long concealed—what then? Is it still your purpose, Prince Khian, to bear our written answer which that messenger has left behind him, to your father, King Apepi, or will you choose to bide on with us, or to fly the land and hide awhile?"

Khian thought a little, then replied:

"Before I knew what fate held in store for me, I accepted this embassy and, according to custom, swore the envoy's oath of loyal service, namely, that I would bear my message and return with its answer, if I lived, making true report of those to whom it was sent. This oath I must fulfil or be shamed, and therefore I cannot hide away disguised here or elsewhere because my task has become dangerous. That I have adopted the doctrines of the Dawn and am affianced to a certain high lady are my private matters, or so I hold; but to sail in that ship which has been summoned from Memphis to await me in the river, and to deliver your answer to the King Apepi, is my public duty. If ill comes to me in the performing of that duty, it must be so, but if I left it unperformed I should be no honest man. I will deliver the letters and, if need be, tell King Apepi the truth, leaving the end of all to fortune, or rather to the will of That which we worship."

Now Nefra looked at him proudly, while the others murmured: "Well spoken."

"These are high-hearted words," said Roy, "and they please me, Prince Khian, who know from them that our Queen has given her love to no base man. The danger is great and until it be overcome you may not marry lest your bride should be widowed almost as soon as she was wed. Yet I believe that it will be overcome and that in the end the Spirit whom we serve will guide your feet to joy and safety."

"May it be so," said Khian.

"Hearken both of you," went on Roy. "I am very old and it is revealed to me that soon I must pass hence, how as yet I do not know. Yes, I, the seeker after light, must enter into the darkness where, as I trust, I shall find light. Prince Khian, you look upon my face for the last time. All my days I have striven to bring about the unity of Egypt, without bloodshed if that might be. Now perchance in the persons of you, Prince and Queen, this unity will be accomplished and Egypt will be one again, if only for a while. That accomplishment I shall not live to see, though I trust that in the after days I may hear of it from your lips elsewhere. Yet being dead I trust also that my spirit may still guide you both upon the earth although you see it not. Come hither, Khian, Prince of the North, and Nefra, anointed Queen of Egypt, that I may bless you."

They came and knelt before the ancient priest who already seemed more a spirit than a man. He laid his thin hands upon their heads and blessed them in the name of Heaven and in his own, calling down joy and fruitfulness upon them and consecrating them to the service of Egypt— of the Order of the Dawn, and of that universal Soul whom they worshipped. Then suddenly he rose and left them.

One by one, according to their degree, the members of the Council followed, and with them went Kemmah and the giant Ru, so that presently Khian and Nefra found themselves alone.

"The hour of farewell is at hand," said Khian sadly.

"Yes, Beloved," answered Nefra, "but oh! when and where will come the hour of re-union?"

"I do not know, Nefra. None knows, not even Roy, but be brave, for assuredly it will come. I must go; but now I saw it in your eyes that, like myself, you thought that I must go."

"Yes, Khian, so I thought, and think. Therefore go, and swiftly, before my heart breaks. Remember all, Khian, and every word that has passed between us. Now one thing more. I charge you by our love that whatever you may hear concerning me, even if they tell you that I am wed elsewhere, or faithless, that you believe nothing, save that while I live, here or in the Underworld, I am yours and yours alone, and that rather than pass into the hands of another man I will surely die. Do you swear this, Khian?"

"I swear it, Nefra; also that as you are to me, so I will be to you."

Then with murmured words of love again they clung and kissed till soon, at a sign, for she could speak no more, Khian loosed her from his arms. He loosed her, he bowed to her, and she bowed back to him. Then he went. At the doorway he turned to look on her. There robed in the virginal white of the Sisters of the Dawn, wearing no ornament or mark of rank and yet looking most royal, she stood still as a statue, gazing after him while one by one the heavy tears welled from her deep eyes. Another instant and like some gate of doom the door swung to behind him and she was seen no more.

In his chamber Khian found Tau, the second Prophet of the Order, awaiting him.

"I come to tell you, Prince, that your ship is ready at the river bank, to which your goods with the presents sent by King Apepi have been borne," he said, adding, "Ru will escort you thither."

"Yes, Tau, but who will escort me back?" he asked, sighing heavily. "I feel like one who has dreamed a very happy dream and awakened to the world and know it but a dream which will never be fulfilled."

"Take courage, Prince, for I hold otherwise. Yet I will not hide from you that the peril of all of us is great. We learn that Apepi masses troops, as he says, to protect himself against the Babylonians who threaten him, but who can be certain? I would that we had questioned that messenger as was my purpose. But he slipped away while we thought that he was waiting for our letter."

"So would I, Tau, but he is gone and now it is too late."

"Prince," went on Tau in a low voice, "it may be that for a while the Order of the Dawn, and with it a certain lady, must vanish from Egypt. Yet if this comes about, do not believe that we are lost or dead who shall but have gone to seek help, whence as yet I may not reveal even to you, though perchance you may guess. We hate war and bloodshed, Prince, but if these are forced upon us, we shall fight, or certainly I shall fight who in my youth was as you are, a soldier and have commanded armies. Therefore, remember that while I live and indeed while a Brother or a Sister of the Dawn lives throughout the world, and as you saw on the night of the Crowning, they are many, dwelling in many lands, that lady will not lack a defender or a home. And now, farewell till perchance in a day to come I see you and that lady wed and afterwards crowned as King and Queen of the Land of Nile, reigning from the Cataracts to the sea. Again, Brother, fare you well."

Once more Khian walked across the stretch of desert that lay between the Sphinx and the palm grove by the bank of the Nile, but this time his companion was no hooded youth with the voice and the hands of a woman, but the Ethiopian Ru who, as he went, addressed him in a kind of soliloquy, after this sort:

"So, Lord, you really are the Prince Khian, as rumour said and the Lady Kemmah and I guessed from the first, and now you are affianced to my Queen, for which I hate you because ever since you came she has hardly had a look or a word for me. Yet to be honest, as such things must happen, I would rather it was to you than to any one else, because you are a soldier and I like you, also a man of courage, as you showed when you learned to climb those pyramids which I should never have dared to do. So I shall be glad to serve you when you are married, though if you do not treat my Queen well, beware of this axe, for then, if you were fifty Pharaohs and a hundred gods, with it I would still cleave you to the chin. No doubt you think that you are very clever to win her love, as certainly you have done, but there you are mistaken. You did not win her love and she did not win yours. It was those old priests of the Dawn who arranged everything and by their magic threw a spell upon both of you because they wished to bring all this about for purposes of their own. Believe me, that as they have joined you together, so they can separate you if they choose, and by their incantations, make you hate each other. Only I don't think they will as that would not suit them, and you see you are both of you members of the Order of the Dawn, and therefore will be supported by them in all things that you may desire."

"I am glad to hear that," interrupted Khian, when at length Ru paused to take breath.

"Yes, yes, Lord, it is a very good thing to be one of the Order, or even its servant as I am, because then everywhere you have a friend. Therefore never be afraid, however desperate your case may be, even if the hangman is putting his rope about your neck; for certainly Roy, or another far away, will utter one of the spells, or speak a word of power, and someone will appear to help you. That is why I am quite sure that in the end you will marry my Queen if both of you continue to want each other, and that all of us will escape from the jaws of that roaring lion, your father the King Apepi, although he does think that he has our heads in his mouth."

"How will you all escape, Ru?"

"Why, Lord, by finding friends who are stronger than Apepi. There is the King of Babylon, for instance, our Lady's grandfather who can put two spearmen in the field for every one of Apepi's, to say nothing of a multitude of chariots drawn by horses, which Apepi has not got. The Order has plenty of brothers at the Court of the King of Babylon; some of them were here on the night of the Crowning, and I know that messages have been going to them almost every day. Never mind how they went—that's a secret. I should not wonder if we went, too, before long, and then perhaps I may see some more fighting before I grow too old and fat to use my axe. As you are affianced to our Queen, I do not mind talking of these things to you."

"No, of course you don't," answered Khian.

"Talking of messages reminds me of messengers," went on Ru, "or rather of one messenger. I mean that fellow who came from Apepi this morning and slipped away afterwards, which he would never have done had I been guarding him instead of those silly priests."

"What of him?" asked Khian.

A COURSE FOR ADVENT

Just how busy will you be getting ready for Christmas?
Shopping, cooking, wrapping etc etc etc
The preparations seem endless.

And how about preparing *spiritually*?
How much time will you be devoting to that?
It's a fair guess that spiritual preparation comes a poor second

In which case - why not come along to our Advent Course?
Begins Wednesday 3rd December
and continues Wednesdays 10th and 17th.
10.30 a.m. at the Methodist Church
7.30 p.m at the Church Halll (Hardy Room)

The old adage applies . . . you get out what you put in.
Put little or nothing into your spiritual preparation for
Christmas and you wil get little or nothing out of it spiritually!

Come and join us -
make Jesus a part of this Christmas.
Make sense?

Know that I am
with you always;
yes to the end
of time.

Produced by the Parish Office
St. Bartholomew's Church, Crewkerne, Somerset.
Some material included is copyright:
© Archbishops' Council 2000
© National Council of the Churches of Christ, USA 1989

You may take this pew-sheet home with you

SECOND READING   *Revelation 1.4b-8*

We are united with Christ as co-workers in the creation of the kingdom on earth. The glory and power are his but he draws us into fellowship with the Almighty through his sacrifice.

[4] Grace to you and peace from God who is and who was and who is to come, and from the seven spirits who are before his throne, [5] and from Jesus Christ, the faithful witness, the firstborn of the dead, and the ruler of the kings of the earth. To him who loves us and freed us from our sins by his blood, [6] and made us to be a kingdom, priests serving his God and Father, to him be glory and dominion for ever and ever. Amen. [7] Look! He is coming with the clouds; every eye will see him even those who pierced him; and on his account all the tribes of the earth will wail. So it is to be. Amen. [8] 'I am the Alpha and the Omega,' says the Lord God, who is and who was and who is to come, the Almighty.

THE HOLY GOSPEL   *John 18.33-37*

Pilate cannot integrate the idea of Jesus as king and yet also a subject. Mighty in his gifts but humble in his bearing, despised by the leaders of his own faith, Christ's authority and his truth remain a mystery to him.

[33] Pilate asked Jesus, 'Are you the King of the Jews?' [34] Jesus answered, 'Do you ask this on your own, or did others tell you about me?' [35] Pilate replied, 'I am not a Jew, am I? Your own nation and the chief priests have handed you over to me. What have you done?' [36] Jesus answered, 'My kingdom is not from this world. If my kingdom were from this world, my followers would be fighting to keep me from being handed over to the Jews. But as it is, my kingdom is not from here.' [37] Pilate asked him, 'So you are a king?' Jesus answered, 'You say that I am a king. For this I was born, and for this I came into the world, to testify to the truth. Everyone who belongs to the truth listens to my voice.'

The Parish Church of Crewkerne St Bartholomew's

Sunday 23rd November 2003
Christ the King

Christ is our King and will draw all people to himself,
presenting the whole restored creation to God.
In this Eucharist we will unite ourselves with Christ our
sovereign and brother, our leader and friend who, in his
majesty, stooped to become one with his people on earth.

Services today
8.30 a.m. Holy Communion
10.00 a.m. Parish Communion

Next Sunday
ADVENT SUNDAY
8.30 a.m. Holy Communion
10.00 a.m. Parish Communion
6.00 p.m. Advent Carol Service

Post Comunion Prayer
Stir up, O Lord,
the wills of your faithful people;
that they, plenteously bringing forth the fruit of good works,
may by you be plenteously rewarded;
through Jesus Christ our Lord

Blessing
May the God of creation reign in your lives.
May Christ our King reign in your hearts and minds.
May the Spirit of God reign over all your days.
And the blessing of Almighty God,
Father, Son and Holy Spirit,
be with you now and always. Amen

COLLECT OF THE DAY

Eternal Father,
whose Son Jesus Christ ascended to the throne of heaven
          that he might rule over all things as Lord and King:
keep the Church in the unity of the Spirit
and in the bond of peace,
and bring the whole created order to worship at his feet;
who is alive and reigns with you,
in the unity of the Holy Spirit,
one God, now and for ever. Amen

FIRST READING   *Daniel 7.9-10,13-14*
The celestial court condemns those who oppose God.
Consolation for Daniel that despite the power of earthly rulers
and their actions against the faithful, the king of heaven will
see justice done.

[9] As I watched, thrones were set in place, and an Ancient One
took his throne, his clothing was white as snow, and the hair
of his head like pure wool; his throne was fiery flames, and its
wheels were burning fire. [10] A stream of fire issued and flowed
out from his presence. A thousand thousand served him, and
ten thousand times ten thousand stood attending him. The
court sat in judgement, and the books were opened. [13] As I
watched in the night visions, I saw one like a human being
coming with the clouds of heaven. And he came to the Ancient
One and was presented before him. [14] To him was given
dominion and glory and kingship, that all peoples, nations, and
languages should serve him. His dominion is an everlasting
dominion that shall not pass away, and his kingship is one
that shall never be destroyed.

Psalm 93
Dominus regnavit
THE Lord is King, and hath put on glorious apparel :
the Lord hath put on his apparel,
          and girded himself with strength.
He hath made the round world so sure :
that it cannot be moved.
Ever since the world began hath thy seat been prepared :
thou art from everlasting.
The floods are risen, O Lord, the floods have lift up their voice :
the floods lift up their waves.
The waves of the sea are mighty, and rage horribly :
but yet the Lord, who dwelleth on high, is mightier.
Thy testimonies, O Lord, are very sure :
holiness becometh thine house for ever.

Glory be to the Father, and to the Son, and to the Holy Spirit
As it was in the beginning, is now and ever shall be,
World without end Amen

"Oh! only that he was a queer sort of fellow, and more, I think, than he seemed to be. Did you see his eye, Lord? It was like that of a hawk, very proud, too, such an eye as a great noble might have, and when he heard the Queen's answer, it grew full of rage and all his body shook beneath those shawls. More—there were other strange things. Thus, when he came to the hall he limped as though he were very lame, but some people who were working in the fields told me that they saw him running down to the Nile like a hunted jackal.

"Now how can a lame man run like a jackal? Also I hear that when he came to the boat which was waiting for him, those who were in the boat or watching on the shore, prostrated themselves as though he were some Great One, but he leapt aboard and cursed them, calling them slaves— as a Great One does. That is why I think he was more than he seemed to be, just like yourself, Lord, who were announced as the Scribe Rasa and yet are really the Prince Khian. But here we are at the palm grove where more than a month ago I stole your baggage while you were asleep, as the Queen, who was only a princess then, put it into my head to do, for from childhood she has loved such jests. And look, there is your ship, the same that brought you hither, and there are the priests with your packages."

"Yes, Ru, there they all are who I wish were somewhere else. And now here is a present for you, Ru, a chain of fine gold that I have worn myself. Keep it in memory of me and hang it about your neck when you attend upon the Queen, that it may make her think of one who is absent."

"I thank you, Lord, though it seems that you seek to kill two birds with this stone of a gift, which I may show but may not sell. Well, lovers will think of themselves first, and I hope that one day if we should stand together in war—— Why, look! Here comes the Lady Kemmah, walking faster than I have seen her do for years. I think she must have some words for you."

As he spoke Kemmah arrived.

"So I have caught you, Prince," she said, puffing. "A pretty task for an old woman to toil across that sand in the heat like a cow after a lost calf, just to please a maiden's fancy."

"What is it, Kemmah?" asked Khian anxiously.

"Oh! little enough. To give you this which a certain one might as well have done herself, had she thought of it, and to pray you to wear it always for her sake, remembering that thereby she acknowledges you as her king as well as her lover, which of course she has no right to do, any more than she has a right to send you what she does. I told her so but she flew into a rage and said that if I would not take it, she would bring it herself as she could trust it to no one else. A pretty sight indeed that a Queen should be seen tearing across the desert after a departing scribe, for so the common people still believe you to be. Therefore come I must or bear her wrath."

"I understand, Lady Kemmah, but what do you bring? You have given me nothing save words."

"Have I not? Well, here it is," and she produced from her robe some small object wrapped in papyrus on which was written, "The gift of a Queen to her King and Lover."

Khian undid the papyrus. There within lay the royal signet of Nefra, the same which he had seen set upon her hand on the night of Coronation.

"This is the Queen's ring," said Khian, astonished.

"Aye, Prince, and the King her father s ring before her, that which was taken from his finger by the embalmers after the battle, and his father's before him, and so on back and back for ages. Look, on it is cut the name of Khafra whose tomb I think you saw the other night, though if he ever wore it I cannot tell. At least it has descended through countless generations from Pharaoh to Pharaoh, and now it seems must pass as a love gift to one who is not Pharaoh but yet is charged to wear it as though he were."

"As perchance he may be yet, by right of another, Lady Kemmah, though the matter does not trouble him over-much," answered Khian, smiling.

Then he took the ancient hallowed thing and, having touched it with his lips, set it on a finger of his right hand that it fitted well, removing thence, to make place for it, another ring on which was engraved a crowned and lion-headed sphinx, the symbol of his house.

"A gift for a gift," he said. "Take this to the Lady Nefra and bid her wear it in token that all I have is hers, as I will wear that she sends to me. Say to her also that on the day when we are wed each shall return to the other that ring which belonged to each and with it all of which it is the symbol."

So Kemmah took the ring and as she hid it away there came that Captain of the Guard who had accompanied him from Tanis.

"Welcome, my Lord Rasa, who I rejoice to see have not fallen a victim to the Spirit of the Pyramids of which we talked when we parted here some five and thirty days ago, or was it more? for time passes quickly in yonder gay city of Memphis. You seem to have found strange company in this holy haunted land," and he glanced with awe at the ebon form of the giant Ru who stood by leaning on his great axe, and at the white-veiled, stately Lady Kemmah who stood near him. "You look thin and changed, too, as though you had been keeping company with ghosts. Well, the steersman says that if you are ready, my Lord Rasa, he desires to sail before the wind changes, or because the sailors are afraid of this place, or for both reasons. So if it pleases you, come."

"I am ready," answered Khian, and while Kemmah bowed to him and Ru saluted him with the axe in farewell, he turned and went to the river bank where the sailors bore him through the shallow water to the ship. Presently he was far out upon the Nile, watching the palm-grove, where first he had met Nefra, fade in the gathering gloom. Still there he sat upon the deck till the great moon rose shining upon the pyramids, and thinking of all the wondrous things that had befallen him in their shadow, until these at last grew dim and vanished, leaving him wondering, like one who awakens from a dream.

CHAPTER XIV

THE SENTENCE OF PHARAOH

KHIAN came to Tanis safely, landing at dawn. Having reached the palace, he went to his private chambers and, putting off his scribe's attire, clothed himself in the robes of his rank. As soon as men began to stir he reported his arrival through an officer to the Vizier, and waited.

From the window-place of his chamber he saw that troops were moving on the plain beneath, also that many vessels flying the royal banner were unmooring from the quays and sailing away up Nile. While he marvelled what this might mean, the cunning-faced old Vizier, Anath, came and welcomed him with bows.

"Greeting, Prince," he said. "I rejoice to see that you have accomplished your mission in safety, for know that here we heard that you were dead by a fall from a pyramid, which we took to mean that you had been murdered by those strange zealots of the Dawn."

"I know that story, Anath, for it was written in a letter which was brought by a messenger from my father, whereon I stepped forward to show myself alive and well, though it is true that I did fall from a pyramid and was senseless a while. Has that messenger returned? He fled away suddenly before I could have speech with him."

"I do not know, Prince," answered Anath. "The man has not been reported to me, but I have only just risen and he may have come in the night."

"I hope he has, Anath," said Khian, laughing, "seeing that although he did not wait for the writing which I bear, he had news that I fear will scarcely please my father who I prefer should learn it from him, not from me."

"Is it so, Prince?" asked Anath, eyeing him curiously. "Already there has come news from these people of the Dawn, enough and more than enough to make His Majesty very wrath, and should it be added to by other tidings of the same sort, I think he will be mad with rage. Would it please you to tell me this news?"

"I think not, Anath, although you are his Vizier and the holder of his secrets, as you know, Pharaoh my father is strange-tempered and might take it ill if I reveal to any one what I am charged to deliver to himself."

Anath bowed and answered:

"As to the temper of his Majesty, you are right, Prince, for since you went away it has been terrible. Would that some evil god had never moved me to put a certain thought into his mind: would that we had never heard of the Order of the Dawn. Because of that thought and them he has even threatened me with the loss of my office, though he knows well that if I were driven from it, evil would come to himself, seeing that for years I have been the shield that has turned arrows from his head and by my foresight have saved him from conspiracies."

"I know that this is so," said Khian.

Anath thought a little while, then went on in a low voice:

"Prince, even Pharaohs fall or die at last. The dust awaits their crowns, the grave their greatness. Prince, I have watched you from a child and made a study of your heart, which I know to be honest and true. Now I will ask you a question, promising to believe your answer as though it were that of a god. Are you friendly towards me and if a time should come when you sit where another sits to-day, would you continue me in my offices, especially in that of Vizier of the North? Weigh the matter and tell me, Prince."

Khian reflected for a moment, then answered:

"I think that I would, Anath; indeed I am sure that I would."

"And of the South also if that great land should chance to be added to your heritage?"

"Yes, I suppose so, Anath, though here another—I mean others—might claim a voice. Why not? If you have watched me, I have watched you, and forgive me if I say I know your faults, namely, that you are cunning and a great seeker after wealth and power. But I know also that you are faithful to those you serve and to your friends, and in your own way the cleverest man in Egypt, also the most far-seeing, as you showed when you schemed that Pharaoh should wed the Princess of the South, though that plan has bred more trouble than you know. So there you have my answer and, as you said, I am not one who breaks his word."

Anath took the Prince's hand and kissed it, saying:

"I thank you, Prince." Then he paused and added: "The day when you are Pharaoh of the North and South I may remind you of these words which from your lips are a decree that may not be broken."

"What does all this mean, Anath?" asked Khian impatiently. "You are not making me party to some plot against my father, are you?"

"By all the gods of the Shepherds and the Egyptians, no, Prince. Yet hearken. I have noted that if he is crossed in his will, his Majesty of late goes mad, and those who go mad seek ruin, especially if they be kings. Moreover, he is very rash and the rash fall into pits from which other men escape. Also in his body he is not as strong as he thinks and rage sometimes stops the heart. If Pharaoh's heart stops, what is Pharaoh?"

"A good god!" replied Khian, laughing.

"Yes, but one who attends no more to the affairs of earth. A month or so gone your father asked your consent to his disinheritance of you and you gave it without a thought. Perchance since then, Prince, you may have found reason to change your mind upon this matter."

Here he glanced at Khian shrewdly and went on: "But

whether you have changed it or not, know that heirs apparent cannot be so lightly dispossessed of their acknowledged rights."

"You seemed to agree at the time, Anath; indeed you did more: it was you who set afoot that new scheme of a certain marriage."

"The rush bends before the wind, Prince, and as to this marriage, perchance I wished to save the People of the Dawn, of whose doctrines I think well, or perchance I wished to save Egypt from another war, or both. The one thing that I did not wish to do was to hurt you, Prince. And yet this came about, and now that knot must be undone."

"Yes, Anath, it came about, or seemed to, for which the gods be thanked, since otherwise I should never have been sent upon a certain mission and certain things would never have happened to me which have made me the happiest man in all the world. I will tell you of them afterwards, perhaps—if I dare. Meanwhile, when will my father receive me? Also, why are those troops gathered yonder and whither do the ships sail up Nile? Is it to make another war upon the South?"

"His Majesty has been upon some pilgrimage of his own, Prince, as he said to make a sacrifice in the desert after the custom of our forefathers, the old Shepherds. He only returned thence last night, so weary or so angered about I know not what that he would not receive me. I believe that he still sleeps but there will be a Court before noon, at which you must appear. As for the soldiers and the ships——"

At this moment there rose a cry without.

"A messenger from Pharaoh!" said the cry. "A messenger from Pharaoh to the Prince Khian. Way for the messenger of Pharaoh!"

The doors burst open, the curtains were torn apart, and there entered one of Apepi's heralds clad in his livery and wearing a sheepskin on his back, after the ancient fashion of the shepherds. He sprang forward and, prostrating himself before the Prince, said:

"Having heard that your Highness has returned to Tanis Pharaoh Apepi summons you to his presence in the Hall of Audience instantly, instantly, instantly! O Prince Khian. And you also He summons, O Vizier Anath. Come, come, come, O High Prince, and O great Vizier."

"It seems that my father is in a hurry."

"Yes," answered Anath, "in such a hurry that we had best not keep him waiting. Afterwards we will talk again, Prince. Herald, lead on."

So they followed the man down the passages and across the courtyard to the door of the Hall of Audience through which were speeding sundry of the counsellors and nobles who were called "The King's Companions," and as it seemed, also had been summoned hastily. At the end of the hall, seated in a chair of state and surrounded by priests, scribes, and a guard of soldiers, was Apepi. Glancing at him, Khian noted that he seemed to be weary and dishevelled in his dress, for he wore no crown, while in place of the royal mantle and apron of ceremony, a coloured shawl was thrown round him which reminded Khian of something, though at the moment he could not remember what it was. Moreover, his face seemed drawn and thin and his eyes were very fierce.

Khian advanced up the hall and, after uttering the customary salutation, prostrated himself before the King, while having made obeisance, Anath the Vizier took his place on the left of the throne.

"Rise," said Apepi, "and tell me, Prince Khian, how it comes about that you whom I sent upon a certain embassy did not report your return to me."

"Pharaoh and Father," answered Khian, "I disembarked at dawn and at once, according to custom, caused the Vizier to be informed of my arrival. The Vizier Anath rose from his sleep and visited me. He told me that your Majesty was still resting on your bed after some journey that you had made."

"It matters not what he told you, and is the Vizier

Pharaoh that you should report yourself to him and not to me, so that I must learn of your coming from the Captain of the Guard, whom I sent with you? Surely you lack respect and he takes too much upon himself. Well, what of your mission to those People of the Dawn? Have you made report of that also to the Vizier? Know that I thought you dead, as my messenger may have told you yonder at the pyramids. Should you not therefore have hastened to advise me that you still lived? Is it thus that a son should treat his father or a subject his king?"

Once more Khian began to explain but Apepi cut him short.

"I received the letter from the Council of the Dawn, an insolent letter giving me back threat for threat, and with it another from yourself, Khian, saying that you had seen this Nefra at some ceremony when and where she purported to be crowned as Queen of Egypt. But I have received no answer to my question as to whether this lady accepts or refuses my offer of marriage. Do you bring that answer, Khian?"

"I do," answered Khian, and drawing out the roll he handed it to the Vizier who on bended knee passed it on to the King.

Apepi undid the writing and read it through carelessly, like to one who already knew what was written there. As he read his brow grew black and his eyes flashed.

"Hearken," he said. "This mock queen refuses to be my wife, as she says because years ago her father Kheperra was killed in battle with my armies. Yes, that is what she says. Now, Khian, do you who have dwelt all this while among the People of the Dawn tell me of her real reasons."

"How am I to know a woman's reasons in such a matter, your Majesty?"

"In sundry ways, I think, Khian, otherwise you are but a poor envoy. Yet before you search your mind for them, stretch out your right hand."

Thinking that he was about to be asked to take some oath,

Khian obeyed. Apepi stared at it, then once more stared at the letter and asked in a quiet voice:

"How comes it, Khian, that you wear upon your hand, where I remember used to be a certain ring that I gave to you engraved with the symbol of our House and your titles as Prince of Egypt, another ring, an ancient ring inscribed with the name of Khafra, Royal Son of the Sun, who once a thousand years ago was Pharaoh of Egypt? And how does it chance that this letter of refusal is sealed with that same ring by Nefra who describes herself as Queen of Egypt?"

Now all present stared at Khian, while for a moment a little smile flickered on the withered face of the Vizier Anath.

"It was a parting gift to me," said Khian, looking down.

"Oh! So this puppet queen makes a parting gift of her royal ring to you, my envoy. And did you perchance make a parting gift to her of the ring of the heir apparent to the Crown of the North?"

Apepi paused, watching Khian, but he made no answer.

Then the King his father went on in a low, roaring voice like to that of an angry lion:

"Now I understand all. Know, Son, that *I* was that messenger who visited the habitations of the Brethren of the Dawn some few days ago. Yes, since he could trust no one else, not even his own son, Pharaoh himself filled that humble office and came for his own answer. See, do you know him now?" and rising from the throne with a quick motion he wound the coloured Bedouin shawl about him so that it hid his face up to the eyes, and limped forward a few paces.

"Yes," answered Khian, "and, my Father, the disguise is as excellent as the plan was bold, for had you but known it, you ran a great risk among people who are worshippers of truth and look for it in others."

Apepi returned to his throne and spoke again in the same roaring voice:

"Aye, I ran a risk because I, too, love truth and desired to know what was passing yonder by the pyramids, also to behold this daughter of Kheperra with my own eyes. So I came and saw that she is very fair and royal, such a one as I desire above all women for my queen. Other things I saw also, among them that again and again she looked sweetly at one clad in the white robe of a Brother of the Dawn, one who presently I discovered to be no other than yourself, my envoy that I believed was dead. Moreover, I heard from a fisherman that there were strange sayings in those parts: namely, that the 'Daughter of the Dawn' had promised herself to the Son of the Sun and that the Spirit of the Pyramids had been unveiled by a man, of which sayings he swore he did not know the meaning, though now to me it is clear enough. Tell me, therefore, Khian, who come from the Home of Truth, first—are you wed or affianced to the Princess Nefra, daughter of Kheperra whose ring you wear upon your hand? and secondly, are you sworn a Brother of the Dawn?"

Now his courage came back to Khian and, looking his father in the eyes, he answered boldly:

"Why should I hide from your Majesty that I am betrothed to the royal lady, Nefra, whom I love and who loves me, also that after thought and study I have adopted the pure doctrines of the Dawn and am sworn of its holy Brotherhood?"

"Why, indeed," asked Apepi with bitter irony, "seeing that these things have been discovered before it pleased you to announce them. So, my son Khian, you whom I sent as my ambassador to ask a wife for me, have stolen that wife for your own, and you whom I set to watch my enemies, have adopted their doctrines and been sworn of their secret fellowship. Why have you done these things? I will tell you. You have broken your trust and robbed me of the woman because, did I marry her, her son might thrust you from your heirship, whereas, if you marry her, you keep it, as you think, and add to it whatever claims this princess

may have on the throne of Egypt. It is clever, Khian,
very clever."

"I became affianced to the Lady Nefra because we love
each other and for no other reason," answered the Prince
hotly.

"If so, Khian, your love and your advantage go hand in
hand, as do her love and her advantage, wherein I think I
see the cunning of that old prophet, Roy. For the rest,
you swear yourself of this Order because you believe it to
be powerful, having friends in many lands, and think that by
their help in days to come you will buttress up your throne
or win mine from me. Khian, I say that you are a thief, a
liar, and a traitor, and that as such I will deal with you."

"Your Majesty knows well that I am none of these.
In order to bring about a certain alliance, your Majesty
was pleased to reduce me from my rank of heir apparent to that of a private person and as such to send me
on an embassy. As envoy I did my duty, but those to
whom I was sent would not listen to your Majesty's proposal which I could not help. Afterwards, as a private
person I chanced to become attached to a certain lady who,
if I had not lived, for reasons of her own would never have
listened to the offer of your Majesty. That is all the
tale."

"That perhaps we shall know when you have ceased to
live, Khian. Learn now how I will deal with these tomb
rats of the pyramids who have defied and insulted me. I
will send an army—already it is on its road—to knock them
on the head, all of them. Only one will I spare—the Lady
Nefra; not because she is born of a royal House, but because
I have looked upon her and seen that she is beautiful, for,
Khian, you are not the only man who can worship beauty.
Therefore I will bring her here and make her mine, and for
a marriage gift I will give her your head, Khian; yes, you,
the traitor, shall die before her eyes."

Now when they heard this decree the high officers who
were named Companions of the King stared at each other

dismayed, for never before had such a thing been told of,
as that a Pharaoh of Egypt should kill his own son because
both of them loved the same woman. Even Anath the
Vizier started and paled; yet all that came from his lips
was the ancient salutation:

"Life! Health! Strength! Pharaoh's word is spoken,
let Pharaoh's will be done!"

As this hideous sentence fell upon his ears and a vision
of all it meant rose before his eyes, for a moment Khian felt
his heart stop and his knees tremble beneath him. He saw
his Brethren of the Dawn slaughtered and lying in their
blood wherever they were trapped in their hiding places.
He saw the giant Nubian, Ru, overcome at last and falling
dead upon a mat of foes that he had slain. He saw the
Lady Kemmah butchered and Nefra seized and dragged
a prisoner to Tanis, there to be wed by force to a man she
loathed. He saw himself led out to death before her eyes
and his gory head laid at her feet as an offering. All these
things and others he saw with the eye of his mind and was
afraid.

Yet of a sudden that fear passed. It was as though a
spirit spoke to his soul, the spirit of Roy, or so he thought,
because for an instant he seemed to appear before him
seated where Apepi sat, venerable, calm, and holy. Then
he was gone, and with him went the terrors of Khian.
Moreover, now he knew what to answer; the words welled
up within him like water welling in a spring.

"Pharaoh and my Father," he said in a bold, clear voice,
"speak not so madly, for I say that you cannot do these
things which you have decreed. Did not the Prophet of
the Dawn repeat to you in his letter his answer to your
threat? Did he not say that he had no fear of you and that
should you attempt harm against the Brotherhood, every
stone of the pyramids would lie lighter on your head than
will the curse of Heaven which you would earn as a butcher
and one forsworn? Did he not tell you that the Order of
the Dawn marshalled hosts unseen and that with it goes the

Strength of God? If not, I, your son, who am to-day a Brother of the Dawn and its consecrated priest, deliver to you this, his message. Try to do the wickedness that you have decreed, O Pharaoh, and speaking with the voice of the Order of the Dawn, as I am taught by the Spirit which it worships, I warn you that you will draw down upon yourself disaster and death on earth, and after you have left the earth, woe untold in the Underworld. Thus say I, speaking not with my own voice but with that of the Spirit within me."

When Apepi heard these dreadful words, he bowed his head and with trembling hands drew the coloured robe more tightly about him, like to one who in the midst of great heat is struck suddenly by a blast of icy wind. Then again his rage possessed him and he answered:

"Now, Khian, I am minded to send you, the traitor, to your gods, your king, your father, and your blood, down to that Underworld of which you speak, there to discover whether this wizard Roy is or is not a liar. Yes, I am minded to do this instantly here in the presence of the Court. And yet I will not, since to you I appoint a punishment more worthy of your crime. You shall live to see your fellow knaves dead, every one of them; to see this maiden whom you have beguiled, not yours but mine. Then, Khian. vou shall die and not before."

"Pharaoh has spoken, and I, an ordained Brother and Priest of the Order of the Dawn, have spoken also," answered Khian in the same clear and quiet voice. "Now let the Spirit judge between us and show to all who have heard our words, and to the whole world, in which of us shines the light of Truth."

Thus said Khian, then bowed to Apepi and was silent.

Pharaoh stared at him awhile, for he was amazed, wondering whence came the strength that gave his son power to utter such words upon the edge of doom. Then he turned to Anath and said:

"Vizier, take this evildoer who is no longer Prince of the

North or son of mine, and make him fast in the dungeons of the palace. Let him be well fed that life may remain in him till all things are accomplished."

Anath prostrated himself, rose, and clapped his hands. There appeared soldiers. Khian was set in the midst of them and led away, Anath walking before them.

CHAPTER XV

BROTHER TEMU

THROUGH long passages and down flights of steps, at the head of which stood guards, the melancholy procession descended almost to the foundations of the vast building of the palace. As they went Khian remembered that, when he was a child, some captain of the guard had led him by this path to certain cells where, through a grating in the door, he had looked upon three men who were condemned to die upon the morrow for the crime of having conspired to murder Pharaoh. These men, whom he expected to see groaning and in tears, he recalled, were talking together cheerfully, because, they said, for he heard it through the grating, their troubles would soon be over and either they would be justified in the Underworld or fast asleep for ever.

The three of them took different views upon this matter; one of them believed in the Underworld and redemption through Osiris, one rejected the gods as fables and expected nothing save eternal sleep, while the third held that he would be re-born upon the earth and rewarded for all he had endured by a new and happier life.

The next day Khian heard that all three of them had been hanged and awhile after he learned from his friend, the captain of the guard, that they had been proved to be innocent of the offence with which they were charged. It seemed that a woman of the House of Pharaoh, having been rejected by one of them, had avenged herself by a false accusation and for certain reasons had denounced two other men, whom she hated, as partners in a plot against Pharaoh. Afterwards, when at the point of death from a sudden sickness, she had revealed all, though this did not help her victims who were already dead.

The sight of these men and the learning of their story, Khian recollected as once more he trod those gloomy stairs, had bred in his mind doubts as to the gods which the Shepherds worshipped and of the justice decreed by kings and governors, with the result that in the end he turned his back upon his people's faith and became one of those who desired to reform the world and to replace that which is bad if ancient, by that which is good if new. So indeed he had remained until fate brought him to the Temple of the Dawn, where he found all he sought, a pure faith in which he could believe and doctrines of peace, mercy, and justice such as he desired.

Now, as innocent as those forgotten men, he, the proud Prince of the North, disgraced and doomed, was about to be cast into the same prison that had hid their sufferings and those of a thousand others before and after them. He recalled it all—the stone-vaulted place lit only by a high-set grating of bronze to which none could climb because of the curve of the walls; the paved floor damp from the overflowings of the Nile which, in seasons of flood, rose high above the foundations of the palace; the stools and table, also of stone; the bronze rings to which the officer had told him prisoners were tied if they became violent or went mad; the damp heaps of straw whereon they slept, and the worn skin rugs that they used for covering against the cold; yes, even the places where each of the three victims lay or stood and the very aspect of their faces, especially that of the young and comely man upon whom the rejected woman had avenged herself. Though to this hour it had never been re-visited by him, his mind pictured that horrid hole with all its details.

Now they had trodden the last flight. There was the massive door and in it the grating through which he had looked and listened. The bolts were drawn by the jailer who had joined them; it opened. There were the table and the stone stools, the rings of bronze, the coarse earthen-ware vessels, and the rest. Only the men were gone—of these nothing remained.

Khian entered the dreadful place. At a sign from Anath the guards saluted and withdrew, looking with pity at the young prince under whom they had served in war and who was beloved of all of them. Anath lingered to give certain instructions to the jailer, then as they were both departing he turned back and inquired of the Prince what garments he required to be sent to him.

"I think such as are thick and warm, Vizier," replied Khian, shivering as the damp cold of the dungeon got a hold of him.

"They shall be sent to your Highness," said Anath. "May your Highness forgive me who must fill this sorry office towards you."

"I forgive you as I forgive all men, Vizier. When hope is dead, forgiveness is easy."

Anath glanced behind him and saw that the jailer was standing at a distance from the door with his back towards them. Then he bowed deeply as though in farewell, so that his lips came close to the ear of Khian.

"Hope is *not* dead," he whispered. "Trust to me, I will save you if I can."

Next moment he, too, was gone and the massive door had shut, leaving Khian alone. He sat himself down upon one of the stools, placing it so that the faint light from the grating fell upon him. Awhile later, he did not know how long, the door opened again and the jailer appeared accompanied by another man who brought garments, among them a dark, hooded cloak lined with black sheepskin; also food and wine. Khian thanked him and put on the cloak gratefully, for the cold of the place was biting, noting as he did so it was not one of his own, which made him wonder; also, that in such a cloak a man might go anywhere and remain unknown.

The jailer set out the food upon the table and prayed his prisoner to eat, addressing him as Prince.

"That title belongs to me no more, Friend."

"Oh, yes! your Highness," replied the man kindly.
"Trouble comes to all at times but it cannot change the
blood in the veins."

"No, Friend, but it can empty the veins of the blood."

"The gods forbid!" said the jailer, shuddering, from
which Khian learned that he had rightly named him friend,
and again thanked him.

"It is I who should thank your Highness. Your Highness
has forgotten that when my wife and child were sick in the
season of fever three years ago, you yourself visited them in
the servants' huts and brought them medicines and other
things."

"I think I remember," said Khian, "though I am not
sure for I have visited so many sick, who, had I not been
what I am, or rather was, would, I think, have turned
physician."

"Yes, your Highness, and the sick do not forget, nor do
those to whom they are dear. I am charged to tell you
that you will not be left alone in this place, lest your mind
should fail and you should go mad, as many here have done
before you."

"What! is another unfortunate to be sent to join me,
Friend?"

"Yes, but one whose company it is believed will please
you. Now I must go," and he departed before Khian could
ask him when this other prisoner would come. After the
door had shut behind him Khian ate and drank heartily
enough, for he was starving, having touched no food since the
afternoon before upon the ship which brought him to Tanis.

When he had finished his meal he fell to thinking and his
thoughts were sad enough, for it was evident that it was
in his father's mind utterly to destroy the Brotherhood of
the Dawn and to drag Nefra away to be made his wife by
violence, for, having by evil fortune looked upon her beauty,
nothing now would turn him from his purpose of making
her his own. This, however, Khian knew would never

happen, for the reason that first Nefra would choose to die. Therefore it would seem that both of them were doomed to death. Oh! if only he could warn them by throwing his spirit afar, as it was said that Roy and some of the higher members of the Order had the power to do. Indeed, had he not felt the thought of Roy strike upon him that morning when he stood before Pharaoh in the hall of audience? He would try, who had been taught the secrets of the "Sending of the Soul" as it was called, though he had never practised them before.

Try he did according to the appointed form and with the appointed prayers as well as he could remember them, saying:

"Hear me, Holy Father. Danger threatens the Queen and all of you. Hide or fly, for I am in the toils and cannot help you."

Again and again he said it in his heart, fixing the eyes of his mind upon Roy and Nefra till he grew faint with the soul struggle and even in that bitter place the sweat burst out upon him. Then of a sudden a strange calm fell on him to whom it seemed that these arrows of thought had found their mark, yes, that his warnings had been heard and understood.

An utter weariness fell upon him and he slept.

He must have slept for long, for when he woke all light had faded from the grating and he knew that it was night.

The door opened and through it came the jailer bearing more food, quantities of food, and bringing with him another man clothed like Khian himself in a dark, hooded cloak. The stranger bowed and without speaking took his stand in a corner of the cell.

"Behold your servant, Prince, who is appointed to wait upon you. You will find him a good man and true," said the jailer. Then he removed the broken meats and went, having first lit lamps which he left burning in the prison.

Khian looked at the meats and wine; then he looked at the hooded figure in the corner and said:

"Will you not eat, my brother in misfortune?"

The man threw back his hood:

"Surely," said Khian, "I have seen that face before."

The man made a certain sign, which, by habit as it were, Khian answered. The man made more signs and Khian answered them all, then uttered a secret sentence which the man, speaking for the first time, completed with another sentence still more secret.

"Will you not eat, Priest of the Dawn?" he asked again meaningly.

"In hope of the Food Eternal I eat bread. In hope of the Water of Life I drink wine," replied the man.

Then Khian was sure, for in these very words those of the Order of the Dawn were accustomed to consecrate their meat.

"Who are you, Brother?" he asked.

"I am Temu, a priest of the Order of the Dawn whom you saw but once in the Temple of the Sphinx, Scribe Rasa, when you came thither on a certain embassy, though then I did not know that you were sworn of the Brotherhood, Scribe Rasa, if that indeed be your name."

"It is not my name and at that time I was not sworn of the Brotherhood, Priest Temu, who, I think, are the messenger sent by the holy Roy with letters for Apepi, King of the North. We heard that you were dead of sickness, Priest Temu."

"Nay, Brother, it pleased Apepi to keep me prisoner, that is all. Had I died, my spirit, as it departed, would have whispered in the ear of Roy."

"I remember now that so the Prophet said. But how come you here, and why?"

"I come because I am sent to help another in distress, by some Great One who visited me in my prison. He gave no name, or if he did I have forgotten it, as we of the Order forget many things. Nor did he tell me whom I was to help, yet I can guess, as we of the Order guess many things. I see that you wear a royal ring, Scribe Rasa. It is enough."

"Quite enough, Priest Temu. But tell me, why were you sent to me? In such a hole as this even a Pharaoh would need no servant."

"No, Brother, yet he might need a companion and—a deliverer."

"Very much indeed, both of them, especially the last. But, Temu, how could even Roy himself open that door or break through these walls?"

"Quite easily, Scribe Rasa, by means of which we know nothing, and if only we have faith perhaps I can do the same, though not so easily and in another fashion. Hearken. During the many days I have spent in prison, bettering my soul with prayers and meditations, from time to time I have given instructions to that humble man who is our jailer, setting his feet in the way of truth. Thus in the end he has become well affected to those who profess our faith, to which I have promised that he shall be gathered in days to come. In reward he has imparted a certain secret to me which, as neither he nor any other will visit this place again to-night, I will now show to you, Brother Rasa. Help me, if it pleases you, to move this table."

With difficulty it was dragged aside, for it was of massive stone. Then Temu took from his robe a piece of papyrus on which were marks and lines. By aid of these he made certain measurements and at length in the roughly paved floor found a stone for which he seemed to have been searching. At this stone he pushed from left to right, for there was a roughness on it against which he could rest the palm of his hand, thereby, it would appear, loosing some spring or bolt. Suddenly a section of the floor, a pace wide or more, tilted up, revealing a shaft cut in the rock, of which the bottom could not be seen, and against its side, also cut from the rock, stone bars set at intervals one above the other, down which it would be possible for an active man to climb.

"Is it a well?" asked Khian.

"Aye, Brother, a well of death, or so I think, though perhaps of that we shall learn more later. At least all is as the Great One whose face was veiled, told me, for it was he who gave me the plan and bade me trust the jailer and do as he instructed me."

"And what is that, Temu?"

"Descend by this ladder, Brother, until at the foot of it we come to a tunnel; then follow the tunnel until it ends in what seems to be the mouth of a drain in the stone embankment of the river. Beneath this hole or drain-mouth a boat should be waiting, and in it a fisherman following his trade by night when the largest fish are caught. Into that boat we must enter and be gone swiftly before it is discovered that this place is empty."

"Do we fly at once?" asked Khian.

"No, Brother, not for another hour, for so I was instructed; why I do not know. Help me now to close the trap, but not quite lest the spring should refuse to work again, and to replace the table over it exactly as it stood before. Who knows that some officer or spy might not be moved to pay us a visit, although the jailer said that none would come."

"Aye, who knows, Temu?"

So they closed the trap, setting a piece of reed from a food basket between its edges so that it did not shut altogether, and dragged back the table to its place. Then they sat down to eat. Scarcely had they done so when Temu pressed Khian's foot and looked towards the door.

He looked also and, though he heard nothing, saw, or thought that he saw, a white face and two glowing eyes set against the grating and watching them, a sight that made his blood turn cold. In an instant it was gone again.

"Was it a man?" whispered Khian.

"A man, or perchance a ghost, Brother, for I heard no footfall, and of such this place may well be a home."

Then he rose, and taking a linen cloth that had been laid over the food, he thrust it into the grating.

"Is that not dangerous?" asked Khian.

"Aye, Brother, but to be watched is more dangerous."

To Khian it seemed as though that hour would never end. Moment by moment he feared lest the door would open and all be discovered. Yet no one came, and indeed they never learned whether they had seen a face at the grating or whether its appearance was but a trick of their minds.

"Whither would you fly, Brother?" asked Temu.

"Up Nile," whispered Khian, "to warn our brethren who are in great danger."

"I felt it," said Temu. Then he rose and packed the most of the food, of which, as has been said, there was much more than they could eat, into two of the baskets wherein it had been brought which were made of reeds and had handles that could be slipped on to the arm.

"It is time to go, Brother. Faith, have faith!" said Temu.

They rose and for a moment stood still to put up a prayer to the Spirit they worshipped for help and guidance, as was the custom of their Brotherhood before they entered on any undertaking.

"I will go first, Brother, carrying one of the lamps in my teeth—the second we must leave burning—and one basket on my arm. Do you follow with the other."

Then he stepped to the door, pulled out the food-cloth from the grating, and having listened awhile, returned, and taking the smaller of the lamps, set its flat handle between his teeth. Next he crawled beneath the table, pushed upon the stone so that it tilted up and stood edge in air, climbed through the hole on to the stone ladder, and began to descend. Khian followed. As it chanced when he had taken some three steps down the ladder, the peaked hood of his cloak touched the stone, disturbing its balance. Instantly it swung to, releasing the spring or catch, so that now there was no hope of return, since this could not be opened from beneath. Even then the purpose of this trap came into Khian's mind. When it was desired to destroy some unhappy captive, unknown to him the spring or bolt was set back. Then shortly, as the doomed one tramped that gloomy cave he would tread upon the swinging stone and vanish into the gulf beneath, for when this was purposed doubtless the heavy table stood elsewhere. Or if his secret end was desired very swiftly, jailers would hurl him down the pit. Khian shuddered as he thought of it, remembering that this fate might well have been his own. Down, down he climbed, the feeble little lamp which Temu carried in his teeth lighting his way. It seemed a long journey, for the pit was deep, but at length Temu called to him that he had reached its bottom. Presently he was at his side perched upon a white and moving pile that crackled beneath his feet. He looked down and by the lamplight perceived that they stood upon a pyramid of bones, the bones of the victims who in past days had fallen or been cast down the shaft. Moreover, some of them had fallen not so very long before, as his senses told him, which caused him to remember certain friends of his own who had incurred the wrath of Pharaoh and, as it was said, were vanished. Now he guessed to what land they had been banished.

"Lead on, Temu," he said. "I choke and grow faint."

Temu obeyed, turning to the right as he had been told that he must do, and holding the lamp near the ground lest there should be pitfalls in the path, which ran down a tunnel so low and narrow that they must walk it doubled up with their shoulders brushing against its walls. For forty or fifty paces they followed this winding burrow, till at length Temu whispered that he saw light ahead, whereon Khian answered that it would be well to extinguish the lamp lest it should betray them. This was done, and creeping forward cautiously for another ten or twelve paces, they came at last to an opening in the great embankment wall built of granite blocks, upon which the palace stood, so small an opening that few would notice it in the roughness of the blocks, and, twice the height of a man beneath them, saw the waters of the Nile gleaming blackly in the starlight.

They thrust their heads out of the hole and looked down, also to right and left.

"Here is the river," said Khian, "but I see no boat."

"As all the rest of the tale has proved true, Brother, doubtless the boat will appear also. Faith, have faith!" answered Temu to whom the gods had given a trusting soul, and when they had waited half an hour or more, he repeated his words.

"I hope so," answered Khian, "since otherwise we must swim before dawn and hereabout are many crocodiles that feed upon the refuse from the palace."

As he spoke they heard the sound of oars and in the deep shadow of the wall saw a small masted boat creeping towards them. This boat came to a halt beneath their hole. There was a man in it who threw out a fishing line, looked upwards and whistled very softly. Temu whistled back, whereon the man began to hum a tune, such as fishers use, then at the end of it sang softly:

"Leap into my boat, O Fish."

Khian scrambled out of the hole and climbed down the surface of the rough wall, which, being accustomed to such work, was easy to him, and presently was safe in the boat. Temu, having first thrown the lamp into the Nile lest it should be found in the tunnel, followed after him, but more awkwardly; indeed, had not Khian caught him he would have fallen into the river.

"Help me to hoist the sail. The wind blows strongly from the north, therefore you must fly southwards; there is no choice," said the man.

As he obeyed, Khian saw his face. It was that of the jailer himself.

"Be swift," he went on. "I see lights moving; perhaps the dungeon has been found empty. Many spies are about."

Then Khian bethought him of the glowing eyes he had seen at the grating.

With an oar the jailer pushed the boat away from the

wall; the wind caught the sail and it began to move through the water, so that presently they were in the middle of the Nile and gliding up it swiftly.

"Do you come with us?" asked Khian.

"Nay, Prince, I have my wife and child to mind."

"The gods reward you," said Khian.

"I am already rewarded, Prince. Know that for this night's work I have earned more than I have done in ten long years—never mind who paid. Fear not for me who have a sure hiding place, though it is not one that you could share."

As he spoke, with the oar he steered the boat near to the farther shore of the river, where at this spot were hundreds of mean dwellings.

"Now go your ways and may your Spirit be your guide," said the jailer. "There is fishing gear in the boat, also you will find such garments as men use who live by it. Put them on ere dawn, by which time with this wind you should be far away from Tanis, for she sails swiftly. Farewell and pray to your gods for me as I will pray for you. Prince, take the steering oar and stand out into the middle of the river where in this stormy night you will not be seen."

As he spoke the man slipped over the stern of the boat. For a moment they saw his head a dark blot on the water, then he vanished.

"At last I have found one who is good and honest, although of an evil trade," said Khian.

CHAPTER XVI

THE PASSING OF ROY

ALL that night Khian and Temu sailed on, for the north wind held strong and steady, and by daybreak were many leagues from Tanis. Once they saw lights upon the water behind, such as might have been borne by following boats, but soon these vanished. At daybreak they found the fisher's clothes of which the jailer had told them, and put them on, so that for the rest of that journey all who saw them believed them to be two fishermen plying their trade; such men as were to be found by hundreds on the Nile, taking their catch to market, or having sold it, returning to their homes in some distant village. Thus it came about that, Khian being accustomed to the handling of boats, they accomplished their journey safely, though during the second night a number of great ships passed them going down Nile.

Catching sight of these ships they lowered their sail and rowed inshore where they hid among some reeds in shallow water until they were gone by, a whole fleet of them. What these might be they could not discern because of the darkness, but from the lanterns at their prow and stern, the words of command that reached them, and the singing of those on board Khian thought they must be war vessels full of soldiers, though whence such came he did not know. Only he remembered what he had heard at Apepi's Court and that on his return to Tanis he had seen armed vessels sailing up Nile, and remembering, grew afraid.

"What do you fear, Brother Rasa?" asked Temu, reading his mind.

"I fear lest we should be too late to give a certain warning, Temu.   Oh! let us play no more with words,   I, whom you call the Scribe Rasa, am Khian, once Prince of the North, the affianced of Queen Nefra, whom my father Apepi would seize to be his wife.   When he discovered that I, his envoy, had become his rival, the King imprisoned and would have killed me, and that is why we came together in yonder darksome vault."

"All this I have guessed, Prince and Brother, but what now?"

"Now, Temu, I would warn the Queen and our brethren of the dangers that threaten them; namely, that Apepi would steal her and kill out the rest of the Order to the last man and woman, for so he has sworn to me that he will do."

"I think that there is no need to take them that message, Prince," answered Temu lightly, "since Roy would learn such tidings quicker than men could carry it.   Still, let us go on, for God is with us always.   Faith, have faith!"

So they sailed forward and shortly after daylight saw the pyramids and at last came to the strand that was near to the palm grove where first Khian had met Nefra disguised as a messenger.

Here they hid away their boat as best they could and wearing the long cloaks that had been given to them in the prison, beneath which were swords that they had found in the boat, set there doubtless for their use, made their way across the sand to the Sphinx, and thence to the temple, meeting no man.   Indeed, they noted that those who cultivated the fertile belt of land were not to be seen and that the crops were trodden down by men and wandering beasts. Filled with fear they entered the temple by the secret way they knew and crept down its passages into the great hall where Nefra had been crowned.   It was silent and empty, or so they thought at first, till suddenly, far away at the end of the hall Khian perceived a white-robed figure seated in the throne-like chair upon the dais, behind which stood the ancient statue of Osiris, god of the dead.   They ad-

vanced swiftly. Now they were near and Khian saw that
it was the figure of Roy or—the ghost of Roy. There he
sat in his priestly robes, down which flowed his long white
beard, his head bent upon his breast, as though he slept.

"Awake, holy Prophet," said Khian, but Roy did not
stir or answer.

Then they went to him, trembling, climbed the dais, and
looked into his face.

Roy was dead. They could see no wound on him, but
without doubt he was dead and cold.

"The holy Prophet has been taken away," said Khian
hoarsely, "though I think that his spirit remains with us.
Let us search for the others."

They searched but could find no one. They went into
the chamber of Nefra. It was undisturbed but she was
gone; even her garments were gone, and so it was with all
the others.

"Let us go out," said Khian; "perchance they are hidden
in the tombs."

They left the temple and wandered far and wide, but all
was silence and desolation. They looked for footprints,
but if there were any, the strong north wind had covered
them up with sand. At length in the shadow of the second
pyramid they sat down in despair. Roy was dead and the
rest were gone, Khian could guess why. But whither had
they gone? Were they perchance on board those ships
which had passed them in the night? Or were they slain?
If so, how came it that they had seen no bodies or signs of
slaughter? So they asked of themselves and each other,
but found no answer.

"What shall we do, Prince?" asked Temu. "Doubtless
all will be well in the end. Still, our food and water are
almost gone, nor can we stay here without shelter."

"Hide in the temple, I think, Temu, at least for the coming night. Listen. I am sure that the Brotherhood of the
Dawn have fled, being warned that Apepi was about to fall
upon them."

"Yes, but whither?"

"To seek the aid of the King of Babylon. The Lord Tau hinted to me, as did the giant Ru, that if it were needful they might go thither, and this doubtless they have done. If so we must follow them, though without guides and beasts to carry food and water, the journey is desperate."

"Fear not, Prince," answered Temu the hopeful. "Faith, have faith! We of the Brotherhood are never deserted in our need. Were we deserted in the prison of Tanis, or on our journey up the Nile? And shall we be deserted though we travel from one end of the world to the other? I tell you nay. I tell you that always we shall find friends, since in every tribe there are Brothers of the Dawn to whom we can make ourselves known by signs, which friends will give us all they have, food and beasts of burden and whatever is needful, passing us on to others. Moreover, I have about me a great sum in gold. It was given to me by that high One whose face was veiled, he who visited me in my cell at Tanis and sent me to join you. Yes, and when he gave me the gold and the jewels, for there are jewels also, he said with meaning that I and another of my fellowship might be called upon to journey into far lands, and that if this were so, the treasure would be needed for our sustenance till we found shelter far from the wrath of a certain king."

Now as he listened the heart of Khian grew bold again, for it seemed to him as though this happy-minded Temu had been sent to him as a very messenger from heaven, which indeed perhaps he was, after a fashion.

"I find your fellowship good in trouble, Temu," he said, "though I know not whence you win such calm and strength of soul."

"I win it from faith, Prince, as you will do also when you have been longer of our Brotherhood. Since Apepi seized me yonder at Tanis and threw me into prison, not once have I been afraid, nor am I now. Never yet have I known harm to come to a Brother of the Dawn going about his duty. The prophet Roy is dead, it is true, but that is because his time had come to die, or perhaps he who was too old to travel chose to withdraw himself from the world. But his mantle has fallen upon Tau and others, and with us will go his spirit, and who shall stand against the freed spirit of the holy prophet Roy who walks with God to-day?"

Then, having determined that they could do nothing more that day, for they were weary and first must rest, also get food if they could from the stores that were hidden away by the Order in case of trouble, of which Temu knew the secret, they set out to return to the Temple of the Sphinx where the dead Roy still ruled as he had done when he was alive. At the edge of the great rock platform upon which was built the Pyramid of Khafra, Khian halted suddenly, for in the midst of the deep silence of the tomb he thought that he heard voices. Whilst he was wondering whence they came, from behind a little neighbouring pyramid that marked the grave of some king's son or princess appeared a Negro running with his head bent down and his eyes fixed upon the ground, as do black people when they track game.

"They have gone this way, both of them, Captain," he called out, "and not an hour ago."

Then Khian understood that the man was following the footsteps of Temu and himself, who indeed had come round that same little pyramid. Whilst he stood wondering what to do, for this discovery seemed to freeze his blood, round the corner of the small pyramid came a whole company of men who by their dress and arms he knew to be soldiers of Pharaoh's guard, forty or fifty of them.

"We have been followed up Nile; they are hunting us, Prince. Now we must escape from them, or we shall be killed," said Temu calmly.

As he spoke the black tracker caught sight of them and pointed them out with his spear, whereon the whole company broke into a run, uttering shouts like hunters when at last they view their game.

Then in his extremity a memory came to Khian.

"Follow me, Temu," he said, and turning, fled back

towards the Pyramid of Khafra, though to do so he must pass even closer to the pursuers.

Temu saw this and stared, then muttering, "Faith! Have faith!" bounded after him.

For a moment the soldiers halted, thinking that they were coming to surrender, but when they saw the pair speed past them they began to run again. Khian, followed by the long-legged Temu, sped along the south face of the great pile and, as their pursuers reached it from the west, were just seen turning the corner of the east face. So swiftly did Khian and Temu run that when the soldiers reached this east face they lost sight of them, who already were speeding along the north face, and not knowing which way they had gone, waited till the tracker came up to guide them by his art.

Meanwhile Khian, rushing along the north face, sought with his eyes for that fallen block of stone which marked where it must be mounted. There were many such blocks, but at last he saw this one and knew it again. Calling to Temu to keep close, he began to scale the pyramid, which to him was easy.

"Ye gods! am I a goat?" gasped Temu. "Well, faith, faith!" and up he went as best he could. Once he would have fallen, but Khian, glancing back, saw and caught him by the hair.

Which was the course of stones? He had found no time to count them as he climbed and each was like to the other. He thought that he must have over-shot it and stopped, trying to remember all that Nefra had told and shown him. Whilst he stood thus, suddenly as though by magic a great block of marble stirred and swung round in front of him, revealing the mouth of the passage beyond, in which he saw a light burning. Not staying to think how this marvel came about, he leapt into the hole dragging Temu after him, for now the tracker had rounded the corner and, though still far away, had caught sight of them on the side of the pyramid, though this afterwards the soldiers would not

believe. Therefore, guessing by the shouting of the man
that they had been seen, in went Khian, though to what fate
he did not know, since he could not guess how the swinging
block had opened of itself and feared some snare.

Scarcely had they passed the stone when it closed as
swiftly and silently as it had opened, and he heard the clank
of the bar. Then panting he turned to look about him and
by the faint light of the lamp that was far off, perceived a
figure standing in the mouth of the recess which Nefra had
shown him was used as a storehouse. The figure came
forward, bowing.

"Welcome, Lord," it said. "Wonderful is the wisdom of
the Prophets of the Dawn, for they warned me that you
might return here thus about this time, and therefore I kept
good watch."

Now as his eyes grew accustomed to the light Khian
knew the man again to be no other than that sheik who had
taught him to climb the pyramids and was called their
Captain.

"How could you watch through a stone wall, Friend?"
he asked, amazed.

"Oh! easily enough, Lord. Come here and I will show
you. Now lie down on the floor and look through that
hole, or if you would see higher up, through that one."

Khian obeyed and perceived that the holes were tubes
which ran slantwise to the face of the pyramid, so cunningly
contrived that a watcher within could see what was passing
at its base, or if he used others, farther away. Thus Khian
saw the soldiers arrive panting and the black tracker with
many wavings of his arms, explaining to them that the
fugitives had run up the pyramid. This tale seemed to
make their captain angry—for clearly he believed it to
be a lie—so angry that he struck the tracker with the handle
of his spear, whereon the man grew sullen, as negroes do
who are beaten unjustly, and throwing himself on to the
sand would say no more. After this the soldiers began to
search for themselves. Some of them even began to climb

the side of the pyramid, till one of them rolled down and
hurt himself and was carried away groaning. Then others
of them went on and vanished, to hunt among the tombs
beyond, or so Khian supposed. But the Captain and some
officers sat down on the sand at the base and took counsel
together, for they were bewildered. So they remained till
nightfall when they lit a fire and camped there.

Having seen these things, or certain of them, Khian bade
the sheik tell him what had become of the Brotherhood of
the Dawn and why he was here alone inside the pyramid.

"Lord, this is the story," answered the man. "Some
hours after you had sailed away down Nile, bearing letters
for the King of the North, news reached the Council of the
Dawn. Whence or how it came I do not know who am
not in their secrets; a spy may have brought it or it may
have been revealed from Heaven, I cannot say. At least
this happened: all of the Brotherhood were gathered together; then the women and children and some men who
were too old to travel far were sent away across the desert
southwards in the direction of the other pyramids where is
the burial-place of the Apis bulls, though whether they were
to stay there or go further I did not hear. At least they departed quietly that very night, and next morning had vanished, doubtless to seek shelter with friends of the Order in
some appointed place where they will be safe."

"But what happened to the Lady Nefra and the rest,
Captain?"

"Lord, all that night they made preparations, and the
next morning before the dawn they started eastwards, bearing with them tents and much provision laden upon asses.
Also they took a mummy case from the burial vault, which
I understood contained the embalmed body of that queen
who was the mother of our Lady Nefra. Only one remained behind, save myself, and that was the holy prophet
Roy."

"Why did you not go also, Sheik?"

"For two reasons, Lord. First because the Captain of

the Pyramids is sworn, whatever chances, never to leave
them. Here my forefathers have lived and died for countless generations, and here my descendants will live and
die till the sun ceases to rise or the pyramids crumble
into dust. This is promised to our race so long as we
guard them and keep our trust, but if we break it, then it is
promised that our family will die out."

"You give a good reason for staying where you are,
though in danger and loneliness, Sheik."

"Yes, Lord, and there is a second, just as good. Before
she went the Lady Nefra sent for me and, speaking as
Queen, laid her commands upon me. These were that I
should forthwith see to it that the tomb chamber in this
Pyramid of Ur, of which like her I had the secret, was full
provisioned with food, fresh water, wine, oil, means of making fire, and all other needful things. That this done, I
should take up my abode here and watch all that passed,
and if you came, for, Lord, she seemed to be sure that you
would come, that I should hide you in the pyramid and
tend you there, thus protecting you from all foes. Moreover, she commanded me, as also did the Lord Tau, to tell
you that she with all the Brotherhood had fled to Babylon,
there to seek the aid of her grandsire, the great King
Ditanah, who it seems still lives and had sent messengers
to greet her as Queen of Egypt and, if need were, to guide
her and all her company to Babylon where, it is believed, he
will give her a great army to make war upon Apepi and to
establish her upon the throne of Egypt. She said also that
I was to bid you, so soon as you could escape, to fly to
Babylon where you would find shelter from the wrath of
Apepi."

"I thank the Queen for her messages and forethought,"
said Khian, "though how she learned that I was fated to
revisit this place, I cannot guess."

"I think that the holy prophet Roy knew and told her,
Lord, for to him at the last the future seemed to be as open
as the present, the only difference being that he saw the one

with the eyes of his soul and the other with the eyes of his body."

"Mayhap, Sheik. But how comes it that Roy sits dead in the temple hall? Do you know aught of his end?"

"Lord, I know everything. I was present when, after the departure of the aged, the women, and the children, the Prophet summoned all the Order before him in the great hall, and with them Nefra the Queen and the Lord Tau. There he addressed them in wonderful words, telling them that they must make the journey to Babylon without him as now he was too old to travel. They answered that they would bear him with them in a litter; but he shook his head, saying:

"'Not so, the time has come for me to die to this world and to pass to another whence I will watch over you and where I will await you all when your hours are fulfilled. Here, then, I bide till I am called away.'

"Then while they wept he called Tau to him and, causing him to kneel, with secret and mystical words ordained him to be Prophet of the Order of the Dawn after him, giving him authority over the bodies and souls of men, after which he breathed upon and kissed him. Next he summoned our Lady Nefra, the Queen, and bade her be of a good heart, since it was given to him to know that all things should befall according to her desire, and that, however great his dangers, he whom she loved would be protected and brought back to her at last. Then he kissed and blessed her also, and after her he blessed all the Order, those of the Council by name, charging them to guard its secrets and to keep its doctrines to which they were sworn, pure and undefiled. Moreover, should they shed blood in pursuit of its righteous aims and in defence of their Queen and sister, he absolved them of its guilt, saying that sometimes war was necessary to peace, but that when war was ended, they must show mercy and become poor and humble as before. After this he dismissed them, nor would he speak with any of them again, save to give Tau a writing for the King of Babylon, and another writing addressed to all the members of the Order throughout the world."

"And what happened then, Sheik?"

"Then, Lord, they bent the knee to him one by one and went away, who by dawn were marching for Babylon. When all had gone Roy looked up and, perceiving me left alone, asked why I was not with them. I told him what I have told you, and he said that it was well and that I must tend him till his death. After this he left the throne and laid him down in a chamber near at hand, and there I visited him night and morning, for all the day I was busy preparing this place to which I carried food and water and the rest from the temple stores and, lest I should be seen, hid them here in the hours of darkness. I think it was on the fourth afternoon from the departure of the Brotherhood that, all my tasks being finished, I went to the holy Prophet to give him water to drink, for now he would touch no food. He drank and commanded me to help him to rise and to array him in all his priestly garments. Then at his bidding I led him to the hall and sat him down on the throne with his rod of office in his hand.

"'Hearken,' he said to me. 'Our foes come, thinking to destroy us according to the command of Apepi. I see them landing on the shore; I see the shining of their spears. Man and brother, hide you there and watch, knowing that no harm shall come to you, and afterwards go do as you were bidden.' Now, as the Brother Temu will know if you do not, Lord, all the temple yonder is full of places where only fire or hammers could find a man, into the secrets of which we of the Order have been instructed in case of need. To one of these I went and hid myself, but a little way from the platform on which Roy sat, nor would any have guessed that the calm statue of an ancient god held a living man who could see all through its hollow eyes of stone.

"A while went by, perhaps an hour, for when I came into the temple the sun was still high, but now its beams, striking through the western window-place, began to fall upon Roy and the throne upon which he sat, in shafts of light that clothed him in a robe of flame. Suddenly the silence was broken by sounds that grew ever nearer, sounds of running feet, sounds of rude voices shouting.

"'Here is the path,' they shouted. 'Here is the nest of the white rats of the Dawn, who soon shall be red. Now let us see if their spells can turn Pharaoh's spears.'

"Roaring such words as these, a mob of soldiers burst into the hall through the great entrance, glittering with armour and with lifted swords. The silence of the ancient place seemed to strike and chill them, for their tumult ceased, and after a pause they came on slowly, clinging together like bees. Then it was, Lord, that the red rays of the westering sun fell full upon Roy, revealing him seated, white-robed, upon the throne, his golden-headed staff held like a sceptre in his hand. They stared, they halted.

"'It is a spirit!' cried one.

"'Nay, it is the god Osiris holding the Rod of Power,' answered another.

"The officers consulted together doubtfully, till some captain who was bolder than the rest said:

"'Shall we be frightened by magic tricks? Let us look.'

"He marched up the hall followed by others, and halted in front of the platform.

"'This old god is dead,' he cried. 'Do you fear a dead god, Comrades?'

"Now Roy spoke in a hollow echoing voice, saying:

"'What is life and what is death? And how know you the difference between a dead and a living god, O Violator of Sanctuaries?'

"The officer heard and fell back, but made no answer, for he was afraid.

"'What seek you in this holy place, O men of blood, and who sent you here?' went on Roy.

"Then the officer found courage to answer.

"'Apepi the Pharaoh, whose servants we are, sent us, and our mission is to capture Nefra, the daughter of Kheperra, once King of the South, and to put to the sword the company of the Priests of the Dawn.'

"'Capture Nefra, the anointed Queen of the Two Lands, if you can find her, Man, and put the priests of the Order of the Dawn to the sword, if you can find them. Search the tombs and search the desert, and when you find them put them to the sword, and bear back the heads of the dead to Apepi, the Shepherd dog whom you call a king, and with them the living beauty of Nefra, her Majesty of Egypt.'

"They made no answer and Roy went on:

"'Search, search, to find naught but wind and sand. Search till the Sword of God falls upon you, as fall it will.'

"Now, Lord, it would seem as though that officer drew courage out of the depths of his terrors, for he shouted back:

"'At least, old Prophet, you are neither God nor his Sword, and for you there is no need to search. You we will take to Pharaoh Apepi, that, yet living, he may hang you as a cheat and a wizard above the gates of Tanis.'

"Now Roy arose from his throne and, terrible to behold, stood in the fierce light of the setting sun. Slowly he raised his wand and pointed with it at that officer, saying in a cold, clear voice:

"'Prophet you name me, and now at the last, if never before, Prophet I am. Hearken, Man, and bear back my words to your master, the Shepherd thief Apepi, and lay them to your own heart. It is you and not I who shall hang from the pylon gate of Tanis. Yea, I see you swinging in the wind, you who have suffered that flock to escape on which the Shepherd dog would feed, and must feel his rage, as this Apepi must feel the wrath of God. Say to him from Roy, the Prophet of the Order of the Dawn, that death draws near to him, the breaker of oaths, the seeker of innocent blood, and that soon he shall talk with Roy, not at Tanis but before the Judgment seat in the Underworld. Say to him that his armies shall go down before the sword of the Avenger as corn is reaped by the sickle, and that one whom he would murder shall sit upon his throne and cherish her whom he desired. Say to him that when he stood here in this hall disguised as a messenger, I knew him well, but spared him because his time was not yet and because the humble Brethren of the Dawn, unlike to the King of the Shepherd pack, remember the duties of hospitality and do not seek to stain their hands with the blood of envoys. Say to him, the oath-breaker who would practise treachery, that he shall drink of the cup of treachery and that from the evil he has sown others shall reap the harvest of righteousness and peace.'

"Thus, Lord, spoke Roy and sank back upon the throne.

"'Seize him!' shouted the officer. 'Beat him with rods; torment him till he tells us where he has hidden the royal Nefra, for ill will be our welcome at Tanis if we return without her upon whom the King has set his heart.'

"Now, Lord, very slowly some of the soldiers crept forward, two paces forward and one back, for they were much afraid. At length they came to the platform and climbed it. The first of them, not touching him, stared into the face of the holy Roy, then reeled back, crying:

"'He is dead! This Prophet is dead; his jaw has fallen!'

"'Aye,' answered one in the hall, 'but his curse lives on. Woe! woe to Apepi and woe to us who serve him! Woe! Woe!'

"While the cry still echoed from the walls, of a sudden the sun sank and the hall grew dark. Then, Lord, there arose another cry of 'Flee! Flee swiftly ere the curse strikes us in this haunted place.'

"Lord, they turned, they fled. The narrow passages were choked with them. Some fell and were trampled of their fellows, for I heard their groans, but these they dragged away, dead or living, I know not which. Presently all were gone. I crept from my hiding place, I lifted the hand of the holy Roy. It grew cold and, when I loosed it, fell heavily; I listened at his heart; it did not beat. Then I followed the soldiers, and hiding as I know how to do, saw them embark upon their ships, fighting in their mad haste, and push out into the Nile although a great wind blew. When I came again at dawn they were all gone, only I think that some boat had been overturned, for on the shore were three bodies which I thrust back into the water.

"Such, Lord, was the end of Roy our Master, who now sleeps in the bosom of Osiris."

"A strange tale and a terrible," said Khian.

"Aye," broke in Temu, "but one in which I see the hand of Heaven. But if such is the beginning, Prince, what of the end? Ill for Apepi, I think, and for those who cling to him. Faith! Have faith!"

CHAPTER XVII

THE FATE OF THE CLIFF-CLIMBERS

THAT night, Khian, Temu, and the Sheik of the Pyramids, after they had eaten and drunk, laid themselves down to sleep in the burial chamber of the Pharaoh Khafra, Khian lying on one side of his sarcophagus, Temu on the other, and the Sheik, who said that he would not profane the sacred place with his humble presence, just outside the doorway. But as Khian discovered that night, often enough it is one thing to lie down and another to sleep.

Sleep, indeed, he could not. Perchance he was over-weary, who had rested little for many nights, for on the boat he had laboured hard and scarcely dared to shut his eyes. Perchance all the dangers that he had passed, all that he had suffered, seen, and heard, so filled his mind that it would not cease from troubling. Perchance the hot, still air of the tomb lying at the heart of a mountain of stone oppressed him and took away his breath.

Or there may have been other reasons. Within the great chest against which he lay, silent and stern, reposed the bones of a Pharaoh, the builder of this pyramid, who had been mighty in the world uncounted years before, but of whom now there remained no history and nothing upon earth, save those bones, the pyramid, and, in the temple without, certain statues portraying his royal presence. Such a one as this was no good bedfellow, thought Khian, especially for a man who, as suddenly he remembered, wore to-day the very ring with which, ages past, that departed monarch had sealed his documents of state.

Khian wondered in his wakefulness whether the *Ka* or Double of this Pharaoh, which, as was well known, or so swore all the priests and learned men, dwelt with his body in the tomb till the hour of resurrection, was now looking at that ring and wondering how it came to be on this stranger's hand. As he remembered, already it had brought him trouble, since through it his father, Apepi, with all the cunning of the jealous, had guessed that he and Nefra were lovers, and thereon cast him into prison. He had escaped from that prison to find another, but if this was to be shared with the *Ka* of the mighty Khafra, the second would be no better than the first, for who could deceive a *Ka*? Had he thought of the matter, which in his folly he did not, he might have hidden the ring from Apepi, but where was the pouch that would hide it from the eyes of a *Ka*? Perhaps, however, Khafra had given the ring to him who came after him, from whom it had descended generation by generation, until it came to his hand lawfully enough, in which case the *Ka* might pardon him who wore it to-day.

Oh! his brain grew weak and foolish; he would think no more of *Kas* and rings; he would think of that sweet and lovely lady with whom he had plighted troth in this very sepulchre. Where was she now, he wondered, and when should he find her again? The Sheik said that almost with his last breath Roy had prophesied that they would come together once more, which were comfortable words. Yet Roy might have meant that this would chance in another world since to Roy, especially at the last, there seemed to be little difference between the live and the dead. But he, Khian, desired the breathing woman, not her ghost, for who knew how shadows loved, if indeed they loved at all? How wondrous was the tale of this death of Roy, hurling curses with his last strength upon Apepi and those who violated the sanctuary of the Brethren of the Dawn and strove to steal away their sister and their Queen. He thanked the gods that Roy had not cursed him in such fashion. Nay, he had blessed him, and Nefra also. Therefore, surely, they would be blessed, for he was holy, a minister of Heaven who knew its mind.

Even in that dread habitation and surrounded by so many perils, he would remember that Roy had blessed them, and that his spirit, purified eternally, was watching him, stronger than the *Ka* of Khafra or than any evil ghost or demon that makes its home in tombs. Yes, comforted by that blessing he would cease to stare at the wavering shadow that the lamplight threw upon the arched roof, and sleep.

Sleep he did at last, though fitfully and haunted by bad dreams, for that place was foul-aired, till at length he was awakened by the sound of Temu, who stirred upon the farther side of the tomb and yawned loudly.

"Arise, Prince," said Temu, "for though one would not guess it here, it must be day."

"What is day to those who live in the eternal blackness of a pyramid as though already they were dead?" asked Khian gloomily.

"Oh! a great deal," replied Temu cheerfully, "because one knows that the sun is shining without. Also darkness has its comforts; thus in it, having nothing else to do, one can pray longer and with a mind more fixed."

"But that the sun is shining on others does not comfort me in a stifling gloom, Temu, and I can pray best when I see the heaven above me."

"As doubtless you will soon again, Prince, for be sure that by now, having lost us, those soldiers have departed to report to his Majesty that we have melted away like spirits."

"In which case his Majesty will make *them* into spirits, Temu, that they may search for us elsewhere. Certainly, wherever those soldiers go, it will not be back to Tanis unless take they us with them. Think now. We have escaped from Pharaoh's strongest dungeon which none has ever done before. The Queen Nefra and all our brethren, save Roy who chose to stay behind to die, have escaped his army. What would his mood be, then, towards those who reported to him that they had tracked and hunted us, only at the last to let us slip through their fingers? No, Temu, unless we accompany them, I think that they will not return to Tanis."

At this moment the Sheik appeared bearing a lamp.

"Have the soldiers gone?" asked Temu.

"Come and see," said the Sheik, and turning, led them down the passages. "Now look," he added, pointing to the eyeholes.

Khian looked, and when his sight grew accustomed to the bright light that flowed from without, perceived the soldiers, fifty or more of them, engaged in building themselves huts or shelters of the loose stones that lay about. Moreover, by setting his ear to the hole, he heard an officer call to someone whom he could not see, asking if all were well with the companies that watched the other faces of the pyramid. Then understanding that these men were sure that their quarry lay hid within the pyramid and intended to guard it day and night until starvation or lack of water forced them to come out, Khian motioned to Temu to look for himself and sat down upon the passage floor and groaned.

"Certainly," said Temu after a while, "it seems as though they were going to stop here a long time, for otherwise they would not be building themselves houses of stone. Well, we will outwit them somehow. Faith—have faith!"

"Yes," said Khian, "but meanwhile even faith needs food, so let us eat."

Thus for these three there began a time of terror. Day added itself to day and still the soldiers remained, watching as a cat watches; also others came to join them, and among these, men who were skilled at the climbing of cliffs and other heights, and set themselves to scale the pyramid with the aid of ropes and spikes of bronze, hoping thus to discover the hiding place of the Prince. It was but lost labour, since although often they crept over it, never did they find the secret stone, nor if they had, could they have opened it that was barred within. Still there they remained, believing always that the prisoners must come out, unless indeed they were already dead.

Khian and his companions slept no more in the tomb chambers; the place was too close and dreadful; they could not rest there. So after that first night they laid themselves down in the passage near to the entrance stone, for there some air reached them through the peepholes, also a little light. Indeed, by setting his eye to one of these holes that slanted upwards, apparently to make it possible for any looking through it from within to see the southern face of another of the pyramids, Khian found that he could behold a certain star. For hours at night he would lie watching that star, until at length it passed from his vision, as the sight of it seemed to give him comfort, though why he did not know. For the rest they must lie in the dark, or with the peepholes blocked, lest the lamplight flowing through these should betray them, and therefore were obliged to eat farther down the passage. Soon, however, although there was plenty of it, food began to grow distasteful to them, who must stay still, or nearly so, day after day. The water, too, became flat, stale, and nauseous to the taste, and of the wine they dared not drink too much.

Thus it came about that at length courage and spirit began to desert Khian, who would sit for hour after hour silent, sunk in a gloom as deep as that of the bowels of the pyramid. Even Temu, though still he talked much of faith, reminding his companions of Roy and his prophecy, and prayed for hours at a time, became less happy-hearted and declared that the prison vaults at Tanis were as a palace compared to this accursed tomb. The Sheik, also, grew so wild in his manner that Khian thought that he was going mad. What angered him most was that strangers should dare to scramble about the pyramid of which he was the captain, for of this he talked continually. Khian tried to soothe him by saying that he was sure they dared not climb so very high, even with the help of their ropes, since never would they know where to set their feet.

These words made the Sheik thoughtful, for after hearing them he grew silent, as though he were considering deeply. On the following night, just before the dawn, he awoke Khian and said:

"Prince, I go on an errand. Ask me not what it is, but to-morrow at sunset unbar the stone and wait. If I do not return before the dawn, bar it up again and think of me as dead."

He would say no more, nor did Khian try to turn him from his purpose, for he knew that then the man would go quite mad. So the stone was opened a little, and having eaten and drunk some wine, the Sheik slipped out into the darkness.

The sound of the bar falling into its place again woke Temu, who sprang up, crying:

"I dreamed that the stone was open and that we were free. Why, where is the Sheik? He was lying by my side."

"The stone was opened, Temu, but we are not free. As for the Sheik, he has gone on some wild errand of his own. What it was he would not tell me. I think that he could bear this place no more and seeks freedom in death, or otherwise."

"If so, Prince, there will be more water left for us two to drink, and doubtless all is for the best. Faith! Have faith!" answered Temu, and lying down went to sleep again.

That day passed as the others had done. Of the Sheik they spoke no more, for both of them believed that he had fled, or hidden himself among the stones of the pyramids to get air. Indeed now their miseries were so great that scarcely could they think of other matters and talked little, but, like two caged owls, sat staring at the darkness with large, unnatural eyes. Towards evening Khian, watching through his peephole, saw that some Bedouins of the desert, who

were mounted upon fine horses, had arrived at the camp of
the soldiers who were chaffering with them for corn or perhaps milk, which others on foot carried upon their heads in
jars or baskets. When the bargaining was done the soldiers
talked with the desert-dwellers, telling them why they
were camped there, or so Khian guessed, for the latter
stared at the pyramids as though the tale moved them, and
asked many questions, as he could see by their eager faces
and the movements of their hands. Whilst they were still
talking the sun began to set, sinking swiftly, as it seems to
do in the clear skies of Egypt. Then suddenly one shouted,
pointing upwards:

"Look! Look! Yonder stands the Spirit of the Pyramids, there on its very crest, clad all in white."

"Nay," answered another, "it is clad in black."

"There must be two of them," called a third, "one in
white and one in black. Without doubt these are no spirits,
but those we seek, the Prince Khian and the priest, who all
this while have dwelt not in the pyramid but on its crest."

"Fool," cried a voice, "how can men live for weeks in
such a place? These are ghosts, I say. Have we not heard
that the pyramids are haunted. Look! The thing mocks
us, making signs with its arms."

"Ghosts or men," said the first voice, that of the Captain,
"we will take them to-morrow. To-night it is impossible,
for darkness falls."

Then followed tumult, for all the soldiers spoke at once,
and at that distance Khian could not hear their words. He
noted, however, that the desert-dwellers did not speak.
They sat still upon their horses at a little distance and behind the soldiers, while he who seemed to be their chief
made strange signs with his arms, stretching them out wide,
then holding them above his head with his fingers touching.
After this, very swiftly came the darkness, covering all, and
the shoutings died away, though from the encampment
below where the soldiers gathered round their fires, still rose
the murmuring of eager talk.

"Temu," said Khian later, "what does this sign mean among the Brotherhood of the Dawn?" and first he stretched his arms out wide and then made them into a loop above his head with the fingers touching.

"That, Prince, is the sign of the Cross of Life which members of the Order use for a signal when they are too far apart to speak. It is thus that they know friend from foe or stranger."

"I thought so," said Khian, and was silent. Then he went to the entrance place and took down the bar that closed it.

An hour later or more he heard a sound and for an instant felt the night air blowing sweetly on his face, though because of the darkness he could see nothing. Next he heard the bar fall into its socket and the voice of the Sheik calling him by name. He answered and together they crept up the passage till they came to a spot where a lamp burned and there were food and water.

When the Sheik had drunk deeply Khian asked him where he had been, though he could guess well enough.

"To the top of the pyramid, Lord. I climbed thither in the dark this morning. It was very dangerous; so dangerous that although you are as skilled as I am, I dared not ask you to accompany me. Still, although I am weak from setting so long stirless in this hole, I did not fear who know the road well; also no harm ever comes to the Captain of the Pyramids while he follows his trade of scaling them."

"Why did you go there, Sheik?"

"I will tell you, Lord. First, that I might make those soldier dogs believe that we were living, not in the pyramid, but on or near its crest in some cave among the stones; or if they would not believe this, that I might frighten them, and perhaps cause them to go away. Doubtless they have heard the tale of the Spirit of the Pyramids and that those who look upon it are doomed to death or madness, and if so, having, as they believed, seen it once they will not wish to do so again. Lastly, I had a reason of my own of which perhaps you will not think well. Skilled cliff-climbers have been brought here to scale the pyramid, *my* pyramid and that of my forefathers, on which none has set foot unless he was of my blood, except only a certain lady and yourself by order of the Council of the Dawn. Yet these bunglers have never yet reached the crest; of that I am sure. Now they will try to do so, for the soldiers will force them to the task, and I think that what will happen to them will cause strangers for many a generation to leave the pyramids to be climbed by my race alone."

"That is revenge which would have been displeasing to Roy," answered Khian, shaking his head. Then remembering that to this man the pyramids were as holy as is a temple to its priest, and that to him he who dared to try to conquer them deserved to die as much as he does who violates a sanctuary, he said no more of the matter, but bade the Sheik to continue his tale.

"Lord, I reached the summit in safety just as the dawn began to break, and there lay flat all day in the little hollow that you know, where part of the cap stone is broken off. It was very hot there, Lord, with the sun beating full upon me, nor did I dare to move lest I should be seen. Yet I endured till at last came the hour of sunset. Then I rose up and stood upon the very point clad in my white robe, so that all the soldiers could see me. While they gazed astonished I slipped back to the hollow and covered up the white robe with my black cloak of camel hair, and thus clad, appeared again, bending my knees so as to make it seem as though I were a second man of a different stature. This I did more than once, Lord, and thus those watchers came to believe that unless they saw ghosts, both you and the priest Temu were on the summit of the pyramid."

"A clever trick," said Khian, laughing for the first time for days, "though I know not how it will serve us."

"Thus, Lord. If the soldiers believe that you are on the summit of the pyramid, they will cease to search and watch its slopes, and all night long the eyes of their sentries

will be fixed upon that summit. But listen, there is more
to tell. Whilst I stood thus on high I perceived certain
men mounted on very fine horses who seemed to be Arabs of
the desert and who were, or had been, engaged in chaffering
with the soldiers, selling them milk or grain. Now the
presence of these men caused me to wonder, for I knew well
that no Arabs dared to set foot within the boundaries of
this, the Holy Ground of Dawn, fearing lest, if they do so,
the curse of Heaven and of the Prophets of the Dawn should
fall upon them. Then a thought came to me, sent as I think
from on high, and seeing him who seemed to be the headman
of the Arabs watching me with uplifted face, with my arms
I made certain signs that are known to our Order, and
perhaps, Lord, to you also who now are one of them."

Khian nodded, and he went on:

"Lord, that man answered the signs and so did another
who was near to him, to show me as I think that this was
not done by chance. Then I knew that they were friends
sent here for a purpose and understood why my Spirit had
moved me to climb the pyramid."

"And if so, what of it, Sheik?" asked Khian in a hoarse
voice, for his heart beat high with hope and choked him.

"This, Lord. To-morrow at the sunset once more I shall
stand upon the crest of the pyramid, and if as I think those
Arabs still are there, I shall make other signs to them, showing them where they must wait at midnight, having horses
in readiness. Then I shall return and guide you to them,
for I think that they will know which way to ride."

"It is dangerous," said Khian, "but so be it, for if I bide
here much longer I think that I shall die. Therefore,
better meet fate in the open and swiftly than perish here
in this hole by inches."

Then he called Temu and the three of them took counsel
together. Also the Sheik and Temu talked much of the
secret signs of their Order, and practised them by the lamplight.

Next morning ere dawn the Sheik departed again as he

had done before. As soon as it was light, watching through
their spyholes, Khian and Temu saw that there was much
disturbance in the camp of the soldiers, saw also that the
skilled cliff-climbers, six or more of them with their ropes
and metal spikes, were collected together, talking with the
officers.

At last, as it seemed to Khian somewhat against their will,
they advanced to the foot of the pyramid, and setting his
ear to the hole Khian heard them scrambling up the face of
it. For a long while he heard no more, but noted the
soldiers watching eagerly, talking together and pointing
with their hands, now in this direction and now in that.

Suddenly there rose a scream of horror. Some of the
soldiers stared as though fascinated, others turned their
backs, and others hid their eyes. The spyhole was ob-
scured for a moment as though by something passing between it and the light. Then soldiers ran forward and
presently Khian and Temu saw them returning towards
the huts bearing three shapeless things that had been men.
A while later they saw the remainder of the cliff-climbers
staggering much as the drunken do, towards the same huts
where they cast down their ropes with the air of those who
had done with them, and departed out of the sight of the
watcher.

"The pyramids are avenged on those who thought that
they could master them, and their captain will rejoice,"
said Khian sadly, thinking to himself that had not some
power protected him they would have been avenged upon
him also, as indeed very nearly happened.

Once more it was sunset and again the Arabs, mounted on
fine horses, appeared at the camp. Again, too, there were
shoutings and pointings with much disturbance, in the midst
of which he who seemed to be the chief of the Arabs drew
a little to one side of, also behind, the soldiers, so as not to
be seen of them, and from time to time made motions with
his arms, as those do who, at its rising or its setting, worship

the sun in the desert. Then followed darkness and in it shone the fires round which the soldiers were seated.

Presently they stood up holding their hands behind their ears as though to listen to some sound in the air; then by twos and threes departed like men who are frightened and hid themselves in the huts or elsewhere. A while later the stone turned and the Sheik glided into the passage, but this time he asked for wine, not for water.

"I have been near to Osiris," he said, "who slipped upon the blood of one of those cliff-climbing fools and almost fell. Yet I did not fall who I think was guarded, and for the rest all goes well."

"Except for the three who are dead," said Khian, sighing.

"If they died, it was by no fault of mine, Lord. Without knowledge of the road, in their madness, having scaled two-thirds of the height they came to smooth marble where is no holding place for hands or feet. Then one slid down, dragging the others with him, for they were roped together, after which the rest, seeing the fate of their fellows, gave up the venture and returned. Now, as I think, the pyramids will be safe from these common cliff-climbers for many a year."

"What chanced afterwards?" asked Khian.

"I appeared at sunset as before, and making pretence to toss my arms about, as a ghost or a devil might do, I signalled to him who seems to be the captain of the Arabs. He answered me. We understood each other. After dark I shouted curses at the soldiers telling them that I was the Spirit of Roy the Prophet, and that doom was near to them. They grew frightened at what they held to be a voice from Heaven, and crept away to hide themselves from the words of evil omen, nor, as I think, will they come out of their holes again until the sun is high. Now drink a cup of wine and follow me, both of you."

CHAPTER XVIII

How Nefra Came to Babylon

After he who was known as the Scribe Rasa, the envoy of Apepi, King of the North, had received the betrothal ring from his affianced, Nefra the Queen, and sailed down Nile to Tanis, there to undergo many evil things, at the Temple of the Dawn all came about as the Captain of the Pyramids afterwards described to him and the priest Temu.

Scarcely had this Rasa, who was Khian the Prince, departed, than there arrived at the temple, disguised as Arabs, an embassy from Ditanah, the old king of Babylon. These men, nobles of Babylon, were received in secret by the Council, and bowing before Roy the Prophet, presented to him tablets of clay covered with strange signs.

"Read the writing, Tau," said Roy, "for my sight grows feeble and I forget this foreign tongue which is your own."

So Tau took the tablets and read:

"From Ditanah the aged, Lord of Babylon and King of Kings, whose glory is as that of the Sun, the Mighty One. To Roy the holy Seer, the Friend of Heaven, the Prophet of the Order of the Dawn, and to him who sits under Roy, the first of the Brothers of the Dawn, who in Egypt is named Tau, but who, as I, Ditanah, have heard, in Babylon aforetime was named the High Prince Abeshu, the lawful son of my body, with whom I quarrelled because he rebuked my Majesty as to a certain vengeance which I took upon a subject people, and who thereafter fled away and as I believed was long dead—Greetings.

"Know, O Roy, and O Tau or Abeshu, that I have received your letters informing me of all that passes in Egypt, and that you, Abeshu, still live. Also that it was the desire of my daughter Rima whom I gave in marriage to Kheperra, the Pharaoh of the South and by right of descent the King of all Egypt, that her bones should be brought back for burial to Babylon. Also I have read that her daughter Nefra has in secret been crowned Queen of Egypt and seeks my help to win her throne out of the hands of my enemy, Apepi the Usurper who rules at Tanis.

"Now I, Ditanah, say to you, Roy the Holy, and to you, Queen Nefra my grandchild, 'Come to me at Babylon with all your company. Thither I swear you safe-conduct in the name of my god Marduk, Ruler of Heaven and Earth, in the name of the gods Nebo and Bel, and of all the other gods who are my lords. There, also, you shall be guarded from all harm by the strength of my hands, and there we will talk together of all these matters.'

"And to you who are called Tau, I say, 'Come also, and if you can prove to me that you are in truth my son, the Prince Abeshu, I will give you all things that you desire, who have mourned over you for many years, save one thing only, the succession to my throne after me which is promised to another. But if you have lied to me in this matter, then do not come, for surely you shall die.'

"To the bones, also, of my daughter Rima, whose husband Kheperra, the wolf, Apepi brought to his death, I will give honourable burial in the sepulchre of kings, where it was her desire to lie at last. Nor do I think that I shall refuse her death-prayer, if Nefra, my grandchild the Queen, will obey me in a certain matter.

"Sealed with the seal of Ditanah, the Great King and with the seals of his Councillors."

When Tau had read he touched his forehead with the tablet and gave it to Nefra who sat upon her throne in the centre of the Council. She also laid it against her forehead, then turned to Tau and said:

"How comes it, my Lord Tau, that all these years you

have kept this secret from me, who if the tale that is written here be true, must be a brother of my mother and my uncle?"—a question which caused the envoys to stare at him.

Tau smiled and answered:

"O Queen and Niece, the tale is true enough, as should we live to come to Babylon, I will prove to my royal father Ditanah and his Councillors. I am Abeshu and the half-brother of Queen Rima. But when I left Babylon she was but a little child born of another mother whom I had scarcely seen, since she dwelt with the royal women. Nor did I reveal myself to her afterwards when we met again and I saved her from the plots of Apepi at Thebes, or to you when you grew to womanhood, because of oaths that I had taken when I became a Brother of the Dawn, which oaths bound me to lay down all my earthly rank and to forget that I had been a prince. Yet in those oaths there was a loophole—namely, should it ever become needful to declare myself and my true name and history thereby to help the Order of the Dawn, I was free to do so. To all of which our father the Prophet can bear me witness."

"Aye," said Roy, "it is true. Hearken, Queen and Sister, and you, the envoys of Ditanah. Many years ago a brother of our Order, now long dead, brought to me a man who said that he desired to become one of us, a noble-looking warrior man, stalwart and square-bearded, who, I judged, had drunk of the water of Euphrates. I asked him his name and country, also why he sought the shelter of the Dawn. He told me, and proved his words, that he was Abeshu, a Prince of Babylon, who had quarrelled with his father, Ditanah the Great King, whose General he had been, over the matter of a subject people whom he had been ordered to massacre, but would not for mercy's sake, and because of his disobedience had been banished or left the land. Afterwards he had served under other kings, those of Cyprus and of Syria, as a captain of their armies, but in the end grew weary of fightings and ambitions, of loves who betrayed him also, and determined to bid farewell to the vanities of the world and in solitude and silence to feed and purify his soul.

"Therefore, having heard of the Order of the Dawn, he came to knock upon its gate. I answered to him that among us there was no room for one who only sought salvation for himself and rest from earthly toil, since those of our Brotherhood must be the servants of all men and more particularly of the poor and those bound with the chains of sin, sworn to bring peace to the world, even at the cost of their own lives, sworn, too, to poverty and, except for special purposes, to celibacy and the renouncement of all earthly honours. For thus only, as we held, could the soul of man come into union with its god. Therefore, if he became one of us, it must be as the slave of the humblest and he must forget that he had been a Prince of Babylon and a General of her hosts, he who henceforward would be but a minister of Heaven appointed to tasks, mayhap, that the meanest idolater would refuse.

"In the end, Queen, this suppliant bowed his neck beneath our yoke and laying down all his titles, became known under the humble name of Tau. Yet from Tau the Servant he grew to be Tau the spiritual Lord, and after me, its aged Prophet, the greatest in our Brotherhood, and so acknowledged throughout the world, though until it became necessary to proclaim it to the Great King Ditanah but the other day, none knew that he was Abeshu, the Prince of Babylon."

Now when they heard this strange story the members of the Council rose and bowed to Tau, as did the envoys from Babylon, setting their hands upon their hearts. But Nefra did more, for she rose also and kissed him on the brow, calling him her beloved uncle and saying that now she understood why she had always loved him from a child.

Then Tau spoke, saying:

"All is as has been told, but because of it I neither seek

nor deserve your praise. What I have done I did for my own soul's sake who came to know that there is no true joy save in the service of others and in the seeking to draw near to God. Now for a while it seems that, still in the service of others, I must once more be known as a prince and perhaps as a captain in war. If so, let not my royal Father have any fear lest I should seek to claim the heritage of those whom he has appointed to succeed him, I whose only hope and purpose is that I may live and die a Brother of the Dawn."

At this moment he who kept the door advanced and whispered into the ear of Roy, who said:

"Admit them."

There came in three men, travel-stained and weary, who when they threw open their cloaks and made the signs, were seen to be Brothers of the Order.

"Holy Prophet," said one of them, "we come from Tanis and from the camp of Apepi's army. We have it from those in authority who in secret are the friends of our Order, that Apepi makes preparation, should a certain request of his be refused, to attack you here; to put every one of the Brotherhood to the sword and to drag away yonder royal lady to be his wife. His troops are gathered and in a few days will be upon you."

"I know it well," answered Roy. "Let those mad servants of Apepi come, for I have words to say to them."

Then he commanded Tau to call together all the people of the Dawn, that he might take counsel with them.

They gathered together and in their presence Roy the Prophet laid down his office and consecrated Tau as his successor, as the Sheik of the Pyramids had told Khian and Temu. Then, too, he bade them farewell and blessed them, and they departed weeping, after which all things happened as the Sheik had said. There were some among the Council—Nefra the Queen was one of them—who would have seized Roy and borne him away by force. But he read their minds and forbade it. So at last they went, leaving him

alone according to his commands. Yet that was a sad
parting and at it many tears were shed. Thus Nefra wept
much, for she loved Roy who from her infancy had watched
over this orphan child as though he were her father. He
noted her grief and called her to him:

"Lady of Egypt," he said, "you who to-day are a queen
in name and ere so very long, unless my wisdom fails me,
will be so indeed, wide seems the gulf that is set between
you and the old hermit, the Prophet of a secret faith whose
name will vanish away and who ere long will be utterly forgotten upon the earth. Also between you and me lies the
span of many years, for I am very, very old, while but
yesterday you came to womanhood. Moreover, your lot in
life is far different from that which I have trod and that now
is ending, so it would seem as though there were little in
common between us. Yet it is not so, because we are tied
together by the bond of love which, did you but know it, is
the one perfect, eternal thing in Heaven and earth. Time is
nothing; it seems to be and yet is not, for in everlastingness
what place is there for time? Pomp and glories, beauty
and desire, wealth and want, things lost and things achieved,
all we seek and all we gain, our joys and griefs, yes, birth
and death themselves, are but bubbles on the stream of
being which appear and disappear. Only love is real and
only love endures. For love is God, and being God, is
King of the world; a King with a thousand faces, who in the
end will conquer all and make of hate a footstool and of
evil the oil within his lamp. Therefore, Child, follow after
love, not only that love which you know to-day, but the
love of all, even of those who do you wrong, for this is the
true sacrifice, and through it only shall your soul be fed.
Now for an hour, farewell."

Then he kissed her on the brow and bade her leave him.

Such was the parting of Roy the ancient Prophet and
Nefra the royal maid who all her life through remembered
this his last message, though perhaps its full mystery and
meaning never came home to her until at last she was about

to follow him into the shadows. Never did she forget the sight of him, white-robed and bearded, hawk-nosed and wrinkled, seated alone upon his chair of state within that dusky hall, staring with steady eyes out into the farther gloom, as though there he sought some beckoning hand of light and awaited the signal to follow whither it might lead.

Ere the dawn they marched, fifty or more of them, besides those who bore the coffin of Rima the Queen. Swiftly they marched by secret ways, for already the sick, the young, and the aged had departed to their appointed hiding places, so swiftly that when the sun rose the pyramids were already distant. Then it was that Nefra bade farewell to the Sheik who had accompanied them thus far, and gave him those commands of which he had spoken afterwards.

For always she believed that Khian would return to seek her there, as did Tau and others of the Brotherhood, who perchance had received some message or spiritual instruction on this matter, and bitterly she grieved that it was not possible to await his coming that he might fly with her. The Sheik bowed and went his way, swearing to fulfil her words, and by degrees the pyramids that had been her only home faded and were lost to sight. Then for the first time Nefra wept a little, for she loved those pyramids which she had conquered and where her joy had found her, and did not know whether she would ever see them more.

They came unharmed to the borders of Egypt, and leaving the great gulf of the Red Sea to the south of them, passed safely into the deserts of Arabia. Indeed, on all that journey through Egypt, avoiding towns and villages, they met few in the war-wasted lands, and those few either fled away or made pretence not to see them. It was almost as though some command had gone out that they should not be observed, though whence it came Nefra did not know. Not until she made that journey did Nefra learn how

great was the secret power of the humble Order of the
Dawn.

At length they were out of Egypt and camped one night
by a well in the desert.   Next morning when Nefra looked
at dawn out of the tent in which she slept with Kemmah, she
perceived a caravan of camels and horsemen advancing
upon them and was afraid.

"Now I think that Apepi has us in his net," she said to
Kemmah, who looked also, then left the tent, making no
answer.   Soon she returned accompanied by two of the
envoys from Babylon, with whom came the Lord Tau himself.

"Have no fear, Queen," said Tau, "all has gone well.
Those whom you see are not Shepherds, but troops of your
grandsire, the great King Ditanah, sent by him to escort
you to his city of Babylon.   Behold the banner of the Great
King blazoned with the symbols of his gods."

"Thanks and praise be to Heaven," answered Nefra.
Then a thought took her and she led Tau aside and said to
him: "I believe and you believe that the Prince Khian will
return to the pyramids to·seek us and to give us warning.
There he may be driven into hiding, being pursued.   If so
he will need help.   Cannot some be found to give it to him
in his extremity?"

"I will consider the matter and take counsel; indeed, I
have already begun to do so," answered Tau.

The end of it was that certain high-bred men of the desert,
disguised as Bedouins and mounted on swift horses, Brethren of each other and of the Dawn every one of them, and
sworn to its service to the death, were sent back to watch
the pyramids with certain instructions, of which men we
have already heard.

Then came the General of Ditanah and his officers who
kissed the ground before Nefra, greeting her, she noted, not
as Queen of Egypt, but as a Princess of the House of Babylon.   Also they were led to the tent where rested the body
of Queen Rima, before which they knelt while a priest of

their worship made prayers and offerings. These things done, camels were brought, a great herd of them, on which were mounted all the Company of the Dawn, and with them a chariot wherein were set Nefra and the Lady Kemmah. Then they departed, guarded by squadrons of Babylonian horsemen and led by guides mounted on fleet camels.

Thus they travelled forward very swiftly across the burning deserts of Arabia by the great military road, halting where there were wells of water, or if there were none, carrying it with them in bags of hide. Moreover, at certain places, oases in the desert, fresh camels and horses awaited them, so that bearing the mummy of Queen Rima with them they advanced almost at the speed of the King's post, helped by all and unharmed by any, and within some five and thirty days beheld before them the mighty walls of Babylon.

Built upon either side of the great river Euphrates, filled with towering temples and glittering palaces, there stood the vast city, the wonder of the world, so huge a place that for a whole day they journeyed through its outskirts before they came to its inmost walls. Then brazen gates rolled back, and as night fell they were conducted down broad, straight streets filled with thousands upon thousands of people, who stared at them curiously, half seen in the twilight, till at length they halted before a palace.

Slaves came forward and led Nefra up steps and through doorways guarded by winged figures of bulls with the heads of men, into a wonderful place such as she had never seen, whose home had been in sepulchres and ancient temple halls. Chamberlains received her, princes bowed before her, eunuchs and women surrounded her and Kemmah, bringing them to a chamber that was hung with tapestry and furnished with vessels of gold and silver. Then they were led to a heated marble bath, welcome indeed after their long journeyings, though never before had Nefra seen such a place, and when they had bathed and been rubbed with oils, were brought back again to their chamber where deli-

cate foods and wines awaited them. Having eaten and
being very weary, they laid themselves down upon silken,
broidered beds and slept, watched by women slaves and
guarded by armed eunuchs who stood without the door.

Nefra was awakened at the dawn by the sound of women's
voices singing some hymn to Sames the Sun god, at his
rising. For a while she lay contemplating the splendours
by which she was surrounded, and already hating them in
her heart. By rank she was a queen indeed, but by upbring-
ing only a simple country girl accustomed to the free air of
the desert, to the exercise and dangers of scaling rocks and
pyramids, to narrow sleeping chambers that once perhaps
were tombs, and to the hard, rough fare of the Brethren of
the Dawn which she had shared with the humblest of the
Order. These silks and broideries, these gorgeous chambers,
these scented waters, these crowds of obsequious slaves, these
foreign, delicate foods, this pomp and state, crushed and
overwhelmed her; she loathed it all.

"Nurse," she said to Kemmah whose bed was near,
"I would that we were back upon the banks of Nile, watching the first rays of Ra gild the Sphinx's brow."

"If you were back upon the banks of Nile, Child," answered Kemmah, "and continued to watch Ra at all, it
would be to see his first rays gilding the gates of your palace
prison at Tanis and to hear the voice of old Apepi calling
you by hateful names of love. Therefore be thankful to
find yourself where you are."

"Nurse, I have dreamed a dream. I dreamed that
Khian, my betrothed, lay in danger of his life and called to
me to come to save him."

"Doubtless, Child, he calls to you wherever he is and
doubtless he is in danger of his life, as all of us are in this
fashion or in that. But what of it? Have we not the
promise of my great-uncle, the Prophet, that no harm shall
come to him? Listen. I, too, dreamed a dream. It was
that Roy himself, clothed in light, as I am sure he is, for
doubtless he has been dead for many days, stood beside me.

"'Bid Nefra,' he seemed to say, 'to calm her heart, for though dangers are many they shall be driven away like storm clouds by the keen desert winds, leaving her sky clear and in it twin stars shining.'"

"Those are happy words, Nurse, that is, if you dreamt them at all, which you know alone; words that give me comfort in this strange and gorgeous place. But look, here come those fat, large-eyed women, bearing gifts I think. Nurse, I will not be touched by them. I will clothe myself or you shall clothe me."

The women came, prostrating themselves almost at every step, and laid the gifts upon a table of jasper stone: wonderful and gorgeous garments, royal robes, collars and belts of jewels, and a crown of gold set with great pearls.

"The gifts of Ditanah the mighty King to his granddaughter, Princess of Babylon and Queen of Egypt," said the chief of the women, bowing and speaking in the Egyptian tongue. "Be pleased to array yourself in them, O Princess of Babylon and Queen of Egypt, that Ditanah, the Lord of lords, may behold your beauty suitably adorned. We, your slaves, are here to serve you."

"Then be pleased to bear my thanks to the mighty Ditanah, my grandsire, and to serve me without the door," answered Nefra, throwing the coverlet over her face so that she might see no more of them.

When they were gone, with many protestations and even tears, Nefra arose and by the help of Kemmah, set to clothing herself in these glittering garments. Yet before all was done that chief of the women must be called back again to show them how they should be worn.

At length she was attired after the fashion of a Babylonian royal lady, marvellously attired, and a mirror was brought that she might behold herself. She looked and cast it down upon the bed, crying:

"Am I Nefra, the Egyptian maid, or the woman of some Sultan of the East? Look at this outspread hair sprinkled with gems! Look at these garments in which I can scarcely

walk! Smell these unguents with which my face and flesh
are smeared! Nurse, rid me of this truck and give me
back my white robe of a Sister of the Dawn."

"It is too travel-stained, Child," answered Kemmah drily,
adding with satisfaction, "moreover, you look well enough
as you are, though somewhat sunburned, and that crown
becomes you. Oh! complain no more; in the spirit you may
be a Sister of the Dawn, but here you are a Princess of
Babylon. Would you anger the Great King from whom
you ask so much? See, they summon us to eat. Come, eat,
for you will need food."

"Mayhap, Nurse. But what is it that the Great King
asks of *me?* Something, as we have heard, of which none
will tell us, not even my Uncle Tau, though I think he
knows."

Then, sighing and pouting her lips, Nefra gave way and
ate, but to her question Kemmah made no answer, either
because she could not, or for other reasons.

A while later there came the chief of the eunuchs, a fat,
vainglorious person, and cringing chamberlains wearing tall
caps, musicians fancifully attired, and women of the Household, and officers, and a guard of swarthy soldiers. All
these, gathering together in an appointed order, set Nefra
and the Lady Kemmah in the midst of them surrounded by
the fan-bearers, the women, and the eunuchs and preceded
by the musicians. Then at a word of command they
marched and though they never left the precincts of the
palace, that walk was long. Down sculptured passages
they went, through great chambers, across courtyards where
fountains played and gardens that grew beyond them, till
at last they reached a flight of many steps and up these
climbed to the bull-guarded doorway of a vast hall.

This hall was roofless, but at the farther end, for a third
of its length perhaps, awnings were stretched over it, from
one side to the other. The place was filled with people,
more people than Nefra had ever seen; thousands of them
there seemed to be, all of whom stared at her, and as she

passed, bowed low.   Up a wide pathway between the crowd
to the right and the crowd to the left went Nefra and her
company, till they came to that part of the hall over which
was stretched the awning.

Here the shadow was so deep by contrast with the bril-
liance without that at first she could see nothing.   Presently, however, her eyes grew accustomed to the gloom and
she perceived that before her was gathered the glittering
Court of the King of Babylon.   There were lords; there
were ladies seated together by themselves; there were soldiers in their armour, there were square-bearded councillors
and captains; there were shaven priests; there were officers
of the Household with wands; there were slaves, black
slaves and white slaves, and she knew not who besides.
Moreover, above all this splendour, its centre and its point,
seated on a jewelled throne, was an aged, white-bearded,
wizened man, wearing a strange headdress who, she guessed,
must be her grandsire, Ditanah the Mighty, the King of
kings.

As they entered the line of shadow a trumpet blew,
whereon all the Court and all the company about her prostrated themselves before the majesty of the King and lay
with their foreheads touching the pavement, yes, even
Kemmah prostrated herself.   But Nefra remained upon
her feet, standing alone like one left living among an army
of dead men; it was as though some spirit within her told
her so to do.   At least thus she stood looking at the little
wizened man upon the throne, while he looked back at her.

Again the trumpet blew, whereon all rose, and once more
her company advanced, to halt near to the throne, on either
side of which stood massed a number of gorgeous nobles
who afterwards she learned were kings' sons, princes, and
satraps of the subject peoples.   For a while there was silence, then the King upon the throne spoke in a thin, clear
voice, an interpreter rendering his words sentence by sentence into the Egyptian tongue.

"Does my Majesty behold before me Nefra, the daughter

of my daughter Rima, the Princess, wife of Kheperra, once Pharaoh of Egypt?" he asked, studying her with his sharp and bird-like eyes.

"That is my name, O Grandsire and Great King of Babylon," answered Nefra.

"Why, then, O Granddaughter, do you not prostrate yourself before my Majesty as all these great ones are not ashamed to do?"

Now again something within her seemed to tell Nefra what to say, and while all stared and listened, she answered proudly:

"Because, Grandsire, if you are King of Babylon, I am Queen of Egypt, and Majesty does not kiss the dust to Majesty."

"Well and proudly said," answered Ditanah. "Yet, Granddaughter, I think that you are a queen without a throne."

"That is so, and therefore I come to you, O Father of my Mother, O Mighty King of Kings, O Fount of Justice, seeking your aid. Apepi the Shepherd usurped my throne as his forefathers did before him, and now seeks to make a wife of me, the Queen of Egypt, and thereby to gain my heritage. But by a little I have escaped out of his hands, helped of your Majesty, and now here I stand and make my prayer to you, the King of Kings from whose body I am sprung."

"Well spoken again," answered the old monarch. "Yet, my Daughter of Egypt, you ask much. Apepi I know and hate; for years I have waged a frontier war against him, yet to cross the waterless deserts with a mighty host to invade him in his territory and drag the stolen crown from off his head would be a great venture that might end ill for Babylon. What have you to promise in return, Lady of Egypt?"

"Nothing, O King, save love and service."

"Aye, thus it stands: you ask much and have nothing wherewith to pay. I must take counsel of this matter. Meanwhile Mir-bel, my grandson, the King of Babylon to

be, lead this lady hither and place her where as a Queen
she has a right to sit, near to my throne."

Now from among the throng of princes came forward a
tall man of middle age, gloriously apparelled and wearing a
diadem upon his head; a strong-faced man with black and
flashing eyes. He bowed before her, searching her beauty
with those hawk-like eyes in a fashion that pleased her
little, and saying in a smooth, rich voice:

"Greeting, Queen Nefra the Beautiful, my cousin. Glad
am I to have lived to look upon one so fair and royal."

Then he took her by the hand and led her up the steps
of the dais to a chair of state that had been made ready for
her upon the right of the throne. There he bade her be
seated and with bows to her and to the King, returned to
his place among the princes.

Nefra sat herself down and for a while there was silence.
At length the old King spoke:

"You say that you have nothing to give, Daughter.
Yet it seems to me that you have much, for you have yourself to give, who are, I hear, unwed. If the Queen of
Egypt," he went on, speaking slowly and in a fashion which
told her that the words had been prepared, "were to take
as her lord the heir of Babylon, so that thereafter, if all
went well, these two great lands were joined into one empire,
then perchance Babylon might be ready to send her armies
to conquer Apepi and set that Queen upon the throne of
her forefathers. What say you, Daughter?"

Now when Nefra heard and understood at length what
was sought of her, the blood left her face and her limbs
turned cold. For a moment she hesitated, in her heart
putting up a prayer for guidance, as Roy had taught her
to do when in difficulty or trouble. It seemed to come, for
presently she answered very quietly:

"It may not be, O King and Grandsire, for thus Egypt
would be set under the heel of Babylon, and when I was
crowned I swore an oath to keep her free."

"That trouble might be overcome, Daughter, in a fashion

pleasing to both our countries of which we can speak here-
after. Have you any other reason against this alliance?
He who is offered to you is not only the heir to the greatest
kingdom in the world; he is also, as you have seen, a man
among men, in the flower of his age, a soldier, and one who,
as I know, is both wise and kind of heart."

"I have another reason, King. Already I am affianced."

"To whom, Daughter?"

"To the Prince Khian, King."

"The Prince Khian! Why, he is Apepi's heir, and yet
you told me that Apepi would have married you."

"Yes, Sire, and therefore Apepi and Khian do not love
each other, but"—here she looked down—"but Khian loves
me and I love Khian."

At these words a whisper went round the Court and old
Ditanah smiled a little, as did many others. Only Mir-bel
did not smile; indeed, he looked angry.

"Is it thus?" said the King. "And where, now, is the
Prince Khian? Have you brought him here in your company?"

"Nay, Sire. When last I heard of him he was at the
Court of Tanis, and, it was said, in prison."

"Where I think he will certainly remain, if, as I doubt
not, your story be true, Child," answered Ditanah, and was
silent.

Just then, when Nefra thought that all was finished and
that her prayer for succour was about to be refused, swelling
sweet and solemn she heard a familiar sound, that of a
certain funeral chant of the Order of the Dawn. She
looked to discover whence it came and perceived Tau followed by all the Brotherhood who had accompanied her
from Egypt, and certain others who were strangers to her,
clad in simple white robes, every one of them, advancing
into the hall by a side entrance to the right. Nor did they
come alone, for in the centre of their company, borne upon
a bier by eight of the brethren, was a coffin which Nefra
knew covered the mummy of her mother, Queen Rima.

The coffin was brought and set down before the throne. Then suddenly the lid, which had been loosened in readiness, was lifted, revealing a second coffin within. This also was opened by the priests who very reverently took from it the embalmed and bandaged body of Queen Rima and stood it on its feet before the King, holding it thus, a sight from which all that saw shrank away, for the Babylonians did not love to look upon the dead.

"Whose corpse is this and why is it brought into my presence?" asked the King in a low voice.

"Surely your Majesty should know," answered Tau, "seeing that this dead flesh sprang from your flesh and that here before you, within these wrappings, stands all that is left of Rima your daughter, aforetime Princess of Babylon and Queen of Egypt, who thus comes home again."

Ditanah stared at the mummy, then turned his head aside, saying:

"What is that which hangs about the neck of this royal companion of the gods, as doubtless she is to-day?"

"A letter to you, O King, sealed with her seal while she was still one of the company of the living."

"Read it," said Ditanah.

Then Tau cut the fastenings and unrolled the writing from which fell a ring. This ring he took, and gave it to the King, who sighed when he looked upon it, for well he remembered that he had set it upon his daughter's finger when she left him to journey into Egypt, swearing to her that he would refuse to her no request which was sealed with this seal.

Next Tau read from the scroll in the Babylonian tongue thus:

"From Rima, aforetime Princess of Babylon, aforetime wife of Kheperra, Pharaoh of Egypt, to her sire Ditanah, the King of Babylon, or to him who sits upon his throne. Know, O King, that I call upon you in the name of our gods and by our common blood, to avenge the wrongs that I have suffered in Egypt, and the slaying of my lord beloved, the King Kheperra. I call upon you to roll down in your might upon Egypt and to smite the Shepherd dogs who slew my husband and took his heritage, and to establish my daughter, the Princess Nefra, as Queen of Egypt, and to slay those who were traitors to her and would have given her and me to doom. Know also that if you, my father, Ditanah the King, or you, that King my kinsman, who sit upon his throne after him, deny this my prayer, then I call down the curse of all the gods of Babylon and Egypt upon you and upon your people, and I, Rima, will haunt you while you live, and ask account of you when we meet at last in the Underworld.

"Sealed by me Rima with my seal upon my deathbed."

These solemn words which seemed almost as though they were spoken by the royal woman whose corpse was set upon its feet before the throne, went to the hearts of all who heard them. For a while there was deep silence. Then Ditanah the King lifted his eyes which had been fixed upon the ground, and it was seen that his withered face was white and that his lips quivered.

"Terrible words!" he said, "and a terrible curse decreed against us if we shut our ears to them. She who spoke the words and sealed them with this seal that once I gave to her together with a certain solemn promise, she who stands there dead before me, was my beloved daughter whom I wed to the lawful Pharaoh of Egypt. Can I refuse the last prayer of my daughter, who suffered so many wrongs at the hand of Apepi the Accursed, and who doubtless stands among us now awaiting its answer?"

He paused and from all who heard him there went up a murmur of "You cannot, O King."

"It is true, I cannot who soon must be as is the royal Rima; whate'er the cost, I cannot. Hearken, priests, councillors, princes, satraps, officers, and people. I, Ditanah the King, make a decree. In the name of the Empire

of Babylon I declare war by Babylon upon Apepi the
Shepherd usurper who rules in Egypt; war to the end!
Let my decree that cannot be changed be recorded and
proclaimed in Babylon and all her provinces."

Again rose the murmur of assent. When it had died
away the King turned to Nefra, saying:

"Fair Queen and grandchild, your prayer and that of
your mother who begat you is granted. Therefore rest
you here in peace and honour till all things are made ready
for this war, and then go forth to conquer."

Nefra heard. Rising from her seat, she cast herself upon
her knees before the King and, seizing his hand, pressed
it with her lips, for speak she could not. Drawing her to
her feet, he bent forward, touched her with his sceptre,
and kissed her on the brow.

"I add to my words," he said. "Knowing your errand,
Child, I made a plan that as a price for the aid of Babylon
you should give yourself in marriage to Mir-bel, the heir to
my throne. Now I put aside that plan, for so my heart is
moved to do, whether because you ask it or for other
reasons. You tell me that you are affianced to the Prince
Khian of whom I have heard a good report, although on
his father's side he comes of an evil stock. Mayhap this
Prince is dead already at the hands of Apepi, or thus will die.
If so, mayhap also you will turn to Mir-bel because it is
my wish and his, though on this matter I make no bargain
with you. Yet if Khian lives and you live to find him,
then wed him if you will and take my blessing on you both.
Look not wrath, Mir-bel, for in the end who knows what
the gods may bring to pass. Learn also from this thwarting
of your desire that they do not give everything to any man,
who to you have given so much. Should this Queen slip
through your hands, the heir to Babylon can find another
to share his throne. It is my will, Prince Mir-bel, that
when the army marches against Apepi, you bide here to
guard me, lest some evil god should tempt you to do
wrong."

When Mir-bel heard this command, knowing that it could not be altered under the ancient law of Babylon, he bowed first to the King and next to Nefra. Then he turned and left the Court followed by his officers. Nor did Nefra see him again till after many years; for at once he took horse and rode for his own Governorship far away, where he remained till all was finished.

When he had gone the King fixed his gaze upon Tau, considering him.

"Who are you, Priest?" he asked.

"I am named Tau, a prophet of the Order of the Dawn, O King."

"I have heard of that Order and I think that certain of its brethren dwell in Babylon and even in my Court. I have heard also that it gave shelter to my dead daughter, Rima the Queen, and to this lady, her child, for which I thank it. But tell me, Prophet Tau, have you any other name?"

"Yes, O King. Once I was named Abeshu, the eldest lawful son of his Majesty of Babylon. Yet many years ago I quarrelled with his Majesty and went into exile."

"I thought it! And now, Prince Abeshu, do you return out of exile to claim your place as the eldest born of his Majesty of Babylon?"

"Not so, O King, I claim nothing, as your envoys may have told your Majesty, save perchance the forgiveness of the King. I am but a Brother of the Dawn and as such dead to the world and all its glories."

Now Ditanah stretched out his sceptre to Tau in token of peace and pardon, and Tau touched it according to the custom of Babylon.

"I would hear more of this faith of yours which can kill ambition in the heart of man. Wait upon me, Prophet, in my private chamber, and we will talk together."

Then waving Tau aside, Ditanah addressed himself to a gorgeous high priest, saying:

"Let this dust that once was my daughter and a Queen,

be re-coffined and borne hence to the sepulchre of kings, where to-morrow we will give it royal burial."

Presently it was done, and as the coffin passed away Ditanah stood up and bowed towards it, as did all in that great place. When it had gone he waved his sceptre and a herald blew upon his trumpet, signifying that the Court was ended. Next the King descended from the throne and, taking Nefra by the hand, led her away with him, beckoning to Tau to follow them.

CHAPTER XIX

THE FOUR BROTHERS

VERY carefully the Sheik of the Pyramids undid the swinging stone and crept out, followed by Khian and Temu, wrapped, all three of them, in their dark cloaks. They closed the stone again and waited, watching. Save one man, a sentry who sat by the embers of a fire, all the soldiers, frightened by what they had seen upon the crest of the pyramid, were gone into the huts that they had built. While this man remained there they dared not descend, fearing lest he should see or hear them and give warning to the others. So there they crouched, among the stones on the slope of the pyramid, drawing in the sweet air in great gasps and gazing at the stars with dark-widened eyes, while Khian wondered what they should do.

"Bide here," said the Sheik, "I will return."

He crept away into the darkness and presently from somewhere above them there arose a sound of hideous howling, such as a ghost or a demon might make, that in the darkness of that solemn place might well curdle a listener's blood. The sentry heard it echoing among the tombs behind him. He rose, hesitated, then of a sudden fled away affrighted and vanished into the huts.

The Sheik reappeared.

"Follow me," he whispered. "Be swift and silent."

They descended the pyramid, Temu, who was no climber, half-blinded, moreover, by many days of dwelling in the gloom, awkwardly enough, and reached the ground in safety. The Sheik turned to the right and ran along its base where the shadows were thick. Now they were clear and darting across an open space towards some tombs. As they reached the tombs a shout told them that they had been seen, by whom they did not know. Following the Sheik, who turned this way and that, they ran on. They came to a hollow in the drifted sand behind a little ruined pyramid, where stood four Arabs holding six horses. Khian felt himself seized and thrown rather than helped on to one of the horses. Glancing round he saw Temu upon another horse, also the Arabs leaping to their saddles. The horses began to move forward, as it seemed to him at some word of command; the Sheik was running at his side.

"What of you?" asked Khian.

"I bide here, as is my duty; fear not, I have hiding places. Say to the Lady Nefra that I have fulfilled her command. Ride fast, for you have been seen; these men know the road. They are our brethren and may be trusted. Prince, farewell!" he said, or rather gasped, and loosing the horse's mane, vanished into the shadows.

They came to open desert and rode on at great speed. All that night they rode, scarcely drawing rein, and at the dawn halted among some palm trees, a place where there was a well of water and hidden away beneath stones, food and forage for the horses. Very glad was Khian to dismount, since, after weeks spent in that tunnel, he was in poor case for hard riding, while that of Temu, at the best no horseman, was worse. They ate a little food, dates for the most part, and drank much water.

"Surely, Brother," said Temu, as he emptied his fourth cup, "we should thank Heaven and our guardian spirits for these mercies. How beautiful is the rising sun; how sweet the fresh air after the heavy heat and blackness of that accursed grave hole. Oh! I pray that I may never again look upon even the outside of a pyramid, and much less upon its tomb chambers. Now we have done with them, thanks to my prayers, and all will be well."

Thus spoke Temu, cheerful as ever, though already he was so sore and stiff that it hurt him even to sit upon the ground. Khian thought to himself that they had more to thank than Brother Temu's prayers; namely, the wit and courage of the Sheik of the Pyramids, also those, whoever they might be, that had sent these Arab horsemen to their succour, if they were Arabs, which as yet he did not know. But he only answered:

"I trust that you are right, Brother, and that all will be well. Yet remember that we were seen as we left the pyramid and that if we escape a second time heads will pay the price of it. Therefore surely we shall be followed, even to the end of the world."

"Faith, Brother! Have faith!" exclaimed Temu as he shifted his seat to find one that was softer.

Just then Khian saw him who seemed to be the leader of the four Arabs, a tall and noble-looking man, standing at a little distance as though he desired speech with him, and alone.

He rose to go to him, and as he came the Arab bowed humbly in salutation and made a certain sign which Khian knew.

"I see that you are of the Brotherhood. Tell me your name and those of your companions; also who sent you in so fortunate an hour to help us, and whither we go."

"Lord, we are four brethren. I, the eldest, am named *Fire*. He who stands there is named *Earth:* the next to him is named *Air*, and the fourth and last is named *Water*. We have no other names, or if there are any we forgot them when we were sworn Brethren of the Dawn, and especially when we were despatched upon a certain duty."

Now Khian understood that for their own reasons, or because of some command laid upon them, these men desired to remain unknown, as was common among the Brethren when they were sent upon any secret service.

"Is it so, Fire?" he said, smiling "But what answer to my other questions?"

"Lord, we were commanded to take six good horses and, disguised as you see us, to go to the Great Pyramids and there bargain with soldiers, if we found any, over such wares as Arabs have to sell. Also we must make ourselves known to the Sheik of the Pyramids, if we could, and give aid to a scribe, Rasa—perchance you are he, Lord—and to his companion, a priest whose name was not mentioned, but whom we have heard you call Temu, if he be the same."

"And then, Fire?"

"Then, Lord, we were to say to the Scribe Rasa that a certain Lady—we know not and, lest we should be captured and questioned, do not seek to know, what lady—with all her following, has passed safely out of Egypt and that the Scribe Rasa and his companion must follow by the road she took. Lastly, we were sworn to bring both of you safely to Babylon, or die at the task, which, Lord, we purpose to do. Now, Lord, we must ride again. These horses are of the most swift and purest desert blood but we have far to go before we can find others, and certainly we shall be pursued. Moreover," he added, eying Temu doubtfully, "I think that yonder priest is more wont to travel on two feet than on four, and until he learns the trick of horsemanship, we must go with care lest he should fall or faint. Lastly, both of you are weak who have, I think, lain for many days in an evil prison."

"True words, Fire," said Khian as he sought his horse.

All that day they rode forward, resting while the sun was high and sleeping at night among some rocks where once more they found food and water for man and beast, and all the next, and the next, travelling at no great speed, till at length Temu, who was brave and active, began to lose his soreness and to win something of that trick of horsemanship of which he who was called Fire had spoken. Also in the strong and wine-like desert air their tomb-bred weakness and languor passed away from both of them, and they grew strong again, as young men do.

One night they slept upon a mound by water where once had stood some village, both men and horses being well hidden by a grove of thorn and other trees that flourished in the rich soil of the mound. As the sun sank behind them, he who was called Fire came to Khian and bade him look through the trees towards the east. He did so and to their right saw that at a distance of perhaps a league, a broad canal or natural sheet of water that may have been the head of a lake was crossed by a ford, beyond which stood an old and crumbling fort built of sun-dried bricks, while in front of them there was no ford and the water seemed to be wide and deep. Beyond this water was a great flat plain that stretched away and away, till very far off upon the horizon it seemed to end in a line of stony hills.

"Listen now, Lord," said Fire. "That water is the boundary of Egypt. That plain is Arabia, and among those hills is the first desert outpost of the army of the King of Babylon, to reach which will be to win to safety. But I tell you, Lord, that we are in great danger. I am certain that yonder old fort is held by horsemen of King Apepi, for I have seen their tracks in the sand, a number of them, fifty men perhaps, and that they watch for us, believing that if we would leave Egypt, we must do so by this ford."

"Why?" asked Khian. "Can we not find another?"

"There is no other, Lord, since below, this water grows into a gulf and above it is deep for many miles, so that to pass round it we must ride through a peopled country guarded by the border garrisons."

"Then it would seem that we are trapped or must fly back into Egypt."

"Where we should be trapped indeed, Lord, for by now the whole land is searching for us."

"What then, Fire? Know that I would sooner look upon the face of Death than upon that of Apepi."

"I have guessed as much. Listen, Lord. All is not lost. These fleet horses of ours were bred in Arabia, yonder among the mountains, and they scent their home and the troops of mares that wander there. The water in front of us will be unwatched because it is so wide and deep and the current

runs so swiftly. Yet I think that the horses will not fear
to face it, and once across, with good fortune we may ride
far before we are seen and perhaps even reach the pass of
the hills in safety. It is a narrow pass, Lord, where one
man can hold back a number for a long while, so that some
of us, at least, should win through to the heart of the hills
and find shelter among the scouts of Babylon," he added
slowly and with meaning.

Then speaking very rapidly, he explained to Khian all
the details of the plan which he and his brethren had prepared. He told him, and Temu, who had joined them, how
they must move down to the water edge before the dawn
and at the first light ride the horses into it, and as soon as
it grew deep, slip from the saddles and swim with them,
clinging to their manes.

Here Temu explained that he could not swim, whereon
Fire answered that he must hang to his horse as best he
might, or drown. He went on to say that those of them
who lived to reach the farther shore must mount at once and
ride for a certain bay in the hills where the pass began,
which bay would become visible to them before noon.
The pass they must climb, on foot if the horses had failed
them, and descend its farther side to the entrenched camp
of the Babylonian company who had orders to succour
all fugitives from Egypt.

Having set out these and other matters, he bade them
drink and sleep while they could, for none knew what might
be their resting place on the morrow.

Khian obeyed, knowing that he must harbour his strength.
The last thing he saw ere his eyes closed was the four strange
brethren grooming the horses and with set faces talking to
each other in whispers as they worked, also, nearer to him,
Temu on his knees, lost in earnest prayer. For with all his
faith Temu remembered that this water was said to be
broad and deep, and that—he could not swim.

It seemed that but a few minutes had gone by when one
of the brethren woke Khian, saying that it was time to be

stirring. They rose by the starlight, set the bridles and the saddles on the horses which had been fed already, mounted them, and followed the brethren down towards the water. They reached it in safety just at the first glimmer of dawn, by the light of which Khian saw that it was indeed wide—scarce could the strongest bowman have shot an arrow from one bank to the other. Also some tide or current seemed to run very strongly through it towards the ford below, which was to this water as is the neck of a wine-skin to the bottle.

"Would it not be safer to risk the ford?" he asked of Fire doubtfully.

"Nay, Lord, for there we should certainly be seen and perhaps killed upon the bank, whereas here, where no man crosses, they may not note us from so far away. Follow me now before the light strengthens."

Then, having patted his horse and whispered into its ear in the Arab fashion, he rode into the flood. After him came Khian, followed by another of the brethren and by Temu. Last of all rode the remaining two brethren, those who were known as Air and Water.

The horses went in bravely enough, and soon Khian saw that Fire's was swimming while its rider had slipped from its back and floated alongside, holding fast to the mane or saddle. Presently Khian's horse also lost foothold and as Fire had done, so did Khian. The swim was long and rough, for the swiftly running water, chilled by the night air, drove them downstream and sometimes broke over their heads. Yet those trained horses held on bravely, smelling the pastures where they were born beyond the desert, and being, as Fire had said that they would be, eager to reach them.

At last they touched the farther shore and Khian, still clinging to the horse, was dragged through the rushes to firm ground. As he came there he heard a shout of "Help!" and looking round, saw Temu's horse struggling up the bank, but unaccompanied by Temu, who indeed, having let go, was floundering in the deep water and being swept down by the current at a distance from the shore. All this the strengthening light showed to them, whereon without a word two of the brethren plunged into the stream and swam to Temu whose shouts grew ever louder. They reached him and with difficulty between them dragged him to the shore, much frightened, but unharmed and still calling to gods and men to save him.

Then one of those strange, fierce brethren drew a knife, saying:

"Will you be silent? Or shall I make you so, who are bringing us all to death?"

"Your pardon," said Temu when he understood, "but my mother always taught me that he who drowns in silence, drowns the most quickly; also I ask you to note that my prayers have saved me."

Muttering words that Temu would have thought evil, Fire helped to thrust him on to his horse and signed to the others to mount theirs.

"Hearken, Lord Rasa," he said, as they pushed their way through the thorn bushes that grew on the bank of the water, "ill-fortune is our companion. The shouts of that mad priest will almost certainly have been heard. Would that he had choked before his throat shaped them. Moreover, he has delayed us, so that the morning wind blows away the mist which I hoped would shroud us for a while. Now there is but one thing to be done—ride straight for the gap in the hills and through the pass. Our horses are better than any the Shepherds have, though theirs will be more fresh, and we, or some of us, may outpace them. At the least, remember this, Lord Rasa, if so in truth you are named, we four brethren will do all that men can to save you, and we pray you, if we meet no more, so to report to a certain Lady whom we serve, and to the Prophet and Council of the Dawn, that our memory may be honoured among men."

Then without waiting for an answer he spoke to his horse

which leapt forward, followed by that of Khian and the others, and sped away.

When they had ridden thus for some minutes and the sun was up, Fire turned and pointed back towards the ford. Khian turned also and saw the bright light glancing on the spears of a great company of mounted men, some of whom were splashing through the ford, whilst others, not more than the half of a league away, were galloping towards them.

They were pursued, and the race for life began.

On they rode for hour after hour towards those hills that scarcely seemed to grow more near. Very strong were their horses and well accustomed to these sandy plains over which they swept at a long and steady gallop. Yet the way was far, also for days already they had been ridden across the desert, and that morning they had swum a wide stretch of rapid water, whereas those of the Shepherd troops were fresh from the stable. Still throughout the burning heat of the day those horses held their own, and when it drew towards evening and at length that pass in the mountains was at hand, still they held their own. Yes, parched with thirst, panting, thin-bellied, still they held their own. Long ago most of the Shepherds had fallen out and vanished, so that when at length the pass was reached, not a score of them remained, men who had remounted upon led horses when those they rode were foundered. But now these were hard upon their prey; scarce a bowshot behind indeed.

Khian and his company stumbled up the pass, for the horses, both of the pursued and the pursuers, had ceased to gallop and at the best could but amble forward Yet step by step the pursuers gained upon the pursued. The sides of that pass were very steep and the pathway was very narrow; one horse filled it all and therefore they must ride one following the other.

Suddenly at a turn in the road, when the first of the

Shepherds was scarcely more than fifty paces away, that Arab or Babylonian, or Brother of the Dawn, whichever he might be, who was pleased to give himself the name of Fire, turned and shouted an order. Thereon the last of those four brethren, he who was called Water, dismounted and with drawn sword took his stand at the turn of the narrow path, while his weary horse followed its fellows, as by certain words and signs he bade it do. Presently those of the party of Khian heard the sound of clashing arms behind them, followed by silence. Then a while later the pursuers appeared again, only whereas there had seemed to be fourteen of them now but eleven could be counted.

Once more they gained, once more they drew near, whereon he who was named Fire shouted a second order, and that brother of his called Air dismounted in another narrow place, leaving a second horse without a rider to follow in the train. Again there was a sound of clashing arms, and, when the pursuers reappeared, there were but nine of them. As before, they gained, and as before, at a narrow place the word of command rang out and the third of the brethren, he who was called Earth, dismounted, waiting. Followed the clash of arms and the shoutings, and when the pursuers reappeared there were but six of them. They gained, they came very near, whereon at a chosen place the first of the brethren, he who was named Fire, halted and leapt from his horse, which he drove forward as the others had done.

"Ride on, Lord," he cried. "Should the god we worship give me strength and skill, for you there is yet a hope of safety. Ride on and forget not the message I gave you by the water."

"Nay," answered Khian wearily, for his head swam and scarce he knew what passed about him. "Nay, here I stay to die with you. Let Temu, who understands nothing, deliver your message."

"Begone, Lord!" cried Fire. "Would you put me to shame and cause me to fail in my trust, making my name a hissing and a reproach? Begone or I fall upon my sword before your eyes."

Then as Khian still stayed swaying in the saddle, that most gallant man called some secret word to the horse he rode and the beast, understanding, stumbled onwards at a trot, nor could Khian stay it.

Once more there came the clash of arms and the sound of shoutings, and presently Khian, looking back, saw that of the pursuers but three remained. He urged his horse but it could do no more. Almost at the crest of the pass it whinnied and stood still.

The three struggled on grimly, for they were afoot, having left their spent beasts behind them. They were strong, soldier-like men, black with dust and sweat, and one of them had been wounded for blood ran down his face and robe, he who seemed to be an officer.

"We are commanded to take you dead or living, Prince Khian, for so you are. Shall we slay you or will you yield?" asked this man hoarsely.

Now when he heard these words Khian's spirit came back to him, and with it some of his lost strength.

"Neither," he answered in a low voice.

Then, changing his sword from the right hand to the left, from his belt he snatched his short javelin and hurled it with all his strength. The officer saw it coming and shrank aside, but in that narrow place it caught the man who stood behind him, piercing him through from breast to back, so that he fell down and died. Then the officer sprang at him and they fought with swords, a well-matched pair, though both were very weary, while the third man who could not come at Khian strove to drag the javelin from the breast of him who had fallen. The officer smote, somewhat wildly, perhaps the blood from his wound had run into his eyes. Khian parried, then bending himself, thrust forward and upward with all his strength, a trick of swordsmanship that he had learned in the Syrian wars. The bronze blade caught the officer in the throat just beneath the chin, and piercing to the neck bone, severed it, so that down he went like a stunned ox, in his fall twisting the sword from Khian's sweating hand. Then it was that the third man, having recovered the javelin, cast it at him, though with no good aim, for it struck him, not in the body, but above the left knee, piercing the leg from front to back.

Khian reeled against the rocky side of the pass, supporting himself there, helpless and unarmed. He who had cast the spear, seeing his state, rushed at him. Perhaps he hoped to take him living, or perhaps he, too, had lost his weapons. At least he seized him with his hands whereon Khian fell backward to the ground with the man above him. Now those hands had him by the throat and were choking the life out of him.

"All is finished," thought Khian.

It was then, just as his senses were leaving him, that he heard the sound of running feet and of a voice crying:

"Faith! Have faith!"

Next there followed the thud of a heavy blow and the grip upon his throat loosened. He lay still, regaining his breath, then sat up and looked about him. There at his side lay the soldier, dead, his head broken like a crushed egg, while over him stood the tall Temu, holding in both hands a great smooth stone.

"None of them will move any more," said Temu in the voice of one who marvels. "Who would have thought that I should live to kill a man in such a fashion, I, a Brother of the Dawn sworn to shed no blood? My brain swam; cooked in the sun; my mind was almost gone; that accursed horse—oh! may I never see another horse—jolted on with me, when I heard a noise, looked over my shoulder, and saw. I could not stop the horse, so I slid over its tail and ran back towards you. I had no weapon—I think I lost the sword in the river; at least, when I looked for it there was nothing but the scabbard. Still I ran, praying, and as I prayed, my eye fell upon that stone. I think that the holy Roy must have sent it there from Heaven. I picked it up and brought it down upon the head of that man of blood, as I used to bring down a flail on corn, and my arms being still strong—well, you see, Brother, the stroke was great and well aimed."

"Very well aimed, most excellent Temu," answered Khian faintly. "Now, if you can, pull this bronze out of my leg, for it pains me."

Temu pulled with goodwill and Khian fainted.

When he came to his mind again, it was to see himself surrounded by tall square-bearded warriors clad in the Babylonian uniform, one of whom supported his head upon his knee and poured water down his throat from a gourd.

"Have no fear, Lord," said the soldier. "We are friends who were warned that fugitives might reach us from Egypt and hearing sounds of war ran towards them, though little we thought to find you thus. Now we will bear you to our camp beyond the pass, there to recover of your wound."

Then Khian fainted again, for he had lost much blood. Yet they carried him to the camp where he was doomed to lie for many a day, for his hurt festered so that he could not be moved and it was thought that he must lose his leg. Moreover, this camp was beleagured by desert men in the pay of Apepi so that escape from it was impossible.

CHAPTER XX

The March from Babylon

Long must Nefra wait in that scented palace at Babylon before the great army, gathered to set her on her throne, was ready for its work. From all parts of the vast empire troops must be collected, hillsmen and plainsmen and men from the borders of the sea; archers, drivers of chariots, infantry, spearsmen, and those who rode upon camels. Slowly they came together and then must be exercised and welded to a whole; also provisions and water for so huge a force must be provided, and companies sent forward with these and to prepare the road. Thus it came about that three full moons went by before ever the vanguard marched out of the brazen gates of Babylon.

To Nefra soon that city grew hateful. She loathed its pomps and ceremonies and its staring crowds. Its religion was not hers and, unlike her mother, to its gods she put up no prayer; indeed, scarcely could she bring herself to bow when her grandsire led her with him to rituals in its enormous terraced temples, she, the pupil of Roy and the Sister of the Dawn who was sworn to a purer faith.

The unending ceremonies of that ancient Court, the adulation accorded to its king, and even to her, his grand-daughter who was known to be a queen; the prostrations, the shouts of "May the King live for ever!" addressed to one who soon must die, wearied and revolted her. More-over, the confinement and the hot airlessness of the place where she could only move in palace courts or in formal gardens, told upon the spirits of this free daughter of the

252

desert, till Kemmah, watching her, noted that she turned from her food and grew pale and thin.

Lastly her spirit was tormented with fear and doubt. Through the secret service of the Brethren of the Dawn, news reached Babylon that the Prince Khian and the priest Temu had escaped from Tanis and repaired to the pyramids, whence they had again escaped towards Arabia, guided by certain men who had been deputed to aid them.

Then after a while came other news, namely, that both of them, together with those guides, had been cut off by Apepi's outposts beyond the borders of Egypt and either killed or taken captive, as it was thought the former, because the bodies of some of their company were reported to have been seen. After this there was silence which, had Nefra but known it, was not strange.

When the Shepherd captain of the border fort learned that those whom he had been commanded to watch for and snare had slipped from his hand, and having killed certain of his people, had, it was believed, reached the Babylonian outpost in the hills alive, although he did not dare to attack that outpost, which was very strongly placed, first because he had not sufficient strength, and secondly because, in a time of truce, it would be an open act of war upon Babylon for which he had no warrant, still he surrounded it with skirmishers with orders to kill or capture any who set foot on the desert roads. Thus it came about that when messengers were sent bearing news that Khian lay sick and wounded at this camp, they were cut off. Thrice this chanced, and when at last, owing to the recall of the skirmishers at the opening of the war, a letter came in safety to Babylon, the army had marched already by another road to attack Egypt, and with it Nefra and the Brethren of the Dawn. Therefore the letters must be sent after it and never came to Nefra's hands till she was far upon her path.

Meanwhile, when first she heard these rumours at Babylon telling her that Khian was dead or captured, her heart seemed to break within her. For a while she sat silent with a face of stone. Then she bade Kemmah bring Tau to her and when he had come, said to him:

"You have heard, my uncle. Khian is dead."

"No, Niece, I have heard a report that he may be dead or captured."

"If Roy were alive he would tell us the truth, he whose soul could see afar," said Nefra bitterly. "But he is gone and only men remain whose eyes are set upon the ground and whose hearts are filled with matters of the world."

"As it seems that yours is, Niece. Yet Roy being dead, leaving me, all unworthy in his place, still speaks. Did he not tell you that however great your troubles, you and Khian would come together at the last, and was the holy Roy an utterer of empty prophecies?"

"Aye, he said that, but he to whom flesh and spirit were much the same, may have meant that we should come together in the Underworld. Oh! why did you ever suffer the Prince to return to the Court at Tanis? Although I could not say it, it was my desire that he should bide with us at the pyramids. Then he might have fled safely with us to Babylon and by now, perchance, we should have been wed."

"Or perchance other things would have happened, Niece. If any knew the decrees of Heaven, that man was Roy, and he held that believing his honour to be at stake, the Prince, his embassy accomplished, must be allowed to follow his desire and make report to Apepi his father. So he departed to fulfil his mission, and since then matters have not gone so ill for you."

"I think that they have gone very ill," she said stubbornly.

"How so, Niece? We know through our spies that the Prince and the priest Temu escaped from Tanis and came to the pyramids where they lay hid a while. We know also that by the help of those high-born warrior brethren of our Order whom I deputed to the task, they escaped,

again from the pyramids and fled safely out of Egypt.
It seems that they were followed and that there was fighting
in which it well may be that those brethren, or some of
them, lost their lives, as they were sworn to do. If so,
peace be to their gallant spirits. But of the death of the
Prince, or even of Temu, there is no certain word, nor,'' he
added slowly, "does a dream or voice tell me or any of us
that he is dead."

"As it would have told Roy," interrupted Nefra.

"As mayhap it would have told Roy, and as mayhap
Roy, being still living though elsewhere, would have told
me who fill his office. Niece, be not so rough-tongued and
ungrateful. Have not all things happened according to
your desire? Has not the royal Ditanah, my father, given
you a great army to set you on your throne? Has he not
at your prayer, and, as I can tell you now, at mine made
in secret, abandoned his policy of wedding you to his heir,
Mir-bel, and sent that prince far from Babylon to where he
cannot molest you? Has he not—though this has been
hid from you—set me in command of that army, that it
may be handled according to your desire and mine, putting
trust in me that when its work is done, I will lay down my
generalship and from a mighty prince of war once more
become a priest, I, who were I evil-hearted might use it to
set the crown upon my head?"

"It seems that he has done all these things, Uncle, but
what of them if Khian be dead? Then I seek no throne;
then I seek nothing but a grave. Nay, first I seek vengeance. I tell you that of Apepi and his Shepherds I will
not leave one living, of his cities not one stone shall remain
upon another."

"Kind words from a Sister of the Dawn, and from her
one of whose titles is Uniter of Lands—not their destroyer!"
exclaimed Tau, shrugging his shoulders, and adding, "O
Child, do you not understand that all life is a trial and
that as we pass the trials, so we shall be rewarded or condemned? You are mad with fear for one whom you love,

and therefore I do not blame you overmuch, though I think that you will live to grieve over those fierce threats."

"You are right. I am mad, and being mad, I will cause others to drink of my cup of fear and sorrows, that cup in which they have mixed the wine. Send Ru to me, my Uncle, that although I be woman he may teach me how to fight. And bid those Babylonian smiths come measure me for armour of the best."

Then Tau departed, smiling. Still he sent Ru and with him came the royal armourer.

So it happened that soon, had there been any to look over the wall of a certain courtyard of the palace, a strange sight might have been seen of a lissom maid clad in silver mail cutting and thrusting at a huge black giant, who often enough cried out beneath the smart of her blows, and once, stung beyond endurance, smote her so shrewdly on the helm with the flat of a wooden sword that she fell headlong to the ground, only to spring up again, while he stood dismayed, and deal him such a thrust beneath the breast bone, that his breath left him and he did likewise. Yes, there he lay, grunting out between his gasps:

"The gods help Apepi if this lion's whelp gets him in her claws!" while she bade him be silent because by all the laws of swordsmanship he was dead.

At other times she would practise shooting with a bow, an art in which she had no small skill, or when she wearied of this, at the driving of chariots in the private circus of the palace, taking with her one of the slave women, a bold, desert-bred girl, for passenger, because Ru was too heavy and Kemmah said that she was mad and refused to come.

"So you thought when I began to climb the pyramids, yet they served me my turn, Nurse," she answered, and went on driving more furiously than ever woman drove before.

Now when her grandsire, the old King Ditanah, heard of these things, he was amazed, and caused himself to be hidden in places whence he could watch her secretly at her

warlike exercises. Having done so and listened to the tale
of her conquest of the pyramids, he sent for Tau and said
to him with a curious smile upon his puckered face:

"I think, Son Abeshu, that I should have given the command of my great army, not to you who, if once a great
warrior, have become a priest, but to this granddaughter of
mine who, if once a priestess, has become a goddess of war."

"Nay, Sire," answered Tau, "for if you gave her that
army, you would never get it back again. Every man in it
would learn to love her and she would use it to conquer
the world."

"Well, why not?" asked Ditanah, and hobbled away,
thinking in his heart that if it had truly pleased the gods
to take the Prince Khian to their bosom, so that Mir-bel
might be recalled to Court, his tears would be hard to weep.
For with such a beauteous and royal-hearted lady for its
queen and that of Egypt, surely the glory of Babylon would
fill earth and Heaven. Indeed—was it too late? Then he
remembered that on this matter he had passed his royal
word, sighed, and hobbled on.

These martial exercises served Nefra in two ways: they
gave her back her health which she had begun to lose in
the soft life of the Babylonian palace and they held her
mind from brooding upon its fears—that is, while she was
engaged in them. Yet at night these returned to her, nor
indeed were they ever quite absent from her thoughts. She
importuned Tau, and even her grandsire the King, who
caused search to be made all along the Egyptian frontier
of his empire. Messages came back from the searchers
that no traces of fugitives could be found. But among
them was another message, namely, that certain hills could
not be approached because they were watched by horsemen
of the army of Apepi. Inquiry was made as to these hills,
and it was found that in a camp among them were stationed
a company of Babylonian troops from which no reports
had been received of late. Therefore, as often happened

in so vast an empire, for a while this outpost had been forgotten by that general in whose command it lay, or if remembered at all, it was supposed to have been overwhelmed by rebellious, desert-dwelling tribes.

When Tau heard this news he went to the King his father and gained leave from him to send a hundred picked horsemen to disperse the outposts of Apepi and search those hills; also he set spies to work. But of this business he said nothing to Nefra, fearing lest he should fill her with false hope.

At length the vast army that had been gathered in the military camps upon the banks of the Euphrates beyond the walls of Babylon was ready to advance, two hundred thousand foot-soldiers and horsemen, a thousand or more of chariots, countless camp followers, and a multitude of camels and asses bearing provisions, besides those which were already stacked at the water holes along the line of march.

Then came Nefra's farewell to Babylon. In state, wearing the crown of Egypt, she visited the Sepulchre of Kings and in its temple laid offerings upon her mother's grave. This duty done, at the Court in the great hall of the palace she bade farewell to her grandsire, Ditanah the Great King, who blessed her, wished her well, and even wept a little at parting from her whom he could never hope to see again; also because he was too old to accompany his son upon this war. With Tau also, now clad in the armour of a General and Prince of Babylon, and looking like one who had never felt the rubbing of a monk's robe, he conversed apart, saying sadly:

"Strange lots are ours, beloved son. Many years ago we were dear to each other. Then we quarrelled, more through my fault than yours, for in those days my heart was hard, and you went your way to become a priest of some pure and gentle faith, and your heirship was given to another. Now for a little hour you are once more a Prince

and a General commanding a great host, who yet purpose,
if you live, to lay down these ranks and titles and, your
mission ended, again to seek some desert cell and wear out
your days in prayer.   And, I the King of Kings, your father,
remain here awaiting death that soon must overtake me,
and oh! I wonder, Son Abeshu, which of us has chosen the
better lot and done more righteously in the eyes of God.
Yes, I wonder much from whom all these pomps and glories
flee away like shadows."

"There is a great taskmaster, Sire," answered Tau,
"who portions out to each of us his place and labours.
Man does not choose his lot; it is chosen for him, to work
for good or ill within its appointed round.   Such at least is
the teaching of my faith, believing which I seek no throne
or power, but am content to build on that foundation as
truly as· I may.   So let it be with you, my royal Father."

"Aye, Son, so let it be, since so it must be."

Then very tenderly they bade each other farewell and
parted to meet no more upon the earth, since when that
army returned to Babylon another King of Kings was seated
on the throne.

So by proclamation Babylon declared war upon the
Shepherds, who long before had learned that this storm was
about to burst upon them and were making ready to meet
it as best they might.

For very many days the great army marched across the
plains and deserts, as the progress of so vast a host was
slow, till at length it drew near to the borders of Egypt.
Then it was that Tau heard from his spies and skirmishers
that Apepi with all his strength, a mighty power, had built
a line of forts upon his boundary and in front of these was
preparing to give battle to the Babylonians.   These tidings
he took to Nefra who sat in her chariot armed in glittering
mail like some young war goddess, surrounded by a body-
guard under the command of Ru.

"It is well," she answered indifferently.   "The sooner
we fight the sooner it will be over and the sooner I shall be

avenged upon the Shepherds of the blood of him whom I have lost." For having received no tidings of Khian, now she had become almost sure that he was dead.

"Do not run to meet evil, Niece," said Tau sadly. "Is there not enough of it at hand that you must go to seek out more? Have I not told you that I believe the Prince to be alive?"

"Then where is he, Uncle? How comes it that you under whose command is all the might of Babylon cannot spare some few thousands to seek him out?"

"Perchance I am seeking, Niece," Tau answered gently.

As he spoke a slave ran up, saying:

"Letters from the King of Kings! Letters from Babylon!" and having touched his forehead with the roll, he gave it to Tau who opened and read. Within was another roll, a little crumpled roll such as might have been hidden in a headdress or a shoe.

Tau glanced at the contents of this second roll and gave it to Nefra.

"A writing for you, Niece," he said quietly.

Seizing it, she read. It was brief and ran thus:

"Again, O Lady, a certain one whose name you may guess writes to say that save for a hurt to his leg which cripples him he is well in health. This he does because he has learned that the enemies who surround the place where he lies may have cut off former messengers. Should he who bears this come safely to you at Babylon or elsewhere, he will tell you all. More I dare not write.

"Signed with the sign of the Dawn which you yourself taught me how to shape."

Nefra finished reading, then fell rather than leapt from the chariot into the arms of Tau.

"He lives!" she gasped. "Or he lived. Where is the messenger?"

As she spoke the words a guard appeared escorting an officer who was travel-stained and weary.

"One who craves audience with you, Prince Abeshu, and at once," said the leader of the guard.

Tau looked at the officer and knew him again.   It was he whom the King had sent from Babylon to search for the missing outpost.

"Your report," he said, and waited with fear in his heart.

"Prince," answered the man, saluting, "we won through to the outpost and found all well there, since it is so strongly placed that the Shepherd skirmishers have not dared attack. Also we found those travellers who were missing."

Again Nefra paled and leaned against the chariot, for she could not speak.

"What of them?" asked Tau.

"Prince, the priest is well.   Four brethren who travelled with them were slain one by one in a certain pass; they died nobly defending those in their charge.   The lord whose name is not spoken, who escaped with the priest, is still sick, that is, he is wounded in the left knee and the wound runs. He cannot walk, and though now it is believed that his leg will be saved, always he must be lame, for the knee is stiff."

"Did you see him?" asked Tau.

"Yes, Prince, I and another of my company saw him. While the rest of us, pretending to retreat, drew off the Shepherds horsemen, we two won our way to the camp which is on a plain surrounded by hills, not to be reached except through two passes, one to the west and one to the east. There we found the garrison, well though weary, for of food they have enough, also the priest and the other traveller who is hurt.   These told us how they came to the place and of the death of their four guides, which is a great story."

"Then repeat it afterwards," said Tau.   "It seems that you escaped.   Why did you not bring these travellers with you?"

"Prince, how could the two of us carry a man who cannot walk, down a mountain path, even with the help of the priest?   Moreover, if we could have brought him to the

plain, it was full of enemies all mounted on good horses
through whom it would scarcely have been possible to bear
him safely, while the garrison had received no orders to
attempt to leave its post. Therefore it was determined
that he should remain where he is safe enough, until a sufficient force could be sent to bring him away."

Then the captain went on to tell how he and his companion had rejoined their men at night and fought their way
through the horsemen of Apepi who watched the stronghold,
though with loss; how also they had learned from some
desert wanderers that the army of the Great King was
marching upon Egypt by a road that ran not more than
thirty leagues from where they were, and how therefore
they had ridden for the army, instead of returning to report
at Babylon.

"You have done wisely," said Tau. "Had you attempted to bring that wounded lord with you, doubtless he
would have been killed or captured."

Then he went away to give certain orders, leaving the
officer with Nefra, who had many questions to put to him.

When Tau returned an hour later Nefra was still question-
ing him. Tau looked at them and asked:

"Friend, how long is it since you slept?"

"Four nights, Prince," answered the officer.

"And how long is it since you and your companions ate?"

"Forty-eight hours, Prince. Indeed, if we might crave
a cup of water and a bite of bread, who have ridden hard
and done some fighting——"

"These await you, Captain, when it pleases her Majesty
of Egypt to dismiss you."

Then Nefra reddened and turned away ashamed. When
the men had gone to eat and rest, humbly enough she asked
Tau what was his plan.

"My plan is, Niece, to send five thousand mounted men,
though we can ill spare them, to clear the desert between
this place and the stronghold where he who was named the
Scribe Rasa lies wounded—*not* dead, as you feared, Niece,

and to bring him with our brother Temu and the garrison
of the camp to join the army on its march which, travelling
in a chariot or a litter, he should do within some six days."

"A good plan," said Nefra, clapping her hands. "I will
go with the five thousand and in command of them. Kemmah can accompany me."

"No, Niece, you shall not go. You stay here with the
army."

"Shall not! Shall not!" exclaimed Nefra, biting her lip
as was her fashion when crossed. "Why?"

"For many reasons, Niece, of which the first is that it
would not be safe. We cannot tell how many troops Apepi
has between here and that stronghold, but we know he
would risk much to capture his son now that the great war
has begun; also the Lady Kemmah could not bear such a
journey."

"If it is not safe for me who am sound and well, neither
is it safe for Khian who is wounded, and if things be thus,
then let the whole army turn and march to the stronghold."

"It cannot be, Niece. This army is a trust placed in
my hands and its business is to push on and give battle to
Apepi, not to wander away into the desert where perhaps
it may be overcome by thirst or other disasters."

"Cannot be! I say it must be, my Uncle, I, the Queen
of Egypt, desire it; it is an order."

Tau looked at her in his calm fashion and answered:

"This army is under my command, not yours, Niece,
and having put on armour the Queen of Egypt is but one
officer among thousands," and he touched her shining mail.
"Therefore I must pray even the Queen of Egypt to obey
me. Or if that is not enough, I must pray Nefra, a Sister
of the Dawn, to accept the word of the Prophet of the Dawn
without question, as she is sworn to do. The safety of the
Queen of Egypt is much, as is the safety of the Prince Khian.
But the safety and the triumph of the great host of the
King of Kings are more."

Nefra heard and was about to answer furiously, for her

high spirit was aflame. Yet there was that on the strong face and in the quiet eyes of Tau that stilled her words before they were uttered. She looked at him a while, then burst into tears and, turning, departed to her tent.

Next morning at the dawn the five thousand horsemen with certain chariots, guided by that officer and others who had brought tidings, departed to rescue Khian and his companions from the stronghold where he was imprisoned.

CHAPTER XXI

Traitor or Hero

The Babylonian host marched on and came in safety to the borders of Egypt, the mightiest host perhaps that ever had invaded the Land of Nile. There it encamped, protected in front by water, to rest and prepare before it attacked Apepi encamped with all his strength some three leagues away around the forts that he had built. The captains of the Shepherds, riding out, saw with their own eyes how terrible and numberless, how well-ordered also, was the army of the King of Kings with its horsemen, its chariots, its camelry, its footmen, and its archers that seemed to stretch for miles; no Eastern mob but disciplined and trained to war. . They saw and trembled, and returning, made report to Apepi at his Council.

"Let Pharaoh hearken!" they said. "For every man we muster, the Babylonians have two under the command of the Prince Abeshu who is reported to be a great general, though some say that he was once a priest and a magician. The spies tell also that with them marches the Princess Nefra, daughter of Kheperra, she who slipped through Pharaoh's fingers and is affianced to Pharaoh's son, who also slipped through his fingers and, if he lives, is hidden we know not where, unless he, too, be with the Babylonians. It is impossible that Pharaoh can stand against such a host as this, which will overrun the land like locusts and devour us like corn."

Apepi heard and rage took hold of him, so that he gnawed at his beard. Suddenly he turned to Anath, the old Vizier, saying:

"You have heard what these cravens say. Now do you give me your counsel, you who are cunning as a jackal that has often escaped the trap. What shall I do?"

Anath turned aside and spoke with certain other of his fellow councillors. Then he came and bowed before Apepi and said:

"Life! Blood! Strength! O Pharaoh! Such wisdom as the gods have given us bids us urge Pharaoh, as do the diviners who have consulted with their spirits, not to join battle but to make peace with Babylon before it is too late."

"Is it so?" asked Apepi. "What terms then can I offer to the King of Babylon, who comes to seize Egypt and add it to his empire?"

"We think, Pharaoh," answered Anath, "that Ditanah does not desire to take Egypt. We have heard from those who serve Pharaoh in secret at Babylon, that Ditanah is bewitched by Nefra the Beautiful. It seems that when those wizards of the Dawn, through help of their magic arts, escaped to Babylon, they took with them the body of the Queen Rima, the widow of King Kheperra. The tale runs that the coffin of Queen Rima was opened before the King of Kings, and that at the bidding of the Princess Nefra and of the head wizards of the Dawn, the body of Rima or the ghost of Rima spoke to Ditanah who begat it, bidding him to attack Egypt or bear the curse of the dead. It bade him also to give Nefra in marriage, not to his grandson and heir, Mir-bel, but to the son of your Majesty, the Prince Khian, to whom she became affianced yonder by the pyramids, and to send a great army to avenge the death of her husband, Kheperra, and her own wrongs by casting your Majesty from the throne and setting the Princess Nefra and the Prince Khian in your place. Moreover, the royal Rima, or her spirit, said to Ditanah, King of Kings, that if he neglected to do her bidding, he and his country should be everlastingly accursed, but if he obeyed, her blessings should come upon them. Therefore because of the words of dead Rima, his daughter, and because of the spells laid upon him by the Princess Nefra and the wizards of the Dawn, Ditanah has sent this army against your Majesty to fulfil the commands of Rima upon you and upon the people of the Shepherds."

"What then must I do to turn aside the wrath of this Babylonian?" asked Apepi of the Vizier, glaring at him.

"That which the King of Kings demands, or so it seems, O Pharaoh—wed the Prince Khian, if he still lives and can be found, to the royal Nefra and give up to them the Crowns of the Upper and the Lower Lands."

"Is this your counsel, Vizier?"

"Who am I and who are we that we should dare to show a path to be trodden by the feet of Pharaoh?" asked Anath, cringing before his master. "Yet, if he takes another and these captains are right, perchance soon there will be a new Pharaoh, and if the Prince Khian be dead, as some believe, the People of the Shepherds will be driven from the Nile back into the desert whence they came centuries ago —and the King of Kings, or the Princess Nefra under him, will rule Egypt."

Now Apepi leapt to his feet roaring with rage and with the wand-like sceptre that he carried smote Anath on the head so hard that the blood came and the Vizier fell to his knees.

"Dog!" he cried, "speak more such words and you shall die a traitor's death beneath the whips. Long have I suspected that you were in the pay of Babylon and now I grow sure of it. So I am to surrender my throne and take Ditanah for my lord, and should he still live, give the woman whom I had chosen for my wife to be the queen of the son who has betrayed me. First will I see Egypt devoured by fire and sword and perish with her. Out of my sight, you white-hearted cur!"

Anath waited for no more. Yet when he turned at the doorway to make the customary obeisance, though Apepi could not see it in the shadow, there was a very evil look upon his face.

"Struck!" he murmured to himself. "I the great officer, I, the Vizier, struck before the Council and the servants! Well, if Apepi has a staff I have a sword. Now come on, Babylon! I must to my work. Oh! Khian, where are you?"

Apepi, the Pharaoh of the North, dismissed his councillors and his generals and sat in the chamber of the fort that he had built, brooding and alone. Although often he was possessed by that devil of rage who sleeps so lightly in the breasts of tyrants, also by other passions, he was a far-seeing statesman and a good general, having inherited from his forefathers the gifts by help of which they had conquered Egypt. Thus he knew that Anath, the old Vizier, the clearest and most cunning thinker in the land, was right when he told him that he could not stand against all the strength of Babylon, drilled and martialled as never it had been before, and marching under the guidance of those wizards of the Dawn who had escaped him, leaving behind them their high priest to lay upon him ere he died the curse of the oath-breaker and the seeker of innocent blood. Yet for telling him this truth he had offered public insult to Anath, smiting him as he would a slave, such insult as the old noble and officer in whose veins, it was said, ran the pure blood of Egypt, never would forget.

Would it not be better, then, to follow the blow on the head with a thrust to the heart and to have done with Anath? Nay, it was not safe; he was too powerful, he had too many in his pay. They might rise against him, now when all complained at being forced into a war they hated; they might destroy him as they believed he had destroyed his son, Prince Khian, whom they loved. He must send for Anath and crave pardon for what he had done when beside himself with rage and doubt, promising him great atonement and more honours, and biding his time to balance their account.

Yet could he accept this Anath's counsel, and to save his

life and the shattering of the Shepherds' power, bow his neck beneath the yoke of Babylon? What did it mean? That he must abandon his throne and in favour of Khian if he still lived, of Khian, who had stolen from him the woman upon whose beauty he had set his heart, and sent her to call up the Babylonian hordes against him, his king and father. Or if Khian were dead, then this Nefra, Queen of the South and indeed of all Egypt by right of blood, would take that throne as the vassal of Babylon and doubtless wed its heir. Therefore what could he gain by surrender? One thing only—to live on in exile as a private man, eating out his heart with memories of the glory of the past and watching the Egyptians and their great ally stamp upon the Shepherd race.

It was not to be borne. If he must fall, it should be fighting as his forefathers would have done. How could he succeed against so mighty a foe? Not in a set battle; there they would overwhelm him, or if he kept to the walls of his forts, surround them and sweep on to capture Egypt. Yet generalship and craft might still give him victory. He had it; he would send all his best horsemen, twenty thousand or more of them of the old fighting Shepherd blood, to make a circuit in the desert and fall upon the rear of the Babylonians as they advanced to give battle, which doubtless according to their custom they would do while it was still dark, in order that they might attack in the uncertain light of dawn. By some such unexpected thrust their array might be confused and broken, so that he would have to deal not with an army, but with a mob. At least since no other offered, the plan should be tried.

The five thousand despatched by Tau came safely to the stronghold in the hills, and reported themselves and their mission to the captain of the outpost, and to his wounded guest whom all knew to be the Prince Khian, though none called him by that name. Khian heard their tale and grew faint with joy when he learned that the great army of Babylon was near to him and that with it, safe and sound, was Nefra his beloved, as a writing in her own hand told him. Sad and heavy had been his long confinement in this place, crippled as he was, but now at length the night of fear and waiting had passed away and there in front of him burned the dawn of joy.

Until the following morning the five thousand rested themselves and their horses; then, taking with them the garrison of the outpost who were glad enough to bid it good-bye, they started to rejoin the Babylonian army that they had planned to meet at a certain spot on the frontier of Egypt. In the centre of their array, in a chariot because he could not ride, went Khian, followed by Temu in another chariot because he would not ride, having sworn an oath, unless Fate forced him, never to mount another horse.

So they passed on safely across the desert, for Apepi's skirmishers who had hemmed them in for so long had vanished away. They could not travel fast because of the soldiers of the garrison who must march on foot; indeed their progress was so slow that Khian, who was on fire to rejoin Nefra, wished to gallop on to the Babylonian army escorted only by a few horsemen. But this the officer in command of the five thousand would not suffer, having been strictly charged by Tau, who foresaw that such a thing might happen, to keep him who was called the Scribe Rasa safe in the heart of his force. In vain did Khian plead. Those, said the officer, were his orders and he must obey them.

On the third afternoon of their march, they learned from desert men that they drew near to the Babylonian host which was encamped over against the forts that Apepi had built. As it was still too far away to be reached that night and those on foot were very weary, its general halted the five thousand to eat and rest at a place where there was water, giving orders that the force was to march again at midnight by the light of the setting moon, which, if all went well, should bring them to the army shortly after dawn.

This plan was carried out. At midnight they broke camp and went forward through the hot desert air by the light of the half moon. When they had marched for about two hours Temu caused his chariot to be brought alongside that of Khian, and though the Prince was somewhat silent, talked on to him after his fashion, for none guessed that on the farther side of a certain rise of ground the five and twenty thousand horsemen whom Apepi had despatched to fall upon the flank of the Babylonians were creeping towards them purposing to attack the camp of the great army at the first break of dawn. Why should it be guessed, seeing that outposts rode ahead of them to give warning of any danger? How could they know that those outposts had been surrounded and captured or killed, when as they thought they were riding into the fringe of the host of Babylon, thus giving the Shepherds warning of the approach of foes?

"Brother," said Temu, "during all this while you have been very impatient, complaining of your wound which will get quite well in time, though it may leave you stiff-legged and lame for life, complaining because you were kept yonder in the hills, instead of thanking the gods that you ever reached them safely by help of those rough-tongued but courageous Arab brethren who gave themselves fanciful names, for which faults as your elder in our Order I have often reproved you, saying that like myself you should have faith. Now you see the end of it, namely, that faith has triumphed as it always does. Within an hour or two we shall reach the mighty host of Babylon and make obeisance to Tau, the Prophet of the Dawn. All our troubles are ended, or rather all your troubles, since because of faith *I* never doubted but that they would melt away——"

At this moment Temu himself melted away, for a javelin or an arrow pierced his charioteer through the heart so that the man fell dead on to the flanks of the horses, causing them to start forward at full gallop in their fright, and charging through the ranks to vanish at speed into the desert, while Temu clung to the chariot rail and grasped wildly

at the reins. The horses were good horses, being indeed
two of those that had borne them on their gallop from the
water to the hills, now fat and strong again. They rushed
on up the rise; they came among the Shepherd troops where
the line was thin, they broke through it unharmed, being
scarcely seen in the dim light before they were gone. They
galloped on across the sands, smelling other horses ahead of
them, or perchance it was water that they smelt. At least
they rushed on while Temu, flung to the bottom of the
chariot, dragged at the reins in vain. That is, he dragged
once or twice, then let them be, muttering:

"Faith! Have faith! These accursed beasts must go
where Fate drives them, and I see no more soldiers."

Presently, however, he saw plenty, for now the chariot,
heedless of the challenges of the sentries, was rushing down
the central avenue of the Babylonian camp. At length
the feet of one of the horses became entangled in the ropes
of a tent, so that it fell, bringing down its companion with
it, and Temu rolled on to the ground in front of a general
who was giving orders to some officer.

"Who is this?" asked the General testily, "and what does
that chariot here? Take it away."

Then Temu, knowing the voice, sat up and said:

"O Holy Prophet, as I understand that you are now that
Roy is dead, O Father Tau, that is, if a Prophet and Father
of the Dawn can be clad in armour which is against all the
rules, I am Temu, a priest of your Brotherhood, as you may
remember, for it was you who sent me on a certain business
to the Court of Apepi, King of the North, since which time
I have suffered many things."

"I remember you, Brother," said Tau. "But whence
come you in this chariot, and why?"

"I do not know, Prophet. One moment I was talking
to him who is called the Scribe Rasa, with whom I have
shared many adventures, but who, I think, has another
name, and the next my charioteer pitched forward with a
missile through his breast, and those mad brutes of horses

on which he fell were dragging me away whither I knew not. All I know is that we passed through a host clad in such armour as the Shepherds use, for the moonlight shone upon it and upon Apepi's banners, which I knew well, for I saw enough of them at Tanis. Then the horses, directed of Heaven, came on here. And that is all the story."

"The Scribe Rasa!" exclaimed a woman's voice, that of Nefra who, seeing the fall of the horses, had come from her tent, accompanied by Ru, to learn its cause. "Where did you leave the Scribe Rasa, Priest?"

"Cease from questions, Niece," broke in Tau. "Can you not understand that the force we sent some days ago to rescue a certain garrison has been ambushed and that by some accident this brother has escaped to bring us tidings. Or perchance," he added, as a thought struck him, "Apepi's army has moved from its defences to attack us from the south presently when the sun rises."

Then he gave certain orders. Trumpets blew, captains ran up, men by the thousand, still yawning, took their appointed places; all the awakened camp burst into active martial life.

Meanwhile, not so very far away, a desperate battle raged. The five and twenty thousand of the Shepherds, attackers who thought themselves attacked, hurled themselves upon the five thousand Babylonians who had marched into their midst. The Babylonians, being alert and well officered, strove to cut a path through the Shepherds, aye, and did so, slowly, losing many men as they struggled forward. Squadrons rushed on them, dimly seen in the moonlight, and were beaten back. There was charge and countercharge. Horses screamed, men fell and groaned out their lives.

The moon grew dark, but still the battle went on in the twilight that precedes the dawn, when it was difficult to distinguish friend from foe. The light of day began to gather and by it the captain of the Babylonians saw that he could advance no more. Nor could he fly, for the cloud of

Apepi's Horse was all about him. Therefore he made a square of those who remained to him, perhaps two thousand or more sound men and many wounded, and gave orders that none must surrender, since this was a fight to the death for the honour of Babylon.

When Apepi's captains in the gathering light perceived with how small a body they had to do, they were dismayed who thought that all this while they had been attacking the flank of the Babylonian host in the darkness. And now the dawn had come and their opportunity was gone; they had failed in their mission and how could they face Apepi with such a tale? In the fighting they had seized prisoners, some of them wounded. Those men they questioned. Under threat of death by torment, or with beatings, from some of these they drew the truth that this was but a force of Babylonian skirmishers sent to relieve an outpost which they were bringing back with them to the army.

"Who, then, is the man that sits in a chariot among the horsemen?" asked Apepi's captain.

The prisoners answered that they did not know, whereon he ordered them to be flogged a while, and then repeated his question. Thus he learned that this lord in the chariot was none other than Khian the Prince whom he himself had been ordered to capture when he was escaping from Egypt, for though the prisoners gave only the name of Rasa the Scribe, well he knew that Rasa and Khian were the same man.

Then that captain saw light in the midst of a great darkness. He had failed, it was true; he had not fallen upon the flank of the army of Babylon at this hour of dawn, or thrown it into confusion and panic, as he had hoped to do, but instead had become engaged with a petty force of which the destruction would help Apepi not at all. But now he learned that with that force was one whose capture would mean as much, or more, to Apepi as a great slaughter of the Babylonians. Instantly he made up his

mind; he would not try to attack the army of the great
King; it was too late. No, he would destroy these horsemen
and take the Prince Khian, living or dead, as an offering to
Apepi, hoping thus to assuage his wrath.

Instantly he gave orders and the attack began. Being
mounted, neither side had bows and now javelins were few.
Therefore the fray must be fought out with swords. The
Babylonians had picketed their horses in the centre of the
square or given them to the wounded there to hold, turning
themselves into foot-soldiers. Moreover, by command of
their general, with hands and stones and cooking vessels
they were heaping the desert sands into a bank which, with
two thousand men or more labouring at it for their lives,
rose as though by magic, for the sand was soft and easy to
handle. At this bank the Shepherds charged from every
side. But the Babylonian square, set on the crest of a
desert sand wave, was small, for its general had drawn up
his men three deep, each line standing behind the other.
Therefore only a few of the clouds of Apepi's horsemen could
come at them at once, and at these the Babylonians stabbed
with their swords, or cut at the horses' legs as they scrambled up the sand slopes, laming them, or causing them to
scream in agony and rush away.

Soon Apepi's captain saw that victory would be slow,
which fitted his plans but ill. Every moment he was in fear
lest the outposts of the great army should discover what
was passing not so very far away and send out a mighty
force to destroy him. He feared also that the wounded
man in the chariot whom he guessed to be the Prince Khian
might be killed in the fighting, whereas he desired to take
him living to Apepi. Lastly he feared that even if he were
not attacked, soon he and his horsemen would be cut off
from Egypt and driven back into the desert, to perish there
of thirst and hunger. Therefore, ceasing from his onslaught, he sent officers under a flag of truce to the Babylonian general, charged to deliver this message:

"Your case is desperate since I outnumber you ten to one.

Surrender and in the name of Apepi I promise you your lives. Fight on and I will destroy you all."

The Babylonian heard, but being a crafty man, would give no immediate answer, for he, too, hoped that news of their plight would reach the great army either through messengers whom he had despatched when they were first attacked, or otherwise. Therefore desiring to gain time he replied that he must take counsel with his officers and presently would let their mind be known. He went to the centre of the square and coming to Khian, told him all.

"Now what shall we do?" he asked. "If we continue the fight, we must soon be overwhelmed. Yet surrender we cannot for the honour of Babylon; indeed, first will I fall upon my sword."

"It seems that you have answered your own question, General," replied Khian, smiling. "Yet here is my poor counsel. Offer to give me up, for you know well who I am and it is I whom they seek. I think that if you do this, that captain will let the rest of you go free."

Now even in his sore strait that general laughed aloud, saying:

"Have you bethought you, Prince, for since you have declared yourself I call you what you are, how I should be greeted by the Prince Abeshu, also named the Lord Tau, who commands the army of the Great King, and by a certain lady who marches with that army, if I return to tell them such a tale? Rather would I die, Prince, with honour upon the field, than shamed before all the host of Babylon. No, I have another plan. I will parley with these Shepherds as one who bargains, asking for the promise of safety in writing, and while I do so all must creep to their horses, taking the lightly wounded behind them and leaving the rest to fate. Then suddenly we will charge upon the Shepherds and, now that we have light, cut our way through or perish."

"So be it," said Khian, but in his heart were thoughts that his lips did not utter. He knew that such a charge made by weary men upon wearied horses could not succeed;

that if it were attempted all who remained alive of the
Babylonian horsemen would perish, together with those on
foot, among them his hosts of the mountain garrison, and
that the wounded would be slaughtered where they lay.
He was sure also that what the Shepherd captain wanted
was himself, not the lives of more Babylonian horsemen,
whose slaying or escape could make no difference to the
issue of the war, and that if he could secure that great
prize, he would turn and ride for Egypt. Therefore certainly it was laid upon him to offer up himself as a sacrifice.
He shivered at the thought, knowing that this meant death,
perhaps death by torture, at the hands of Apepi, and what
was worse, that never more after all that he had suffered
could he hope to look upon the face of Nefra beneath the
sun. Oh! he must choose, and choose at once.

Khian cast down his eyes and with all his soul prayed to
that Spirit whom he had learned to worship, that he might
find guidance in his agony. Lo! it seemed to come. It
seemed as though there amidst the stamp and neighs of
horses, the groans of the wounded, the orders of officers who,
having received the General's word, already were making
preparation for that last wild rush for life, he heard the
quiet, well-remembered voice of Roy, saying:

"My son, follow after duty, even down the road of sacrifice, and leave the rest to God."

Khian hesitated no longer. He was alone in the chariot,
for its driver had descended to give the horses the last
of the forage they carried with them and a sup of water that
remained, and stood at a distance watching them finish their
food as best they could, for the bits in their mouths ham-
pered them. He seized the reins, he smote the stallions with
the whip, and the beasts sprang forward.

Now they had come to the low bank of sand and were
scrambling over it, dragging the light war chariot after
them. Some fifty paces away and as many perhaps from
the first of Apepi's horsemen stood the General of the
Babylonians and one officer talking to the Captain of the

Shepherds, also accompanied by one officer, a man whom he knew well enough for they had served together in the Syrian wars. They had turned and did not see him coming or hear the chariot wheels on the soft sand. Apepi's captain had grown angry and cried in a loud voice:

"Hear my last offer. Give up to me the Prince Khian who is with you, and you and your soldiers may go free. Refuse, and I will kill you every one and take him, living or dead, to his father, Apepi the Pharaoh. Answer. I speak no more."

"*I* will answer," said Khian from the chariot, whereon they turned in amaze and stared. "I am the Prince Khian, and you, Friend, know me well. I, too, know you for a man of honour and accept your promise to let these Babylonians go their way unharmed, taking their wounded with them, and in payment I surrender myself to you. Is it sworn?"

"It is sworn, Prince," said the Captain, saluting. "Yet remember that Apepi is very wrath with your Highness," he added slowly, as though in warning.

"I remember," answered Khian. Then he turned to the Babylonian General, who all this while had stood like one transfixed, and said: "Say to the Lord Tau and to the Lady of Egypt that I have gone where my duty calls me and that if it be decreed that we should meet no more, I trust that they will not think ill of me, seeing that what seems false often is the truth and that sometimes ill deeds are done for good ends. For the rest, let them judge as they will of me, who follow my own light."

"Lord," exclaimed the General like one who wakes from sleep, "surely you do not desert us for the Shepherds?"

"Am I not a Shepherd?" asked Khian, smiling strangely. "Farewell, Friend. Good fortune go with you and your company, no drop of whose blood shall be shed for me."

Then he called to the horses and they went forward while the General wrung his hands and muttered the names of strange Babylonian gods.

"I do not understand your Highness," said Apepi's captain as he walked by the chariot back towards his horsemen, "which is not strange, since always you were different from other men, and I am wondering whether those Babylonians will write you down as a traitor or as a hero. Meanwhile, I who know you to be honest, ask your promise that even if you see opportunity you will not escape to them lest I should be forced to kill you."

"It is yours, Friend. Henceforth, like a certain Temu, I walk by faith, though whither faith has led him this day I do not know, who last saw him vanishing into the heart of your host."

"Mad!" muttered the Captain. "Still if he has lost his wits, he will keep his word, and that may save my head."

CHAPTER XXII

KHIAN RETURNS TO TANIS

SWIFTLY the Shepherd horsemen galloped back towards Apepi's forts across the border line of Egypt, leaving their wounded to follow after them as best they might or perish, and in the centre of their array, surrounded by a guard, raced the chariot of Khian. Their captain knew there was no time to lose, for soon those Babylonians whom he had spared would be at the camp of the Great King—and then——! What he did not know was that two hours before Temu had reached that camp and that already a mounted army was sweeping down to cut him off.

Far away in the desert appeared a cloud of dust. It grew nearer and more near, and now through the dust shone helms and spears and burnished chariots. Then the Shepherds knew the worst. Their path was blocked, Babylon was upon them! Flight was impossible. Their case now was that of the five thousand whom they had surprised not twelve hours before, and they must charge as these had done, and with as little hope of victory.

They drew together; they lined up their squadrons to the shape of a wedge, skilfully enough, as Khian noted, and rushed forward bearing somewhat to the right, that they might strike the Babylonian line where it was thinnest. The two armies drew near together, some twenty thousand of the Shepherds against fifty thousand of their foes who were massed in dense squadrons divided by companies of chariots. A roar of triumph went up from the Babylonians, but the doomed Shepherds were silent.

Apepi's captain appeared by the chariot of Khian.

_280

"Prince," he cried as he galloped, "the gods are against me and I think that our end is near. Yet I trust to you to remember your oath, upon faith of which I spared your company, and to make no effort to escape. If you are captured, it is so decreed, but while you are able, I repeat I trust to you to head straight for the boundary which is near, and to surrender yourself to Apepi or his troops. Do I trust in vain?"

"My honour has never yet been doubted," Khian called back.

Then that captain saluted with his sword and, spurring his horse, vanished away.

With a shock and a sound like thunder the hordes of horsemen met. Deep into the Babylonian array cut the Shepherd wedge, throwing men and steeds to either side of it, as a gale-driven ship throws waves of the sea. Yet slowly Apepi's squadrons lost their speed as more and more of the Babylonians poured upon their flank. The point of the wedge, passing through the first group, became engaged with fresh squadrons beyond, that escorted a company of chariots which had raced in front to cut them off.

The fighting grew desperate. Slowly those before him were killed, scattered, or trodden down, so that Khian found his chariot in the forefront of the battle. At a little distance he perceived a throng of the Shepherds, some of them dismounted, attacking a few of the Babylonians who were gathered round a splendid chariot that had outraced the rest, whereof the wounded horses were struggling on the ground. In this chariot, sword in hand, was one clad in mail that seemed to be fashioned of silver and gold, whom he took to be a beautiful youth, doubtless some princeling of the royal House of Babylon sent out to look upon the face of war, while on that side of it on which the Shepherds, six or eight of them, pressed their attack, stood a black-faced giant hung about with plates of brazen armour that clanked as he swung his great axe aloft and brought it crashing down upon those within its reach. One glance told Khian that

this was the mighty Ethiopian, Ru himself! Then with a
sick heart he understood that the figure in the chariot was
no noble Babylonian youth but none other than Nefra, his
betrothed.

Oh! she was sore beset. Horsemen were coming to her aid,
but the nearest of them were still a full bow-shot away, for
in her fierce folly she had outdriven them all. Ru smote
and smote, but he could not be everywhere, and while some
drew him to the rear of the chariot which they were striving
to enter from behind, others, five or six of them, ran together at its side, purposing to rush forward and kill or drag
away her who stood therein. It was as if they knew that
this was a prize indeed, one for whose sake all must be
risked, and as he came nearer, Khian perceived how they
knew, for now he saw that about her silver helm she wore the
snake-headed coronet, the royal uræus with the sparkling
eyes that proclaimed her Egypt's queen. The men gathered, watching Ru as with savage war cries he beat down foe
after foe, and waiting their chance to spring upon their prey
and pierce her through or capture her.

Khian thought for a moment.

"I swore not to escape, but never that I would not fight
upon my way to doom," he said to himself and pulled at the
reins, turning the rushing horses straight upon that knot
of men. As he came the first of them leapt at Nefra. She
smote with her sword and the blow fell upon his thick
headdress. He shot out his long arms, for he was a great
fellow, and gripped her round the middle, dragging her to
him. The others stood waiting to seize her as she fell to
the ground and carry her off if they could, or kill her if they
could not. So eagerly did they watch that they never saw
or heard the white-horsed war chariot thunder down upon
them from where they knew there were no foes. Khian
called to the stallions, beasts trained to war, and turning
neither to left nor right they rushed on. They smote those
men and down they went beneath the hoofs and wheels.
Only one remained standing, he who dragged Nefra from

the chariot. In Khian's hand was a spear. He hurled it
as he passed and it pierced that man through and through,
so that, loosing his grip of Nefra, he fell to the ground and
died.

Now Ru had seen and was rushing back. Nefra, freed,
stared at her deliverer—and knew him.

"Khian!" she cried. "Khian! Come to me."

Ru knew him also and shouted:

"Halt, Lord Rasa!"

But Khian only shook his head and galloped on.

Then the Babylonian deliverers came up as a flood comes
along a dry river bed and covered all. But already Khian
was far off with the remnant of the Shepherd Horse.

The battle rolled away. Of the twenty thousand Shepherds or more but some few hundreds escaped; the rest were
cut or hunted down before they reached the border line of
Egypt. But among those who came unharmed to the army
of Apepi was the Prince Khian, for through all that fray it
was as though some god protected him and the horses that
drew his chariot. On he drove till he saw where a general's
standard flew. Then he halted the bloodstained, weary
beasts and called aloud:

"I am the Prince Khian. Come, bear me hence for I am
hurt and cannot walk."

The officers who heard him saluted and their men cheered,
for they thought that the Prince Khian whom they loved
and who had been their comrade in the Syrian wars had
escaped from the Babylonians that he might fight against
them with his own people. Tenderly they lifted him from
the chariot and gave him wine and food, the best they had,
then placed him in a litter such as they used for wounded
men and bore him to the royal encampment in and around
the new-built forts. Over these forts flew Pharaoh's banners, yet when they came to them they found confusion and
open gates. Pharaoh, heralds announced, had been called
back to Tanis, leaving orders to his armies to follow after

him, that they might re-form there to protect the great city and Egypt.

Now when the captains heard these commands they stared at each other and murmured. But Khian, looking back across the frontier line, learned their reason. Yonder the sands were black with all the ordered hosts of Babylon. On they came, foot and horse and chariots, a mighty flood of men, before the shock of whose onslaught the army of the Shepherds must have broken and gone down. Therefore it was that when he learned that his flank attack had miscarried and saw all the might of Babylon sweeping down upon him, Apepi had fled to Tanis, leaving his troops to follow as best they could.

Understanding at last how matters stood, some of the chief officers came to Khian and prayed him to take command of the army, by right of his rank and repute in war. But he smiled and remained silent, as they thought because he was sick and could not stand upon his feet. While they still pressed him there came that captain to whom he had sworn the oath and who, like himself, had escaped the slaughter of Apepi's horsemen. Calling them aside he told his comrades of how he had captured the Prince among the Babylonians, and the rest. Then they pressed Khian no more, though had he chosen to put another colour on the tale perhaps they would still have listened. Or had he offered to go to the Babylonians and pray the clemency of the Queen of Egypt and of the Prince Abeshu their General, for Pharaoh's army, perhaps they would also have listened. But as he did neither of these things, they yoked fresh horses to his chariot and setting him in it, took him with them in their flight to Tanis.

Thus it came about that when the Babylonians poured up to the camp of the Shepherds to give them battle, save for some sick and wounded men, they found them gone. Learning the truth from these men, who by Tau's command were spared and cared for, also that the Prince Khian had come in safety to the camp and been welcomed there and, as some said, was now in command of the retreating army, at once they started in pursuit.

At their first bivouac Tau, with some of the generals under him, waited upon Nefra, there being present also Ru, Temu the priest, and the Lady Kemmah. By the wish of Tau, Nefra and Ru told all the tale of their meeting with Khian in the battle of the horsemen and of how he had driven his horses over those who attacked Nefra, thrust his spear through him who was dragging her from the chariot, and then, when they called to him to stay with them, had shaken his head and fled away, making no attempt to check the horses, as he might have done, thereby escaping from the Shepherds if he were their captive.

Now when he had heard this strange tale, Tau asked those present to interpret it. The Babylonian Generals, one and all, answered that either this Prince was mad, or evidently he was a traitor. It was clear, they said, that otherwise he would have escaped when he had opportunity, and it was also clear that being a Shepherd and the son of their King, he had followed his heart back to the Shepherds and to his father. Kemmah, who spoke next, held that certainly he was mad, for how, she asked, could a sane man fly away from the loveliest woman in the world, to whom he was affianced, and one who was a queen as well?—Unless, indeed, she added as an afterthought, since they parted he had met one yet lovelier, words at which Nefra sharply bid her be silent.

Then Temu, who had been the Prince's companion in his captivities and flights, was called upon. But all he could do was to mutter, "Faith! Have faith!" adding that in this matter it was easy because he could not believe that any one who had once tasted of the palace dungeon at Tanis or of the tomb chamber in the dark of the pyramid could wish to return to either of them again. Then he began to set out the tale of their escapes and of all that he had suffered on horseback and in the chariot, until an officer pulled him back to his seat.

Then spoke Nefra, asking angrily of the Babylonian Generals:

"Have you ever known, Lords, of a man who wished to play the traitor, who began his treachery by killing sundry of those to whom he had sold himself? Do you not understand that if this Prince wished to be rid of me in order that in future he might lay an undisputed claim to the double throne of Egypt, all he needed to do was to pass on and leave those Shepherd knaves to kill me as—Ru, after his fashion, being elsewhere when he was wanted—doubtless they would have done. Yet he drives his chariot over four of them and pierces the fifth through with his spear. Then— the gods alone know why, though I doubt not for some good reason, other than that advanced by the Lady Kemmah," she added acidly, "he departs, shaking his head, and so swiftly that he could not be caught, as yonder priest says, to taste once more of Apepi's dungeons, or"—here her voice grew faint and her eyes filled with tears—"of worse things."

When they had finished Tau said:

"All who know the Prince Khian have learned that in some ways he is different from most men, and it is probable that among those differences the truth may be found. Indeed I think that I have discovered it, but if so, as we have talked enough, I will keep it to myself until I know whether I be right or wrong. Meanwhile, I would ask you all to listen to the prayer of our brother, Temu, and have faith, such as that which her Majesty of Egypt showed when she rushed forth alone into battle against the commands of those set over her, and now again shows in him who preserved her from death."

Then he rose and departed from the tent, leaving Nefra abashed and yet indignant.

Those who remained of the army of the Frontier came at length to Tanis which was strongly held by Apepi's second army of reserve. They were not many, for the Babylonian pursuit had been sharp and captured thousands. Moreover,

when in this way or in that it became known that none of
these were put to the sword or set aside to be sold as slaves,
but that all asked of them was that they should take an oath
of fealty to Queen Nefra of Egypt and serve under her
banner, other thousands grew weary of that rapid march
and lagged behind until they were overtaken by the Babylonian pickets.

Among the faithful that at length straggled through its
gates, however, were the Prince Khian and that captain
to whom he had surrendered and sworn a certain oath.
Together these two, between whom there was now a bond
of lasting friendship, were brought to the palace and to the
wonder of Khian placed in the apartments that had been
his own when he was Prince and heir apparent of the North.
Here slaves waited upon him, his own slaves, and doctors
came to treat his knee, now much inflamed and swollen
with so long and rough a journey. Yet, as Khian noted,
with all of these were mingled spies and guards: spies to
watch and note every spoken word and guards to frustrate
any effort at escape. In short, he was now as close a
prisoner as he had been in that dungeon whence he escaped
with Temu.

There in his own place Khian, who had been brought to
it at dawn, rested till the third hour after sunset, sleeping
the most of this time, save when he bathed and ate, for he
was very weary. At length came an officer and soldiers
with a litter to bear him into the presence of Apepi, his
father. At the head of this company was Anath the Vizier
who, as Khian noted, had grown thinner and more gray and
whose quick black eyes darted from place to place as though
everywhere he expected to see a murderer, and following
after him a sharp-faced scribe whom Khian took to be a spy.

Anath bowed a greeting nicely judged, neither too scanty
nor too full, saying:

"Welcome home, Prince, after long travels and many
adventures. Pharaoh needs your presence. Be pleased to
accompany me."

Then he was set in his litter borne by eight soldiers, at the side of which walked Anath, while the captain followed after. In turning the corner of one of the passages the long litter tilted and Anath put out his hands to steady it, or to save himself from being pressed against the wall, while the spy for a moment was left out of sight and hearing on the farther side of a corner. Swiftly Anath whispered into Khian's ear:

"The danger is great. Yet be calm and keep courage, for you have friends, ready even to die for you, of whom I am the first."

Then the spy appeared and Anath straightened himself and was silent.

They came into the presence of Pharaoh who sat in a low chair clad in mail with a sword in his hand. The litter was set down and its bearers helped Khian to a seat that was placed opposite to that of Pharaoh.

"You seem to have taken some hurt, Son," said Apepi in a cold voice. "Who gave it to you?"

"One of your Majesty's soldiers during a fray in a pass of certain hills, who overtook me when I was flying from Egypt a while ago, Pharaoh."

"Oh! I heard some such tale. But why were you flying from Egypt?"

"To save myself and to win another, Pharaoh."

"Yes, again I remember. The one you have done so far, though with damage; the other you have not done and shall never do," Apepi said slowly. Then he looked at the captain, who accompanied Khian, and asked:

"Are you that man whom I sent in command of some five and twenty thousand horse to fall upon the flank of the Babylonians? If so, tell me why you failed in your task?"

In brief, soldierlike words the captain told him all the story: how he had met the body of Babylonian Horse during the night and become engaged with them; how in the end Khian had bought the lives of those of them who remained by his surrender of himself; how they had fallen in with

the great force of mounted Babylonians and chariots which
in the end destroyed them nearly all; how the Prince Khian
had kept his word when he might have escaped, and thus
was now a prisoner at Tanis, and the rest.

Apepi listened till he had finished and said:

"Enough, man. You have failed and by your failure
have brought me to the gates of ruin. My army is dispersed
and the Babylonians, under the command of one of the
accursed wizards of the Dawn, sweep down on Tanis to
capture it, after which they purpose to seize all Egypt and
set this girl Nefra as their puppet on its throne. All these
things have happened because you failed in the task I laid
upon you and instead of falling upon the Babylonian flank,
were trapped and wasted your strength and time in a petty
fight with some few thousand men. For such as you there
is no more place upon the earth. Get you down to the
Underworld and there learn generalship, if you may."

Then he made a sign whereon certain armed slaves ran
forward. The captain, answering nothing to Apepi, turned
to Khian and saluted him, saying:

"Now, Prince, I am sorry that I did not loose you from
your oath and bid you escape while you could. For if I am
treated thus, what chance is there for you? Well, I go to
make report of these matters to Osiris who, I have been told,
is a just god and an avenger of the innocent. Farewell."

Before Khian could answer the slaves seized the man and
dragged him behind a curtain, whence presently one of them
reappeared holding up a human head to tell Pharaoh that
his will was done. At this sight for the first time Khian
hated his father and hoped in his heart that Apepi himself
might be overtaken by the fate which he had brought upon
a loyal servant who had done his best.

Now father and son were left alone and stared at each
other in silence. At length Khian spoke.

"If it be the will of your Majesty that I should follow on
the path that has been trodden by yonder victim, I pray that
it may be soon, since I am weary and would sleep."

Apepi laughed cruelly and answered:

"All in good time, but not yet, I think. Do you not understand, Son, that you are the only arrow left in my quiver? It seems that by aid of the arts of these wizards of the Dawn you have bewitched this royal Egyptian in such fashion that she dotes on you, she, the chosen of your father, from whom you stole her. Now how do you think it would please her when she appears before the walls of Tanis with the Babylonians, as doubtless she will do to-morrow with the light, if she saw you, her darling, set upon the eastern gate and there about to die as that fool died or in worse fashion?"

"I do not know," answered Khian, "but I think that if such a thing chanced, very soon Tanis would be given to fire and all that breathe within its walls would also die, and with them one—who does not wish to die."

"You are right, my Son," mocked Apepi. "An angry woman with a hundred thousand men behind her might commit such crimes upon the helpless. Therefore I propose to keep your head upon your shoulders, at least for the present. This is my plan—tell me if you do not think it good. You shall appear upon the gateway and heralds shall announce, or perhaps this would best be done by messenger, that you are about to suffer death for treason in the presence of Pharaoh and his Court, or as many of them as can find standing room upon that gateway. It will be announced, however, that Pharaoh, out of his great pity and love, will spare you upon certain terms. Can you perhaps guess those terms?"

"No," answered Khian hoarsely.

"I think you lie; I think you know them well enough. Still, Son, I will repeat them to you, that you may never say you have not been fairly dealt with. They are short and simple. First, that having surrendered all its treasure and some trappings such as horses and chariots and signed a perpetual peace with us, the Shepherds, the Babylonian army retreats whence it came.

"Secondly, that the Princess Nefra gives up herself to me, that in the presence of both armies and of the holy gods the priests may declare her my wife and queen who brings to me as her dower all the rights and inheritances that are hers by blood in Egypt."

"Never will she consent," said Khian.

"Of course, Son, that is the danger, since no one can tell what a woman will or will not do. But do you not think that if such should chance to be her mind and that she should determine that you must be sacrificed to what she holds her duty, you who otherwise would be set free among the Babylonians, the sight of a little torture and the sound of your groans might work the needful change? There are some clever blacks in this place and by the way, that knee of yours is still swollen and painful, is it not? They might begin there. Hot irons—yes, hot irons!"

Khian looked at him and said in a low voice:

"Do your worst, devil who begat me, if indeed I am your son, which now it is hard to believe. You speak of the priests of the Dawn as wizards. Know that I am a priest of the Dawn who share their wizardry or their wisdom, and it tells me that all your plots will fail and that your wickedness will fall back upon your own head."

"Ah! does it? I understand your scheme. You think that you will kill yourself. Well, this shall not happen, for be sure that you shall be too well watched. Nor will you escape from the palace for the second time. Good-night, Son. Rest while you may, for I fear that it will be necessary to awake you early."

CHAPTER XXIII

THE QUEEN OF THE DAWN

BEFORE the hour of dawn Khian was carried up the pylon stairs to the top of the eastern gate of Tanis. It was a large flat place where fifty or more might stand with comfort, and being lame he was seated in a chair upon its eastern edge. Ra the Sun arose and showed him all. Beneath him was a wide moat filled with water from the Nile, but the bridge which spanned it had been hoisted up by the aid of ropes and pulleys and was made fast to the gateway pillars.

Beyond the moat and almost at its edge, for in their overwhelming might they seemed to fear nothing from their broken foes, appeared the heart of the host of Babylon, whereof the wings already encircled the city of Tanis, cutting off the escape of those who were within its walls. A little way back from the edge of this moat, though out of the reach of arrows, pavilions were pitched, over which, side by side, flew the royal ensigns of Egypt and Babylon, showing to Khian that there rested Nefra and the Prince Abeshu who was also called the Lord Tau. For the rest the walls on either flank of the gateway were garrisoned by Shepherd troops who seemed restless and ill at ease, while on its top, attended by Anath and other councillors, sat Pharaoh Apepi gorgeously attired and wearing the double crown of the Upper and the Lower Lands.

Trumpets blew and guards gathered about the royal pavilions, after which there was silence. On the farther side of the moat behind the outposts, the ordered ranks of the marshalled Babylonian soldiers stood staring up at the gateway crest; wall upon wall of white faces, every one, as

it seemed to Khian, turned towards himself. Presently a
messenger bearing a white flag appeared crossing the moat
upon a boat and from its farther bank was escorted through
the lines to the pavilions where flew the standards of Babylon and Egypt and there handed a letter to the captain of
the General's guard who entered and delivered it to Tau.
Tau opened it and read, then said to Nefra who stood beside
him, large-eyed and haggard-faced:

"These are the terms of Apepi: That having given up all
its treasure and signed a treaty of perpetual peace, the
Babylonian army must march back to Babylon."

"What else, my Uncle?"

"That you, the Queen of Egypt, surrender your person
forthwith to Apepi and with due ceremony be wed to him
in front of the gateway and in sight of the people of the
Shepherds and of the armies of Babylon."

"What else, my Uncle?"

"That if these terms be refused, then the Prince Khian
will be tormented before our eyes until they are accepted or
until life leaves him. Now what answer, Niece and Queen?"

Nefra's face grew ashen. She bowed her head until it
touched her knees and rocked her body to and fro; then she
straightened herself and asked:

"What would Khian wish that I should do? I know! I
know! He would wish that I should defy Apepi, leaving his
fate in the hand of God."

"Have faith! Have faith!" muttered Temu who was
seated behind her with papyrus on his knee.

"Aye, Brother," went on Nefra, "I have faith, and if it
fails me, well, there is always death behind and in death I
shall find Khian. Shall I of the ancient blood, his sworn
betrothed, come to him beyond the grave, defiled, the
woman of that dog of an old Shepherd king? Never! Shall
Babylon, my great ally, bow herself before these runaways
who did not dare to await the battle? Never! Let Khian
die if die he must, and let me die with him. But if so, not
one man shall be left living in Tanis, and not one man of

Shepherd blood throughout the North. Write it down,
Temu, as the Prince Abeshu shall tell you, and let the
messenger take it back to that cruel crossbred cur Apepi,
and let heralds call it out to those who stand upon the gateway and the walls, while the captains bid the attack begin
at every other mouth of Tanis."

Tau heard and smiled in his slow, secret way. Then to
officers mounted on swift horses he issued certain orders
on receipt of which presently thousands of men began
to move to the onslaught upon the great city. This done,
he turned to Temu and other scribes, saying to them the
words that they should write. Also he summoned heralds
and caused them to learn those words by heart and depart
to shout them out at every gate.

At length all was ready, and the messenger, having received the roll, departed to the moat escorted by Ru, who
gave him another message on his own account. It was:

"Tell that Sheep herder who calls himself a king, and tell
all his councillors and the captains who remain to him, that
if a finger is lifted against the Prince Khian, presently I, the
Ethiopian Ru, will twist out their tongues and drive in their
eyes with my own fingers, and afterwards cast them into the
desert to starve. Aye, and yours also, Messenger, if you
fail to report this my message so that I can hear you from
this shore of the moat."

Now the messenger looked up at the giant Nubian who
glared down at him grinding his great white teeth and
swore that he would do his bidding. Then he entered his
little boat and, crossing the water, was admitted by a tiny
door in the gateway tower, so that presently he appeared
upon its crest and handed the writing to Apepi. Moreover,
as he had sworn to do, he repeated the message of Ru in a
loud voice, the words of which seemed to please those upon
the gateway little, for they gathered into knots debating
them fearfully. Heralds also called out that which had
been written in the roll, so that all upon the wall might
learn and understand.

Khian, bound upon the edge of the gateway so that if spears were thrown or arrows shot these might pierce him first, heard the proclamation and was glad, because now he knew that not for his life's sake would Nefra be shamed. Yet he turned his head and spoke over his shoulder to Apepi who stood behind him, and to Anath and the other councillors, saying:

"Pharaoh and Lords, what the Prince Abeshu and the royal Nefra have sworn most certainly they will do. Torture and kill me before their eyes if you desire, but be sure that it will not change their purpose, for not with my poor life can you buy their honour. For myself I fear not death, but I ask of you—is it your will to follow me, every one of you, and to give all the people of Tanis and the nation of the Shepherds to the sword? If you spare me and set me free, you and they will be spared. If you lift a hand against me, you and they will die. I have spoken; do what you will."

Now, although because of his bonds he could not see what passed, Khian heard tumult behind him. He heard Anath the Vizier and other councillors praying Pharaoh to forego his purpose because their case and the case of the whole city was desperate, beleaguered as they were by the countless hosts of Babylon, and it seemed mad to die that Pharaoh might satisfy his hate upon the Prince his son. Moreover, crowds from the city who had also heard the proclamation were rushing into the open space behind the gate, sweeping aside the soldiers by whom it was guarded, and shouting such words as:

"Pharaoh! Spare the Prince Khian! Must we all die because you would torment and murder him who was born of you?"

Then above the tumult Anath spoke again, saying in a high cold voice, like one who threatens rather than prays:

"Pharaoh, this is a very evil business. The Prince is beloved in Tanis and it is not well for kings to kill those whom the people love when the enemy is at their gates."

Now Apepi answered, hissing like one mad with rage:

"Be silent, Anath and the rest of you, or as I serve this traitor, so shall you be served. Slaves, to your task!"

Behind Khian arose guttural murmurings. It seemed to him that the black tormentors shrank from their office. Again the furious Pharaoh commanded, but still they hung back. Then came the sound of a blow and groans and Khian knew that he had cut one of them down and guessed that the others would no longer dare to resist his will. On the farther side of the moat he saw Ru the giant marching to and fro like a caged lion and shaking his great axe. Beyond him now were ranged a company of archers, their arrows set upon the strings, waiting the word to loose, while behind the archers he perceived Tau, and leaning on him Nefra clad in her glittering mail. Then he lifted up his voice and cried:

"Ru! Hear me—Khian. Bid the archers shoot, for thus would I die, rather than in torment."

He could say no more for Apepi, stepping forward, struck him heavily upon the face and bade the torturers gag him, a sight at which the army of Babylon groaned, as did the inhabitants of Tanis who now packed the Place of the Gateway in thousands. Ru roared out a curse that sounded like the bellow of a wounded bull, then turning, repeated Khian's words to the archers who lifted their bows and looked to Tau for the order to shoot. But Tau gave no order, only motioned to them to hold their hands, while Nefra sank to her knees as though she swooned.

Khian became aware of black hands tearing at his garments, then there was a smell of fire and an agony darted through him. The slow sacrifice was begun! He shut his eyes, making his soul ready to depart.

There was a sound behind him, a very strange sound of wrestling and blows. He opened his eyes and looked. Past him, staggering backwards, went the form of Pharaoh, and in his breast was fixed a knife. At the edge of the gateway platform he stopped, clinging to the seat in which Khian was bound.

"Dog!" he gasped, "Dog of a Vizier! I have spared you too long; it should have been done last night. But I waited——"

"Aye," answered the voice of Anath, "you over-shot yourself, Pharaoh, and gave the dog time to bite. Away with you to Set, son-murderer."

A withered form, that of Anath, leapt forward, its black eyes gleaming in the yellow wrinkled face, a thin arm smote with the tormentor's heated iron at the hands that gripped the seat, crushing and burning them. Apepi loosed his hold and with a cry fell backwards into the moat beneath.

Ru saw him fall and leaped into the water, swimming with great strokes. As the Pharaoh rose he seized him with his mighty hands and dragged him to the bank where he broke him like a stick, then cast him to the shore.

"Pharaoh Apepi is dead!" piped the thin voice of Anath, "but Pharaoh Khian lives! Life! Blood! Strength! Pharaoh! Pharaoh! Pharaoh!"

So he cried as he hacked at Khian's bonds and dragged away the gag, and all the multitude beneath took up the ancient greeting, shouting:

"Life! Blood! Strength! Pharaoh! Pharaoh! Pharaoh!"

It was evening. Khian lay upon a couch in the royal pavilion of the Babylonians, whither by his own command he had been brought, since as yet Nefra could not enter the city. The Lady Kemmah and a leech bathed his bruised face and bandaged his swollen knee, while Nefra, who stood near, shivered at the sight of a long red burn upon his flesh made by the touch of hot iron.

Then suddenly a question burst from her:

"Tell me, Khian, why did you fly away from me in the battle, when you might have escaped and spared us all this agony?"

"Did not some two thousand sound men and with them very many wounded rejoin this army upon that day, Lady," asked Khian, "being the survivors of the force which was sent to rescue me and the garrison of the mountain stronghold?"

"They did, and were questioned, but knew nothing except that you drove out your chariot and surrendered yourself to the Shepherds, after which the attack upon them ceased."

"Then do you not understand that sometimes it is right that one man should offer himself up for many?"

"Yes," answered Nefra, colouring, "I understand now—that you are even nobler than I thought. Yet, when you could have escaped, why did you fly away, as I saw you do?",

"Ask the Prophet Tau," replied Khian wearily.

"Why did Khian fly away, my Uncle? Tell me if you know, since he will not."

"Does not the oath sworn of those who enter into the fellowship of the Dawn demand that they shall never break a promise, Niece? Perchance our brother here had vowed to deliver himself up in Egypt, and did so, even when he might have stayed at your side. So at least I have believed from the first."

"Is that so, Khian?"

"It is so, Nefra. With this oath I bought the lives of those men. Would you have had me break it even to win my own—and you?"

"I cannot say, but oh! Khian, you are noble, who did this knowing that if you died, all my life I should have been ignorant *why* you died, seeming to desert me."

"Not so, Nefra, since Tau knew and would have told you at his own time."

"How did you know that which was hid from me, my Uncle?"

"My office has its secrets, Niece. Enough that I knew, as I knew also that it would never be necessary for me to set out the truth to you."

"So you let me suffer all these things when there was no need, my Uncle!" exclaimed Nefra angrily.

"Perhaps, Niece, and to your own good. Why should you alone escape from suffering which is the medicine of the soul, you, who if you be the Queen of Egypt, are, as I would pray you to remember, first and foremost a sister of the Dawn and the servant of its laws? Be humble, Sister. Sacrifice your self-will. Learn to obey if you would command, and seek, not self-will or glory but the light. For so, when these little storms have rolled away, you shall find the eternal calm."

"Faith! Have faith!" muttered Temu who stood behind.

"Aye," went on Tau, "have faith and humility, for by faith we climb and in humility we serve—not ourselves but others, which is the only true service. I say these things to you now even in the hour of your joy, for soon we must part, I to my hermitage and you to your throne, and then who can reprove Pharaoh on the throne?"

"You could and will, I am sure, my Uncle," Nefra answered, tossing her head.

Then suddenly her mood changed and, turning, she threw her arms about him and kissed him on the brow, saying:

"Oh! my most beloved Uncle, what is there that I do not owe to you? When I was a babe you saved me and my mother from the hands of those traitorous Theban nobles, with whom soon I hope to talk if they be still alive."

"I think that the Lady Kemmah and Ru here had something to do with that, Niece."

"Yes, yet they did but fulfil their offices, whereas you travelled up Nile to rescue us."

"Fulfilling *my* orders, Niece."

"Then you brought us to the pyramids and there you watched over my childhood, teaching me all the little that I know. Afterwards it was you who led me to Babylon and in secret worked upon the heart of the Great King, so that, as though at my prayers, he abandoned his plan of wedding me to Mir-bel and gave me this great army that has brought us victory and peace."

"God, for His own purposes, changed the heart of my father, Ditanah, on that matter, not I, Niece."

"Afterwards," she continued, taking no heed of his words, "you comforted me in a hundred ways; also it was you who held me back from accompanying the five thousand to the mountain stronghold which, had I done so, would have brought me to death or shame. Oh! and I know not what besides. And how have I paid you back? Often enough with pride and angry words and rebellion against your commands; aye, and disbelief when you told me that if I found patience all would work for my good and that of Khian, whom I believed dead, even when you bade me hope on. Yet," she added in another voice, "if I behaved thus, it was your fault, not mine, for who was it that spoiled me in my youth, giving me my way when I should have been taught obedience?"

"The holy Roy, I think; also the Lady Kemmah," answered Tau with his quiet smile.

At this moment guards challenged without. Then the curtain of the pavilion was drawn and, heralded by Ru, there entered the old Vizier Anath and with him others of the councillors and captains of the Shepherds.

Anath and his company prostrated themselves thrice, to Nefra, to Khian, and to the Prince Abeshu, the General of the armies of Babylon.

"Queen and Princess," he said, "on behalf of all the Shepherds we come to surrender to you the city of Tanis and to pray your clemency for those who have fought against you and for every one who breathes within its walls. Is it granted?"

"Be my mouth and answer," said Nefra to Tau. "Your mind is my mind and by your words I will be bound, as I think will his Highness, the Prince Khian, who is still too sick for ceremonies."

"It is granted," said Tau. "To those who will be loyal to Nefra, Queen of Egypt, and to Khian, Prince of the North, whom she purposes to take as husband, all is forgiven. To-morrow we enter Tanis and proclaim the great peace."

"We hear and thank you, Queen and Princess," said Anath. "Now I have a word to say to the Prince Khian, I who come before him with the blood of Pharaoh on my hands, for which deed I crave pardon. Let the Prince hearken. When the Prince was cast into prison, it was I who saved him with the help of yonder Brother of the Dawn and a certain jailer. Being suspected of this deed by Pharaoh I was disgraced and myself imprisoned. Therefore I could not rescue him when he was shut up in the pyramid or prevent his pursuit to the mountain outpost of the Babylonians where he took refuge. Afterwards I regained power because Pharaoh knew that I alone might perchance save him from the fangs of the Lion of Babylon. When the great host poured down upon Egypt I counselled Pharaoh to surrender and, if the Prince still lived, proclaim a marriage between his son, Khian and the royal Nefra. For answer he struck me like a dog—see, here are the marks"—and he touched his head. Afterwards Pharaoh fled, his attack having failed, and the Prince Khian, through his own nobleness, fell into his power. I pleaded for his life in vain, both in the palace and on the gateway, but Pharaoh was mad with jealousy and hate and would have put the Prince to death by torment before the very eyes of the royal Nefra and of the host of Babylon. Then, before it was too late, I smote, and saved the Prince and the people of the Shepherds. Have I pardon for this deed?"

Now Tau went to where Khian lay upon his couch and talked with him apart. Presently he returned and said:

"Anath, what you did must be done. To-morrow make sacrifice in the temple of your gods and receive the forgiveness of your gods for the shedding of royal blood to save other royal blood and the lives of tens of thousands who are innocent. Then appear before us in the palace of Tanis that there may be given back to you the wand and chain of office of Vizier of the Upper and the Lower Lands. The

word is spoken. Record it, Scribe Temu. Anath, withdraw!"

Thirty days had passed. Tau had handed over the command of the host of Babylon to the general next in rank to
him at a great ceremony, and putting off his mail and royal
emblems, had donned the white robe of the Prophet of the
Dawn and returned to the Temple of the Pyramid, leaving
Temu behind him because such was the will of Nefra and
Khian. Save for a force of ten thousand picked men who
remained to guard the grand-daughter of the Great King
until all was accomplished, that army had marched for
Babylon. There were ceremonies at which all who served
his father, now known as "Apepi the Accursed," swore
fealty to Khian his son, but at these Nefra was not present,
nor as yet had there been any coronation, for indeed none
knew whether Khian of the North or Nefra of the South
ruled over Egypt. Some grumbled that this should be so,
but others glanced at the encampment of the ten thousand
Babylonian guards and bade them be silent.

Khian recovered but slowly. With skilful tending his
leg healed indeed, though now he knew that all his life he
must be lame, but the sufferings which he had undergone
had left him shaken in both mind and body. First there
was the palace dungeon, then the long confinement in the
bowels of the pyramid, then the flight from the pursuers to
the Babylonian outpost; also the wound that would not
heal, while for moons he must lie upon his back among
strangers whose tongue as yet he did not speak, com-
panioned only by Temu with his prayers and maxims, and
ignorant of the fate of Nefra.

Afterwards followed the wild joy of the knowledge that
she lived and was near, the rescue by the five thousand, the
desperate battle in the desert, the surrender and the sacrifice, the sight of Nefra in the second battle, and her aban-
donment for honour's sake, knowing that she would not
understand; the coming to Egypt and to Tanis, the meeting

with his father Apepi; the pain of the hot iron and the agony
of suspense upon the pylon top while Nefra watched below.
All these events, young and strong though he was, had
broken his body and eaten into his spirit, so that he must
rest and keep himself apart by day, while at night, when at
last sleep found him, he was visited by evil dreams and
tremors, so that at length it was said throughout the city
that soon the Pharaoh to be would join his forefathers in
their burial place.

Anath came to him with reports of affairs, to which he
listened patiently, saying little. Temu read to him from
ancient rolls, or offered up the prayers of the Order of the
Dawn at his side, and talked of faith. Ru visited him also
and spoke of battle or of the wonders of Babylon, and how
Nefra there had learned the arts of war, a tale at which he
laughed a little. Lastly, from time to time, accompanied
by Kemmah who stood far off gazing through the window-
place, came Nefra herself and spoke softly of love and marriage when he should be well again.

Still he did not grow well, so having talked with Tau by
messenger, Nefra took another counsel. Telling Khian that
Tanis in the low land was too hot for him, she set him in a
ship and travelled with him slowly up the Nile, till at last
the pyramids appeared. At the first sight of these pyramids
Khian's manner changed: he became alert and eager as he
used to be, even gay, talking to her of all that had befallen him among them. Rejoicing at this change, that
evening she caused him to be borne ashore to a camp that
had been set in the midst of the palm grove where first
she had found him sleeping and whence, after Ru had taken
his goods, disguised as a messenger, she had conducted him
to the secret home of the Brotherhood.

Here that night Khian slept better than he had done
since, many months before, wearing Nefra's betrothal ring
upon his finger, he had left this spot to return to Tanis and
make report of his mission to Apepi.

On the following morning, while it was still quite dark, Ru

entered his tent and assisted him to rise. Then he set him in a litter in which Khian, asking no questions, was borne across the sands till they came to a great shape outlined against the starry sky, which he knew to be that of the Sphinx. Here he descended from the litter, which departed, leaving him alone.

At length the dawn began to break and in its tender light he saw that he was not alone, for by his side, wrapped in a gray cloak, stood a hooded figure that might have been that of a lad or a slender woman.

By the gods! he knew this figure: it was that of the "Young Person" who—oh! years and years ago—had guided him from the palm grove to the Sphinx and there had tied a bandage about his eyes. The height was the same, the very cloak and hood seemed to be the same.

"So, Young Person," he said, "you still ply your business of guiding travellers across the sands."

"That is so, Scribe Rasa," answered the figure in a gruff voice.

"And do you still steal their packages—or hide them? My litter I think has gone."

"I still take that which I desire, Scribe Rasa, who must live and be happy if I can."

"And do you still blindfold messengers?"

"Yes, Scribe Rasa, when it is necessary to hide secrets from them. Indeed, be pleased to suffer that I do so to you for the second time, and bide here a while alone."

"I obey," he answered, laughing, "for although you may not know it, Young Person, since first we met I have suffered many things and learned one great lesson from them, also from the lips of a certain Temu, namely, to have faith. Therefore bind on and I will submit as gently as though I were sure that when sight is given back to my eyes they would behold a vision of heaven come to earth. See, I kneel, or rather stoop, for kneel I cannot."

The gray-cloaked figure bent over him, the silken kerchief once more was bound upon his brow—oh! how well he re-

membered its soft substance and its odour! Then, leaning
on his guide's shoulder, he limped a little distance till the
feigned voice bade him be seated upon a bank of sand and
wait.

Presently voices, men's voices, prayed him to rise. He
did so with their help, and those men supported him down
passages in which their footsteps echoed, to some chamber
where they clothed him in new garments and set a headdress on his brow, what headdress or what garments he did
not know, and when he asked they would not answer.

Again he was helped forth, as he thought into a large
place where whisperings ran as though from a gathered
multitude. Someone bade him to be seated and he sank on
to a cushioned chair and waited.

Far away a voice cried:

, "Ra is risen!" and from all round him rose a sound of
singing.

He knew the sound. It was that of the ancient chant
with which on days of festival the Brotherhood of the Dawn
greeted the rising of the sun. It died away; there was deep
silence; he heard a rustling as of robes. Then suddenly and
in unison from a hundred throats there rose a great cry of:

"The Queen of the Dawn! Hail! Queen of the Dawn!
Hail, Light-Bringer! Hail Life-Giver! Hail, Consecrated
Sister! Hail, Heaven-appointed Uniter of the riven Lands!"

Khian could bear no more. He snatched at the bandage
about his eyes. Perhaps it had been loosened, at least it
fell. Lo! there before him stood Nefra glittering in the
rays of the risen sun, wearing the robes of Egypt's queen and
crowned with Egypt's crown, a living loveliness; a glory to
behold.

For a moment she stood thus while the shoutings echoed
from the vaulted roof of the great temple hall. She lifted
her sceptre and there was silence. Then she turned and
came to him who, he found, was seated on a throne. To
Kemmah and to Ru she gave the sceptre and her regal
symbols. From her head she lifted the double crown and

set it on his brow. She kneeled and did him homage; yes, with her lips she touched his hand.

"Egypt's Queen greets Egypt's King!" she said.

Khian stared at her, astonished. Then, though of a sudden pain and weakness struck him once more, he struggled from the throne, purposing to offer it to her. But she shook her head and would none of it. Supporting him with her strong young arm, she led him to where stood Tau the Prophet in front of the gathered Councillors of the Dawn. Tau joined their hands. In the presence of the Brotherhood, living and dead, and in the name of that Spirit whom they worshipped, he blessed them, giving them to each other, uniting them to all eternity, on earth and beyond the earth.

So it was finished.

Nefra and Khian stood together gazing by the light of the moon at the mighty mass of the Pyramid of Ur.

"Our holiday is done, Wife," he said, "and to-morrow, ceasing to be but a Brother and a Sister of the Dawn, we must become the rulers of Egypt united at last from the Cataracts to the sea. Strange has been our lot since first side by side we looked upon yonder pyramid. Yet, Beloved, I think that the Strength which preserved us through so many perils and now, from sickness and the gates of death has brought me with joy to those of health, will be with us in the years to come."

"So Roy the holy prophesied, and in him, if in any man, lived the spirit of Truth, Husband. At least, thanking the gods for what they have given us, let us go straight forward in humility, remembering that though we be King and Queen of Egypt, first and foremost we remain Brother and Sister of the Dawn, sworn to its holy faith and to the service of mankind."

At that moment this royal pair heard a sound behind them and, turning, beheld the lean and withered Sheik of the Pyramids.

"Would your Majesties wish to ascend?" he said, bowing and pointing to the mass of Ur. "The moon is very clear and there is no wind; also I desire to show Pharaoh the spot whence those accursed cliff-climbers rolled to their doom on the day of his escape."

"Nay, Captain," answered Khian, "of Ur I have had enough who am lamed for life. Henceforth be you its king."

"And its spirit also," added Nefra, "for no more may I stand upon the crests of pyramids who am doomed to a dizzier pinnacle of power. Farewell, you gallant man. Our thanks be yours with all you seek and we can give."

Then Khian and Nefra turned and, hand clasped in hand, wandered back to where Ru and Kemmah waited with the escort to accompany them to the vessel that made ready to sail with the night wind.

"Now," said Kemmah the white-haired to Ru the mighty Ethiop, "now I understand the meaning of the vision that I saw when yonder Queen was born, and why the goddesses of Egypt gave to her the name of Uniter of Lands."

"Yes," answered Ru, "and I understand why the gods of Ethiopia gave me a good axe and the strength to use it well on a certain Theban stairway."

THE END

Printed in the United Kingdom
by Lightning Source UK Ltd.
9743800001B